Knox County Public Libra
500 W. Church Ave.
Knoxville, TN 37902

WITHDRAWN

The
Moon
Stops
Here

By the same author

MY FATHER'S GEISHA

James Gordon Bennett

Doubleday
NEW YORK LONDON TORONTO SYDNEY AUCKLAND

The Moon Stops Here

FICTION

PUBLISHED BY DOUBLEDAY
a division of Bantam Doubleday Dell Publishing Group, Inc.
1540 Broadway, New York, New York 10036

DOUBLEDAY and the portrayal of an anchor with a dolphin
are trademarks of Doubleday, a division of Bantam
Doubleday Dell Publishing Group, Inc.

All of the characters in this book are fictitious, and any
resemblance to actual persons, living or dead, is purely
coincidental.

Book Design by Gretchen Achilles

Library of Congress Cataloging-in-Publication Data
Bennett, James Gordon, 1947–
    The moon stops here / James Gordon Bennett.
        p.   cm.
    1. Automobile travel—United States—Fiction.   2. Family—United
States—Fiction.   I. Title.
PS3552.E54635M66   1994
813'.54—dc20   93-3691
                                                                    CIP

ISBN: 0-385-47095-9
Copyright © 1994 by James Gordon Bennett
All Rights Reserved
Printed in the United States of America
January 1994

10   9   8   7   6   5   4   3   2   1

Thanks to my editor, Nancy Nicholas,
and my agent, Lisa Bankoff,
for making the trip possible.

For James and Matt

July
1969

It isn't until the halo appears over my mother's head that I recognize all the other signs: colors shimmering, the tingling in my toes, the air crackling like woolen socks pulled from the dryer. But just as I'm about to say something to her, the aura flickers like a string of Christmas bulbs and goes out. Only another false alarm.

My cousin Bobbie, meanwhile, is trying to force her suitcase into the already stuffed trunk. She's decided finally that her husband Lou can fend for himself for two weeks.

"Just what we need," my sister Cora mutters, fanning herself with one of her movie magazines. "Like we're not already packed in here like goddamn extras."

My mother twists around in the driver's seat. "I don't want your cousin hearing that kind of language out of you," she says. "Now roll your window up. I'm putting the air on." She's been studying me skeptically in the rearview mirror and reaches back to feel my forehead. "You all right, sweetheart? You look a little peaked."

I nod, trying not to stare at the fading nimbus above her.

When Bobbie at last bounds into the front seat, there's a subtle shift in the load of the car.

"Just like the astronauts," she declares and finds a spot at her feet for her pedicure set with its five snap-on attachments.

"Just like," my sister says irritably, "an outtake from *The Grapes of Wrath*."

My mother finishes taping the auto club's emergency road service number to the dashboard and announces that she wants this to be a pleasant trip for everyone. "So the grousing can stop here. Understood?"

Leaning over the seat, I remind her to release the hand brake and notice that my cousin's wearing her suede go-go boots. Not only does Bobbie dress like a cheerleader, Cora likes to say. She *thinks* like one. However, just because my smart aleck sister quit Mensa doesn't make my cousin a bimbo.

"We'll take it nice and easy," my mother says. She's still suspicious about my coloring and aims the air conditioner vents back at me. "No reason to overdo it."

It isn't our first cross-country trek. Just our first without my father. But we're dependents and used to the long haul. Only this time my mother wants things to be more scenic than sonic (she accuses my father of always trying to break the land-speed record for a family of four). As long as we board our ship on schedule in San Francisco, everything should be copacetic.

Where we are headed is that tiny speck in the ocean called Formosa. The same place, my sister says, where everything in the world under a dollar ninety-eight is made. In his last letter home, my father talked about the cook and live-in maid he planned to hire. But my mother worries more about our education since we're supposed to attend something called Taipei-American Institute. Cora says it sounds like one of those places over a laundromat where they teach karate. My sister is just bitter that she doesn't get to stay behind and board at a girl's academy somewhere. Somewhere like in the Hollywood Hills, for instance.

As soon as school let out, my mother surprised everyone by

suddenly agreeing to put us all on a slow boat to China. Although she won't admit it, I know that my condition helped change her mind about joining my father overseas. She believes that I aggravate my affliction by taking on the sad cares of our separated family and warns me that I'll have plenty to worry about when I have my own brood. Until then, I'm to try to relax and enjoy the scenery.

Bobbie, who knows about engines, advises my mother to let the car idle a moment longer, secretly hoping, I suspect, that Lou will race out to beg her not to leave. But it's almost time for "Mike Douglas" and the rest of the talk shows, which, now that he's been laid off at Tic Toc Children's Shoes, Lou never misses.

"Here we go," my mother says and backs the sagging Oldsmobile out onto the street, the bumper scraping the concrete.

Cora disappears behind her *Photoplay* with Julie Christie on the cover. And for a moment I try to imagine what it would be like to cross the country with the famous actress in the backseat with me instead of my sullen sixteen-year-old sister.

The car is cluttered with household goods too delicate, my mother insisted, to be trusted to military movers. This includes Betty, her butterfly fish, in a bowl wrapped with towels at her side. At the last minute, she refused to leave it with my aunt Irene (or, as Cora suggested, to give it a burial at sea).

"First bump's the worst bump," my mother says as the water sloshes.

My sister lowers her magazine and rolls her eyes back.

But I'm watching my cousin as she struggles to keep any tears from spilling over. She is having a hard time of it right now. Already this month Lou has strained his back again. The manager of Tic Toc's, an old boyfriend of Bobbie's, is convinced that her husband is a slacker. "If the shoe fits," Cora said but my mother wants us to try to be charitable. Years before Bobbie got married, no matter where we were stationed, she'd confess her problems to my mother long distance. "I been dialing your momma collect since before my first French kiss," she would say. "If it wasn't for her I'd of probably shot Hammuck in the back by now." Hammuck is her married name.

Cora believes that Bobbie deserves what she got: someone who ties shoelaces for a living. My sister has always been jealous of how my mother treats her niece like a daughter. "Maybe if she stopped baby-sitting her," Cora will say, "the woman might grow up."

With my aunt Irene already at the Spalding plant where she stripes basketballs for a living, there's no one to see us off. We've been renting a small house near my mother's sister ever since my father was shipped off to command an infantry battalion in Vietnam. Our stay in Chicopee, Massachusetts, has not been a popular one with Cora who will tell you that nothing is worse than a town without a decent movie theater. Nothing except maybe being assigned to a hellhole like Taiwan.

"Do we really have to be subjected to that?" Cora says as soon as Bobbie flicks the radio to a country and western station.

"We'll each get our chance," my mother says, signaling to merge onto the turnpike. "We got a long way to go."

It's hard to find a station where they're not gabbing about the moon launch. They send the rocket up Wednesday and it's on everybody's mind.

My sister plugs in her headphones already sorry that Bobbie has had to come along for the ride.

But I'm glad for my cousin's company. Maybe her IQ isn't as high as Cora's but then whose is? "We have to be patient with your sister," my mother will plead whenever Cora is being particularly obnoxious. This is my mother's way of saying that her first-born is a genius and her second born should try to be more understanding. What exactly I'm supposed to understand is never made clear. Only that the usual rules don't apply to the gifted. And that being such, my sister is allowed to get away with murder while her average brother must bite the bullet. That is the way my mother thinks and it's only one of the reasons I miss my father.

Except for Christmas, my father hasn't really been Stateside since they rotated him out of Nam. He was crazy, my mother told him over the holidays, if he imagined she was going to fly across any ocean with the kids. Cora would summarize for her the plots of *Lifeboat* or *The High and the Mighty* or any other movie she could think of where people crash-landed or wound up on rafts in the water. Even though my sister has been miserable in Chicopee, she's afraid that the only movies we'll ever get to see again will star Doris Day dubbed in Taiwanese.

When my father's new assignment kept him overseas, my mother stubbornly vowed to keep the rest of us here until he returned. But she's changed her mind and now the Army will send us all over at government expense. Only Bobbie's return fare from California will have to be paid by my parents. That is, *if* my cousin decides to go back to her husband. Already she's talking about how her absence might make Lou's heart tic toc a little stronger.

It's too early for lunch when my mother pulls into a Gulf station to let Bobbie use the ladies' room. After getting the key from the manager, my cousin sashays past one of the gawking attendants.

"How do you figure Lou keeps throwing his back out?" Cora says, lifting her headphones free.

With the air conditioner off, the car quickly warms up and I roll my window down.

"Bobbie's your widowed aunt Irene's only child," my mother points out to Cora. "She didn't have all of the advantages you had when she was growing up. Just remember that."

My sister slumps down in the seat. "What the hell's that supposed to mean? She only had Waylon Jennings to listen to?"

"Let's just try to be understanding," my mother says. "And I want you to watch the language."

"*You* be understanding," Cora says. "The woman's on another wavelength."

"Just because you think you know so much," I say. "Well, movies aren't everything."

My sister glowers at me from across the stack of magazines she keeps between us.

"There's going to be a lot to see," my mother says. "And I want the two of you to cooperate."

"Fine," Cora says. "Just keep him out of my hair."

"You'd have to be batty to get in your hair," and I grin at my mother who only sighs wearily. "Which is probably why no one wants to go near it."

My sister's face hardens like plaster of Paris.

"You don't know . . ." and she mouths the letters "s-h-i-t."

But I know from her sour expression that boys are still the biggest chink in her armor.

"That's enough," my mother says. "Not another word from either of you."

I pucker my lips at my sister who glares at me stonily.

Bobbie returns the key ring to the manager who watches her saunter back through the island of gas pumps. It's nothing new for my cousin. Men seem to stop whatever they are doing when she is around. Cora says it's only because she's built like Anita Ekberg but I believe that my mother's right and that it's because my cousin has such a big heart. When she smiles it's as if she's known you all of your life but wouldn't mind listening to your life story again anyway. "There's a certain type of man to take advantage of a girl like Bobbie," my mother will say. "And so far it's all she seems to run into."

My cousin's husband Lou never talks about his first wife. Another thing he never talks about is what he did for a living before he met my cousin. He spends most of his time resting his injured back and switching to Betsy Palmer or the Linkletter show whenever Steve Allen has on a black woman or an author. Lou isn't much of a conversationalist, which might account for his liking all the talk shows. Cora thinks he looks like an ugly Alan Ladd ("without the lifts"). Anyway, none of us can see what my cousin sees in him, if she still does.

The astronauts are big business this week and Bobbie comes back waving a free Gulf Oil bumper sticker (MOON STOPS ONLY HERE). She takes her turn driving and finds a call-in station on the radio. "Maybe Hanoi Jane's the one we ought to be sending to the moon," a listener says and my mother laughs. She doesn't think much of the war but she thinks even less of the antiwar people.

There isn't a whole lot to take in on a thruway that your average Army brat hasn't taken in a hundred times before. Still, my mother believes that it broadens our horizons to travel as long as it doesn't involve commercial aviation. When I point out that Daddy has flown around the world at least a dozen times without any trouble, she reminds me that he is also a paratrooper. That's what I mean about trying to argue with my mother. You can't.

The rule is no stopping for lunch until noon. And so at exactly twelve, Bobbie turns into a Howard Johnson's. When she gets out of the car to stretch, her blouse sticks to her back and I can see the outline of her bra. It looks a lot heftier than the ones Cora hangs over the shower rod to dry. But then my cousin has a lot more to heft.

The restaurant is crowded and we stand in front of the sign that tells you to please wait for the hostess.

"I'm dying for a patty melt," Bobbie says. "I've been dying for a patty melt since we passed New Haven."

When there's finally a clean booth, the hostess unhooks the padded chain to let us through.

"I love this part," Cora says as we follow the woman around the salad bar. "Being seen by all the movers and shakers."

We were stationed at Fort Polk when my sister read *The Prince and the Pauper* and decided that she wasn't really an Army brat after all. Somehow her papers had gotten mixed up in the post infirmary and soon her rightful parents, Joanne Woodward and Paul Newman, would come to claim her. In the meantime, she had to play the role of an officer's daughter who suffers through life with an idiot sibling.

"Save me the little flag from your sandwich," Cora says to Bobbie after the waitress collects our menus. "I'm keeping a scrapbook."

My cousin half smiles, uncertain how to take my ironic sister. In fact, I doubt that Bobbie has ever really known how to take Cora. Since dropping out of high school, she has gone from one dead-end, blue-collar job to the next. She admires my sister for doing so well in school and makes a point of encouraging Cora not to wind up like her. But the idea would never have crossed my sister's mind. After the cinema studies program at the University of Southern California, she plans to become Hollywood's first girl wonder director. It's a future that doesn't include working for minimum wage at any of the fast-food chains in Chicopee.

After three hours in the car together, even my mother chooses to eat in silence. So we sit in our booth looking off in four different directions.

Once we arrive in San Francisco, Bobbie will fly back East while the rest of us board the USS *Anderson* to the Nationalist Republic of China. It will take two weeks to get to Taiwan but my mother, who's not optimistic about my sea legs, has brought along a month's supply of Dramamine pills. The only time I've ever gone fishing, I never even got my pole out ("The story of your life," my sister likes to say.). Ten minutes out to sea, my father didn't care for my pallor. It made him think of Army camouflage. And there hadn't even been a small craft warning.

"We should have held out for Stuckey's," Cora says, pushing her plate away.

Bobbie raises her chin slightly, eyeing Cora's french fries. "You're not going to eat those?"

My sister turns her head away as if from a freeway pileup. "Enjoy."

"Driving makes me hungry," Bobbie says and pops the bottom of the ketchup bottle with her palm. "Must be from having to concentrate so much."

Cora looks over at me but says nothing.

As soon as the waitress wipes the table for dessert, my mother has the map out.

"We'll just take it at a comfortable pace," she says, drawing her finger along the route. "There's no rush. We've got plenty of time."

She's helped lure Bobbie along by promising tickets to the Elvis concert in Las Vegas. It's his first public performance in nearly ten years and my cousin's a big fan. My mother will pass the time playing the slots. She's stashed half a dozen pairs of Army socks filled with change in the spare tire well. As a compromise with Cora, she's agreed to swing far enough south to take in Los Angeles and the Celebrity Tour of Homes.

"Teddy," my mother says to me. "What's the latest?"

I know that she wishes I would change my mind. That instead of the Lindbergh estate in New Jersey, I'd pick some place less morbid. Some place like the Luray Caverns where we could see the blind albino shrimp. Only I haven't changed my mind. I still want to see where the baby was kidnapped.

"What about Memphis?" Bobbie says. "God, what I wouldn't give to see the shrine."

My mother looks back at her blankly.

"The King," my cousin says, pressing her hand to her heart.

"Get with it," Cora says to my mother. "She means the druggie."

My sister takes everything she reads in the tabloids as gospel.

"Now hold it right there," Bobbie says and sets her french fry back down. "Just hold it right there. The only medication Elvis ever takes is for his sinuses."

"Well, that might explain *Clambake,*" Cora says, "but what about *Harum Scarum?*"

When the waitress returns I notice that something is different about her. This time she's aglow.

"I ought to pass," Bobbie says, shaking her head at the color pictures of dessert on the menu. "But lord that shortcake looks appealing."

"It's one of our favorites," the waitress says.

I squint at the woman's ballpoint, which has turned into a roman candle. When her check pad goes off like a flare, I look up at her but she's only waiting for my order. Like neon, a tube of light snakes along her shoulders before the entire restaurant explodes into the aurora borealis.

I know what's happening, of course. Everything is starting all over: the fireworks, the cool breeze, the prickling down my spine. It's the falling sickness. And it's time to fall again. But don't ask me why. It's idiopathic, the doctors have told us. Without any known cause.

"Mom," I say. "I think . . ."

"**So,** Lazarus," Cora says. "How we doing?"

I sit up too quickly and my ears whine like a tuning fork.

Bobbie and my mother are smiling warmly at me, their empty coffee cups before them. My cousin's shortcake has been left uneaten, the strawberry sauce congealed into a red plastic puddle.

My mother opens her pocketbook. "You need an aspirin, sweetheart?"

My head is listing. "I've been asleep?"

Bobbie nods. She's heard tell of my condition but seen little evidence of it for herself.

I clear my throat. "Was I twitching?"

My cousin looks away, embarrassed for me.

"You remember the frog experiment?" my sister says.

My mother slides her glass of water across with the aspirins. "Never mind," she says. "It's over."

I glance at her watch but it can't be right. I've been out for over an hour.

"Sorry," I say when Bobbie looks back at me.

Cora springs from the booth. "What the hell are you apologizing about? You didn't have anything to do with it. Jesus."

At first, I think it's just my excitable sister. But as she troops out of the restaurant, fists clenched, I can tell that it has to be something more. Through the wide, plate glass window I watch her march across the parking lot to lean sullenly against the car.

My mother shrugs her shoulders. "Cora's a little touchy today." This is code for what the Army doctors have diagnosed as an overactive thyroid. My sister has her own diagnosis, of course, and blames my mother's "oppressive personality."

"Well," Bobbie says, tapping her long nails on her coffee cup. "She was very sweet to her brother. Like a little nurse."

My tongue feels as if it's gone to sleep. "Which one's our waitress?" I say. "I'm kind of thirsty."

My mother takes her keys out. "Your sister gave her a pretty hard time," she says. "The woman made the mistake of lingering."

Bobbie laughs. "She was like a tiger with her cub. And I'll tell you what. That manager sure knew better than to tarry."

Outside, Cora is still braced against the hood, her Lolita sunglasses halfway down her nose. It's her James Dean pose: hands tucked under her armpits, shoulders slouched, legs crossed at the ankle.

"There's a Coke in the cooler," my mother says to me. Our waitress still hasn't appeared.

I slide out of the booth and the acoustical tiles in the ceiling seem to shift place.

"How we doing, buddy?" My cousin has wrapped her arm around my shoulder to draw me up straight. "Still a little wobbly?"

At the register, the hostess rings up our bill and when she steals a sidelong glance in my direction, I feel like a freak. And yet I know that I'm lucky. Public performances are rare. Very few nonrelatives have ever really seen the show. It's become just another skeleton in the family footlocker.

Still, for the next few miles down the interstate everyone gets quiet and looks philosophical. Even Bobbie. A thousand years ago doctors called epilepsy "The Great Teacher" because it taught them that the brain was a lot more complicated than they thought.

Sitting behind my mother I'm reminded of how prematurely gray her hair has gotten. She blames my father and sister for it, arguing that I've never given her a minute of trouble since the day I was born. But I know that seeing me keel over into my New England clam chowder isn't going to make her look any younger.

Usually it's the back of my father's head I'm staring at whenever we're on the road. Our cowlicks swirl identically but it's just about the only thing we have in common. My father looks like a movie star. Cora thinks he could have been Jimmy Stewart's stand-in if Jimmy Stewart had been handsomer. He's tall and slender and his teeth look capped. I wasn't even born yet when he came back from Korea with a Purple Heart and a punctured eardrum ("the one I turn toward your mother."). He won't tell me what he did to earn his Silver Star and only makes fun of all the other ribbons on his dress uniform. But how many fathers have ever jumped out of a helicopter at night behind enemy lines? That's what I mean about us being so different.

By the time we get to the other side of Newark on the interstate, it's started to drizzle, and Bobbie and my sister have fallen asleep. I keep the road atlas open in my lap with Hopewell circled in red. Every once in a while, just to make conversation, my mother asks me something about the kidnapping.

"I don't understand the fascination," she admits for the hundredth time. "Why you wouldn't rather do Disneyland, for example."

"Guess how he identified the body?" I say. "I mean, it was lying out in the woods all that time. It didn't look much like a baby anymore."

"They've got Fantasyland and the Jungle River Cruise and every ride you can imagine," my mother says.

"Two of his toes curled over his big toe," I say. "It was lucky it was his right foot because the left one was eaten off by wild—"

"Teddy, that's enough," my mother says. "I don't want to hear about it. Most fourteen-year-old boys would jump at the chance to do the Magic Kingdom."

Raising one knee to steady the steering wheel, she reaches over to unwrap the bath towel from the fishbowl.

"We don't have to go," I offer. "I could just do it on my own sometime."

My mother's already shaking her head. "A promise is a promise. If you want to see the place then we'll see the place. That's all there is to it."

Twenty minutes later, we pass our first Princeton exit.

"Well," my mother says, signaling to get over. "If nothing else, you can start thinking about a good boy's college."

Cora suddenly sits up to squint out her window at the light rain. "It's not just all-male anymore," she says groggily. "They've come out of the stone age."

"Who says I'm going to college?" I say. "Maybe I'll just enlist and see the world like Daddy did."

My mother continues to cock one eye at me in the mirror. She's still worried about the seizure.

"You're smarter than to grow up and be cannon fodder," she says. "Your father's a different case."

"Whereas you're just a case," Cora says.

When my mother turns the wipers on, Bobbie nestles closer to the door and mumbles Lou's name in her sleep. Our ears prick up as we all lean in her direction.

"Howdy." My cousin grins crookedly at my mother and straightens up in the seat. "Was I saying something?"

"You were saying how Lou beats you," Cora says.

My cousin looks anxiously back at Cora. "Did I say that?"

"You're going to have to get used to smarty pants," my mother says. "Know when she's just pulling your leg."

Bobbie wags her finger at my sister. "This one's too fast for me," she says. "I never even graduated high school."

It's true that Lou wears cowboy boots and has a tattoo on his forearm: Jane, his first wife's name. But my sister has a knack for blowing things out of proportion.

And yet Bobbie's reaction, even if she was only half awake, still surprises me. For a moment, I almost expected her to confess. To admit that Lou *does* occasionally take a swing at her but that she probably deserves it. That would be just like Bobbie—to blame herself. Anyway, I've decided that there's more than meets the eye with my cousin. Which, in her case, is saying something.

As we approach the small, Ivy League town, I start to recognize a lot of the street names from all the books I've read about the kidnapping. Perfect lawns slope down to private residences the size of most officers' clubs.

"Now this is the kind of place I want my boy to go," my mother says as we pass through the imposing stone gates to the university. "Let him mix with the muckety muck."

"And who do you want your daughter to mix with?" Cora says indignantly. "Just the muck?"

My mother shakes her head.

"Honey, I forgot it's not just a boy's school anymore. That's all. You know I only want the best for both of you."

Remarkably, my sister's eyes shine with tears. "It's the twentieth century," she says. "They're all co-ed now. If this is where I wanted to come, I'd come."

"Of course you would," my mother says. "And Daddy and I would love for you to."

This is only another of my hypersensitive sister's complaints: that her younger brother is the more loved. "Rosemary's Baby," she calls me (my mother's name). Which is nonsense. If anything, my mother has to dote on my sister just because she's so touchy.

It's too dark to make out much on campus besides the hulking silhouettes of great limestone buildings. And so we cut our tour short.

There are only a few motels on the outskirts of town and their "no vacancy" signs are already blinking in the rain. Cutting back through the stately, tree-lined streets, my mother slows down then pulls over.

"What do you think?" she says, peering out at one of the Victorian mansions. Hanging from its porch is a bed and breakfast sign.

"Looks cozy," Bobbie says.

"You want me to go up with you?" I ask my mother.

Whenever my father is away, she takes me along for things like this because I am the male. My mother's old-fashioned that way. Cora is at least right about that.

It feels good to get out of the car and stretch my cramped legs. I walk with my mother up to the broad front porch and bang the brass knocker twice. Through the door's beveled-glass window I can see a staircase. And I think how the house probably hasn't changed that much from the day almost forty years ago when everyone was suddenly racing over to Hopewell.

A man Bobbie's age peeks out at us through the sheer curtains before unlocking the door. He's wearing tight jeans with a cat wrapped around his shoulders.

"We're interested in a room," my mother says and turns for him to see the Oldsmobile. "There are four of us." And she smiles at me. "Four adults."

The innkeeper's name is Ernest and he holds the cat's paw out for us to shake. "Say hello to our guests, Julio."

The cat licks my mother's fingers.

"He smells the fish food," she says and explains about Betty.

When the man steps back, I notice that he has on slipper socks with a cat face on each foot.

"I'm sorry," he says, his whole expression having changed. "We can't permit pets."

My mother blinks once. "No pets," she says as if trying to take this in.

After an awkward silence, during which Ernest does not budge, they both turn to me.

"What about if we just left it in the car?" I say.

Ernest shifts the cat on his shoulders, settling it into a more comfortable position. "If you don't mind leaving her unattended."

"We'll just crack the window a tad," my mother says.

Ernest points the cat's tail where we can pull the car up.

"People can get a little eccentric," my mother explains to me as we walk back to lock Betty up for the night. "Especially the ones that live alone."

Upstairs, Ernest shows us the rooms, proudly noting how everything has been elegantly maintained: the hardwood floors, the moldings, the claw-foot tub, the transoms. There are two connecting suites with a four-poster bed in each.

"And, of course, complimentary coffee and toast in the morning." He holds the cat like a muff. "Now I have to put Granny to bed. She's ninety-two and we have our little ritual."

The first thing Cora notices when she comes up with her suitcase is the TV.

"Look at that dinosaur," she says. "It's twenty years before color."

My mother has already changed into her pajamas in the room she'll share with Bobbie.

"Why don't you just talk to your brother," she says. "You can live without that thing for one night."

Cora flings herself theatrically onto the bed. "It's like Sleepy Hollow out here, for god's sake."

The bathroom is at the end of the hall and Bobbie pads barefoot back from it wearing baby doll pajamas. They barely reach past her bottom but I try to act as if I'm paying attention to my sister.

"That's why Lindbergh picked it," I say, watching my cousin

hang up her clothes in the other room. "He wanted to get away from people."

My mother has the phone book open on the bed and is thumbing through the yellow pages.

"Tell us something nice about the man," she says. "You're giving your cousin the wrong picture."

Bobbie has wandered in filing her nails, her breasts swaying beneath the cotton top.

When I don't say anything, my mother looks up from the directory.

"You okay, honey?"

Sometimes, hours after a seizure, there will be brief lapses of consciousness. Petit mals, the doctors call them. Even Cora is eyeing me now.

"Sure," I say.

My mother smiles nervously at me. "Well, then? You're the expert."

I try to recall the question.

"Lindbergh," my mother prompts me. "Tell your cousin something else about him. About why you admire him so much, for instance."

Bobbie has stopped filing and is half sitting on the mattress, her painted toes pointed.

"Okay," I say.

For my oral report in Miss Clark's world history class, my mother tried to persuade me to talk about the flight instead of the kidnapping. "Who wants to hear about that poor baby?" she would say each time I came back from the post library. I did, I told her. And I knew my eighth-grade audience.

"Well?" my mother says.

My cousin and sister are both waiting hopefully, their expressions pained and expectant.

"All right," I say at last, concentrating hard. "How about this?

Lindbergh was so honest he didn't want the police to copy any of the serial numbers down from the ransom money. He'd promised the kidnappers he wouldn't."

My mother shakes her head at Bobbie. "Tell me he doesn't take after his father. They've got that same stubborn streak in them."

"Sounds like he was a real man of his word," my cousin says.

"Jimmy Stewart played him," Cora says. "Way too long in the tooth for the part though."

"Did you know that your grandfather was in New York for the ticker tape parade?" my mother says to Bobbie.

My cousin hands me a bottle of nail polish. "Can you open that, honey?" She looks back up at my mother. "Rosemary, Mom's never said two words to me about my *own* father, never mind my grandfather."

"Well, he used to say it was like a snowstorm," my mother says. "A million people throwing confetti."

"Four million," I correct her. "Eighteen thousand tons of paper."

Only the flight never much interested me. It was the kidnapping I did my report on. And it included an exact scale model of the Lindbergh estate constructed from over two thousand popsicle sticks. I put the crib together with matches and made a miniature nursery above the colonel's study. Miss Clark gave me an A+ but questioned whether some of the material was absolutely necessary. The picture of the baby in its shallow grave, for example. The one where you can still make out some of its face and hair. Curly blond hair just like its father's.

But what kept me up nights reading with a flashlight under the covers was something else. It had got me thinking again about how no family was ever really safe. Not even the most famous family in the world. At any time, when your parents least expected it, a dirty German could sneak up a ladder and into your nursery.

And not even if your father was Lucky Lindy himself, and he was right there in the room under yours, were you safe. So what chance did the rest of us eighth-graders have? What would keep some truck driver, stopped to take a leak in the woods one day, from finding your tiny, decomposed body buried in the leaves?

That was the question I asked my classmates. Except no one had an answer. And neither did I. Still, it would be nice to think that my father worried about the same things I did. Things like our family, for instance. Though I know that wasn't what my mother meant by my father and me being alike.

Cora moves her hand like a crossing guard in front of my face. "Houston to Apollo."

I look down at the small bottle indented in my fist.

"We've had a little staring spell," my mother says, taking the nail polish from me and giving it back to Bobbie.

"I was only daydreaming," I say. "Really."

My mother leads me over to the wing chair.

"How about Italian?" my cousin says cheerfully, folding the page over in the phone book. "I could go for some pizza."

"If you want to know what I was thinking about," I say, "it was whether the Lindbergh place still looks the same as it does in all the pictures."

It's quiet for a moment and everyone seems to nod at the same time.

"Sweetheart," my mother says, "I'm going to bring you out there first thing in the morning. That's the deal."

Cora groans but doesn't put up any resistance.

Since I'm the only one still dressed I volunteer to watch for the delivery boy. Sicily's promises a free pizza if it's not there in thirty minutes.

The house creaks as I come down the staircase and at the

landing I listen for Ernest but there are no lights on in any of the rooms.

Drawing the brass bolt back on the front door, I step out onto the porch. The rain has stopped and I sit in the rocker that's chained to one of the milled railings.

While the trial was going on up in Flemington, over a hundred thousand people sought rooms in the neighboring small towns. And I wonder if any of them came out here to stay. It's only one of the questions I would have liked to ask Ernest's grandmother.

"Teddy?"

Bobbie stands jangling the car keys, a sweater over her pajamas.

"I thought I'd get your mother's fish," she says. "Who's going to know, right?"

She tiptoes across the lawn to the car and I watch her lean into the front seat, the sweater riding up until my eyes water. She comes back with the fishbowl tucked under her arm like a bowling ball.

"I wouldn't have been able to sleep," she says. "I'd start thinking about her soon as the lights went off."

Her fingers are splayed out to grip the bowl and I notice that her wedding ring's missing.

"You need to listen to your momma," my cousin says, nodding at me as if trying to make up her mind about something. "Let me tell you, honey, I probably wouldn't be standing here today it wasn't for her."

I reach back to feel my pants. They're damp from sitting in the wet rocking chair.

"I don't worry half as much as she thinks I do," I say.

"Half's too much. You got to cut back, Teddy. Take it easier on yourself." She shifts the bowl to her other hip. "What do you say?"

"We could prick our fingers."

She smiles. "We're already blood relatives, honey. You just listen up. Your cousin knows what she's talking about in this department, let me tell you."

I wait until she's back in the house before turning around. The whole seat of my pants is soaked.

I'm trying to find the moon through the clouds when a Volkswagen with an illuminated cone on its hood does a sharp U-turn into the driveway. The delivery boy leaves the engine running and trots up the brick walk, the pizza kept warm in a padded, zippered bag.

"Half green peppers, half sausage, extra cheese, extra sauce?" he says.

The generous tip surprises him. I want to ask about the Lindbergh estate.

"Sure," he says. "Had a delivery out there once. No trespassing signs all over the place."

I'd read how it was turned into a reformatory and when I mention this, he rolls his tongue around his mouth as if there's something stuck between his teeth.

"Now the man tells me."

The Highfields number is unlisted and I ask if he thinks they'd mind someone just coming out to see the grounds.

"Hey, what you got to lose?" And he jumps down from the steps, spinning the empty zippered bag on his finger. "Bring a ladder."

Back upstairs, Bobbie has carried the phone into the other room to call Lou.

"Every man for himself," Cora says as I set the large white box down on the bed.

I'm not real hungry. All I can think about is seeing the Lindbergh place. And now it looks as if I won't get past the gate.

My mother is watching me as she crumbles a piece of pizza crust over the fishbowl.

"You need to eat something," she says. "You'll get a head-ache." It's one of her theories that not having enough body weight makes me seizure-prone.

She suddenly raises her hand for us to be quiet. Walter Cron-kite's describing what the astronauts will have for breakfast.

"Cora," my mother says excitedly. "Tell your brother how your father was involved in all this."

My sister refuses.

"Old news," she says and peels up her first slice of pizza.

When my father was over at the Natick Labs, the military scientists there were trying to come up with something for the Mercury program more appetizing than puree squeezed from a toothpaste tube. That's when they started freeze-drying everything and letting the astronauts just add water to rehydrate it.

"Doesn't appear as if they're going to suffer," Walter is saying as he surveys the mock breakfast of bacon bars, peaches, sugar cookie cubes, pineapple-grapefruit drink and coffee. "At least not with a seventy-item menu to pick from."

When Bobbie sharply raises her voice in the other room, my mother leaps over the ottoman to turn the TV down. After a long silence, she moves to the door and knocks once.

"Honey?"

My cousin doesn't answer at first and we all wait.

"Maybe she slit her wrists," my sister whispers, sweeping in a long string of cheese with her tongue. "Or maybe—"

"Quiet," my mother says. She knocks a second time. "Bob-bie?"

A chair scrapes back and my cousin says, "Right there."

My mother turns away from the door to glare at my sister. Cora only looks up from studying the *TV Guide*.

"Slim pickings," she says. "This stupid coverage is screwing up the regular scheduling."

My mother steps into the other room without knocking again.

"Just our luck they'll preempt 'Laugh-In,' " Cora says.

I sit on the bed with the last batch of pictures from my father. Over half the roll are shots of different religious temples. He pays guides, usually faculty from the national university, to take him out to see them on weekends. I thought it was because he was lonely without us over there. But my mother believes that it's all part of his upbringing. He can still recite the Latin from when he was an altar boy. Cora has her own theory, of course. My father's just enjoying his life as a bachelor. And she pointed out that every guide was female and attractive. Even if they all *do* look alike.

When my mother comes back in, she puts her finger to her lips. "Your cousin's gone to bed," she says to Cora and nods at the TV. "I want you to keep that down."

She's wearing a rolled-up pair of my father's pajamas. Cora claims that Mom's a ringer for Tammy Grimes, whoever that is. There's a streak of silver in her widow's peak that comes, she jokes, from worrying about her daughter's social skills. Cora doesn't have what my mother calls her own "little friends." My sister argues that this is because we're never in one place long enough to bother. Cora's a snob, but it isn't, I think, the only reason she keeps to herself.

While Walter introduces Wally Schirra, the former astronaut, who will help with the technical terminology coming from Mission Control, I flip through the rest of the photographs my father's sent of the countryside. In one, there's a statue of Buddha sitting cross-legged, his beer belly poking out from his kimono. My mother had been surprised by how big the mountains appeared in the background. But I'd read about aboriginal headhunters still living on the island. I didn't say anything, of course. That was all she needed to hear.

After each letter that included new pictures, Cora would complain that my father had no consideration for us as a family. "Like we give a damn about some idiot statues." What she wanted to see instead were things like the commissary or the PX.

At eight-thirty my sister switches to a special on the National

Gallery of Art narrated by Mrs. Edward Kennedy. The senator's wife leads a tour of thirty-five of the most appealing children's portraits in the museum.

"Where are *my* kids?" my mother says.

"Over in the Ripley's 'Believe It or Not' wing," Cora says and changes the channel to the NBC coverage.

My mother is stretched out on the bed, a pillow folded under her feet. "Who's fixing something to drink?" she says. "I'd get up but my gams are killing me."

Ernest had included kitchen privileges with the room.

"There's a Coke left in the ice chest," my mother says when I volunteer. "If you can find some lemon to go with it, sweetheart, it'd be much appreciated."

She won't watch Frank Reynolds or any of the other anchormen she considers biased against the war but she's still too wound up from the driving to fall asleep.

Downstairs, the kitchen has the same musty, old-house smell as the rest of the rooms. Running warm water over the metal ice tray, I start thinking again of what Cora said about the pictures. Pretty young women *did* seem to pop up in a lot of them.

I turn the tray over and several ice cubes slip out into the porcelain sink.

The night before we saw my father off at Logan International, my parents spent the evening arguing until my father finally closed the bedroom door. Well into the morning I could still hear my mother shouting and my father trying to quiet her down.

The Coke cracks the cubes in the glass and fizzes noisily. Ernest sleeps in the same room with his grandmother on the first floor. But it's a big house and there are too many heavy oak doors between us to worry about waking them.

When I carry my mother's drink up to her she's sitting back against the headboard. Cora and I watch her spike the Coke from the small flask she brought along to help her sleep. My sister turns off the TV and we can hear Bobbie snoring in the other room.

"Cinderella," Cora says. "You'd think she could have seen through that shoe salesman." She stops and looks at us for a moment and then shakes her head. "Let me retract that last statement, your honor."

My mother sets her glass down. "Why don't we try a little Ouija? See what the future holds."

Cora has brought her board along but doesn't feel like digging it out of the car.

"You're right," my mother says. "I better let you two get to bed in here anyway."

As soon as she closes the door behind her, Cora looks over at me. "She's going to wind up like Judy Garland," she whispers. "It's not the ride keeping her awake."

I pull my toothbrush from my travel kit. "And I guess her legs don't really bother her either," I say.

My sister inspects the thumbnail she's been chewing. "As a matter of fact that's right. It's psychosomatic. Like how she gets if you talk about flying."

I want to say something about her own hyperthyroid but instead take my pajamas with me to change in the bathroom. After undressing, I decide to step into the stand-up shower. The hot water feels good on my scalp and I squint up at the warm spray. I wish that my father could be with us. He would know how to take care of three women at once. My mother suspects that her children bring on their own medical problems and refuses to believe that anything is idiopathic. And probably in a hundred years some scientist will prove that she's right. In the meantime, all I can do is hope that my sister calms down, that my cousin cuts back on her long distance calls, and that our new house has air conditioning.

When I come back down the hall, Cora's sitting cross-legged on the bed, eyes closed and fingers resting lightly on the planchette of her Ouija board. She'd had the game in her suitcase all along.

I pull the covers back on the roll-away.

"It keeps telling me I'm going to meet a tall, dark stranger," she says. "That must be Dad."

"I don't know what I'm going to do with her," my mother said at one of the many pit stops we made for Bobbie this afternoon. Cora had strayed over to see whether the McDonald's sign was really claiming two billion hamburgers served. "Your father knows how to deal with her. She'll listen to him. I can't even get her to take her pills. Everything I say goes in one ear and out the other."

"I was asking Ouija about Daddy's pictures," Cora says in her taunting voice.

They're the ones of my father at the Taipei Zoo with some of his coworkers. Some of whom appear young and pretty.

"Old news," I say and turn my head away on the pillow.

Without an audience, Cora loses interest in the photographs and reads her magazines, occasionally laughing out loud over something in Rona Barrett. "Listen to this," she'll say and then make a snorting sound to show how you can't take any of it seriously. "I mean, who does the woman think she's kidding?" My sister trusts nothing any of her favorite stars say. They lie about their age, their children, their marriages ("even the nose on their face"). Everything and everyone in Hollywood is suspect. To Cora the movies are just like life. What you see is never what you get. And so the only place you can really suspend disbelief is in a darkened movie theater. Which is also the only place my sister ever seems to relax and not try to make something out of nothing.

When I can't fall asleep I sit up.

"Dad makes friends easy," I say. "But you have to make a big production out of everything."

My sister looks over at me.

"Been cogitating, have we?" She smiles. "To reflect upon. Verb transitive. Ten across."

She's been working one of her stupid celebrity crosswords.

"You can stay here for all I care," I say. "There'll be that much more room for the rest of us."

"In the hut he's renting," she says, "you'll need it."

She clicks off her light and bellyflops on the mattress.

My sister's doubts about my father are nothing new. Because he looks like a movie star she believes that women are always throwing themselves at him behind my mother's back. Whenever I point out that Dad isn't an actor, she only grins knowingly. How many naive baby brothers, she will say, can you stand on the head of a pin? Then I'll tell her that not everything is filmed in Hollywood. Maybe she has Daddy cast in the wrong role. Maybe he isn't even in it. Oh, he's up there on the giant screen all right, she'll say. Bigger than life. It's her dim bulb brother who isn't getting the picture. But then he's been closing his eyes at the scary parts for as long as she can remember.

In the morning, Bobbie's the first up to use the shower and I'm waiting in the hall when she steps barefoot from the bathroom.

"Sorry, buddy," and she lifts the wet hair off her neck. "Guess I been dawdling in there."

The guest towel is tucked at her breasts and I pretend to be only half awake.

"It's okay."

My cousin wears a retainer at night for the gap between her front teeth. But she isn't vain and looks no different without makeup, only less colorful.

"I must of been sawing some logs last night," she says, hitching the towel up. "Your momma had to plug her ears with the cotton from her aspirin. She thinks I ought to see somebody about it." But she already has. Several times. Once, a specialist even filmed her sleeping. "Lou ripped the bill up. He said he wasn't paying anyone to make movies of his wife in the sack." She stops to look down at the small puddle at her feet. "I'm dripping."

At the end of the hall she does an about-face, her soles squeaking on the hardwood floor. "Know something, buckeroo?"

I'd been watching how her backside shifted beneath the towel.

"You're starting to remind me a lot of your daddy." She appears to scrutinize me critically. "It's real interesting the kind of things get passed on. *Real* interesting."

My cousin sounds Southern even though she was born and raised in Massachusetts. Cora says it comes from listening to nothing but hick music. I think it's because Southern just sounds friendlier to her than New England.

In the bathroom, I stand in front of the clouded mirror of the medicine chest and look for any pale sliver of my father in me. But everyone agrees that it's Cora who's a chip off the old block. "One of your father's enough," my mother will console me. "My boy's his own man."

Afterward, Ernest (whose skin appears sallow in the bright light of morning) fixes us a continental breakfast. It isn't much more than fresh juice and toast out on the brick patio but he's trimmed the crust off the bread and decorated the glasses with the orange rinds.

"I guess this house must go back a few years?" my mother says when he carries the marmalade out on a silver tray and seems not to want to leave. "Has it been in your family long?"

Ernest nods at the empty chair. Bobbie has gone back up to the room to call Lou. She wanted to try to make up for whatever their argument was about. It's the first time since their honeymoon that they haven't spent the night together (although Cora believes it goes back farther than that).

"Please," my mother says and Ernest lowers himself like an old man into the wrought-iron chair.

"Oh yes," he says proudly. "But I'm the last of the breed."

My sister, who has the Sunday *Times* scattered about, noisily unfolds the entertainment section.

When my mother asks about his parents, Ernest cocks his head as if there's a kink in his neck.

"We're a fair-weather family," he says bitterly. "It's just my grandmother and me now. She was born in this house."

Cora has some dark suspicions about Ernest's mental health but my sister specializes in making something out of nothing.

"Then she must remember the Lindbergh trial," I say.

Ernest turns to me as if one of his potted plants had just talked. "She does," he says evenly. "She was on the jury."

My heart does a little stutter step. This seems miraculous. Earlier, I'd seen the old woman sitting in the parlor flipping through the sign-in register.

"We thought we'd drive out to see the place," my mother says, relieved with the change in subject. At the mention of his parents, Ernest's cheek had begun to twitch.

"She hated the prosecutor," he says. "A little piker from the Bronx who thought he was George Raft."

Cora sits up.

"Wilentz," I say.

Ernest narrows his eyes at me.

"It was one of my son's school projects," my mother says. "Teddy's read all about it."

There was a famous picture of the jury published in the papers. One of the women was caught blowing her nose. I ask if that was his grandmother.

"Ethel Stockton," he says. "My grandmother's sitting behind her next to Rosie Pill from Califon. That's a little town outside Flemington. Shortened for California."

"Small world," Cora says, gathering up the *Times*.

I ask Ernest about the Lindbergh estate.

"It's a home for delinquent boys now," he says. "So there aren't as many tourists, thank god. There used to be a gentleman who'd sell you a piece of the original ladder." He pats his knee and the cat hops up into his lap. "Is pussy thirsty?" The cat's paws are wet and Ernest dries them with a napkin.

"I'll be loading the car," my sister says.

"You do that, honey," my mother says. Then she smiles at me. "Maybe Ernest could tell us how to get out there."

Ernest allows that there isn't a lot to see but copies down the directions anyway.

I ask if he knows what became of the Hospital for Epileptics in Skillman.

"In this country?" His voice rises an octave. "It wouldn't surprise me if they were still locking them up. Nothing this government does would surprise me anymore."

My mother and I are both nodding vigorously.

"It's like the war," he says and his arms and legs seem to quiver with rage. "It's a vicious joke." He stops to steady himself. "Anyway, you'd have to ask my grandmother about Skillman. She might remember."

"Why don't you?" my mother says to me. She pushes her chair back, eager to get upstairs. "And I can finish packing."

Ernest leads me back through the house to the parlor where the old woman is sitting. The shutters are closed and it's a moment before my eyes adjust to the light.

"Sometimes she has a little trouble connecting," Ernest says, gently taking up his grandmother's hand. She'd been plucking at the Victorian sofa with her nails. Now she looks about as if her grandson's voice is coming from outside.

"Dearie," Ernest whispers, "our guest wanted to ask you a couple of questions. Do you think you could remember about the time you were on the jury?"

The old woman blinks and seems momentarily to emerge from her reverie. "Oh yes," she says brightly. "That would be no trouble at all. He was such a fine boy, such a sweet boy. Like Mary's little lamb."

Ernest strokes her arm. "What was it like sitting on the jury, Grandmother?"

Her face tightens. "The Lone Eagle flew right into that courthouse. He was a great American and from the best family. So I said to Charles . . . Charles, we've got to find out who's responsible for this."

Ernest looks over at me. "Charles Walton, the foreman. He died a while back."

"Yes, he did," the old woman says. "And Charles Walton did the right thing. He burned that evil man. That Nazi. Stealing our babies right out of their nurseries. You'd think a carpenter could make a ladder that wouldn't break. That was what Rosie tried to tell us but we didn't go for it. Not for a minute."

"Rosie Pill," Ernest says. "She was the last one to win over. They deliberated seven hours. Some of them had some questions."

"His wife was there every day," his grandmother adds. "She had her own little boy. A little German. But he didn't have curly hair. They were Krauts."

"She's still alive," Ernest says. "She even called once to try to get my grandmother to go back on her vote."

"Oh yes," the old woman says. "And I told her we should have electrocuted all of them. There wouldn't be this terrible war giving our babies ulcers now."

Ernest squeezes her hand to get her attention. "That's fine, dearie. That's fine."

"They took that little boy from his mother's arms," she says, raising her voice. "And now they're trying to take mine from me. Look at him," and she reaches over to pinch her grandson's elbow. "Not an ounce of fat. Nothing stays down."

Ernest's ears have turned red and he quickly asks about the hospital for epileptics. But she ignores him.

"He doesn't weigh any more than that baby. And what's happened to *my* baby's curls?" She smoothes the few wisps of hair remaining on her grandson's head.

"The Skillman place," Ernest interrupts, repeating his question.

"They didn't know what to feed him," she says. "So they followed the mother's special diet in the newspapers. A half cup of orange juice on waking. One baked potato or rice. Two tablespoons of stewed fruit daily." She stops and turns to her grandson. "You're late with my prunes. This is the second time this week. I don't want to have to remind you again. How do you think the Lone Eagle made it all the way to Germany?"

Ernest looks at me and we both stand up.

"I'm going to get those for you," he says to her. "You just wait right here, dearie."

I thank her for talking with me but she's gone back to dreamily plucking at the cushion.

"Grandmother has her clear days and Grandmother has her cloudy days," Ernest says as soon as we're out in the hallway. "Today things are a little overcast for her."

We can hear Cora complaining about something upstairs.

"My sister doesn't like to go anywhere in a car," I say. "She'd rather fly."

"I absolutely hated to travel in an automobile with my family," Ernest confesses. "I've always been a stay-at-home person. Now I just want to stay in this big old house and take care of my grandmother. Is that so un-American?"

I shake my head and glance up at the long banister. Cora is still bitching loudly.

"Well," Ernest says, his slippers flapping as he crosses the foyer. "Toodle-loo."

Upstairs, the door to my mother's room is open and I stand outside it a moment before Cora sees me.

"Wait till you hear this one," she says.

My mother is sitting on the bed and smiles sadly at me.

"The cat ate Betty."

I look over at the empty fishbowl on the dresser.

"It's what she gets for bringing the damn thing in the first place," my sister says. "This family—"

"How do you know it was the cat?" I say, fingering the damp lace doily beneath the bowl. There's water on the floor and wet paw prints leading out into the hall.

"Inspector Clouseau," Cora says.

"It's my own fault," my mother says. "I should have listened to your father."

"Why can't we do things like normal human beings?" my sister says. She appears more upset than my mother. "Why do we have to have a domestic scene every fifteen minutes?"

"Now Betty has to pay for my stupidity," my mother says. I rest my hand on her shoulder but it feels awkward.

"We should finish loading the car," I say. "It's getting hot out there."

"The first sound suggestion of the day," Cora says. She's sitting on her suitcase unable to snap the locks shut.

"Where's Bobbie?" I say.

"Probably walking back to Chicopee," my sister says. "Soon as she heard that shoe salesman's voice."

"Your cousin has her own problems," my mother says. She dries the fishbowl but then doesn't seem to know what to do with it and sets it back down on the dresser. "I don't want us adding to them."

Cora opens the suitcase and finds the top to her Ouija board caved in. "Shit."

"Well," my mother says. "That wasn't very smart, was it?"

Cora holds up the bent planchette. "It runs in the family."

I'm trying to figure out how to move things up onto the rack so the driver can see out the back window when Bobbie appears wearing shorts and a tank top that Cora will no doubt have a comment about.

"All I do is make your mother stop the car so I can tinkle," she says. "You people must be ready to kill me."

"It doesn't matter," I say, wiping the damp hair out of my eyes.

"Lou says for all he cares I can cash my plane ticket in now."

I stand next to her and put my hand on her shoulder. With my cousin it doesn't feel uncomfortable.

"He's just jealous," I say.

"Lou carries a grudge. He still carries a fierce one for his first wife. I wouldn't want to be her."

"You aren't."

She exhales heavily. "That's right. I'm wife number two. Now he's got a double grudge."

I ask if she heard about Betty but she only looks at me.

"Mom's goldfish," I say. "Ernest's cat ate her."

She seems to ponder this a moment then opens the front door and sits down behind the wheel.

"That's what happens," she says. "One minute you're swimming around and the next minute something blows you right out of the water. You never even knew what hit you."

The sun is already blistering and her bubble hairdo has begun to sag.

"Mom's going to drive me out to the Lindbergh place," I say. "We don't have to stay or anything."

But she's found a Willie Nelson song on the radio and is miming the words as if they addressed her personally.

"Why don't you get out of the car until we can put the air conditioner on?" I say.

My cousin gazes distantly at me, her forehead beaded. She hasn't heard a word.

I pass Cora on the porch. Her face is flushed from lugging her suitcase down.

"Just what I want to do in this heat," she says. "Drive out to some lunatic asylum in the middle of New Jersey."

Upstairs, I find my mother arranging the fishbowl on the bureau. She's decided to leave it behind.

"You want me to pay Ernest?" I ask her.

She points to the check on the dresser.

"We could just get on the interstate," I say. "We don't have to bother with Hopewell."

She smiles at me. "What would I do without my little man?"

When I bring my mother's other suitcase down, Cora's sitting in the shade reading a magazine.

"It's got to be two hundred degrees in there," she says, glancing in the direction of the Oldsmobile.

Bobbie's still in the front seat with the radio on.

"Why doesn't she just put a hose in the exhaust pipe?" Cora says. "Melting's going to take her all day."

"Lou doesn't know what he's got," I say.

My sister grins at me. "And what's that, Duke?"

I cross the driveway with the heavy suitcase banging against my ankle. When I open the trunk the heat rushes out as if from a furnace.

"How can you stand it in there?" I say to Bobbie but she has the radio blaring.

At first, when I come back around to the driver's side, I think my cousin is only listening intently to the song. Her eyes are closed and she's slumped a little in the seat. But the radio's too loud.

"Bobbie?"

As soon as Cora sees me shaking her, she comes over.

"Christ," my sister says and together we pull my cousin from the car.

Even for the two of us, she's an armful.

"Get some water," Cora says.

There's a coiled hose in the ligustrum and I race back up the driveway.

My mother opens the screen door just as I low-crawl out of the bushes. "What's the matter, honey?"

But she can see Bobbie now, flat on her back, my sister fanning her with her magazine.

"Oh, my god!"

The hose won't reach so I turn the water up full blast.

"Jesus," my sister shrieks, dancing out from the shower.

I keep the nozzle pointed at my cousin as my mother ducks under the spray.

"Okay, okay," she shouts back at me when Bobbie sits up. "That's enough."

My cousin is glassy-eyed.

"Did you take something?" my mother is asking her. "I have to know, sugar. Did you take anything? Answer me."

Cora flaps her soggy magazine down on the hood of the car. "She doesn't have the brains to come in out of—"

"All right," my mother says sharply.

My sister shakes her head and the water sprays from her hair like a sprinkler. "Like that moron Lou's even worth—"

"Just find something dry for your cousin," my mother tells her.

I pull Bobbie's suitcase from the rack.

"How about a Greyhound bus back to Chicopee?" Cora mumbles as she roots out a pair of jeans and a blouse.

Bobbie flicks the water from her chin. "It's all right," she says. "I just got dizzy."

My mother's watching her cautiously. "We'll get you in some clean clothes."

Afterward, the three of them walk back up the driveway, their footprints black on the bleached concrete.

Surprisingly, Ernest doesn't come out with all the commotion, and after returning the hose, I find him sitting at the pine table in the large kitchen.

"My mother wanted me to give you the check," I say.

He takes it without bothering to look at the amount.

"Pussy's sick," he says. "I had to walk him across the street to Dr. Burke's. Julio's eaten something disagreeable. And he can't tell me what. It's the most frustrating feeling in the world."

I ask him if his cat has ever gotten a bone caught in his throat. We had a tabby once who choked on some bass my father caught in the Salton Sea.

"A fish bone!" Ernest says, rising up in his chair. "Pussy eats whatever Grandmother and I eat. Everything goes through the blender. She's one of the family." He eyes me coldly. "A bone!"

But then our cat was only a stray, I admit, and backing out of the kitchen, I thank him again for breakfast.

As I pass by the parlor, the old woman sees me and starts back up about the trial.

"You must always lock the shutters," she says, pointing an accusing finger. "If you don't want your fat little lamb stolen."

I have the engine idling and the air conditioner on high when Bobbie and my mother come down the front steps.

"Everything tight?" my mother says, glancing up at the rack.

I nod and run around the car to open the door for my cousin. She slides in and slaps a damp handkerchief over her forehead.

"We don't have to do the Lindbergh stuff," I say, looking past her at my mother. "It's too hot. Let's just get back on the interstate."

My cousin peels the handkerchief off. "No," she says firmly. "Teddy already planned it. We're going."

Cora climbs into the backseat.

" 'Dehydrated with Love,' " she mutters. "We're talking country and western Top 40."

The ride out to Hopewell reminds me of the country in my father's pictures. The narrow, paved road winds through hills thick with loblolly. Lindbergh picked the Sourland Mountains so he could build a private airstrip where there wouldn't be any problem with fog. He also wanted privacy even though his widowed mother-in-law lived nearby in a mansion with over thirty servants.

While Bobbie naps and Cora reads, my mother daydreams at the wheel. She'll call my father from the motel tonight. But I know that they'll only wind up arguing again. Just as they have all summer at nearly a dollar a minute.

This is a mystery to me since my mother's already agreed to bring us over. Cora, naturally, has all the answers. Every picture tells a story, she'll say, pointing out the incriminating evidence in each photograph. In other words, the camera doesn't lie even if Daddy does.

When my mother turns off Princeton Road and passes the spot where the baby's body was found, I don't say anything. Everyone is depressed enough just being out here.

This morning we watched the *Columbia* liftoff from Cape Kennedy. All the scientists in their white short-sleeved shirts and skinny black ties stood staring at their monitors until the rocket cleared the platform. Then the camera showed thousands of tourists along the beach jumping up and down cheering. Later, when there wasn't as much to talk about, Walter Cronkite pointed out Jack Benny in the VIP stands telling jokes to the Vice President.

I can see that my mother's worried about a flat tire and so I mention how the famous comedian once drove down this very same road to attend the trial.

"Really?" she says. "Jack Benny?"

I ask Cora if she can guess some of the Broadway stars who turned up.

"It's practically right around the corner," I say. "They'd bus over after the matinee."

My sister keeps her magazine open in her lap. "Like whom, *par exemple?*"

"Like Ginger Rogers, for one. She had clues she wanted to pass along to the family."

My mother steers around a deep pothole. "Is that true, Teddy?"

I cross my heart. "It got her name on the front page. But I guess that's why they were celebrities. It's not like they were human beings or anything."

Cora makes a pained expression at my mother. "He's so full of it."

I think of faking some names but know better than to try to trip up my sister.

"The day Hauptmann took the stand sixty thousand people waited outside the courthouse," I say. "Even movie stars got turned away. It was a bigger story than the First World War." I don't mention the reason why: that the Lindberghs were America's most famous family and then suddenly they weren't a family anymore. It isn't what my mother wants to hear from me. She's convinced that it's the kind of thing that brings on my seizures. And that if I don't start learning how to relax I'll wind up in some state institution for epileptics like Skillman.

"He's such a bull artist," Cora says.

My cousin seems to come out of a trance.

"Well, I believe it," she says, wiping the back of her neck with the handkerchief. "It's the same as they pester Elvis."

Cora looks over at me but then only picks her *Cosmopolitan* back up.

The Oldsmobile dips heavily with the sharp ruts in the road, the dust billowing up behind us.

"It's certainly isolated enough," my mother says. Her knuckles are white on the steering wheel. "Nothing but trees for miles."

"The better to hide all those stars of stage and screen," Cora says.

The temperature drops as we climb higher into the mountains until, in the shade, it's almost cool enough for a sweater. There's the smell of pine and I begin to appreciate why Lindbergh wanted to settle here.

"What's that?" my mother says.

I lean forward to see past her. Up ahead a gang of teenaged boys has stumbled out of the woods. They're all dressed in the same style dark drawstring pants and T-shirts.

"Are they going to move?" my mother says, lifting her foot off the gas.

But they only stare defiantly back at us until finally she has to come to a complete stop.

"I guess that answers that," Cora says.

My mother checks to be certain our doors are locked. "I don't like this," she says.

There are five boys. The oldest, and the only white, looks to be about Cora's age. The youngest can't be much older than me. "Highfields" is printed across the front of their T-shirts.

"What are they?" Cora says. "Some kind of chain gang?"

"Highfields is the rehabilitation center," I say. "It's what they turned the estate into."

Bobbie swings her door open before my mother can stop her.

"Right back," my cousin says and all we can do is watch her amble down the road toward them, her hands in the back pockets of her tight jeans.

"They don't look rehabilitated to me," Cora says.

When I unlock my door, my mother lurches about in her seat. "Sit!"

"I was just going to—"

"Just sit."

Bobbie, meanwhile, has come up to the group and is agreeing with something the oldest boy is saying. The others stand about ogling her. When one of them points at a large leaf bag in the road, the smallest boy walks back and drags it into the ditch.

"Disposing of the body," Cora says.

But they've just been policing the area.

"I wish your cousin would be more cautious," my mother says. "She's been this way since she was a girl."

"Hey," my sister says. "These are her people. Salt of the earth."

Halfway back to the car, Bobbie turns to wag her finger at the youngest one who's said something to her.

My mother unlocks the door and my cousin's perfume wafts in ahead of her.

"It's right around the bend," Bobbie says, ignoring my mother's reproachful look. "They live there."

"Why don't you just back the car out," Cora says. "You can turn around when it's safe. Like in Philadelphia."

My mother seems to study the steering wheel as if it hadn't been there before.

"They're just kids, Rosemary," my cousin says. "You want me to drive?"

My mother looks straight ahead before slowly depressing the gas pedal. "Are they going to move?" she says more to herself than to us.

Bobbie rolls her window down and sticks her head out. "Come on, guys," she shouts.

They slouch sullenly as we inch toward them and only grudgingly step to the side.

"I think we ought to make this a short trip," my mother whispers.

"Highfields is for orphans," I say. "That's what the Lindberghs wanted it used for."

"They've been in a little trouble," Bobbie says, giving the boys a thumbs-up as we pass. "Who hasn't? They just got caught. That's all."

"Doing *what* is the question," Cora says. She twists about to see out the back window. "That tall one looks right out of *Lord of the Flies*."

I can tell that we're close now and my heart begins to race. The kidnapper had to have stolen back down this same dirt road.

Then abruptly the woods open on to an old white stone house. And I'm reminded of all the pictures in all the books.

"Very nice," my mother says when she pulls the car up. She turns to me. "Was there anything else you wanted to see, Teddy?"

I'm straining to make out the second-floor window on the side of the house. It's shaded by trees that forty years ago hadn't even been planted yet.

A man has stepped out onto the porch and Bobbie waves to him. He comes over to her side of the car and stoops down.

"I'm afraid we're closed up for the day," he says.

My mother leans over to see out my cousin's window.

"There are some boys back there on the road," she says. "They were a little frightening."

He continues smiling at Bobbie. "That's today's cleanup crew.

I'll have the superintendent speak to them. They forget their manners sometimes."

He introduces himself as Dr. Ivey, the curator of the estate, and explains that unfortunately visiting hours are over.

"So early?" Bobbie says.

When she edges out of the car to stretch, Dr. Ivey admits that things have been slow this week. Perhaps he could offer us an abbreviated tour.

My mother turns off the engine reluctantly.

"Do I have to come?" Cora says but she can tell from my mother's look not to press things.

Bobbie seems surprisingly buoyant. "It's not as big as Graceland," she says. "But it's roomy."

"The residence was given over to wards of the state," Dr. Ivey begins, leading us into the house. "Everything's pretty much as the Lindberghs left it."

I stop to read a small plaque on the wall that commemorates a "young son who once lived in this home with his loving family."

My mother trails behind us, on guard for any reappearance of the cleanup crew.

We move into a living room with two brick fireplaces at either end. There are signs for visitors not to touch the furnishings.

"Comfy," Bobbie says and plops down on one of the couches.

Dr. Ivey winces. He appears to be about my father's age and, taking off his glasses, smoothes his long hair back behind his ears.

"You've of course read about the kidnapping," he says. "Our guests are always curious about the baby's room. So if you'll follow me."

As we step back into the foyer, I point to the end of the hall. "Is that where he was reading?"

"The colonel?" Dr. Ivey says, watching Bobbie start up the stairs.

My cousin pauses. "You want to see in there first, Teddy?"

I look at Dr. Ivey who's smiling at her. "Certainly."

Cora comes up beside me and does her disc jockey voice. "This is now a free concert."

At the door, Dr. Ivey faces the chair that "Mr. Lindbergh" was sitting in when the maid rushed in to ask if he had the child.

"But, sadly, the colonel didn't," he says to Bobbie.

The ladder was outside the window. Everything had gone on right in front of Lindbergh's eyes. Only it was too dark for him to see.

"When the colonel was still in the living room he heard something crack," Dr. Ivey tells us. "Like wood splintering."

It sounded like an orange crate to him. Perhaps one of the help had dropped it in the kitchen. He hadn't bothered to get up and check.

The curator pats his hair with his palm and grins at my cousin. "Shall we go up to the bedroom now?"

Cora gazes over at me and mouths the word, "Doctor."

"So the house is for delinquent boys?" my mother says.

"Orphans of the storm," Dr. Ivey says. "Ages eight to eighteen."

"I guess it cuts down on your tourists," my sister says.

The doctor tails my cousin as she climbs the stairs ahead of him.

"They still come," he says distractedly. "They still come."

Cora looks back at me and mouths the word "Doctor" again.

Even without air conditioning the house is as cool as a wine cellar. It's the stone walls and mountain elevation. There's an eeriness about the place, like an abandoned monastery, and I wonder if anyone else feels it.

At the nursery, we all stand behind the velvet rope and peek in at the high-ceilinged room. Everything is just as it was the night of the kidnapping, Dr. Ivey assures us. The crib stands against one wall. There are stuffed animals and a small school desk.

And the window. The sun glows in its frame and I think of the boy. He'd been stolen from his home through this window.

The doctor nods at Bobbie who stands twisting her hair about her finger.

"The colonel wouldn't let anyone touch the ransom note," he says. "He was afraid they'd ruin any fingerprints. So they waited for the police."

In the end, so many inspectors and lieutenants had handled everything that the experts couldn't uncover a single unaccounted-for pair.

"But I think we got our man," Dr. Ivey says. "There can't really be any doubt about that."

My mother peers back down the hall nervously. "My son's very interested in the story," she says. "He's read all about it."

Bobbie suddenly ducks under the rope.

Dr. Ivey's face flushes. "I'm afraid that's against the rules."

"What about I promise to keep my hands to myself?" my cousin says.

The doctor stands rigidly. "It's not that," he stammers, holding the rope up. "It's just so many people come through here. What would happen if everyone touched everything?"

Bobbie ignores the raised rope. "I don't know," she says. "The furniture would get smudged?"

"Honey," my mother says to her. "You're upsetting the doctor."

My cousin takes a last look at the crib then dips back under the curator's arm, bumping his hip.

My mother and Cora drift down the hall for a glimpse at the Lindberghs' adjoining bedrooms. Dr. Ivey follows, apologizing to Bobbie for having to be so rule conscious. As soon as they're out of sight, I step back into the nursery.

There's a small quilt in the crib. That night, the nurse had used two large safety pins to keep the blanket from slipping. This is where the baby was taken from, and I draw my hand across the soft mattress. There seems nothing really special about any of it. No different really from any other nursery. It even reminds me of pictures of my own.

I try to imagine what the baby must have thought when, without a word, a stranger's hands scooped him into the air. How his eyes must have narrowed to make out the familiar face of his nurse: the kindly Betty Gow who just an hour before had rubbed his chest with VapoRub to soothe his cold. Only nothing in the end had protected him. Not the great warm house. Not his loving parents. Not his thoughtful nursemaid. Nothing.

I move to the window to touch the sill. The note was found here. Outside, directly below, is the cobbled courtyard where the carpenter's chisel was dropped. And I think, if only someone had closed the shutters. Or the baby's father had gotten up to see about the splintering sound. Or just this once his mother let him sleep with her. Or an older sister had been there to look in on her brother. But it had all happened differently.

"Teddy?" My mother stands in the doorway. "Honey, what are you doing?" She's giving me her X-ray look. "What's the matter, sweetheart?"

I low-crawl back under the rope. "Just thinking."

She shakes her head. "About what?" And she sweeps her hand in front of her to take in the room. "This?"

"I guess."

"What am I going to do with this kid?" she says. "This doesn't have anything to do with you."

"Okay."

"Why do you get yourself so wound up? Was it something Cora said?"

"I don't listen to her."

"Good. Because we both know better, don't we?" She's still studying me. "Don't we?"

"Sure."

She crosses her arms. "I know what you're thinking. You're not fooling anyone. I hope you know that. This is your mother talking to you."

I look down at the worn floorboards. It's where, for the first time, they would have seen the open window and understood it all.

"You're thinking how not even a little baby's safe," my mother says. "Not even in his own nursery. All somebody has to do is sneak up a ladder in the dark. Am I right?"

"You should know," I say. "I can't fool anyone, remember?"

She doesn't smile. "Well, I can at least tell you this, sweetheart. The only time you'll ever go out a window on me is if you decide to elope. And that's why your mother's going to keep the shutters nailed down." Then she reaches out to brush the hair from my eyes. "Honey, no one's ever going to be around my boy except people who love him."

"What about Dad?"

She looks at me as if I'd just spoken in tongues. "Your father?"

"Sure," I say. "He's never around. How do I know he loves me?"

"Now you're talking crazy," she says. "Your father loves you as much as any of us. Maybe you'll understand that when you're a daddy. What kind of crazy thing is that to say."

"All right."

My mother gazes at me for a moment. "I'm going down and wait in the car," she says finally. "This is not one of my favorite conversations."

"I was just thinking," I say.

"Well, maybe you shouldn't then," and she presses the heel of her hand against her forehead. "Anyway, I think the doctor's fallen in love with your cousin."

"I guess I'll poke around a little more," I say.

She looks down at her feet as if she'd dropped something. "What am I going to do with him?"

"Trade me in," I say.

My mother nods. "Your sister I'd consider."

At the end of the hall, I step over the rope to the master bedroom and sit down on the corner of the mattress. It's bigger than my parents' bed. Whenever, as a boy, I wandered into their room after a nightmare, they would let me fall back asleep between them. And in the dark, I could imagine myself nestled between two mountains, protected against whatever monsters might lurk in my dreams. But the Lindbergh baby was never big enough to find his way here on his own.

In the bathroom, I ease into the claw-foot tub and rest my neck against the rim of the cold porcelain. The colonel had been six foot three so there's plenty of room to stretch out. My mother has told me that she had a difficult time ever leaving me alone in the tub when I was a child. This was because Cora had nearly drowned once. She'd seen Esther Williams in a movie endlessly hold her breath underwater and then tried it herself. When my mother stepped back into the bathroom after answering the phone, she found my sister bug-eyed and sputtering.

Downstairs in the den, I sit where the colonel sat reading when the ladder was hoisted against the wall. One summer, when we were stationed at Fort Lee, Virginia, someone cut a screen open and stole my mother's monogrammed dresser set, an anniversary gift from my father. According to the MP's the thief had simply hooked his arm in the window and snatched the pieces right off the bureau. It wasn't much consolation to my mother but I remember being relieved that the person hadn't actually come into the house. That seemed to me far worse than any theft. That a stranger had wandered through our rooms, leaving his fingerprints on things that didn't interest him. Turning his nose up at what he knew wouldn't be worth stealing. That would have seemed a kind of judgment of my family and I would have hated him for it. I would have wanted to hunt him down with the MP's, and when we caught him, show no mercy.

After the insurance came through, my father replaced the dresser set, my mother no longer left the windows open, and we all forgot about the robbery until six months later when some AWOL Spec-4 was picked up for looting the PX. I remember seeing a picture of him in the *Post Reporter* and thinking how skinny and harmless he looked. But I know that I would have felt different if in taking the dresser set, he'd even stepped one foot into our house. That was where my mother and my father and my sister lived and I would have been unforgiving.

The colonel's leather armchair has a heavy, thick cushion. He liked to sit up late and read. This he did nearly every night after his wife and child were asleep on the second floor. Coming back down the ladder from the baby's bedroom, the kidnapper would have clearly been able to look in through the picture window to see him: the most famous man in America but no longer a father since he no longer had a son.

From the living room window I can see the Oldsmobile parked in the shade. My mother sits with her head slightly bowed and seems to be studying her travel brochures. More than likely she's thinking about the big telephone call to-night. In his last letter home, my father told me to pack an egg timer to keep any long distance conversations from going over. Cora said that he was just worried about Mom: that the longer they talked the better chance there was for her to ask the wrong question.

The Highfields boys live like recruits in the other half of the house. Their Army surplus bunk beds are tightly tucked in, their names stenciled on their metal footlockers. Each day on their cleanup detail they troop through the woods where the baby's body was finally found. And I wonder what they must think about to pass the time. Whether they daydream of being adopted, of ever being part of a real family. Dr. Ivey says that it's a good bet most of them will wind up back in a reformatory.

The morning after the kidnapping, students from Princeton volunteered to help search for clues. They formed human cordons to sweep through the hills but found nothing and eventually went home. Now orphans wander through the same dense forest and sleep in the same stone house the Lindbergh baby once slept in.

I walk out through the kitchen to the backyard. In pictures taken just before the house was built, this whole area had been bulldozed. And it's a moment before I notice the pup tents pitched just inside the tree line. Dr. Ivey had mentioned how boys guilty of house infractions are penalized by having to sleep outside. Some of the hard cases, he explained, would spend most of the summer in the woods.

Two of the tents are empty but the third is littered with camping gear: a nylon rucksack, a rusted portable cookstove, half a dozen utensils (but no knives), mosquito repellent, some crockery. The tent flaps are open and there's a stack of comic books and a Boy Scout flashlight. Dirty socks and underwear are balled up in one corner.

I lie down on the sleeping bag. There's no cushion of leaves beneath it and the ground is as hard as marble. At night, with the cicadas screeching in the dark it must be difficult to sleep. But the real punishment, of course, is being isolated from the others even though they're orphans and used to being alone. It must seem the worst sentence of all: to be rejected all over again. To understand that there's no one else, not a single soul in the world who wants you.

For the most part, Dr. Ivey tells us, the boys seem to care little about what actually happened here. They prefer to make up their own stories. He hears of the latest variation whenever a visitor complains. A favorite seems to be that the baby, after being murdered by his parents, was buried right on the grounds of the estate. And for an extra dollar the exact location would be pointed out by their knowledgeable guide.

Strolling back up to the house, I notice that one of the storm doors to the basement has been left open. At the bottom of the concrete steps, I peer into the darkness, hands on my knees. The windowless stone walls are covered with soot and I can barely make out the large furnace that looks as old as a steam engine. I'd read how a detective once led Mrs. Lindbergh down here to have her face the black hole of the empty grate.

Several months had passed without the baby being found and different rumors had started up around the country. For instance, that its famous parents only faked the abduction because the child was horribly deformed. And so the detective wondered aloud if perhaps Mrs. Lindbergh (who was pregnant again) hadn't cremated the colonel's son when it turned out to be retarded. If, and he'd glanced down at her swollen belly, she only wanted to clean the slate. Start all over as America's perfect family.

Back up in the sunlight, I breathe in deeply the clean mountain air. There's a waist-high, stone wall that borders the patio and I follow it around to the side of the house and sit down.

Yesterday, in the car, a bulletin on the radio made us all think the *Columbia* had crashed. Instead, a girl in West Virginia had murdered her parents and ten brothers and sisters. "I put gasoline into every room but the bathroom," she'd told the police in Parkersburg. "Now I don't have them to worry about."

We were all a little relieved that the spacecraft hadn't been the story. Still, it was something to think about.

"You wonder what could possess a child," my mother had said, looking up at Cora and me in the mirror.

My sister had shrugged her shoulders. "These kids today."

Cora comes up the driveway, her cheeks pink from the heat. "If it isn't Humpty Dumpty."

I ask her if she's seen Bobbie.

"I just looked at the map," she says and leans against the wall. "Do you have any idea how many more miles we have to be in the same vehicle together?"

"Maybe we could rent you a sidecar," I say.

My sister does her snorting laugh. "You don't get it, do you?"

And she rolls her eyes as if trying to explain the obvious to a four-year-old. "All you worry about is this moronic family. Like staying together's some kind of answer to everybody's prayer. Well, it's not mine. I'm sick of being carted off from one foxhole to the next. I'm not interested in wearing chopsticks in my hair. But does anybody ask me what *I* want to do?"

"Okay," I say. "What do you want to do?"

"I can *do* without graduating from Tiger Lily High," she says bitterly. "And my diet can *do* without eighteen months of moo goo gai pan."

"But if it was the south of France," I say, "that would be different."

"Damn straight it'd be different. Because it's exactly the kind of place Daddy never gets assigned. And you want to know why?"

"Sure."

She seems to hesitate, as if considering whether to answer her own question.

"All right," my sister says finally, "you're a big boy. I'll *tell* you why." But she doesn't and suddenly appears to want to change the subject.

"Go ahead," I say. "I haven't heard your cockeyed-theory-of-the-day yet."

She pushes off from the wall like a swimmer, turning about to face me with her arms folded.

"Okay, smart ass, I'll tell you. It's because the worse the overseas assignment, the less likely Mom's going to drag us all over. Think about it. Think of the dregs Daddy's come up with. Two tours in Nam? Both voluntary. Seoul? A misnomer if ever there was one. Formosa? Not exactly Aix-en-Provence, is it?"

"Mom's bringing us, isn't she?" I say.

"And doesn't Daddy sound ecstatic about the prospect." Cora breathes on her sunglasses, wiping each lens on her blouse. "Trust me. I know good acting when I see it."

"He doesn't really want us to come over then?"

"It's a script, buddy. He's reading the lines. But the heart ain't in it." She holds her glasses up to the sun.

"You're saying he's just pretending. He'd rather be over there alone."

"Hate to be the one to break it to you," and she stops as if to see whether all of this *is* being too hard on me.

"I'm all ears." In fact, her voice is like the roar of a giant conch shell: so close and overwhelming that I can't quite take it all in. Which is the only reason my sister hasn't stopped. I haven't registered *any* reaction. For once, her baby brother seems to be facing the truth like a big boy.

"Mom's hardly in the picture anymore," she says. "But listen, as far as supporting roles go, I've got to hand it to her."

"Dad's just going through the motions then?" I say.

She starts walking backward, trailing her hand along the top of the wall. *"Exactement.* Only I don't care for my part. It's getting old. They can take their little domestic farce on the road, if they like. I'm just not interested in being in it."

"You mean with us," I say.

My sister's voice almost seems pitying. "It's playacting, Teddy. And it's a lousy play."

I watch her cross the gravel drive, her long shadow pointing back at me.

After a while, I come around the nursery side of the house and stop beneath the window. The sun reflects brightly off the white stone house and I pick up a pebble. Mrs. Lindbergh had tossed one of them up at the window just before the baby was put down for his nap. His nurse then held him up for her to see. If he hadn't come down with a cold they would have spent the night at his grandmother's. If the shutter hadn't been warped it wouldn't have been left unlocked. If the rung on the ladder hadn't broken, the kidnapper might not have dropped him. But there was a long list of if's. None of which happened. Or any Ouija board could ever have predicted.

My mother has the ice chest open and, when she sees me, pulls a drink out.

"What's with your sister?" she says. "She walked right by a minute ago and didn't say a word."

I scoop an ice cube from her glass and I can smell the alcohol.

"She mentioned something about jumping out of a window," I say.

"Sounds like your sister, doesn't it?" My mother feels my forehead, her hand cool from holding her glass. "You all right, honey?"

Typically, after a seizure, I'll have a whopping migraine that lasts the day.

"We can skip the Hospital for Epileptics," I say. "Dr. Ivey thinks it's just a federal rehab center or something now."

"A lot of rehabilitating going on around here," my mother says.

"We ought to drop Cora off."

She smiles slyly at me. Having a drink this early, even just a mildly spiked one, is something new for her. Occasionally she'll have a nightcap to help her dull the pain in her legs. But according to Cora she's started slipping shots into her Coke long before bedtime.

"Speak of the devil," my mother says.

My sister comes back down the driveway chewing her lip. A stranger would look at her and suspect she was deranged. But I know that she's only feeling put-upon.

"Something the matter?" my mother says as Cora flings open the back door of the car.

"Let's just get out of here, could we?" She cranks her window halfway up. "Brother's had his little visit."

I shrug my shoulders at my mother whose eyebrow is already arched.

"You two," she says exasperatedly, imagining that Cora and I have had another fight.

When Bobbie and Dr. Ivey emerge from the house, they shake hands politely on the steps. The doctor waves to us but keeps his distance as my cousin crosses the driveway to the car.

Because my mother believes Bobbie to have more credibility with "our little friends," she asks her to drive. Before Lou, my cousin had gone steady with a semi-professional stock car racer named Ron. He was from Worcester and often picked her up in one of his funny cars. But after they were married Lou made Bobbie sell the souped-up Monte Carlo Ron had sold her. Now she drives a brown Nova that rattles dangerously in fourth. Still, my cousin knows better than to push the overloaded Oldsmobile. Or my mother.

"It's great getting out on the open road," Bobbie says and angles the mirror to take both Cora and me in.

My mother already has the map and her red crayon out. She's decided that Amish country might be educational for the kids.

As we descend through the Sourland Mountains, I think about the Hospital for Epileptics over in Skillman. It was the first place the cops thought of looking the night of the kidnapping. Everyone agreed that the ransom note must have been written by a German ("the child is in gut care") who was probably a carpenter (the three sections of the abandoned ladder were handmade to fit in a car). And mentally ill. Who else would even think of stealing the son of Lucky Lindy?

At the bed and breakfast last night, I dreamed I was a patient at the clinic and the prime suspect. How could I be certain, the authorities wanted to know, that I hadn't wandered off the grounds after a seizure? And, of course, I couldn't be sure about anything. Perhaps, after all, I *was* guilty. A jealous, epileptic orphan living only miles from the most adulated family in America. Why shouldn't they suspect me? Especially when I told them who my real father looked so much like. Only handsomer. And braver. And a paratrooper besides.

At the first Ho-Jo's on the Pennsylvania Turnpike, I order German pancakes and wind up eating most of Bobbie's french toast as well (she's having "plumbing" problems again). We've called ahead for reservations in Dutch Country. One of the Visitors' Bureau pamphlets advertises a three-star motel just outside Paradise.

My mother's few surviving relatives are scattered in the western part of the state. But she has no interest in visiting any of them. "They're distant," she says and leaves it at that. Bobbie tells us that the last she heard of her only uncle (my mother's half brother), he was on another bender up in Bethlehem. Cora has always wondered about us not having any grandparents. "I mean, what are the odds? Four of them bought the farm before they hit sixty? Something doesn't strike you as a little funny there?" What I *did* find unusual was that neither my mother nor my father ever talked about them. My aunt Irene has been our only source. And even she is tight-lipped. "Your mother's father was a stubborn man," she'll say. "That's what killed him. Going deer hunting without a poncho and catching pneumonia. You couldn't tell him anything." His wife, my maternal grandmother, passed away in childbirth bringing an alcoholic into the world. That, we assumed, must have been Uncle Bill, the half brother no one heard from except when he was out of bar money.

Our lack of relatives feeds my sister's favorite fantasy. "You're theirs, all right," she'll say to me. "Had to come from the same shallow little pond. Whereas with me we're talking a different gene pool entirely." Then she'll launch into her popular fairy tale. "Once upon a time a beautiful child was plucked from the reeds by a passing lieutenant and his overbearing wife. There followed her sad odyssey from one base, in every sense of the word, to the next . . ."

"We'll go on in to Lancaster," my mother says. "It's too early to check into our room."

We pass our first Amish horse and buggy on the interstate. And I catch a quick glimpse of the family. They're all in black. A girl my own age is wedged between her parents on the bench. She wears a bonnet, her long hair braided. They pay no attention to the traffic that whisks past. The driver only concentrates on keeping the horse clomping safely along the shoulder of the road.

"It's a long way from rockets and moon landings," my mother says. "You have to wonder what they must make of it all."

We'd just been listening to some commentator on the radio talking about what would happen if the astronauts were forced down in alien territory. According to him they were authorized by international treaty to use a special frequency picked up by short-wave receivers around the world.

"Might make an interesting Bond movie," Cora chimes in. She's been sulking the last hour, which also happens to be the limit to how long she can keep her mouth shut. "The capsule crash-lands in Amish country and 007's sent to rescue the crew from a stone age civilization."

Bobbie rests her head against the window. "I'm sorry," she says. "I have to wee-wee again."

"I see Grace Kelly as the love-starved widow," Cora says. "After a brief fling with Connery she marries Buzz Aldrin who reveals his mother was a Quaker."

"Almost there," my mother says to Bobbie. "Five miles."

It's beautiful country. Dirt roads lead back to hundred-year-old farms where white barns big as airport hangars shimmer in the heat.

As soon as our exit comes up we get stuck behind a procession of buggies that move slowly toward town.

"My idea of hell," Cora says. "Spending my life watching the wrong end of a horse."

"Who are you kidding?" I say. "You wouldn't even *know* the wrong end of a horse."

My sister cracks the knuckles of both hands. "That's what comes from having a jackass for a brother."

"All right," my mother says. "Your cousin's not feeling well."

But we all have a little cabin fever. It's too pretty a day to spend it couped up in a car.

The outskirts of Lancaster look a lot like Chicopee. But Cora will tell you that *everything* in America looks like Chicopee now. It's only one of the reasons my sister is so bitter about our assignment. Most Army brats her age, she complains, have already lived in Europe. If not Paris then at least Milan. She predicts that Taipei will turn out to look like Chicopee too. That, after all, is what the Taiwanese do best: make identical copies.

With all the tourist traffic it takes us nearly twenty minutes to get in to town. There are more buggies than cars along the main street and as soon as my mother finds a meter, Bobbie bursts from the front seat.

"I'll be in the drugstore," she says and is gone.

Cora shakes her head. "This how it's going to be the next two thousand miles? Peeing our way across the country?"

"She'll settle down," my mother says. "This business with Lou's just got her a little tense."

We're parked in front of Van's General Store. Next to it are Whitworth's Hardware and the Royal Café.

"I'm going to catch up with your cousin," my mother says after changing her shoes (her ankles are swollen from the heat). "How about we meet back here in half an hour?"

"Plenty of time," my sister says.

I watch my mother limp across the street. Lately, even an hour in the PX will send her home to soak her ankles in Epsom salts. She shrugs off seeing a doctor, arguing that it's just poor circulation. As if at forty that's an expected ailment.

"I keep thinking of Ernest Borgnine," Cora says, shading her eyes as she surveys the storefronts. My sister possesses what she calls "TMR"—Total Movie Recall. "He played this Amish farmer who stabs Lee Marvin with a pitchfork."

I feed the meter and we wait for a buggy to pass. The driver is Cora's age but already appears round-shouldered and weary. He doesn't look over at us, only gives the reins a little flick of his wrist.

We walk down to the grocery store on the corner. There's a Pine-Sol-scrubbed scent to the place. The worn, hardwood floors shine with hand wax but the shelves are filled with the same brands you see in any chain supermarket. Behind the dimpled glass of the display cabinets are boxes of Bit-O-Honey's and Baby Ruth's.

Cora finds a Coke machine (Bobbie's gone through the ones in the cooler) and pries the top off, taking a deep swig.

"There'd be two options if I lived here," she whispers. "Convert to Judaism or go buggy. No pun intended."

I know that my sister only wants to argue. But it's impossible not to come up for her bait.

"What do you know about how they live," I say. "Maybe they know something you don't."

Cora leans back against the machine, amused by my tone. "And what did *thee* have in mind?"

"Maybe living this way keeps them together," I say, feeling my face get red. "Maybe some things are more important to them than stupid movies."

Only my sister could get me riled up about the Amish.

"To my brother," she says, raising the bottle in a toast. "The philosopher king."

"You don't think they've learned anything?" I say. "Like we've got all the answers?"

Someone with two cameras wrapped around his neck rattles a shopping cart past us. Cora waits until he's down the next aisle.

"You read a two-page brochure on the 'plain people' and suddenly you're Brother Theodore." She isn't smiling. "You wouldn't know 'Ordnung' from cow shit. That's because you live in a dream world." She keeps her voice down, clipping her words sharply. "Come to think of it, you'd fit right in. But tell me this. Dad's a soldier, right? Willing to give his life for his country. You've heard the spiel. So what do you think these jokers are?" She expects an answer but I only take the Coke from her. "Conscientious objectors is what they are. All the way back to the Revolutionary War. But then you knew that. Right?"

I take a swig of the Coke and hand it back to her.

"Who you figure's going to come up with a cure for your little problem?" my sister says angrily. "Some Amish neurosurgeon? It'd be a neat trick on an eighth-grade education. Which is as far as they let the kiddies go. Real smart. But you're right. I *don't* think they know anything." She shakes her head and I can't tell who she's more disgusted with—me or the Amish.

Back out in the street we stand blinking in the stark sunlight when I see Bobbie sitting in the phone booth.

I point her out to my sister and we both move back into the shade of the grocery store's awning.

"He's probably mad she woke him up," Cora says.

We aren't close enough to hear anything even though the booth's open.

After a while, Bobbie sets the phone down and leans her shoulder against the meshed glass. She slumps on the stool with her back to us, her head lowered.

Just then my mother comes out of the drugstore, a large brown bag in one arm and a sack of ice in the other.

"You seen your cousin?" she says and hands me the ice. "The pharmacist was telling her about some things to see."

"I don't think the Amish are into Grand Ole Opry," my sister says.

"Did you ask about the Homestead?" I say. One of the guidebooks had recommended it: an authentic farm opened during the day to visitors.

"I forgot to, honey. But we ought to be able to find it."

"I'm going to draw the line on wax museums," Cora says.

"As a matter of fact," my mother says, "he mentioned one out on Route 30. Not far from our motel." She turns to me. "And something called Dutch Wonderland right next door to it. His own kids swear by it."

At the car, I empty the ice in the chest while my mother unfolds the map on the hood.

"I vote we go check into the room and see what we want to do," she says.

"I'm going to pass on the wax museum," Cora says. "I just don't think there'd be any real difference to the untrained eye. I mean, given the subject matter."

"I want this trip to be educational," my mother says. "It's an opportunity for us to learn a few things."

Bobbie returns with her mascara smudged so that she looks like a raccoon.

"I probably ought to stop calling," she says. "He just gets me flustered."

My mother is already nodding. "That's a good idea, honey. Let him cool off awhile."

Cora fans herself with the *Screenland* my mother has bought

her. "Tell him we've got tickets for 'The Mike Douglas Show,' "
she says. "Tell him you'll be in the audience. You're hoping Mike
lets you ask a question."

Bobbie listens to all of this uncertain how to take my sister.

"She's just kidding," I say when my cousin looks over at me.
"It's taped in New York."

"Tell him it was a special," Cora says. "What's Lou know?"
She stops and pokes her tongue into her jaw. "Anyway, it might
give him pause."

My mother signals for us all to get in the car. "We'll let your
cousin work this out," she says. "She doesn't need our advice."

In fact, that's exactly what I think my cousin is looking for:
someone to tell her what to do. On this, at least, I have to agree
with Cora. Bobbie's father, my uncle, used to be the one to counsel
her. But she wasn't much older than me when he dropped dead
trying to start up the lawn mower. Everyone still tells stories about
Uncle Sal, the mechanical genius. He was a tinkerer. Someone who
would spread an old sheet out in the front yard and take apart
whatever he thought needed taking apart: my aunt's Singer sewing
machine, a broken juicer, the abandoned hot rod of one of Bobbie's ex-boyfriends (she was already dating sixteen-year-old me-
chanics). Anything around the house that plugged in worked like a
top. "He'd lay all the parts out till he found what was causing the
problem," Bobbie will still proudly recall. "Then he'd clean everything up. Oil what needed oiling and throw out what needed
throwing out. He was that way with me too. All he had to do was
look at me and he'd know what was wrong. And he always knew
how to make it right."

Cora believes that her cousin's problem is textbook material.
That Lou is just a father substitute to fill the void. The only trouble, my sister argues, is that Bobbie filled it with another void. And
that you didn't have to be a psychiatrist to see Lou coming down
the pike.

It's true from the photographs I've seen that my uncle Sal did look a lot like my cousin's husband. And coincidentally when they got married Lou was exactly the same age as Bobbie's father when he yanked the starter cord on the refurbished mower for the last time. My sister hopes that with any luck history will repeat itself although she admits that it's hard to picture Lou doing any kind of strenuous yardwork.

As we drive out Route 30, half a dozen billboards advertise Dutch Wonderland, which Cora suspects is some kind of tax dodge for the "plain people."

Bobbie sits in the front seat staring blankly out the window. My mother has given up trying to talk to her.

We pass another barn with a bright red hex sign. In the middle of the field a father and son sit on an ancient-looking plow. The boy holds the leather reins out in front of him, a straw hat shading his eyes. My mother has always told me that if Korea hadn't come along, my father probably would have wound up a farmer.

"Listen to this," Cora says and reads to us from her travel book. A celibate cloister of Seventh Day Baptists had once lived in nearby Ephrata. However, by the early 1800s, its members had all died off. "I guess nobody cheated."

But up ahead, a woman is sitting in a rocker set back from the road, quilts stacked high on a table beside her.

"Let's stop," my mother says.

The woman doesn't bother to look up as we pull over.

"We'll just see what she has first," my mother says. "Let's not start flashing money around."

The woman sits beneath a large beach umbrella wearing the

traditional Amish garb: a triangular shawl and white prayer cap. She glances up from her knitting, touches the stacked quilts, and smiles politely.

Cora studies several exorbitant price tags and then wanders back to the car, her sneakers crunching on the gravel.

"How large are they?" my mother says, shielding her eyes from the sun. "I mean, are they big enough for a double bed?"

The woman tilts her head. Her face is tanned and deeply lined. "Yes, they are all the proper size."

"Mom might like a quilt," Bobbie says to herself.

My mother gives her niece a pained look. She's an accomplished flea market haggler and knows better than to show any enthusiasm.

"I didn't think Irene was that big on blue," she says when my cousin presses one of the quilts to her cheek.

"It's her favorite color," Bobbie says.

The woman doesn't take her eyes off her darning needles. She's going to let my cousin do the bartering for her.

When I glance back at the car, Cora flings her head and arms out the window as if from sunstroke.

"Why don't you think about it?" my mother says to Bobbie. "It's a little more than you probably want to invest."

My cousin hasn't stopped fingering the quilt.

"I don't get the impression she wants to come down on the price anyway," my mother says as if the seller weren't there. "I think she's going to stand firm."

Bobbie looks over at the woman who pretends not to be paying any attention.

After a while, we all trudge back to the car where Cora's chewing an ice cube.

"She's probably not even Amish," my sister says. "That getup looks mail-order."

My cousin leaves her door open.

"I won't see another one that pretty," she declares. "It's just the kind Mom would pick out for herself."

"Irene's like me," my mother says. "She likes a bargain."

"Lou Hammuck was supposed to be a bargain," Bobbie says and we're all stunned by her tone. "And look what that got me."

She tramps back along the shoulder of the road, her blouse black with sweat.

"Lou Hammuck a bargain?" Cora says. "That must of been some basement."

"Your cousin's distraught," my mother says. "She's not herself today."

When Bobbie returns it's only for her billfold.

"I'm getting two," she says, reaching under the seat for her pocketbook. "One for a single bed."

My mother tries to grab her hand.

"Don't spend your money," she says. "You're just tired."

"That's right," my cousin says. "*Sick* and tired."

She doesn't wait for my mother who quickly catches up with her.

Cora and I watch them argue in front of the woman's stand. I can't remember ever seeing my cousin raise her voice to my mother. It's like coming in on a strange drive-in movie.

Bobbie suddenly brings her fist down on the table and the stack of quilts jumps. We can hear everything she says. Lou doesn't love her. He couldn't care less if she ever comes back. If her father hadn't died she never would have married him. She would still be single and happy.

"Talking sense for a change," Cora says.

My mother tells her she's going to have a stroke in this heat. If the quilt is that important then she'll buy the both of them for her.

The Amish woman has moved several feet away from the table, keeping her chair out in front of her.

Then just when it appears that Bobbie has settled down, she seizes one of the quilts and hurls it into the road.

"Great," Cora says and we both get out of the car to see my cousin trample it in a crazy war dance. Now even my mother seems to think it best just to keep her distance. To let her niece work it out of her system. She only continues to watch for traffic in either direction. But it's a flat stretch of highway and there are no cars in sight.

Bobbie finally backs away from the quilt as if from a coiled snake and I quickly gather it up from the hot pavement.

A car at last approaches, its passengers gawking at the curious roadside spectacle.

"Don't worry about it," my mother says. "It's none of their business."

She looks over at Cora and me. "Get the change from the woman." And she smiles at Bobbie as she leads her away, one arm around her waist.

They walk back to the car, my mother whispering into my cousin's ear.

The woman is waiting for us at the table. She replaces a rubberband around a thick wad of bills.

"I don't know what I'm doing anymore," my cousin is saying to my mother as I stuff the quilts in the back of the car. "You know I'm not mad at you, Rosemary."

Afterward, half a mile down the road, Cora finds something in the paper to share with the rest of us.

"What's that?" my mother says, happy to hear anything that might lift the tension in the car.

Cora holds the front page so I can see that she's not making it up.

"Mrs. Armstrong's not worried about being a celebrity," my sister says. "She said, 'If Neil has to spend a great deal of time with other things then we'll try to make the most of our time together.' " Cora rattles the paper in her lap and grins at me. "Isn't that inspiring?"

But I'm watching a pickup come toward us in the other lane. Bound in big bundles in the back of the truck are dozens of colorful quilts.

"It is," my mother says and smiles cautiously at my cousin. "When you think of all the pressure on that woman right now."

My mother unfolds the slip of paper with my father's fourteen-digit number on it even though she knows it by heart.

"You can have Daddy when I'm through with him," she says to me. "Think of what you want to talk about."

What I really want to talk about, of course, no one wants to hear. Serious questions are against house rules but where exactly these rules come from, no one seems to know. "If this family had a coat of arms," Cora likes to say, "it wouldn't be *Veritas Vos Liberabit* [The Truth Will Make You Free]. It'd be *Noli Me Rogare* [Don't Ask]."

Glancing at her watch, my mother dials the long distance number and as she listens to the circuits clicking across the Pacific, she winks at me. When, at last, my father's cheerful voice filters through the other end of the cable, her whole expression changes.

"Darling?" she says excitedly. "Is that you?"

Cora looks over at me and makes a gun with her thumb and forefinger, putting it to her head. She believes that my mother is too much the perfect housewife and should assert herself more. It's the reason, she argues, that my father takes advantage of us all.

"We're in Paradise," my mother says and laughs girlishly.

Tired of the moon coverage, Cora puts her headphones on to listen to the soundtrack to *Doctor Zhivago.*

Bobbie has been sitting at the desk writing a letter to Lou on motel stationery. She crumples up another sheet of paper and pitches it into the wastebasket. Every once in a while she has stopped to ask me how to spell a word. So far I've spelled "nauseous," "hypocrite," and "annulment."

I can't concentrate on my book. It's one my father started after a trip up to Thule, Greenland, to test some Arctic gear. That was when he was still in the Quartermaster with Research and Development. Anyway, it's about the Negro explorer who went to the North Pole with Commander Robert Peary. His name was Matthew Henson and regardless of how terrible the conditions were or how much he suffered from the cold, "Matt" never complained. At the end of each day, he would build two igloos, one for Peary and one for the Eskimos and himself. The commander treated him poorly but never went anywhere without his "manservant." Once, when Peary came down with frostbite and lost nearly all of his toes, it was Matt who gave him morphine and nursed him back to health.

My mother laughs at something my father says. "It's a good thing this isn't a party line," she says, uncoiling the cord from her chair leg. Her voice is teasing and after a long silence, she gets up, smiles at us, and steps into the bathroom, easing the door shut after her.

"They're like newlyweds," Bobbie says.

I'm studying a picture of Matthew Henson. His grandmother had been half white and his smile reminds me a little of my father's.

My cousin comes over and stands beside me a moment. She glances in Cora's direction and then collects a letter from the desk. There's a mail slot in the office.

"How about we step outside for a minute?" she whispers. "Got something I want to ask you."

When I follow her to the door, my sister rolls over on the bed and lifts the headset from her ears.

"We'll be right back," Bobbie says to her, waving the envelope.

"Get me a Hershey Bar from the machine," Cora says and scoops up some change from the top of the TV. "Hey, it should be fresh. Right?"

Outside, my cousin walks ahead of me, chewing her nail.

"I ought to keep this to myself," she says. She stops in front of the shrubbery that borders the parking lot. "You're my favorite boy cousin."

"I'm your *only* boy cousin."

"It doesn't matter," she says distractedly. "You'd still be my favorite."

She paces along the edge of the concrete as if afraid to take the step from the sidewalk. I can see the glow from the amusement park rides in the distance.

"Your cousin's a coward," Bobbie says and holds the envelope out for me. "You see where it's from?"

I nod. "Planned Parenthood."

"You see the postmark?" she says.

It was stamped over two weeks ago but is still sealed.

"Why do you think I been afraid to open it?" she says.

But Cora had been suspicious from Day One.

"Because it's about whether you're pregnant or not?" I say.

We both look out at the Oldsmobile parked in the motel lot.

"How come all the brains got on your side of the family?" She exhales, her breath whistling. "I had them send it to work so Lou wouldn't get a call at home."

The reason she didn't want to know was because it might have influenced her decision about coming along with us. Then on Saturday she ran into the doctor at the post office. She'd never once seen the guy outside of the clinic and she bumps into him waiting in line. That was when she suddenly realized what she was doing in the post office. She'd made up her mind to go with us and was buying stamps to send postcards to Lou.

"Anyway, he just sort of smiled at me and I didn't know if he was smiling because he thought I was happy with the news or whether he was just smiling because I'd been dumb enough to come in thinking I was pregnant." She steps out onto the lot but then backs up. "Lord have mercy, Teddy, what am I doing telling you this stuff?"

"I'm fourteen," I say. "I'm not a baby."

She looks at me without saying anything and then her bottom lip starts to quiver. "You're not," she says. "You're not a baby at all. If I had a kid, I'd want him to be just like you."

"But you don't want to have one?"

She contemplates the condition of her nails for a moment. "With Lou?" And she sits down on the curb, drawing her legs up against her chest. "That's the thing. I guess that's what's kind of up in the air."

I notice that the bathroom light in our room isn't on. Whenever my mother talks to my father long distance, she likes it to be in the dark. She says it makes it easier for her to think.

"We used to go to the drag races together," Bobbie is saying. "Or roller derby when it was in town. We used to do a lot of things together before we got married. Now he's not interested."

"Lou's crazy," I say.

My cousin stands back up, her ankles cracking. "It takes two to tango, honey. He ain't any crazier than me. I mean, I married him, didn't I?"

She pulls the car key from her jeans.

"Want to do your crazy cousin a favor?"

She'd already tried to open the letter herself after we got back from dinner at the Wagonland Grill. But once again she'd chickened out.

"Go sit in the car and read that thing for me." She holds the key out. "Just read what it says and then pitch it in the bushes. I don't want to see it."

"You mean, you just want me to tell you if the test was positive?"

"That's right, darlin'. That you got yourself a cousin, once removed."

I can feel the key sticking to my damp palm. "But you want me to go to the car?"

"If I could wait here," Bobbie says, "it'd be a real favor I'd owe you."

The Oldsmobile is coated with dust from all the back roads we've been on. The rear tires appear deflated even with several of the suitcases unloaded, and as I come up to the passenger side my legs feel feeble and I reach out for the door handle as if it were a life preserver. My cousin is still sitting on the curb, her chin resting on her knees. And I think of Lou lying on the couch watching television. He'll have my aunt Irene call in some excuse for work tomorrow and then reset his alarm for "Art Linkletter." Cora thinks Bobbie should have thrown the TV in the tub with him as a parting gesture. A little shock treatment to loosen up his back.

In the front seat, I set the letter on the dashboard for a moment. My mother's right about her niece. She's a poor judge of character. How else can you explain a character like the one she married? Still, I want to believe that Lou could change. And that Bobbie's coming with us might scare him enough to unplug the talk shows for good. Cora thinks there's as much chance of that happening as him getting his tattoo burned off. Certain traits are ingrained, she likes to say. It's the same word she uses to describe how Dad's such a lady-killer. "It's why Bobbie's always been able to spill her guts out to Mom," she'll say. "They're birds of a feather. The kind that clip their own wings and then sit in a cage the rest of their lives." My sister likes to talk tough. She's subscribed to *The Village Voice* since the seventh grade.

My hand is shaking as I pick up the letter. This is how I'm so different from my father who's always graceful under pressure. He would know how to comfort my cousin. In Saigon, while my father was picking out tomatoes in a downtown vegetable market, his bodyguard was shot to death. Of course, he told us nothing about this until years later. And only then because my mother overheard the story during Happy Hour at the officers' club. A captain tipsy on half-priced whiskey sours had started bragging about how "the old man" never told war stories even though he had more to tell than anyone. My mother confessed how much all of this embarrassed my father. And it was easy for me to picture him standing there holding his gin and tonic trying to steer the conversation in another direction. "That's your father for you," my mother said. She frets about his career and how he never takes credit for himself. But it's also the reason, I believe, that he's always been so popular with his troops.

Bagging groceries at the commissary or setting pins at the post bowling alley, I would be told by enlisted men how my father was the only officer to ever listen to them as a person and not just as a soldier. Even though Cora accuses me of making him into some kind of five-star Buddha, I know that she feels the same way I do. "There's nothing wrong with a boy putting his father on a pedestal," my mother will defend me against my sister. "As long as he's lucky enough to have a father like the one you've got."

The letter feels as light as junk mail. The address has been personally typed, my cousin's last name misspelled as it always is. And I think of how the Oscars are announced the night of the Academy Awards when each presenter rips open the sealed envelope and the camera pans to the delirious winner who kisses everyone in his aisle before leaping onto the stage to seize the gold statuette.

I open the letter and stare at the single sentence, knowing that it's useless to hope there's been some mistake. That the results are somehow in error.

There's only one typed line above the two signatures, the word itself followed in parentheses by the positive mathematical symbol (+).

Bobbie is up pacing again, suspicious that I'm taking so long. It doesn't seem right that I should know what I know before her. She could have asked my mother to come along or even Cora who is older and a girl.

The car door cracks shut like a pistol shot and my cousin stands squinting at me in the dark. Already she can see for herself. Her shoulders slump and she bows her head. Even at fifty paces I've given it away.

Then everything starts all over again: my hair lifting as if charged with electricity, the itchiness in my toes. And I bite my lip, praying that it will stop. It isn't what Bobbie needs: her favorite boy cousin left twitching pathetically in the middle of the parking lot.

When she reaches me, I'm holding onto the aerial.

"Teddy?"

She grasps my elbow, her own face as contorted as mine.

"Sugar, what's the matter?"

I try to speak but only saliva curls from the corner of my mouth.

"Your cousin's right here."

The halos have sprouted. But at least I'm conscious, which is something new: a waking seizure.

Bobbie wrests my fingers from the antenna and together we slide down the side of the car to the pavement.

"We're going to hold on," she says, her soft hands wiping my chin. "We're going to sit this one out."

And I'm thinking: this is definitely something different. Not only do I taste my own tears but I can feel my cousin's hands and smell her unmistakable scent. My tongue is dead. My legs have folded beneath me like a yogi's. Yet I'm conscious. Not out of it.

"Bobbie?"

"Right here, honey."

The light's come back on in the bathroom. My mother has either hung up or it's Cora's turn with my father.

"I think I'm okay," I say. "See," and I tug one leg out.

"That's good, tiger. That's real good."

"I can get up now."

She pins both hands behind my shoulders and I lean forward. "Bobbie?"

She's trying to blink away the tears that have welled up.

"You're pregnant," I say.

My cousin smiles weakly and now it's my turn to comfort her. But my arm, twisted behind my back, has fallen asleep and I can only flop it out in front of me.

"I guess I already knew," she says.

For once, I feel as brave as my father. I've kept from blacking out. I've stayed awake to be with my cousin.

"Can you stand up all right?" she asks.

I can. There's nothing to it. I could jump from an airplane.

But I'm frightening her. The crazy smile. The way I lose my balance and crash back up against the car.

"Can you walk?"

I'm trying not to appear so pleased in my light-headedness and brush my dead hand across the back of my pants.

"No problem," but when I turn, the glare of the Paradise Inn sign stops me. Finally, like a drunk I toe one foot out in front of the other. "Really."

My cousin is crying and she watches me as if I were edging out onto a high wire.

"You're just going to scare my mother," I say.

This makes sense and she agrees.

"Okay."

My hand itches but I keep from scratching it.

Five minutes later, standing outside the door, I can hear Cora on the phone. She's hyper, talking excitedly to my father. And I remember we were supposed to get her a candy bar.

"Maybe we shouldn't say anything yet," Bobbie whispers. "What do you think?"

I think that it's probably a good idea, although halfway back to the machines, I can't decide whether she means my seizure or her being pregnant.

By the time Cora hands the phone over, my father is antsy to get off the line.

"We're going to have to cut this short," he says. "Your mother's worn off the reentry shield on my ear."

He jokes about how I'm the one earning the hazard duty pay and not the astronauts ("In the same bunker with those three."). And that when Mom rings him up again, I can pull rank. Our brief chat goes the way all our brief chats do. With nothing really ever getting said.

Afterward, my mother follows Bobbie into the bathroom to recount her conversation while my cousin soaks in a bubble bath. To avoid any questions about my pallor, I let Cora talk me into wandering over to the amusement park, which is within walking distance of our motel.

"I don't want the two of you out of each other's sight," my mother calls out to us from the door.

"Scary thought," Cora says, pocketing the five-dollar bill my mother has given her.

It's a beautiful night. There's the smell of hay and horses in the air. This afternoon, everything was lit up a primary color and even

Cora stopped reading her magazines to look out the window at the sunny fields.

At the gate to the park, a small band of Amish boys loiter about. They're dressed in scruffy jeans with their white shirts and straw hats.

"Rebels with a cause," Cora says.

They move in a pack up the midway, pushing and shoving each other like any teenagers at a shopping center.

My sister buys us a string of tickets and steers me toward something called the Magic Carpet. She's like my father when it comes to carnival rides. Nothing scares her.

"We'll start you out slow and work your way up," she says, pointing to the roller coaster in the distance.

There are few people on the rides and the operator of the Magic Carpet sets his paperback down when we come up to him.

"Two," Cora says and hands him tickets for the both of us. "My treat."

The man is wearing a T-shirt that's several sizes too small for him. When he lifts the safety bar, Cora and I dip under his huge arm.

"Liftoff," he says, cranking back a great metal stick that releases the car's brake.

We lurch forward, our chests pressed against the cold iron. Cora is suddenly all smiles. "Your sister's always been that way," my mother will tell me. "Ever since she was a baby, she's liked things like Ferris wheels. No one else would go on them with her except your father."

I take after my mother. But I don't want Cora blabbing to Bobbie about what a pantywaist her brother is.

As we start to whirl and dip I clench the side of the car and make pleading faces at the burly operator each time we hurtle past him. He ignores us, his head lowered, one hand resting on the control stick. We've paid, after all, and he'll give us our money's worth, perhaps even an extra spin or two since there's no line.

My bored sister taps her foot beside me, already plotting her next ride without her thin-skinned brother. She sits with both arms folded in her lap, gazing coolly out at the dark, rolling farmland.

I open my eyes to see Cora laughing, her hair whipping about her head as my white fingers clutch the safety bar, the lattice of girders beneath seeming as flimsy as matchsticks.

After several revolutions, my sister looks over at me and quickly signals the operator to stop the ride. Within seconds the car rattles over the last arch, shimmying to the bottom of the final loop where we jolt to an abrupt rest.

"What do you say, bub?" The man is leaning all his weight against the control stick.

I stagger across the platform to the plywood stairs while Cora continues patting my back as if to urge me to throw up and get it over with.

I sit down in the grass, head between my knees.

"You don't feel like you're going to have a seizure or anything?" my sister is saying.

I can tell that she's upset. My sister has always taken my condition harder than anyone.

"You want something?" she says. "A Coke?"

When I manage to lift my head I can see an Amish boy staring at me. He looks away.

"A Coke," I say.

Cora studies me a while longer before standing up. "Right back."

I close my eyes and take several deep breaths, trying not to make any sudden movements. If I can keep perfectly still there's a chance I won't puke. But as soon as I start thinking this way, I know it's over. And the next moment I'm on my hands and knees heaving up the Wagonland Grill's buffet.

When at last I can raise my head again the Amish boy is standing nearby.

"This happens to me too," he says sympathetically and introduces himself.

Tears have worked their way down to the tip of my nose as I wipe my arm across my face. "I just need to sit for a second," I say.

Nodding, he scatters a fistful of hay over the spot where I've been sick. He's Cora's age. His eyes are deep-set and his fair complexion reminds me of the Dutch boy on the cleanser.

When my sister returns he shyly backs off several paces.

"They wouldn't take cash," she says, eyeing my new friend. "You have to use your goddamn tickets."

"This is Daniel Stoltz," I say.

Cora makes a face as she hands me the Coke. "Were you sick?"

I get up slowly, my feet feeling detached.

"Maybe we ought to head on back to the motel," she says.

But I can tell that she's curious about Daniel. The Amish rarely volunteer to speak to the "English." They keep to themselves and in town move only in groups.

"I'm okay," I say and sip cautiously at the Coke.

My sister surprises me by being half sociable.

"How come you're by yourself?" she asks Daniel. "I mean, isn't that against the rules?"

He seems to have half expected the question.

"We have still to take the oath," he says. "We do not belong."

It isn't often that I'm in mixed company with my older sister. And for a moment I wonder if it's simply my dizziness that makes me imagine she's actually flirting. Then it strikes me that Daniel is handsome. And I wonder who my sister has already cast him as.

As we make our way back toward the gate, Daniel explains how they are free to do as they please. Sometimes this means being rowdy and racing their buggies into town.

He is so soft-spoken that Cora has to lean toward him like a deaf person reading lips. Half of what he tells her is lost on me and I catch only snippets of their conversation.

Apparently his family lives in nearby Strasburg. There are four younger sisters and an older brother who has left the settlement.

We stop to watch the roller coaster clatter overhead. It's empty except for the last couple of cars. They're filled with the boys we'd seen earlier. Their straw hats strapped at their neck flutter like kites behind them.

"Your brother," Cora says and I have to keep from staring at my own sister. It's a tone I've never heard from her before. "He doesn't practice the faith?"

Daniel scuffs the dirt with the heel of his boot.

"He writes to us. But I must go to Lancaster to read his letters."

"Lancaster?" my sister says.

"Poppa will not allow the postman to deliver them."

"They save them for you," Cora says. "At the post office."

He keeps his hands in his pockets. "The English understand this. I believe it is because it happens to them."

"What about your mother?" Cora says. "She doesn't have any say in it?"

Daniel looks blankly at me.

"Your mother won't let you see your brother?" I say.

He shakes his head. "This is for Poppa to decide."

The ride rumbles past again, the cars shifting heavily on the tracks. One of the boys is holding onto the safety bar while his friend tries to pull him back down into the seat.

"Benjamin Lapp," Daniel says. "He has come back from living in Ohio and wishes to be going gay."

Cora smiles. "There's a lot of that going around." But it isn't how she would have said it to me. Nothing she says to Daniel is how she would have said it to me. "You mean leave his family?"

"Yes," Daniel says. "Cutting his hair."

He sees that we're puzzled and looks down at his rumpled slacks. "Benjamin has promised himself to Rebecca but she will not join him."

The operator is waving a red flag as a warning and the boy is coaxed back down into his seat by his companion.

"So what will he do?" I ask.

Daniel shrugs his shoulders, saying something only my sister hears.

Cora walks with her hands behind her back and suddenly everything about her seems new to me. Later, I know, she'll have some excuse. It was like an old science fiction movie, she'll say. The one where the expeditionary team finds a prehistoric man frozen in the Arctic and manages to bring him back to life. It will be her reason for not wanting to let Daniel go. He was a curiosity.

"So how'd you get here?" she asks. "I mean, did you come with your friends?"

Daniel points to the row of buggies just outside the grounds.

Males wait to join the Old Order at sixteen, he tells us. In the meantime, because of their age certain behavior is tolerated by the others.

Cora has heard the word *rumspringa* before.

"It's when they get to run around, right?" she says. "Sow their oats."

We follow Daniel back out through the gate where he proudly shows us his horse and buggy. The harness is studded with silver buttons, which eventually will have to be taken off.

Several other boys are jostling each other beside the fence. They're passing a bottle back and forth. One of them is smoking. They see us and call to Daniel in German but he only waves back at them.

"They have come from the barn dance," he says. "They have been looking for *Madels*."

"Girls," I say.

The boys pile into one of the buggies and when the driver yanks at the reins, the horse rises up on its hind legs.

"They belong to the Groffies," Daniel says. "That is their group. Now they will race their horses on the highway until the English arrest them."

I support my weight on the wheel of Daniel's carriage and the horse turns its huge head toward me.

"You still shaky?" Cora says.

Daniel runs his hand down the horse's mane. He seems to have nowhere to go.

"Perhaps you would like to take a ride," he says finally.

When Cora climbs up after him onto the buggy, I'm left standing alone. Truly this is remarkable: my sister at ease with someone of the opposite sex.

Cora's face shines in the moonlight and if I didn't know that it was my sister's I would have had to describe her expression as radiant. My own expression must seem equally bewildering to her. And so I allow her to believe that it's only petit mal to blame.

Once we are out on the highway, Daniel keeps to the shoulder of the road and continues to speak coaxingly to his horse. As we pass our motel, I'm tempted to ask him to stop but I know that Cora would never let me hear the end of having bailed out.

So I inhale in shallow, rhythmic breaths and try to remember not to look down.

As we move farther from the lights of Dutch Wonderland the sky begins to glitter with stars.

Daniel sits with the perfect posture of a military cadet. Occasionally he lifts his chin to gaze at the moon and I wonder how much if anything he knows of the launch.

A mile out into the country, few telephone wires extend from the main lines to the farmhouses. When they do, Daniel remarks that it's Mennonites who live there. They are the ones with the big cars and electricity. This afternoon, Cora had spotted a black Cadillac with enormous tail fins. It was stripped of any ornaments. Even the chrome bumpers were missing.

"You are from where?" Daniel says unexpectedly. It's the first question he's asked about us and for a moment we're both too surprised to answer.

"Out of state," Cora says.

"Our father's in the Army," I say. "So we move around a lot."

Daniel turns to us as if we'd just told him we were only visiting from Mars.

"This is true? You are from the Army?"

"Sad to say," Cora say.

"Our father's overseas right now," I say. "We're on our way to join him. We'll catch a ship in San Francisco."

It almost seems too much for him to take in all at once.

"The Army," he says at last. "This is where my brother has gone."

For the next half mile or so he reflects on so remarkable a coincidence.

"Jonathan has tattoos on his arms," Daniel says. "A dragon and a woman's name."

I can tell that my sister is holding her tongue. This is not an everyday occurrence.

"He cannot come home again," Daniel says. "He is too English. He would be shunned."

There's only the sound of the crickets and the soft clomping of the horse's hooves. I've read how the Amish will turn their back on their own. But in Daniel's hushed voice I hear what it really means. It means that his brother is lost to him.

"What about you?" Cora says. "You'd shun him too?"

I suck in a breath of air. My head is spinning again. My sister isn't afraid to ask anything.

"Yes," Daniel says in a way that makes it clear how his family would have no other choice.

"So," Cora says and resists the urge to say something about happily switching places with him. "Where we headed?"

Daniel hesitates and then glances over at us both. The whites of his eyes glow fiercely in the dark.

"There is a barn dance," he says. "Everyone has been invited."

For once, Cora is speechless. We sit staring at a black sea of buggies parked before an enormous white barn. Hundreds of young people mill about in the fields surrounding the farmhouse, their cigarettes flickering.

"Gideon has been left to do as he pleases," Daniel says and loops the reins over the armrest. "His father and mother have gone to visit."

"Chance to let their hair down," Cora says.

Like the others, Daniel's hair is cut short as a sign of his rebellion.

He reaches down to pull from under the seat several water-stained magazines.

"*Life,*" Cora says, taking the top one.

The mailing label is addressed to a barbershop in Lancaster.

"My father warns me of chairmindedness," he says.

"Book learning," Cora says to me, the pages crinkling as she turns them. "Look at the things your father's missing," and she holds the magazine open to a picture of Mick Jagger. He's strutting across the stage wearing one of Marianne Faithfull's dresses.

But I'm watching two figures that are moving toward us, their broad-brimmed hats silhouetted in the dark. One stops to drink from a bottle then pats his companion on the back before they stagger down the embankment.

As soon as Daniel sees them he hops from the buggy.

"Maybe we should just head on back," Cora says.

A few of the young people, Daniel has warned us, especially those who are members of groups, don't care for the English to come too close.

With everyone dressed alike and singing German songs, Cora is reminded that we're "not that far from Hamburg actually."

Daniel has led the two boys away from the road where he stands between them, head lowered as if considering some grievance. Then the one with the bottle starts shouting something, his companion echoing his threats.

Daniel only raises his palms, his voice barely audible. He is the peacemaker. But others have begun to drift over, attracted to the commotion. There are no girls. Only young men in their mid-teens, their straw hats tipped back cockily.

When the horse flaps its tail and whinnies, I nearly vault from the buggy.

"Christ," Cora says and shakes her head angrily.

I'm trying to think what my father would do. By now he'd probably have convinced everyone to join him at Dutch Wonderland for a German waffle. Except for my mother no one can stay angry with him for very long.

Daniel walks slowly back toward us. At the ditch, he holds his hat and jumps to the other side.

Cora scoots over to make room for him on the bench.

"There is much unfriendliness," he says and draws the buggy around. As soon as the horse picks up its pace, the boys run alongside the embankment. Suddenly a fistful of small rocks sprays about us like buckshot.

"The little creeps," Cora says, spinning around as if to crawl out of the buggy.

But we're already far enough away that it's impossible to make them out anymore.

Daniel keeps to the service road that parallels the highway.

"It was that one in the baggy pants," Cora says. "The one about the size of Roddy McDowall."

We ride in silence, listening to the occasional car that zips by on the main road.

"Some pacifist," my sister says finally.

My ears are ringing. Seizures are unpredictable. But like hurricanes there seems to be a season for them. Too much excitement, my mother's persuaded, can bring them on, and so when I suspect one might be coming, I'm to try to concentrate on something pleasant. Something that relaxes me. And so I gaze up at the moon, trying to imagine how the astronauts will feel when they are completely free of the world.

Daniel points out to us the large mechanical baler in his father's field. This is the kind of compromise that the Amish tolerate, he tells us. "If it is able to be pulled by horses then you might have it." And so his family has gradually accumulated mowers, sprayers, and corn pickers—all horse-powered. Still, I notice that the baler has steel wheels. Half the field is mown. Parked beneath a tin shed is a rusted tractor while behind it a huge silo rises into the black sky.

What appears to be the farmhouse is in fact the barn. His family's house turns out to be made of brick with aluminum gutters and Sears storm windows. As commonplace-looking as any junior officer's quarters on any Army post in America.

It's as close as Daniel cares to bring us. Everyone is already asleep.

In the dark countryside the gray craters of the moon are as clear as the first pictures back from the command module. Like silhouette cutouts, the low hills roll across the horizon. If the war hadn't come along, my father might have chosen this, and in some ways we might even have made a good Amish family. Cora, of course, excepted. My father might then have realized his dream of creating the tomato capital of the world. Other than my hothouse sister we might all have sported year-round tans and taut, muscular bodies.

Daniel sits with the reins loosely held in one hand, attentive to Cora's polite banter. It's amazing to hear my sister volunteer both halves of a conversation. With only the creaking of the buggy as backdrop her voice seems very nearly giddy to me. But then the more I consider it, the more Daniel seems the perfect boyfriend for her: they barely speak the same language and after tonight she's unlikely ever to see him again.

Watching Daniel I wonder how it is that he hasn't come to share his family's faith. Cora and I have inherited our own parents' indifference to any organized religion. It would have been the biggest stumbling block for us as an Amish family. My mother would never have been able to tolerate the weekly custom of sharing one's home with fellow worshipers. The idea of company is alien to her. The notion of family extends no farther than her half sister and niece.

Daniel suddenly interrupts Cora's monologue to draw our attention to what looks like a large corncrib in the distance. But it isn't until we've passed it that we can look back to see why. Parked behind the ramshackle shelter is a car. And even in the dark I recognize it as an older model T-Bird.

"Yours?" Cora says.

Daniel smiles and my sister prattles on about having her own wheels soon. Where we're headed, I'm tempted to remind her, it's more likely that her first car will be a pedicab.

Daniel explains that it's as close to the house as his parents will allow him to keep it. I know that the Amish fear the automobile for the same reason they fear modern appliances. Without machines they're forced to work together more as a family. There's far less idle time on their hands.

In our motel this afternoon I'd looked through the latest copy of the *Intercourse News*, Lancaster's weekly newspaper. Mostly it's made up of local advertisements for tourists: the Toy Train Museum, the Gast Classic Motorcars Exhibit, the Village Greens Miniature Golf and Snack Bar. The only real article was a short piece on Amish children. The half-dozen black and white photographs were each briefly captioned: "An Amish daughter guides the horse while her father plows the family garden," "An Amish boy on his scooter," "Amish learn at an early age to visit when the chores are finished." It was like looking at daguerreotypes with everyone tinted gray. The author noted that the children were secure in knowing that they were surrounded by their family and community. In the last picture, four girls stood talking beside a main thoroughfare "oblivious of the cars of the non-Amish that speed by." I studied the photograph, trying to make out the children's blurred expressions. And it seemed to me that the writer was right. They *did* look secure.

Every so often Daniel switches the reins to his other hand but otherwise seems engrossed in my sister's soliloquy. What Cora is yammering about now is how much she's convinced herself she has in common with her new friend. Like him, she is an unwilling prisoner of her parents. While he is stuck among country people, she is being dragged off to another country entirely. Neither is left a say in their own lives. They are both expatriates. But as soon as the law allows she will strike off on her own. Even if it means hijacking a Far East Airlines jet. She is sick of sitting in the backseat all the time. Just once she wants to get behind the wheel for herself. That's why she can appreciate Daniel's own situation. Their mothers could be sisters. Cora goes on like this with Daniel seeming to hang on her every word. It's impossible to know, of course, how much, if any of it, he's actually following. But he periodically peers over at her, his soulful eyes seeming to soak up her harangue completely.

Most boys would have leaped from the buggy after ten minutes of my sister's nonstop gabbing. Daniel is different. He appears genuinely smitten. And this astonishes me more than anything: that my loony, motor-mouth sister might actually seem attractive to a male her own age. I had to have seen it with my own eyes. But then Daniel is no doubt happy for any excuse to get out of the house.

Once back up on the highway he steers the buggy carefully along the edge of the road. Cars thunder past on our left but the horse merely clomps along as if still on the dirt path. The Amish are hard on the public roads. The hooves of their horses tear up the expensive macadam. Still, the locals accept why the tourists are here and know better, as Cora says, than to look a gift horse in the mouth.

At the motel, I jump down from the buggy and walk around to shake Daniel's hand.

"I'm sorry about your brother," I offer, not knowing what else to say.

Cora doesn't budge from beside Daniel even though there's now plenty of room to slide over.

"Next time we come through we'll have to get together," I say.

Daniel smiles politely. Cora's eyes have clouded over. They are both waiting for me to leave them alone.

"Take your time," I say, tripping back over one of the concrete speed bumps. "I'll tell Mom you're here."

My sister yawns widely. "Do that."

I skirt the hedge around the front of the motel and stop under the orange neon sign that hums "Vacancy" overhead. Even this far away I can see how Daniel has shifted toward my sister who's still sitting in the middle of the buggy. By just leaning forward slightly their faces seem close enough to touch.

But this is more than I really want to think about and so I turn and follow the numbers down to our motel room. At first, I listen for a moment outside, barely able to hear Bobbie's voice over the television. Cora claims that *Psycho* was responsible for the extra thickness of motel doors all across America.

Every once in a while my mother says something that sounds comforting. But it's my cousin doing most of the talking. Only bits and pieces of the conversation come through and they're mixed in with Johnny's monologue. He's describing how women act when they go to a male strip show. Then Bobbie says something about Lou getting kind of rough with her. Once or twice he's even shoved her hard enough to leave a bruise. My mother doesn't say anything to this. And then Johnny jokes about how women act silly whenever they go out to a club together. Men, he says, are different. They're serious. They get the same look watching a woman strip as a tiger gets spotting a nearsighted gazelle. Then Bobbie starts crying and my mother says something about Lou that's drowned out by the audience's laughter.

After the commercial, I step back from the door and knock twice, raising my voice to let my mother know that it's me and not Tony Perkins.

The following morning, as soon as Cora is in the shower, my mother sits up in bed.

"So who's your sister's little friend?" she says.

Bobbie's awake but has wrapped her pillow over the back of her head.

"You didn't talk to him?" I say and reach over for the map on the bedstand.

Last night, she'd put on her bathrobe and walked out to the parking lot. Any other time my mother would have been upset with us for being late. But as soon as she saw Cora chatting with Daniel, she backed off.

"I stopped worrying when I saw the buggy," she says.

Bobbie suddenly flips over.

"I hope she's a better judge of boys than I was," she says. "It'll save her a lot of heartache."

"Well, if that's what she's trying to avoid," my mother says, "I guess she's doing all right."

I unfold the map, smacking the corners down. "Maybe she's just choosy," I say.

My mother continues to look at me as if I'd just blown cigar smoke in her face.

"Sweetheart, I wasn't being critical of your sister. You know I only want the best for her."

"That's what you keep saying. But maybe if you didn't put so much pressure on her, she'd relax a little more."

Bobbie fingers a loose thread on her pillowcase.

"You think I put too much pressure on your sister?" my mother says. "Is that what you think?"

I don't know what I think. I only know that for once I feel sorry for my sister.

Bobbie rips a Kleenex from the box beside the bed. "You have the sweetest two kids in the world, Rosemary. Do you know that?"

My mother focuses on me like sunlight coming through a magnifying glass.

"If you think I'm too critical, Teddy, I won't say another word. I'll avoid the subject completely."

The only way Mom knows to argue, Cora insists, is by going for the guilt jugular.

"She'll never see him again," I say. "So what's the difference? It's probably the only reason she can talk to him in the first place."

Bobbie takes another swipe at the box of Kleenex. "Your kids look after each other is what they do," she says. "They take up for each other when no one's looking."

The water is turned off and we can hear my sister flick the shower curtain back in the bathroom. My mother lifts her legs out from under the covers like an invalid and carries her clothes from the closet.

"Another day," she says, "another interstate."

Bobbie uncaps her eyeliner and examines her plucked brows in her portable makeup mirror.

"We got some serious tweezing here," she says.

I locate Asheville, our next stop, on the map.

When Cora at last steps from the bathroom, she's already dressed and her hair blowdried.

I can tell that my mother is desperate to ask her about Daniel. But she also knows better than to try. Bobbie, on the other hand, doesn't.

"Your hair looks different," my cousin says. "I used to change my style every time I'd meet a new guy."

Cora stares at her.

"It was wet," my sister says. "I dried it."

My mother sees her opening.

"Your cousin's just saying how nice it is you've met someone," she says. "That's all."

"I didn't *meet* anyone," Cora says.

"Then who's the boy you were out talking with half the night?"

Cora turns her back on my mother, pretending to look for her sunglasses.

"So," I say. "We shooting for Asheville?"

My sister spins about as if to pounce on my mother.

"Why can't you just back off?" she says. "What business is it of yours anyway? I talk to someone and I have to give you an annual report? I mean, what am I?" And she points at me. "Fourteen?"

My mother picks up my sister's socks from the floor and turns them right side out.

"I can't be interested in your little friends?" she says. "A mother's not supposed to take an interest in her daughter's life?"

"He's as tall as Daddy," Cora says icily. "You make it sound like he's a goddamn dwarf."

"Why don't we stop over in Roanoke," I say. "Then we could sort of coast into Asheville tomorrow."

Bobbie carries her makeup mirror into the bathroom. "Roanoke sounds real nice," she says. "That sounds like a real good idea, Teddy."

My mother sets Cora's neatly folded socks on top of her suitcase. "I'm not going to listen to that kind of language, young lady. I ask a civil question, I expect a civil answer."

My sister sweeps her socks up, stuffing them into her pocket. "Maybe when you *ask* a civil question I'll answer it." She turns and offers me a fractured smile. "You want to get something to eat, I'll meet you in the restaurant."

As soon as Cora is gone, my mother sits down on my bed. "What did I say, Teddy? Did I ask her anything so terrible? You tell me."

She doesn't know whether to blame Cora's hyperness or herself for raising her daughter so permissively.

"I try, honey," she says. "Honest to god I try to be patient with your sister. And this is the thanks I get. I'm not supposed to involve myself in my children's lives? I can't ask them a simple question?"

I pull my jeans on under the sheet. It's useless to argue with her.

"Look at my little man," my mother says as I lace up my sneakers. "He's going to be every bit as big as his father."

I can hear Bobbie start the shower.

"I don't think so, Mom," I say. "I've seen pictures of Dad my age."

"The camera lies, sweetheart."

She's already biting her upper lip and so I quickly back over to the door.

"We'll get a booth," I say. "Maybe start with some orange juice or something."

My mother's eyes have watered. "You're my peacemaker, sweetheart. It's what I tell your father all the time."

Cora's sitting in the far corner of the restaurant even though the place is empty.

"Can you believe that woman?" she begins, handing me the

other menu. "Where does she get off prying into my life? Like her own isn't disastrous enough."

My stomach feels a little queasy and so I tell the waitress I'll order when the others come.

"Fine, darlin'," she says. "Get you some coffee?"

It's the first time a waitress has ever asked me this and even Cora has to smile.

"It'll put some hair on your chest," my sister says, stirring her own cup.

"All right," I say and the woman winks at me, clicking her ballpoint.

There's no traffic out on the street. Either everyone's on the road early or it's an unpopular spot.

"It's Daddy gets her like this," Cora is saying. "Every time they're on the phone together, she takes it out on me. Like her own life's not screwed up enough, she's got to screw up mine."

Ours is the only family I know that can get this wound up before breakfast. My sister is like the experimental jet my father told me about that can take off without a runway.

"She just worries about us," I say. "So what if she's overprotective? I mean, what do you expect, she's your mother."

"There's mothers and then there's mothers. And we've got one mother, kiddo."

"Why can't you ignore her? Or just make up something. How's she going to know?"

Cora stirs her black coffee as if looking for her reflection in it. "You don't see how she operates yet."

The waitress comes back with my coffee and while my sister starts in again on my mother's plans to twist her children's lives to compensate for her own pathetic relationship with her husband, I take my first sip.

"That's the way you'll come to feel about Mom," Cora says when my right eye closes involuntarily. "Real bitter going down."

None of this is anything new, of course. Only now my sister wants me to understand that Mom's clutches will start to dig into me next. And that I should get ready.

My mother at last comes in without Bobbie. "Your cousin's on the phone," she says and slides in next to me in the booth.

She studies the menu a moment before ordering what she always orders for breakfast: a poached egg and dry toast.

"There's another party coming," she tells the waitress. "So go ahead and add two eggs over easy, sausage, buttered toast, a large orange juice, and a side order of hash browns."

The waitress copies all of this down before asking if the "gentleman" also cares for coffee.

"Soon as she puts her lipstick on," my mother says. She smiles brightly across the table at my sister. "Pretty day."

Cora aligns her silverware. "Perfect," she says and smiles back just as brightly.

This is fine with me. They'll pretend to be polite commuters who've agreed to share the same booth in a crowded diner.

"I hope cousin Bobbie's not calling home," Cora says, dipping her fork in her water. "It's almost time for 'Let's Make a Deal.'"

"They're adults," my mother says. "They'll work it out."

My sister dries her fork with her napkin and looks up at me. "Personally, I think it'd be easier just to go straight to court."

My mother shifts sideways so that she's facing me in the booth. "I hope when your sister grows up that all her problems have such easy solutions."

Cora continues to grin at me crookedly. "I guess when people grow up there's always that chance."

I stare out the window and then crane forward when a silver T-Bird cruises past. It stops at the light before disappearing down the incline toward the railroad tracks.

"Teddy?" My mother has her hand on my shoulder. "Did you hear the lady?"

I turn to see the waitress holding the coffeepot out. "You want that heated up, darlin'?"

My mother carefully slides my cup back across the table. "He doesn't drink coffee," she says.

Cora taps her own cup for the waitress to refill. "Why don't you let him decide," she says.

They're both suddenly looking at me as if I've had a staring spell. And when I glance back out the window for the T-Bird, I'm not so sure that I haven't.

"That's okay," I tell the waitress.

My sister shakes her head as if I've already lost the war.

When our breakfast comes, Cora wolfs down her Belgian waffle while I only peck at my food, hoping for Bobbie to show up.

"I'm taking a hike," my sister says at last. "I get enough sitting in the car."

"Don't wander off," my mother says. "It's almost checkout time."

As she slides out of the booth, Cora's bare legs make a farting sound on the vinyl.

"Excuse me," she says, smoothing her skirt down. "Must be all this road food."

My mother takes in my sister's red blouse. It's the one my father sent from Hong Kong for Cora's sixteenth birthday. Although it's made out of silk and looks expensive, it's too mod for my sister ever to have picked it out for herself.

"Are you going to be comfortable in that?" my mother asks her.

Cora lowers her chin. She's only wearing it because she knows how much it irritates my mother.

"I'll let you know," she says.

"Your father thinks anything that's Oriental is somehow exotic," my mother says.

"Maybe I should have my feet bound," Cora says.

"Why don't you start with your mouth," I say.

"Your father means well," my mother says, smiling tightly at me. "It's just I hate to see him spending money on some of the stuff he thinks is so different."

"It *is* different," I say.

Cora puts her sunglasses on and glares at me. "You're going to explain taste to *him?*"

I watch my sister walk out of the restaurant. She doesn't often wear skirts even though I have to admit that there's nothing wrong with her legs. She has my father's height but the blouse is too small for her and strains the buttons. And her coffee cup, I notice, is rimmed with lipstick smears. None of this is like my sister at all.

My mother finally asks me to go see what's keeping Bobbie. The waitress has kept her breakfast under the warming light.

Coming out of the restaurant, I don't at first see the T-Bird idling just beyond the pool's chain-link fence. It's my sister's red blouse that stops me. She's leaning into the passenger side of the car but the windshield is tinted dark enough that I can't make out the driver. I don't want to seem to be spying and so I turn and take the long way back around the pool.

The cleaning woman has moved her cart past our room and when I come up behind her, she gives me a dirty look. There's a "Do Not Disturb" hanger out.

I open the door. Bobbie's sitting on the bed with her elbows on her knees blowdrying her hair. She doesn't hear me and it's a moment before my pupils adjust to the light. Then I see that she's in her underwear and I quietly back out of the room, easing the door shut after me.

The cleaning lady refills a bottle of Windex and eyes me suspiciously.

I can hear the hair dryer inside and so I turn and pound loudly on the door. Meanwhile, the woman has pulled out a squeegee stick as if she thinks it a good idea to have something in her hand.

Bobbie cracks the door, tilting her head to look out at me.

"It's you, Teddy," and she steps back to let me in.

She's put her jeans on but is still only in her bra. It isn't the first time my cousin has forgotten to cover up around me. Already this summer my mother has had to remind her several times that I'm a big boy now. Bobbie can be forgetful, especially when there's something else on her mind.

It isn't one of her see-through bras, but more like the top of a bikini. Still, it's hard to concentrate when instead of throwing her robe on, she only leans back against the bed's padded headboard and starts in on how she's just about had it with Lou.

"I swear to God, Teddy, the man can't hear a word I'm saying. I could tell him I'm nine months' gone and he'd still say to just get it fixed. It's like it's too much trouble to hear so he doesn't. You understand what I'm saying?"

I say that I do.

"Course you do, honey. What am I asking you that question for? You always listen to your cousin."

Then she tells me how Lou hadn't even turned the television off. She could hear the host of "Hollywood Squares" the whole time she was trying to explain about missing her period again.

"So I scream at him and what does he do?"

She sits with her arms crossed, which makes her breasts look like they're going to pop free.

"What does he do?" I repeat.

"He turns the TV down low enough he can still hear it. That's what he does. I'm telling him he could be a daddy and he's trying to figure out some game show." She glances over my shoulder. "What do you think your cousin did then?"

Her expression is blank as if she's only talking to herself now.

"You did something?" I say and turn finally to see what it is she's staring at.

From the jagged black hole of the television screen a cord curls like some animal's long, corkscrew tail. Several shards of glass stick straight up from the thick carpet.

"You threw the telephone," I say.

My cousin nods. "I believe the man heard me for a change."

To avoid involving the authorities, my mother agrees to the manager's terms: the replacement cost of an identical nineteen-inch color Zenith. As soon as we're back out on the road, Bobbie writes a personal check to my mother, who, of course, will never cash it. Her niece is sharing the driving with her and that is payment enough. When my cousin argues that everyone would probably be better off if she just caught the train back home, Cora immediately looks up the nearest Amtrak station. But my mother won't hear another word of it. The best thing her niece can do for the time being is to put on hold any more calls to Chicopee.

To cheer my cousin up, my mother proposes that we go ahead and shoot for Asheville. There's a public lodge in the mountains that the North Carolina State Tourist Commission advertises as the highest lookout east of the Mississippi.

"The cabins seem very reasonable," she says. "We could do the Vanderbilt place first and then stay in the lodge afterward."

"Let me see if I've got this straight," Cora says. She's opened the pamphlet to the picture of the cathedral-ceilinged lodge. *"You're* going to climb a mountain?"

"We'll take it easy," my mother says. "They have rest spots along the way."

"How about a cardiovascular unit?" my sister says.

"Your mother's not *that* old," Bobbie says. "We'll just have to watch out for her."

"Thank you," my mother says coldly.

"Well, at least we'd get to see a *real* house," Cora says. "As opposed to some dinky pilot's hovel."

In the mirror, my mother gives me her please-don't-get-your-sister-started expression and so I pick up my book on the explorer Matthew Henson. I'm at the part where Commander Peary gets sick and they have to turn back from trying to reach the Pole. In a little shack near a place called Fort Conger, Matt gives the commander morphine to ease the pain in his legs. But when he pulls Peary's boots off by the heels, eight of the commander's toes, blue from gangrene, snap off like icicles.

I flip forward to the photographs. In one of them Matt is standing on the deck of the *Roosevelt*. He's wearing a parka but it's warm enough to leave it unbuttoned. He couldn't be happier because once again the commander has chosen him, his Negro manservant, for the trip north. Peary has even used the word "indispensable" in talking to the reporter from the *New York Herald*. Years later, he would call him his assistant but for now manservant is enough for Matt. It's more than enough. The commander's like a father to him and that's all that he's ever wanted.

In another picture, Henson's skin appears cocoa-colored. His great-grandmother had been kept by one of the overseers of a plantation in Maryland where Matt was raised as a boy. In the caption, the commander tells the reporter that he believes that there's enough white blood in his manservant to save him from being lazy and shiftless. Peary means this as a compliment.

Less than an hour down the interstate, Bobbie needs to take another pit stop. She hasn't said anything yet to my mother about being pregnant. My cousin believes that my mother has enough on her mind right now without having to listen to her niece's troubles.

At a Shell station, Cora and I get out of the car while my mother follows Bobbie into the rest room.

"So," I say when my sister thinks better of leaning against the overheated Oldsmobile and stares in the direction of the exit ramp. "What do you hear from Daniel?"

Cora turns her head without moving her shoulders.

"One word and you're dead."

None of this makes any sense. Why would a boy want to follow my sister this far? Just to talk to her every time we pull in for gas? Or did he plan to tailgate us for the next two thousand miles? All I can think is that maybe one of the rocks hit him in the head.

"Not a word," Cora whispers when she sees my mother. "*Nada.*"

"Tell him to turn back," I say. "It's crazy."

My sister opens her door. "That's *his* problem."

Bobbie comes around to the driver's side. It's her turn to take the wheel.

"Got to do something about all these stops," she says to me. "Your cousin's holding up the parade."

"We're not in any hurry," I say. "You heard Mom."

She lowers her voice. "You going to help me out, Teddy?"

I nod without really knowing what I'm nodding about.

As soon as we merge back onto the interstate, I turn around to see if Daniel is anywhere in sight. Cora kicks my foot. But it's hard to believe that my mother would ever suspect that an Amish teen-ager was chasing her antisocial daughter in a T-Bird with tinted windows. Usually the only males my sister ever pays any attention to are thirty feet high and in Technicolor.

Bobbie listens to the radio while my mother works on her letter to my father. She never finishes them in one sitting but adds a page a day until they're fat enough that she has to use masking tape to keep the envelope shut. Her sentences all run on into each other for ten or fifteen lines. Cora says it doesn't matter because my father probably just skims them anyway. His own letters aren't much longer than what you could get on a postcard: sentences short and clear enough that even a stranger would have no trouble following them. Which, my sister says, is exactly why they aren't worth reading. There's never anything personal in them. They could have been written by his warrant officer. "One of these days," she complains, "he's going to get the addresses mixed up and we'll find out he's got six kids in Seattle. And they're the ones been getting the *real* letters home."

Whenever Cora comes across anything about someone's double life being uncovered, she'll tape it to the refrigerator. Usually it's some movie star but just before we left she'd found a piece in the *Chicopee Times* about a man at whose funeral his two families showed up. It turned out that my aunt Irene actually knew him: some auto parts dealer Uncle Sal had once had dealings with. The man had willed his shop to both his wives, and the executor wound up having an auction to settle the inheritance. At the sale, the two women bid against each other for everything from a fan belt to a customized Harley (which my aunt Irene recalled my uncle Sal had admired).

I turn to the last few pictures in my book. The story of Peary and Matt Henson trying to get to the Pole is a sad one. In the end, Peary lied to his assistant about where they were. Matt didn't know how to read a sextant, one of the few things the commander wouldn't teach him how to do. And so when Peary claimed that they'd finally reached their destination, Matt was confused. He thought they had at least another hundred miles to go, which, of course, they did. But with only two toes left Peary couldn't go any farther and knew he'd never have another chance because of his age. So he lied. And Matt tried to convince himself that it wasn't a lie. Despite the way the commander had always treated him, Peary was his hero.

I study the photograph of Henson in his caribou-lined parka. It was taken on the ship after their return from the Pole. His skin is sunburned, the tip of his nose still white from frostbite. But while everyone else is happy about their success, he looks depressed and anxious. The commander has retreated to his stateroom on the *Roosevelt* and won't show himself much on deck the entire trip home. Nor will he call for his Negro assistant. Matt is expected to keep his secret but Peary will never speak to him in public again.

There are two pictures of the black explorer that show him right before the last assault on the Pole and another right after it. He hardly seems the same person. He's come back defeated even though everyone is claiming theirs the greatest victory in polar history.

"So how long's it supposed to take us to get to the top?" Cora asks my mother.

My sister isn't athletic and it pains her to think of having to climb a mountain.

"I mean, is there some kind of ski lift or something we can take?" she says.

My mother caps her pen and stuffs her letter back in the glove compartment.

"We just hike up, sweetheart. The book said maybe a couple of hours at the most. It's very scenic."

"Aren't we getting enough of that looking out the window?" Cora asks peevishly. "We have to climb Mount Everest too?"

"I want us to do some things," my mother says. "And you can't do things cooped up in a car."

My sister tilts her crossword for me to see. With her ballpoint she's scribbled in the margin: "Bet your niece disagrees."

"I think Cora misses Amish country," I say. "I think she wants to go back to Dutch Wonderland."

My sister is quiet and for the first time I realize the power this gives me over her.

"Maybe it's just the buggy rides," I add. "Or it could be the people she misses so much. Their Amish ways."

My mother turns around. It isn't like my sister to take abuse silently from her younger brother.

"Did you really enjoy it, honey?" my mother says.

Cora smiles halfheartedly. "It could have been worse."

But this is like some psychedelic drug. I don't want to give it up.

"I think it really surprised her," I say. "I don't think she ever expected to fall in love so quickly with a place."

My mother is studying me now. "Are you teasing your sister?"

"Me?" I say, lifting my shoulders. "Tease Miss Unteasable?"

If we were going any less than fifty, my sister might have shoved me out the door. She turns away, her face reflected darkly in the window. I will pay for this, her expression says. If not in this life then in the next.

"Okay," my mother says and switches off the radio when Jefferson Airplane starts singing "White Rabbit." "One guess who came into the world not too far from here."

A hundred miles east actually. At the Fort Bragg Army Hospital. My father had already gotten his next assignment by the time I was delivered.

"He had the sweetest disposition," my mother says. "You could tell even then."

Bobbie is looking up at the mirror. "Teddy was born here?" she says. "I thought he was a Yankee."

"That's because we were gone in three months," my mother says. "You're an Army brat you get used to that early."

"Speak for yourself," Cora says.

My mother shakes her head at my sister. "Sweetheart, you're not fooling anyone. The last thing you'd want is to stay in one place all your life."

"Who's talking about all my life? I just think a move every fifteen minutes is a little excessive."

My mother turns to Bobbie. "She'd be miserable without a change of scenery."

"You're right," Cora says. "And that's exactly why I *am* miserable. The scenery *never* changes. Take away the guard hut and the cannon at the gates and that stupid tape of reveille every morning and what have you got? A bunch of barracks."

We've begun to climb into the foothills and I can feel the Oldsmobile working harder. I'm a Tarheel even though I can't remember anything about Fort Bragg. Nearly all of the photographs in our albums seem to have been taken indoors. And in most of them I'm asleep, my face buried in a quilt.

Once, when I asked my father if he'd gone into the delivery room, he smiled as if recalling it fondly.

"Your mother started having contractions about five in the morning," he said. "So I went on to work."

When I looked at him, he smiled.

"Duty first," he said.

And I thought, What about family? Wasn't that his *first* duty?

"You were born at noon," my father told me. "I got the news a little after one."

His first sergeant had stuck his head in his office and announced, "It's a boy," and then closed the door after him.

"So that's how I got the word," my father said. "While I was sitting at my desk looking over some procurement orders."

This was typical of the kind of story my father liked to tell. It reminded me of the few war stories we'd ever gotten out of him. He volunteered nothing. "Name, rank, and serial number," Cora would say. "Everything else you're pulling teeth." It wasn't that he didn't enjoy sharing things with us, my mother would try to console me. "It's just your father's an officer. And officers can't swap stories with their men." But I wasn't a man. And he wasn't an officer to me. He was my father. My mother would only shrug her shoulders and say that maybe when I grew up and had my own son, I'd be able to understand my father better. But I doubted it.

"I was nursing you the last time we were on this highway," my mother says. "Your father had to keep pulling over because I'd get dizzy looking down at you."

"I know the feeling," Cora says.

"Your brother was a dream baby," my mother says. "He never fussed. His eyes would be closed and he'd be fast asleep but he wouldn't give up the nursing."

"Breast fetishes run in the family," Cora says. "Dad's the original boob man."

"There's no denying that." My mother laughs. She can laugh because like Bobbie she's busty.

But I can see my cousin grimacing in the mirror.

"Every boy I ever went out with," she says, keeping her eyes straight ahead on the highway. "It was the same thing. I could never figure that out."

"Figure what out?" my sister says. There's an edge to her voice. She hasn't filled out yet even though my mother promises that she's just going to be a late bloomer. "Why American men are obsessed with boobs? That's supposed to be some kind of mystery?"

My mother shifts uncomfortably in her seat already regretting the drift of the conversation.

Cora brags that she'll only consider marrying someone ten years older than her, a European who speaks at least half a dozen languages.

"American men are all momma's boys," she says. "I wouldn't touch one with a barge pole."

"How about a pitchfork?" I say.

My sister has to bite her lip to keep from coming back at me. And I suddenly feel bad for taking advantage of her. Once in the last hour Daniel passed us, slowing up as he came alongside. But no one else appeared to notice anything suspicious about a ten-year-old T-Bird with black windows hanging beside us like a pilot fish.

If he didn't leave a note Daniel's parents will have begun to wonder where he is by now. It's hard to understand what he has in mind. Or maybe he likes not having anything in mind. After sixteen years in Amish country that might be especially appealing.

As we rise into the mountains outside Asheville the scenery becomes like a series of captioned postcards: Mist Over the Treetops, Craggy Rock Formation, Deer Crossing.

When suddenly something like a large bird flaps loudly overhead.

"What was that?" I say.

My mother turns the radio down. "What?"

"Outside," I say. "That noise."

"Long as it didn't come from under the hood," Bobbie says.

"Probably electrical," Cora says to me, lifting her headphones. "Like a synapse in your brain."

My mother has slowed down around the curve but when we don't hear anything else, she gradually builds back up to the speed limit.

I continue to lean forward in my seat, one ear cocked, until there's a clicking sound coming from right outside my window.

"What about that?" I say.

My mother lifts her foot off the accelerator again. "You're right," she says finally.

But when we come to a stop on the shoulder of the road so does the clicking sound.

"You check," my mother says to Bobbie. "I don't want to open my door this side."

There are no cars but my mother and I wait while Cora and Bobbie get out. They both step back and look up. Then my cousin closes her eyes and Cora kicks the gravel, showering the hubcap with pebbles.

I climb over my sister's pile of junk and tumble out of the backseat. Bobbie and Cora are still staring up at the roof. The canvas belt I'd used to strap down the suitcases hangs limply from the empty rack.

"Swell," my sister says. "Just great."

My mother waits until there's no traffic before trotting around the front of the car.

"That's what you heard," she says.

All of us stand with arms crossed. I'd spent half an hour this morning rearranging the luggage. I didn't want us up in the mountains with the driver unable to see out the back.

"Every goddamn stitch of clothing I brought," Cora says.

"If you'd kept your stupid magazines out of the window," I say, "we might have seen it."

My mother moves up beside me. "Your father warned me about taking too much along," she says. "I didn't listen."

But we all know that it's because of Bobbie that everything had to be untied and reorganized.

"It's my fault," my cousin says at last. "This wouldn't have happened if it hadn't been for me."

Cora slides back into the car and slams the door shut after her.

"We could backtrack," I say.

Bobbie stands on her tiptoes, squinting. "Let's go," she says. "I'll drive."

My mother looks at me. "We could try, honey."

It's another mile before we can turn around and Cora nervously watches the opposing traffic.

Then I realize that she might be more interested in spotting a T-Bird. This could put Daniel off our trail. Unless, of course, they already arranged a rendezvous in Asheville.

"This about where you heard it?" my mother asks.

Across the median there's only the same barren strip of interstate gleaming in the sun.

"I'm trying to remember if there was any identification on them," my mother says.

"Like maybe an old airline tag," Cora says. "So American can have everything waiting for us in San Francisco."

"You can feel sorry for yourself," my mother says. "But we all had something up there."

"Some of us more than others," my sister says.

Bobbie lowers her visor. "She's right, Rosemary. Half my things are in the trunk."

"Well, good," my mother says. "Then we can just share."

"That's right," I say. "Cora's about the same size. More or less."

My sister lifts her middle finger up so that only I can see it.

"That must be how we get the expression 'knothead,'" she says to me. "One incapable of tying a simple knot."

"I don't want to hear anymore," my mother says and pats Bobbie's knee. "Why don't you turn around up here, honey?"

My cousin signals to pull into the passing lane. "We can find a department store," she says. "I have Lou's credit card."

"Let's not worry about it," my mother says. "None of us is going to go without."

Cora has started penciling in an inventory in the margin of her magazine.

As soon as there's an opening, Bobbie U-turns into the southbound lane. Then, as if trolling, she puts on her blinkers and drives slowly along the shoulder.

"I don't like this," my mother says. She's faced about in her seat, afraid someone will rear-end us. "Let's just call it quits."

"We're okay," Bobbie says. "I'll just keep it at twenty. They can see us."

"It was right in here," I say. "I remember we'd just passed the ravine."

The road angles sharply. We'd been in the right-hand lane the whole time and so it's unlikely that the suitcases would have bounced anywhere but down the steep slope into the woods.

"You'd think we'd see at least one of them," my mother says.

"Maybe some good Christian picked them up," Bobbie offers. "We can call the Motor Bureau in Asheville."

"Four blouses," Cora reads from her list. "Two of them brand new. Three pairs of shoes—"

"We're all going to be a little inconvenienced," my mother says. "We'll just have to live with it."

"It's my fault," Bobbie says. "That's what I get."

"You mean, that's what *we* get," my sister says. "None of your stuff—"

My mother taps her window. "Nobody's blaming anyone. We'll deal with it together. That's the way we'll deal with everything on this trip. As a family. Is that understood?"

Cora rolls her magazine up and drums it on her knee. "A family," she says, looking at me. "Gotcha."

When it's apparent that we've gone well past the probable spot, Bobbie eases back up onto the road and accelerates.

I try to think of what's left in the trunk. Mostly it's personal things my mother was afraid to leave with the movers: photo albums, mementos, jewelry. There's an extra spare tire and a couple boxes of grocery items my father hadn't been able to find in Formosa: a can of Steen's maple syrup, his favorite brand of stewed tomatoes, several jars of Red Wing peanut butter, and a dozen bags of barbecued potato chips. The only clothes left are those on our backs and whatever Bobbie has packed. It's no real disaster. Except for my autograph book: the one my father gave me when I was a boy. There's the entire starting lineup of the Yankees, including Mickey Mantle and Whitey Ford. I don't say anything because it would only upset my mother more and no one will ever miss them except me since over the years my father has been gone too often to keep up with the league standings anyway.

Leaning against a wall of jagged slate, I watch Cora work her way up the steep path. She's wearing a pair of Bobbie's flowered shorts and a T-shirt with a silk-screen likeness of Slim Whitman (worn inside out to prevent anyone from imagining she's a fan).

"How's Mom doing?" I ask her.

My sister lifts the carry bag from her shoulder and sits down. "She's got it in her head we have to sleep in that idiot lodge tonight. So she's down there killing herself to keep up."

I look out at the clouds below us. We passed the six-thousand-foot marker half an hour ago. "Bobbie staying with her?"

Cora pulls a Coke from the bag and takes a long swig before holding it out to me. "You remember that scene in *The Postman Always Rings Twice?*"

She means the film not the book. But I haven't seen the movie either.

"Well, anyway," she says. "We'll drop Lou a postcard. Maybe add something like, 'Easy come, easy go.'"

We didn't stop anywhere. My mother was afraid we wouldn't make it up to the lodge by dark. So she had Cora pick out something of Bobbie's for climbing.

"What about Daniel?" I say. "Think he's gone home?"

Cora glances over her shoulder. We can hear Bobbie encouraging my mother that they're almost there.

"I've been dropping bread crumbs," my sister says.

Bobbie appears on the path, ducking beneath a low-hanging branch. I step past Cora and come down halfway to help my mother.

"I'm holding up the formation," she says and exhales heavily. "The rest of you could have been up there an hour ago."

Her borrowed tie-dyed blouse is dark with sweat.

"I thought we were supposed to do everything together," I say.

My mother smiles weakly. Her face is flushed, her hair sticking to her forehead. She's had to leave the top button of Bobbie's jeans open.

I trudge ahead to see if there's any sign of the lodge but only pass more posters warning hikers to remain alert. We're high enough now that wandering off the beaten path could actually be dangerous.

"I'll pay for this later," my mother says, massaging her calves. "Maybe they'll have a nice sauna to sit in."

Cora rests in the shade with her back against a scrub pine. "Right," she says to herself. "Along with Sven, the masseur."

Bobbie has said little all day. She feels bad about the suitcases and insists again that my mother reoutfit us all as soon as we can find a Penney's.

Suddenly, two male hikers come thrashing through the brush and out onto the trail, the older one leading the way. He's barrel-chested, the sun glinting off his wire-rimmed glasses. Both men carry sleeping bags tightly rolled in protective rain gear.

"Howdy," my cousin says.

The younger one stops to retie his red bandanna as his friend troops past us with barely a nod, his desert boots crunching on the packed dirt.

"How much farther you think we got to go?" Bobbie asks him.

"To the lodge? Less than a kilometer."

He looks to be in his mid-twenties, his dark hair swept back from his deeply tanned face, his forearms bulging beneath a snug rugby T-shirt.

"You taking a shortcut or something?" Bobbie says.

He glances past me to see where his companion has reentered the woods.

"We try to stay off the trail," he says. "It makes it a little more interesting."

He's obviously eager to catch up with his friend.

"Maybe we'll see you up at the lodge," Bobbie says.

"We'll just be taking a shower," and he shifts the enormous backpack on his broad shoulders.

As soon as he's out of earshot, my mother struggles to her feet. "He was a nice-looking boy," she says. "Reminded me a little of that one on the wildlife program your father watches."

"Jim," Cora says. "Mutual of Omaha."

"That's the fellow," my mother says.

"Always downriver wrestling something," Cora says. "Which, of course, rivets Daddy to the tube."

"The 'Wild Kingdom,' " my mother says. "I don't think your father's ever missed an episode."

"Maybe they'll run out of kingdoms and take in Taiwan," my sister says. "Jim could slop around in a rice paddy with a water buffalo."

"I don't know what your father sees in that show," my mother admits. "It's the same thing every week."

"That's because Daddy likes nature," I say. "He loves animals."

"So how come he shoots them?" Cora says.

My sister exaggerates everything. My father once went on a turkey shoot with a bunch of second lieutenants who'd invited him along. He doesn't even own a gun.

My mother gets to her feet slowly. "How far's a kilometer?" she says.

"Point six two of a mile," Cora says.

"Not far," I say. "Less than half an hour."

"Good," my mother says. "That's about all this girl's got left in her."

Bobbie unsnaps her compact mirror.

"I'm going to start watching that show," she says. "If that's what Jim looks like."

Cora steps around her. "I feel like a damn Von Trapp."

Clouds billow in the valley below and I think about how my father and I have never camped out together even though we've lived on plenty of Army bases surrounded by woods. "Don't take it personally," my mother told me when my father discouraged any Scouting. "Daddy got his fill of that stuff in the Infantry."

On the trail, I stop and wait for my mother again. Like Cora, she walks slightly pigeon-toed.

"One last push over the top," she says, staggering up beside me. "Then I'm going to soak these gams."

I tell her that I don't think she should expect the Holiday Inn or anything.

"I mean, what makes you think there's even going to be hot water?"

My mother leans into the path. "Blind faith," she says. "Sheer blind faith, honey."

Twenty minutes later, we come upon a dozen small gray huts scattered about a clearing.

"Didn't Bob entertain the troops here?" Cora says.

The main lodge is set off from the cabins but built from the same weathered logs. There's a flagpole out in front of it.

"Rustic," my mother says hopefully.

Bobbie looks around for some sign of life.

"Maybe they've got a ski lift back down," Cora says.

My mother bends over, both hands on her thighs. "I bet the sky's beautiful at night," she says. "The Milky Way."

"Why don't we go ahead and check in?" Bobbie says. "I wouldn't mind cleaning up before dinner. Maybe someone's got a little calamine lotion."

Every half-hour or so she's had to detour into the woods and more than once come back asking me to describe what poison ivy looks like. I even drew a little sketch on a napkin for her but she wound up having to use it for toilet paper. "Probably too late anyway," she told me. "I been squatting more this afternoon than hiking."

Except for sharing the rest of Cora's candy bar, we haven't had anything to eat in over six hours and we're all a little cranky and tired.

The lodge looks like an Army barracks. Its wooden porch sags with age. My mother holds onto the railing and the boards creak with her weight.

Bobbie peeks through the screen door. Someone is sitting inside behind a makeshift desk reading the *Whole Earth Catalog*.

"It's open," he mumbles.

We all follow my cousin in. The room is small and damp and smells of mildew. There's a large antiwar poster on the wall and a picture of Eldridge Cleaver giving his raised-fist salute. Like recruits reporting for duty we line up in front of the desk.

The man folds his page over in the catalogue. He has a thick, reddish beard and is wearing the faded green uniform of the park's personnel.

"We were interested in a reservation," my mother says.

He looks up at her.

"You mean a cabin?"

Cora crosses her arms but my mother quickly says yes.

The man turns slowly in his swivel chair and slides open one of the drawers in the dented file cabinet behind him.

"Boarders?" he says finally, studying a yellow legal pad. "Is that your intention?"

Cora clears her throat but my mother smiles pleasantly and assures him that it is.

"Just the one night," she says. "We're delighted to be able to spend that."

Dinner will be served promptly at six in the mess hall, the man tells us. Breakfast at seven. There will be four cups in our cabin and we're encouraged to bring them with us to our meals. Because of the wildlife problem, any perishables are to be stored in the main lodge's facilities. All of this he announces as if reciting from a printed program.

"A tight ship," Cora says.

He only fingers his catalogue without looking up again. "There's coffee served till three."

Bobbie turns her wrist to check her watch. The crystal is steamed over. It's already after five.

"The beard looked a bit dry," Cora says as we march out onto the porch. "If I'd had a match I would have lit it."

"I guess they can get a little testy living this isolated," my mother says.

"The word's surly," my sister says.

Our assigned cabin is near the camp's water pump and as we come back across the grounds, Bobbie stops to splash her arms and face.

"It's cold all right," she says, smiling sympathetically at my mother. "I guess you could get used to it."

A woman has leaned out of the front door to the mess hall.

"Shower's down a ways," she shouts at us. She's wearing the green park uniform, her hair in a braid that slides around her shoulder. "That water's just for drinking."

My cousin wipes her chin. "Sorry."

"Jesus," Cora says when the woman closes the door after her. "Where'd these people train? Dachau?"

"I guess there's not going to be any tub baths," my mother says to herself.

"How about a home massage?" Bobbie says. "I got some cream packed that might work."

"A massage," my mother says. "That sounds wonderful."

"One massage coming up," my cousin says cheerfully. "Lou'll tell you I got the magic touch."

I look down at her red fingernails. They're lacquered and shining.

"Honey?"

My mother has her hand on my shoulder. She's asked me something and now even Cora is waiting for my answer.

"I thought after we got settled you could do a little reconnoitering for us," she says. "Maybe go down and see what the shower's like. Give the girls a chance to change."

"All right."

She continues to look at me.

"You weren't spacing out on us there, were you?"

She doesn't like to use any of the medical terms she's heard from Army doctors. They scare her. And so she's made up her own list. Petit Mal is spacing out. Grand Mal is a blackout. Both, she's convinced, are controllable. It's one of the reasons she encourages me to take naps and to go to bed early.

Cora surveys the row of gray cabins. Their tin roofs are rusted and covered with brown pine needles.

"Why do I have this feeling I'm going to bump into the seven dwarfs?" she says.

Signs posted by the water pump warn boarders to carry their valuables with them. Our own cabin turns out not to have a lock. But no one says anything until we're all crowded into the small single room. Twin sets of bunk beds are separated by a space too narrow to allow two adults to get out at the same time.

"This ought to bring us together," Cora says, lying down on the lower bunk's thin mattress.

"At least we'll be warm," my mother says. She smooths her hand across one of the Hudson Bay blankets. "The brochure says it gets a little cool at night. Even in July."

There's a single bedside table with a kerosene lamp on it. The glass funnel is coated with soot.

Bobbie empties her bag on the other bunk and unravels two pairs of wadded-up panties.

"Why don't you see about that shower," my mother says to me. "I'd like us to be cleaned up for dinner."

I look up at the cross beams that support the tin roof. The top bunks are high enough that you can barely turn over on the mattress without getting a splinter in your shoulder. Blackened initials and phone numbers are gouged into the wood.

"I'll start then," I say to my mother.

She unfolds one of the towels and hands it to me.

"Don't use all the hot water," she says.

Cora lies on her side, her hand propped under her chin. "What a dreamer."

"She's probably right, Mom," I say. "I don't think you should get your hopes up."

My sister flips over onto her back. "We should have that stamped on our license plate."

Bobbie has set all her underwear out on the other bunk. "That ought to hold us till we get back," she says. "Long as we stay dry."

In the last hour or so it's gotten overcast.

"Let's not even think about it raining," my mother says.

"There's a lot I don't want to think about," Cora says. "For instance, spending the night in a Skinner box."

I back out onto the steps and hold the door open in front of me.

"I guess if it's real cold I'll be right back," I say.

My mother covers the window with a towel. "That's all your father used to get in boot camp, sweetheart."

"Boot camp," Cora says. "Exactly."

The outdoor shower stalls are another fifty yards down the path and enclosed in a wooden fence. Even though there's a sign designating which side is for women and which for men, the fence boards are warped and dotted with punched-out knotholes.

Water is running through the aboveground pipes and I can see now that a couple of the stalls are being used. On the bench outside the fence are the clothes and backpacks of the two hikers we'd passed on the trail.

I sit down and slowly unlace my sneakers. No steam is coming up from behind the fence and I watch the soapy water spill out from under the boards.

Years ago when we were still at Fort Campbell, my father would bring me with him to the motor pool to wash the car each week. There was an area where the tanks were scoured with a high-pressure hose, the dirty water draining into a large uncovered manhole. On Saturdays with the radio blasting, my father would soap the car down and puff away on his cigar while I played with my toy soldiers in the sun. He would warn me not to stray from his sight and every once in a while glance over his shoulder to be certain that I was safe on my blanket. There was no reason for him to worry. I wasn't going anywhere. That uncovered manhole monopolized my dreams, sucking me down into its black oblivion. And even though I would appear to be content with my miniature soldiers and jeeps, it was only a show for my father. I didn't want him to think that I was afraid. I looked forward to this time I spent alone with him without my mother or older sister. But the sight of that steady stream from the hose washing down into that dangerous pit terrified me. I would venture no farther than the edge of my safe blanket. So that even when my father swept me up into his arms to admire his gleaming car, I stiffened against his chest.

"All yours."

I'm staring at a man's face that's leaning toward me, water dripping from his wet hair.

"How we doing?" he says.

Now his companion is beside him and together they hunch over, eyes fixed on me.

"Had a little too much sun?" one of them says.

There are towels wrapped about their waists. And then I recognize the one with the red face and freckles. The hiker.

"Yes," I stammer. "Maybe so."

The older one glances about before whipping his towel free to rub down his legs. His friend is already in his underwear and sits on the bench to pull his shorts on. They dress quick as firemen. No movement seems wasted.

"You back in commission?" the younger one asks me finally.

To prove that I am, I try to stand up.

"Okay, buddy," one of them says, his arm suddenly hooked under my own.

"I'm fine," I say but now they're on either side of me, lifting me back up onto the bench.

"Maybe some oxygen deprivation," the younger one is saying. "Kind of took a little dive there."

I stare at the loop of shower pipe above the fence and then down at the pool of water that seeps into the ground at the edge of the concrete.

"It's passed," I say.

The older one asks if I'm still with my friends.

"Back in the cabin," I say. "I'm supposed to test the water."

"Well," the older one says when they're dressed. "Should we go on back and tell them the water's fine?"

When I agree they both take up their positions beside me, their forearms hard as banisters. Before we're halfway back up the trail I can see Bobbie and my mother on the steps of the cabin. To keep from scaring them, I let go of my friends' arms.

But when I open my eyes again, half a dozen hands are reaching down to pull me up. Only this time I decide to sit and wait until I can tell whose legs belong to whom.

I awake in the bottom bunk of the empty cabin. It's cold and dark out and I light the kerosene lamp. A note from my mother tells me that they're up in the lodge and if I'd rather just sleep I'm not to worry about joining them. My dinner is under the towel on the bedstand.

The cabin is strewn with my cousin's clothes that my mother and sister wore this afternoon. Damp towels hang from the railing of the top bunks.

The small cast-iron stove takes up one corner with its black door half open. There are cinders still in the grate. The wide planks of the wooden floor are worn smooth from the heavy soles of hiking boots.

I raise the towel from my dinner: fried chicken and a large piece of cornbread with a bite taken out of one corner. Cora.

And I wonder if Daniel has tracked her this far. But it's hard to imagine *anyone* climbing a mountain just to get to my sister.

Outside it's thirty degrees cooler than it was and the sky is black and filled with stars. I haven't seen Venus so clearly since our desert days in Yuma. All of the other cabins are dark and silent, and I follow the path back around the water pump and up the slight incline to the lodge. There are no curtains and the big picture window is a yellow rectangle in the chilly dark. Everyone is playing Monopoly at the long pine table. Bobbie sits between the two hikers, their thick hair identically slicked back from their broad foreheads. Across from them Cora and my mother study the board. There are no park personnel. They have the lodge to themselves.

My mother laughs at something the older hiker says to her then reaches across the table to squeeze his wrist. She's landed on one of his properties.

The cups from the cabin are on the table and the younger hiker pours from a ceramic pitcher into each of them. Except Cora's. When he's done he rests his arm on the back of my cousin's chair.

My sister rolls the dice, concentrating on the game. Her stacks of colored money are neatly piled in their separate denominations. She's the only one who already owns the red plastic hotels. The others are enjoying their conversation too much to follow her moves. But even if they all suddenly took their turn seriously, it wouldn't matter. Cora would still win. Next to Ouija, Monopoly is her favorite board game. The goal is to put your opponents in your debt and nothing appeals to my sister more.

Farther up the trail, past where the park personnel have their own enclave of cabins, the woods open up to permit a nearly panoramic view. Here the Milky Way stretches across the black sky like a wisp of smoke and I stand and count the constellations until my eyes sting. When I was ten my father bought me a telescope for Christmas. This was in Yuma and each night we would sit on the patio and aim it up at the stars. Even Cora would stay out for a while, staring at the moon without saying anything, unwilling to admit that she was enjoying herself. My mother would fix something to drink and we'd spend an hour together sitting on the lawn furniture taking turns with the telescope. It was the last time the four of us ever sat still together for that long. Eventually we lost interest in figuring out which stars outlined which mythological figure's sword, and the telescope wound up collecting dust under my bed with the electric football game and the beginner's rock polishing kit.

But the real reason I'm putting off going back to the cabin is simple: I'm afraid of the dark. Last year, just before school let out, I rode my bike home from a classmate's party to discover that no one was home. My mother had left the front door unlocked and a note explaining that they'd decided to take Cora to the movies. I knew why. My sister was feeling sorry for herself. None of her classmates ever invited her to parties.

I could tell from her short note that my mother hadn't wanted to leave me alone. I knew as well that she would do so only with my father's prodding. The day after coming back from a month-long maneuvers in Labrador he complained to her that she was turning me into a real momma's boy. All of this I overheard during what Cora liked to call their Friday night imbroglios. They'd closed their bedroom door but with their voices raised and our common wall, there were no secrets. I was turning into a sissy and a pantywaist and it was my mother's fault. If she kept it up, she'd have a goddamn fairy on her hands before her little man ever hit high school. I listened barely able to believe my father's fears. That his only son wouldn't exactly be the kind of material the service academies had in mind. Well, that was just fine with her, my mother argued. She didn't want any child of hers growing up with no more prospect in life than as cannon fodder. And back and forth it went for over an hour, my ears red and then finally numb from their strident voices. But what they were *really* arguing about, (and it would take me another year to figure it out) had nothing to do with me. It was just my father's understanding as a military man that the best defense was a vigorous offense. And he knew that my mother was upset about his being sent off to the Far East again and that we would be unlikely to join him.

This was right before Chicopee when my father had been assigned to the Pentagon and we were temporarily living in civilian housing in a suburb of the capital. Typically we knew none of our neighbors and that night I walked my bike back down to the street. It felt safer outside. There were streetlights on and cars would drive past. I circled the block repeatedly, checking each time around to see if the Oldsmobile was parked in the driveway. I knew that Cora had wanted to see a mature-only movie and thus needed parental accompaniment. It wouldn't let out until after eleven. Plus, my father would suggest getting an ice cream afterward to give his soft son a better chance of hardening up. What this proved to me as I spun about the neighborhood was that he was right. His son *was* a sissy. Practically a teenager and still in need of a baby-sitter.

When at last I talked myself into returning, I flung open the front door, shouted my parents' names, and then slammed the door shut behind me. After switching on every light in the house, I opened the drapes wide in the living room and turned up the TV so that it could practically be heard next door. Then I sat down in the middle of the couch and waited, my heart leaping in my chest at whatever noise I imagined outside even with the television blaring.

As soon as the headlights flashed in the driveway, I quickly rushed from room to room slapping the lights off. Then I composed myself on the La-Z-Boy and pretended to be reading.

"Too much," Cora said when she came in through the kitchen, a box of popcorn tucked under her arm. "What were you doing, sending Morse code?"

I closed my book nonchalantly and told her I didn't know what she was talking about.

My sister made her favorite snorting sound. "Next time why don't you get a couple flags and try semaphoring."

Later, my mother came in to my room to tell me good night. "I thought we'd be back before your party was over," she said and sat down on the bed. "You have every reason to be upset."

I turned my face away from her on the pillow.

"You're just used to living on a post," she said finally. "This is an entirely different experience for you. You're not accustomed to it."

The truth was I was old enough to be alone.

"There'll come a time when you won't want any of us around," she said, leaning over me. "You'll see."

But I *couldn't* see. And it was impossible to believe I ever would.

Back at the cabin, I hesitate on the top step. I'd heard a rustling sound inside like leaves swept across the wooden floor. When I push the door open gently, the hinges creak and I squint at the blanket on the bottom bunk. There's the kerosene lamp on the nightstand and Bobbie's bag in the corner. One of Cora's magazines, turned over on her pillow, is a black steeple in the dark. Behind me there's the faint sound of voices filtering down from the lodge. And the ping pat, ping pat of water dripping from the pump.

Then I see it. The flicker of a tail. Perched on the sill is a rat. And sucking in my breath I feel the cold air like a karate chop to the throat.

With one hand still on the door I reach into my back pocket for my new, empty wallet (Bobbie had picked it out for me in the drugstore). I can't take my eyes from the pointed silhouette of its snout, its long tail as thick as my finger. I don't really aim and only want to scare it but it seems to vanish even before the wallet slaps against the wall.

I wait until my heart stops pounding then light the kerosene lamp to find where a board has rotted out in the windowsill.

I sit on the bed for a few moments before folding several of my sister's magazines in half and wedging them into the opening in the sill. Then, gathering up the dirty clothes, I tuck one of the towels under the door. After holding the lamp up to inspect each corner of the tin roof, I force Cora's *Photoplay* into a slot between the floorboards. The rim of the vent to the coal stove is just wide enough to plug up with my jeans and I stuff my socks into the larger cracks in the mortar.

Standing naked finally in the middle of the cold cabin, I feel my hair damp with sweat. I think of getting dressed again and walking back up to the lodge but then I think of what Cora might say in front of the two hikers and decide against it. Instead, I get under the covers on the bunk and open my book up.

The last picture of Matt shows him outside an igloo he'd built himself not far from what would be their most recent Farthest North. Like my father, Matthew Henson would think nothing of sleeping alone in a cabin where a rat had just been nibbling at their dinner. More than likely they would wind up giving it some funny name and eventually adopting it as a pet. I, on the other hand, am neither a fearless Arctic explorer nor a war-decorated paratrooper but a seizure-prone momma's boy who won't be able to fall asleep again until his mother, sister, and cousin have all come back to be with him.

In the morning, a chorus of voices wakes me and through the cabin window I watch a parade of old people winding toward the dining hall.

Cora opens one eye. " 'Onward Christian Soldiers'?"

I duck back under the covers. It's only seven and my mother and Bobbie are still asleep.

"You missed 'Go Tell It on the Mountain,' " I say.

Cora reaches up to pull the towel from around the stove pipe. "So what'd you have in here last night," she says, "some kind of black mass?" She slides down from the top bunk, Bobbie's nightgown riding up on her stomach.

The only time my sister is ever halfway pleasant to me is after a seizure. But this soon passes and she's once again her usual snotty self.

"I wouldn't mind getting something to eat," I say.

Cora studies me as if to decide whether I'm still to be treated with kid gloves.

"You have a headache?"

"Just hungry."

My mother sleeps with one arm folded over her ear. Bobbie

lies on her back, both legs drawn up and her knees nearly touching the tin roof.

"You should have seen those two with Wilbur and Clark," Cora whispers. "I practically had to drag them from the lodge." She sorts her clothes out from the pile on the floor and I turn my back for her to dress. "Nature boys had them eating wheat germ out of the palm of their hand."

"I thought you wanted Mom to be more liberated," I say, keeping my voice down.

"Being liberated doesn't mean you have to be indiscriminate."

"Are they still around?"

"You missed it," she says. "It was priceless. After I killed everyone in Monopoly, the old man slings his backpack on and tells junior they have to hit the road."

"They're father and son?"

Bobbie stirs in the other bunk, pulling the blanket over her shoulders.

"Anyway," Cora says, "after we said our good-byes they head straight into the woods. It's pitch black out but they don't believe in trails. The girls were impressed."

We step outside and I ease the door shut behind us. It's overcast and cool.

"So where were they going?" I ask.

My sister raises her hand as if to swear an oath. "You won't believe this one," she says. "Mom's jaw must have dropped two feet." She bends over to yank at her sagging socks and grins up at me. "Dig this. Allen got a low number so he's on his way up to Canada." She double knots her laces. "But here's the fun part. Dad's against it. Turns out he's some kind of retired Navy captain. Nonstop war stories about steering ships through the Panama Canal. Mom was all ears."

Although Cora plastered her bedroom door in Chicopee with antiwar stickers ("Draft Beer, Not Boys"), I was never sure how much of it was just to irk my mother. Her mocking of the captain and his son seems to me more personal than political.

Up ahead we can see the last of the old folks shuffling into the dining hall.

"Great," Cora says. "Just who I want to break bread with."

Like the lodge, the dining hall is built out of enormous rough-hewn logs. Inside, a dozen picnic-style tables are lined up like a military encampment.

My sister takes the empty table nearest the door even though several couples wave for us to join them.

"Ho-Jo's never looked so good," Cora says to me out of the corner of her mouth.

Park personnel move about the tables pouring milk from earthenware pitchers.

Suddenly, a man with a shock of silver hair stands up, stilling the noise.

"Let us thank the Lord," he begins and the others immediately bow their heads.

The workers appear unsure of whether to continue serving or not, their empty trays held at their side.

"Lord," the pastor pronounces in a deep, stagelike voice, "we have come all the way from our beloved state of Arkansas to be reminded once more of your boundless beauty." He pauses. "And please bring our brave astronauts home safely to us."

Cora turns to me and makes her where-did-they-get-this-guy face but waits with the rest of us to eat.

Afterward, one of the servers comes up to our table holding a coffeepot.

"You didn't bring your cups," she says.

Cora toys with the shaker of brown sugar. "Weren't any," she says. "We looked."

The girl retrieves two from the table behind us. "We get robbed blind," she says, a bulky mitten extending to her elbow.

Her face is pink. She's been standing all morning in front of the kitchen's cast-iron stove.

At the next table over, two couples sit with their hands folded in their laps. They're still praying silently, their stacks of pancakes steaming in front of them. Both of the women have hair as white as the bleached cotton tablecloth. Their husbands wear sporty tam-o'-shanters that are rimmed with souvenir pins. It's difficult to believe that they've made it up the mountain without help. I try to imagine my mother and father ever belonging to a church that sponsors group activities. It's impossible. I can't even imagine them as grandparents.

"You're not hungry?" Cora says, having caught me staring.

I haven't touched my breakfast.

"You need to eat something," she says and surprisingly reaches over to cut my pancake in half. "Come on."

A couple stops as they pass our table.

"It's a real pleasure to see," the woman says to my sister. "You don't find young people doing for each other anymore."

Cora looks up, her knife and fork frozen in mid-slice.

"My brother's mentally deficient," she says gravely. "He gags if the pieces are too big."

The woman's husband places his wrinkled hand on his wife's shoulder.

I wait until they've tottered out the door and then I turn on my sister.

"Jerk."

Cora pours syrup over my pancake. "Eat," she says and mimics bringing a fork up to her mouth. "Like this." And she pretends to chew in exaggerated bites.

Later, we wander about the camp, waiting for my mother and cousin.

The congregation from Arkansas, meanwhile, has moved in a pack to a camp area where they can meditate.

146

"Maybe we should get Bobbie up," Cora says. "They look like Elvis's kind of people."

But my sister is curious to see where the "rangers and ranger-ettes" live and so we follow one of the well-worn trails to a fenced-in clearing marked "Restricted."

Cora inhales deeply, rising up onto her toes.

"That ain't bread I smell baking," she says.

Beyond the fence the terrain forms a natural hollow ringed by a cluster of cabins. Several couples in swimsuits sit on aluminum lawn chairs, passing a cigarette among them, a tape recorder playing Jimi Hendrix. And then I notice the woman who'd yelled at Bobbie for using the pump. Although it's cloudy she's sunbathing and wears only the bottom half of her swimsuit.

"The staff at rest," Cora says.

One of the men twists about in his folding chair. Now they're all staring at us, the one holding the cigarette keeping his arm stiff at his side, his palm cupped.

"*Exeunt* stage right," my sister says, turning away from the fence.

I catch up with her. "I guess we were sort of trespassing," I say.

Cora picks up a large brown pinecone. "Just checking out the natives. No harm done. We're taxpayers."

Back at the cabin Bobbie and my mother are both dressed but not interested in breakfast.

"We can get something in town," my mother says.

My cousin sits on the bottom bunk. She looks pale and not especially eager to hike back down the mountain.

Afterward, before we're half an hour on the trail, the clouds have darkened and there are ominous rumblings off in the distance.

My mother shouts ahead for my sister to slow down to allow the rest of us to catch up. Cora is eager to get to a shopping center and out of her cousin's hand-me-downs.

"I feel like a damn backup singer on 'Hee Haw,'" she says when I find her leaning against one of the elevation markers. The pair of Bobbie's cutoffs she's wearing are stone-washed and the ragged threads hang to her knees. "You should see the alternative." And she pats the carry bag. "A little number Lou gave her for her birthday."

We watch my mother and cousin inch down a steep drop in the trail.

"The woman's a marvel," Cora says. "Truly."

My mother has to take another rest and so we all find something to sit on. When Bobbie wanders back into the woods, Cora asks about the hikers.

"You mean George and Allen?" my mother says.

"Right," my sister says. "Barry Sadler and son."

"It's very sad," my mother says. "What this war's done to families." She looks over at me. "Allen's seeking immigrant status in Canada."

"In other words, a draft dodger," Cora says.

"I feel sorry for the boy," my mother says. "I feel even sorrier for his father."

My sister twists the loose threads of her shorts around her finger. "Why? Because he's got a turncoat for a kid?"

But my mother doesn't want to get Cora started, which, of course, only gets her going all the faster.

"You're telling me you feel sorry for a little quisling?" my sister says. "Now what would Daddy think of that?"

My mother gazes tiredly at me. "If it were your brother," she says, "I'm sure your father would feel the same way I do, honey. We'd do whatever it took to keep Teddy out of harm's way."

Cora's eyes are bulging and I can see the pulse in her throat. She's not accustomed to losing arguments with my mother.

"In other words," she says, "send everybody over but your own kid."

But my mother's too exhausted to argue. "You're right, sweetheart, your mother's a hypocrite. What can I say?"

"You've already said it," Cora says and rips the thread from her shorts.

When Bobbie comes back she stares up at the threatening clouds.

"That one looks like a warship," she says. "The way that big gun comes out of it."

Cora looks over at me but doesn't say anything.

"George was telling us how he guided ships through the Canal Zone," my mother says. "He did it for ten years after he retired. Apparently the Panamanian government hires a lot of ex-Navy officers. Their own people don't quite have the know-how yet."

"Let George do it," my sister says. "Good thinking."

"Actually he's a very interesting man," my mother says. "Not much older than your father. In fact, he reminded me of Daddy a little."

"Daddy?" I say.

My mother stops rubbing her sore calves. "I don't mean physically, sweetheart. I just mean the way he obviously enjoys a new challenge. It's the kind of thing I could see your father doing when he retires."

"That," Cora says to me. "Or maybe teaching the CIA how to sky dive into Cuba."

"You don't want to underestimate your father," my mother says without taking her eyes off me. "Plenty of people in private industry would love to have his expertise."

"So how come he doesn't go for the gold?" Cora says. "What's keeping him? The prestige?"

My sister doesn't think of the Army as any kind of profession. Movie stars have a profession. Soldiers have a sentence. My father, for example, has served twenty years of his. And where besides Formosa has that gotten him?

Bobbie pulls herself up and steps into the thick brush.

"What's with her?" Cora says.

My mother puts her shoes back on. "Let's just leave your cousin to herself right now," she says.

My sister springs to her feet, tucking in her loose T-shirt. "Great idea," she says.

And we watch her troop back down the trail.

"We're going to have to keep those two separated," my mother says.

"It's not Bobbie's fault," I say. "She's not the one."

"There's always been something about her that sets your sister's teeth on edge," my mother says. "Don't ask me what."

It doesn't seem that big a mystery to me. Cora is just jealous. We can't go into a Howard Johnson's without every male in the restaurant spinning around on his stool. My sister is invisible beside Bobbie. And that's what irritates her. That someone with half her IQ should get twice the attention.

"What was that?" my mother says, holding her hand out.

It's begun to sprinkle and we listen to the patter of the rain on the leaves.

Bobbie scrambles back in from the woods. "I think we're in for it," she says.

"What's a little shower," I say.

But we're soon shouting at each other to be heard over the rain. My mother wants me to go ahead and catch up with Cora. And when I do, she says, mouthing her words slowly for me to read her lips, I'm to wait for them. I'm to stay beside the trail with my sister and not go any farther. Do I understand?

My cousin comes over next to my mother. It's pouring and together they lean toward me, their hair pounded flat on their heads.

Cora's stubborn enough to try to make it back to the car. My sister isn't athletic. She's always talked her way out of P.E. and here there are only dim markers and no barriers to prevent her from pitching headfirst off the side of the mountain.

The rain rushes down the slick trail as I start out cautious as a roofer, pinecones clattering through the trees. But all I can think about is my crazy, uncoordinated sister who'd rather risk plunging off a cliff than sitting out a storm.

Ten minutes later, the rain stops as abruptly as it began, the air seeming to clear magically. My sneakers make a wet sucking sound in the ankle-deep mud and at a bend in the trail, I stand peering over the edge at the rain-washed valley, the trees as green and misted as supermarket produce.

But then just as I'm about to turn away, I see something. Halfway down the ledge, draped over one of the larger boulders, there appears a white patch of cloth. But the longer I stare at it the more I begin to shake until to steady myself I have to reach out and grab the elevation marker. I want to believe that it's what happens when you strain your eyes. They can play tricks on you. Tricks like imagining the image of Slim Whitman in a rock.

After a while the dark clouds begin to scatter and between them the sun shines through in great shafts of light. Already the birds are singing again and the squirrels chattering and once more I crane forward to see far below me the same T-shirt stuck to a boulder as if set out to dry.

"Teddy?"

I turn just as my sister grabs my shoulder.

"Jesus," and her voice catches as she pulls me back. "I mean, what if you had a . . ." She drops the carry bag, shaking her head exasperatedly. "Christ, Teddy."

I touch the sleeve of her dry blouse.

"You changed," I say.

She kneels beside me and I point down at the boulder. My sister takes her hand away from her mouth.

"What'd you think?" she says angrily. "What?" She stops, her eyes blazing. "Jesus, Teddy."

She gets up and wipes her knees. Then, without looking back to see if I'm behind her, she detours into the woods where the thick mulch of leaves will keep our feet from sinking in the mud.

I trudge dutifully after my sister even though my mother made me promise to wait for them beside the trail. But Cora has never been taken with the great outdoors ("I *hated* Heidi") and is eager to get back to the car. After a while, she's bored enough that I can try conversation and so I ask when she thinks Daniel will return to his family.

"Family?" and she steps gingerly over an enormous rotted log. "Those people were your idea of a family?"

I'm tempted to ask *her* idea of a family. But I know that she'd only tell me what she always tells me. My sister doesn't care for the American version. The one with the father who knows best and his wife who thinks she knows even better. No, she prefers the European model. With Marcello Mastroianni as the harried poppa and Anna Magnani as his hysterical wife. In other words, a couple who allow their children to go their own bilingual way.

Cora stops to look about. "We're lost," she says. "And I mean with a capital L."

This is a painful admission for my sister who *never* gets lost. But the trail is nowhere in sight. We've wandered too deep into the woods to keep track of the beaten path.

"Talk about not being able to see the forest for the trees," Cora says.

I stand on my toes trying to peer over a thicket of vines. We've given up being careful about touching anything doubtful looking and rip barehanded at the seaweedlike undergrowth that wraps around our ankles.

When we seem finally to have worked our way to the bottom of the mountain, we've been stumbling around so long in the dense woods that it's impossible to know if we're even at the bottom of the *same* mountain anymore.

A branch suddenly whacks sharply across my ear and Cora turns to check on me.

"It's just a scratch," I say, smearing the trickle of blood with my palm. "It's not that deep."

My sister backs away, satisfied that I'm not going to bleed to death. "The only reason it's not that deep is because *you're* not that deep."

I'm not worried about finding our way out. I'm worried about my mother realizing that we haven't.

"She'll have gone bananas by now," Cora agrees. We've stopped to rest and she peels a chunk of bark from a moss-covered pin oak. "It'll be Cape Cod all over again."

We were stationed at the Army Research Labs in Natick when my parents took us out to Martha's Vineyard for the weekend. After a large picnic lunch on the beach, Cora was getting too much sun and my mother walked her back to the car to find something to put on her. They were gone no more than five minutes but my father still managed to fall asleep watching his infant son dig in the sand with his plastic shovel. As soon as my mother returned (my sister's nose lathered with ointment), all hell broke loose. Within seconds everyone on the island was combing the shore for a thirteen-month-old.

My mother, who couldn't swim, repeatedly rushed into the surf and had to be dragged back out by my guilt-ridden father. This went on until I wandered out from one of the Port-O-Lets not twenty feet from where our towels were still spread out beneath a rental umbrella. Clutching me to her breast, my mother thanked everyone for helping with the rescue. My embarrassed father tried to hide behind a pair of experimental sunglasses (a lab prototype that supposedly filtered out actinic rays) but as soon as my mother managed to catch her breath she was merciless. According to Cora the tirade didn't cease even after we were back on the road, cutting our vacation short. Twice my mother made my father pull over so that she could pound his shoulders again without fear of killing us all on the highway.

"Soon as the sun goes down," my sister says, "I expect Mom will have the helicopters out circling."

I try to remember which side of the tree moss is supposed to grow on. Not that even a compass would do us much good. It's the trail we need to find.

"The way I see it," Cora says, "we can either sit and wait or we can try to get back to Amish country on our own."

Each time we seem to make some headway a cloud will burst leaving us drenched and breathless. Even with the tree cover the rain slices down through the leaves as cold and stinging as sleet.

"Another hour or so and it's going to start getting a little cool out here," Cora says after yet another sudden shower.

"We'll be on the trail by then," I say.

But we wander about aimlessly all afternoon: slipping in creek beds, hacking our way out of wild berry patches, avoiding what look like animal burrows.

Though we're sweating, by dusk it's become chilly enough that we huddle next to each other in the gray light. Cora's been thinking how my mother will have imagined by now that we've been abducted by wild mountain men, the first victims of cannibalism in a recreational park.

"Maybe Bobbie will keep her calmed down," I say.

My sister shakes her head.

"What is it about her that Mom clicks with?" she says. "I'm honest to god nonplussed."

"Bobbie?" I say.

"She wears clothes like they're Saran Wrap. Blows off school to spend her life flipping burgers. And then goes and marries a troglodyte."

"She's not as dumb as you think, you know."

Cora picks at the burrs sticking to her shorts. "And how dumb is that?"

"You don't learn everything in a book," I say.

"Listen," she says. "The last book cousin read was the first book she read."

I hold my watch up, trying to see the time.

"Maybe what Mom likes," I say, "is how Bobbie doesn't blame her mother for all her problems."

When my sister doesn't respond immediately, I know to brace myself for the worst. But I'm still stunned at how deeply aggrieved she winds up sounding.

"Maybe," she says, "that's because her mother *isn't* her problem."

"But Mom's yours."

"That's right," she says. "Mom's my problem. And she's Daddy's problem and some day soon when you're not looking she's going to be your little problem too."

"I don't think so."

"You don't think is right."

"Everything's Mom's fault with you," I say. "She's the reason you don't make friends. She's the reason you're a hermit. She's the reason you've got brown hair. Or whatever else you don't like about yourself on any given day."

But before I can add something about why a boy who's probably never talked to another girl might be attracted to her, my sister's voice is barely a whisper in the still woods.

"I don't like my eyes."

We're not a family to confess our secrets. It's our number-one unspoken rule. Never to embarrass each other with any personal anguish we might suffer.

"They look like a frog's," Cora says.

It's a symptom of my sister's condition that her eyes protrude slightly. I could tell her that Ava Gardner's do too and that she's more critical of her appearance than any leading lady. Except Cora would take any kind of reassurance from her baby brother as coddling.

"They're bloated," she says. "I don't even look the same anymore."

"Then what are you complaining about?"

She looks up, surprised. "That's very good. You see what happens when you hang around me long enough?"

Cora despises feeling sorry for herself in front of me and so predictably she lashes out.

"And you know who I blame too, don't you?" she says bitterly.

I do.

"She's diabolical, Teddy. She'll get those claws in you and she won't let go."

My sister's gotten herself worked up and right now her eyes *do* look bloated. But because her symptoms aren't reversible, she refuses to continue using her medication.

"I should have gotten out when I was your age," she says. "Gone and lived with Aunt Irene or something."

"And risk winding up like Bobbie?" I say.

Her brows glisten. "It almost would have been worth even that."

This is as close as my sister will get to sharing any confidence with me and she stares uneasily over my shoulder.

"We're not getting anywhere here," she says at last and stands up.

I want to add that we're not hurtling off any cliff either but instead follow closely behind her in the dark, imagining how it must have been for my father leading his troops in the jungles of Vietnam. Two tours of duty and half a dozen combat ribbons, including the Purple Heart with the oak leaf cluster for all those shrapnel scars that wrinkle the back of his neck, the ones I see sitting behind him in the car. You don't get the Silver Star for jumping every time you step on a twig in the woods. Or for letting your sister lead the way at night. But then I'll always be my mother's son and my sister will always be my father's daughter.

The air's cold enough to see my breath and I stop to pry the mud from my sneakers with a stick.

Cora waits holding her watch up to her face when I suddenly drop the stick at my feet.

"What was that?"

My sister casually cups her ear. "I don't know. Suitcases?"

But now we can both hear it: the unmistakable sound of human voices.

"Over here," Cora shouts. "This way."

I keep my hands tucked under my armpits.

"Who is it?" I whisper.

My sister only touches my shoulder. "Relax."

Then like one of the enormous ships he steers through the Panama Canal, George, the pilot, emerges from the shadows, his teeth gleaming in the moonlight. Allen thrashes out after him and together they stand over us.

"How you guys doing?" George says.

"You were going in circles," Allen says. He holds a thermos out for me.

There's coffee in it but I take a deep swig anyway.

"How's Mom?" Cora says. "Catatonic?"

George studies the luminous hands of his watch. "We promised to have you back by midnight," he says with all the confidence of an accomplished outdoorsman.

Even after being hopelessly lost, Cora resents the thought of being rescued and so my suspicious sister asks them how it is that they're still here.

"I guess we sort of got derailed," Allen says and explains that they're amateur mycologists and last night they'd run into a wonderful patch.

Cora passes the thermos back. "The study of mushrooms," she

says to me and it's clear from her tone that she doesn't believe a word he's said. What she *does* believe is that they've fallen in love with Bobbie and my mother.

"Get any?" she asks.

"Some puff balls," George says then smiles at me. "You ready to hit the trail again?"

When I nod he points over my shoulder with his walking stick. "Why don't you two stay between us and we'll save some time cutting across the trail."

Allen immediately sets out in the exact opposite direction Cora and I had come from. This is humbling to my sister and so it's no surprise when, to pass the time, she recalls the complicated plot of some B movie where the victim was killed by slipping him poison mushrooms. "They were called 'Angels,' " she says. "I remember the hero saying how they looked just like puff balls. Apparently only an expert can tell the difference." Neither Allen ahead of me nor his father behind us admit to ever having seen the film and continue to march in silence, the only sound the squishing of my sneakers.

Less than fifty feet from the parking lot, George comes up front to lead us back out onto the trail.

"Recognize where you are now?" he asks.

We would never have found our way without him. Still, I wish it could have been anyone else. Even one of the self-satisfied park personnel from the camp would have been better.

"So where are the squad cars?" Cora says. "The blood-hounds?"

Allen grins, surely thinking of my cousin and his own reward.

I look down at the back of my sister's legs, which are crosshatched with scratches. Our clothes are splattered with dried mud so that we look like a couple of painter's apprentices.

The pilot and his son, on the other hand, appear as fresh as when they set out from camp earlier in the day. Neither of them wears a jacket, their muscular arms uncovered and unspotted. Even their hiking boots look as if they've just been spit-shined.

The Oldsmobile is the only car still in the lot. My mother sits in the front seat biting her nails. She has the doors locked and the small overhead light on. Bobbie sleeps in the back, her heels pressed up against the smudged window. It's after midnight and I try to persuade myself that my mother's an Army wife and used to waiting.

"Let's get it over with," Cora says.

As soon as my mother hears us her head pivots sharply and she squints out into the blackness.

My sister glances over her shoulder at me. "This is not going to be pleasant."

My mother springs from the driver's side as if the engine has caught fire. The parking lot has been churned up from all the cars leaving in the rain.

"Just stay there," George calls out to her.

My mother gazes down at her feet as if wondering what's preventing her from lifting them.

Bobbie pushes her door open and peers out at us. "The car's stuck," she says. "It won't budge."

My mother steadies herself.

"We must have taken an inch of rubber off the back tires," my cousin says.

Allen shouts for her not to get out.

"No point in it," he says, unlacing his boots.

Cora and I watch the pilot and his son step barefoot into the mud.

"I didn't know better," my sister says, "I'd say this had all been staged."

Allen places his own feet in his father's deep footprints. There's nothing for Cora and me to do but wait, our teeth chattering from the cold.

When at last George reaches her, my mother is giddy and he squats down in front of her.

"He's going to sweep Mom off her feet," Cora says.

Bobbie is being carried piggyback, her arms wrapped about Allen's neck. They all plunge forward.

My sister and I move over to stand beside the split-wood fence that encloses the parking lot.

"You had us a little worried," my cousin says as Allen gracefully lowers his shoulder for her to slide off.

George bends from his waist and my mother rolls to one side until her feet touch the ground.

When she sees Cora backing away from her, she tries to calm herself down by taking several deep breaths.

"We probably ought to just wait till morning on that car," George says.

Allen delicately flicks a clod of dirt from Bobbie's eyebrow. "And hope for a little sunshine," he says, draping a poncho over my cousin's shoulders.

With mud creasing the corners of my mother's mouth, she smiles beatifically.

"What's one more miracle," she says and points to where Bobbie's leaning against a spruce whose needles form a wide skirt about its trunk.

And there like abandoned presents beneath a scraggly Christmas tree sit our half-dozen scuffed and dented suitcases.

"Then there was a rainbow," Bobbie says. "Right over the parking lot."

We're sitting around a fire George has somehow managed to start.

Behind us, Allen finishes tying down a second shelter constructed of ponchos and rain gear. Our rescuers don't believe in carrying tents.

"And there was our luggage," my mother adds, shaking her head in disbelief. "Like it had all come to rest under that one tree."

"They didn't even leave a note," Bobbie says.

My sister is quiet.

"There's nothing missing?" Allen says. "You've gone through everything?"

"We were on the interstate," my mother says. "So they got a little banged up. But unless Cora finds something, I don't think so."

She looks over at my sister who's warming her hands before the fire.

"I think you're right, Rosemary," my cousin says. "It's a miracle. How else can you explain that rainbow?"

Cora keeps her head bowed, palms outstretched. "By light filtering through moisture," she says. "It's a simple prismatic effect."

My mother is wearing one of George's flannel, long-sleeve shirts.

"Maybe," she says. "But it's a little harder to account for the suitcases."

Cora pretends not to hear her over the crackling of the fire.

"Whoever returned them had to be some kind of Christian," I say.

"You don't come across them everyday," Bobbie says. "I'd say we've been pretty lucky."

My mother nods appreciatively at George who drives a sharpened stick into the ground.

"We have," she says. "And we've got our own Good Samaritans right here."

Allen steps back into the light with his arms piled high with dry twigs.

"There's an unwritten code in the wild," he says. "Next time it might be you out there."

"It's true," Bobbie says thoughtfully. "The world can be a cold place."

"Well," Allen says, turning toward his father, "I've found that hiking can bring people together."

George only finishes hammering the stick in.

Afterward, with only room for the four of us in the two makeshift shelters, father and son decline to sleep in the car, insisting that doing without is part of their survival training.

"You can share that with your brother," my mother tells Cora when she claims the larger lean-to.

My sister's tired enough not to argue.

"It'll be light out in a few hours," George says to coax my mother into taking the other sleeping bag. "It's no sacrifice, believe me."

When Bobbie follows Allen back into the woods to help gather some more wood, I quietly crawl into my sister's tent.

"Just keep your feet out of my face," she says.

Through the open triangle, I can see my mother kneeling on the bedroll, her profile aflame. She's smiling up at George who's said something to her about his flannel shirt reaching down to her knees.

I close my eyes. It's unfair to hate him but I do. It doesn't matter that he helped save my sister and me from possible frostbite and exposure. What matters is that my mother is whispering to him in the dark so as not to keep her jealous son awake.

Cora has already fallen asleep. My sister doesn't worry about her mother running off with a retired Naval officer. Or, for that matter, her father with some geisha. If that's what her parents care to do then she'll only wish them godspeed. In the meantime, she'd appreciate it if I keep to my side of the bed-roll.

My mother has moved back beside the fire with her pilot. Across from them, Bobbie and the draft dodger lounge with their backs against the same tree. The fire crackles loud enough to mute their hushed voices. It's possible only to see their lips moving. In the flattering glow of the firelight my mother appears as young as my cousin.

Cora snores at the other end of our unzipped sleeping bag. Her socks press warmly against my shoulder. It doesn't trouble my sister that her mother wears a stranger's clothes and is practically reclining beside him. She would only remind me that Mom and Dad are adults, and that what's good for the goose . . . etc. This is easy enough for her to say. She doesn't worry about us as a family.

In fact, Cora will tell you that the first picture she'll direct will be a *real* family movie. There won't be any Andy Hardys or Tim Considines. No Robert Youngs or Jane Wyatts. Just what my sister's script will be all about she won't say. Only that the guilty will recognize themselves in living color.

Whenever I mention this to my mother, she only smiles. "Cora's right about one thing. She was made for Hollywood." But I shouldn't take her too seriously. Some day my sister will come to learn how lucky she was to be able to take us all for granted.

I open my eyes to see Bobbie and Allen tossing twigs into the fire as the flames curl up over their heads. My mother is rubbing her ankles either because of the cold or soreness. They're all silently staring into the fire as if hypnotized by its warmth. And I wonder what they must be thinking. If perhaps my mother is recalling her last conversation with my father. And if Bobbie is considering giving Lou a second chance. Or if, instead, my mother is reflecting on how attractive and youthful the pilot appears for someone retired. Or if Bobbie has already fallen in love with the draft dodger who seems so at home in the woods.

Cora grunts and kicks me in the chest. She's half out of the sleeping bag and I get up to roll her back onto the poncho.

"She keeping you awake, honey?"

My mother crouches before me. Her eyes appear to water in the firelight and I almost imagine that she's about to cry.

"Tomorrow I'm going to get you the warmest, biggest motel bed on the interstate," she says, her breath frosting in the cold. And she tugs the poncho up over my shoulder. "Don't let your sister take it all."

"I'm okay," I whisper but she stares at me unconvinced.

"What's the matter, sweetheart?"

She doesn't, of course, even have to ask. She only has to squint at me in the dark to see.

"What do you think?" she says at last. "Your frumpy old mother's going to run off with a sailor?" She tucks the corner of the sleeping bag under me. "They've been very kind to us, don't you think?"

I nod reluctantly.

"We're all military," she says, "so we have a few things in common."

"He's Navy," I point out.

My mother glances back over her shoulder toward the others. They keep their voices down with Cora asleep.

"George joined up just about the same time your father did," she says. "We figured out they were over in Vietnam exactly the same time."

Hearing her use his first name feels like a betrayal.

"Dad was in the jungle," I say. "The Navy just floated around in the gulf. It's a big difference."

My mother looks down at me. "Your father's a very brave man, sweetheart. No one's making any comparisons."

Hot tears well up in my eyes and I know if I try to say anything they'll spill over.

"We're all proud of Daddy," she says. "He doesn't have to prove anything to any of us."

"Then how come you compare him to someone you don't even know?"

Cora shifts beneath the covers, her toes digging into my arm.

"Daddy's Daddy," my mother says. "Nothing anyone says is ever going to change that."

I draw one hand up out of the sleeping bag to keep the tears from curling into my ear.

"Not every boy has a father like yours to look up to," she whispers. "And that you do makes your mother very happy."

"So how come you make everything sound like it's over with," I say, swiping at my cheek.

My mother shifts to take the weight off her legs. "Like it's over with, honey? I don't understand."

"Like Daddy's a stranger or something."

Her expression is unchanged. My mother's only trying hard to make sense of what I'm saying.

"You think I've forgotten your father?" she says finally.

I nod, afraid that my voice will crack.

When my mother exhales, the gray cloud of air obscures her face. "You're tired, honey," she says gravely. "Half of what you're saying now won't make any sense to you in the morning. You'll see. It'll all seem silly once the sun's up."

She's right, of course. When it comes to talking about my father, I *don't* make any sense. "That's because he's your idol," Cora likes to say. "Other kids have Batman or that fetus-face John Glenn but you've got Daddy." Even though this is true—my father always *has* been my hero—I come back at her angrily. "What about you?" I'll say. "You don't worship dumb movie stars? At least I don't hang up idiot posters in my room." Cora will then point out that no one has made a poster of Daddy yet. "A fan club of one does not a celebrity make."

My mother rejoins the others about the fire and every once in a while squints in my direction but I pretend to be asleep.

With my eyes closed I listen to the crackling of the fire and my sister's snoring. Yesterday, in the car, Cora picked up my Matt Henson book and made her guffawing noise, saying how the dust jacket made it sound a lot like our assignments. "Dad gets to ride the sled while we're left to put up the igloo." I guess we always have set off hoping things would turn out half as good as my father promised. Yuma was going to be a desert paradise and Natick a winter wonderland. In the end, though, no matter what the temperature, none of us ever warmed up to our assignment.

Still, Matt never complained. He was orphaned before he was my age and went off to sea as a cabin boy. By the time he teamed up with Peary, he'd traveled as much as any Army brat. Yet he always seemed content, smiling brightly in all the photographs. It didn't matter that they'd just come back from another failed attempt to reach the Pole. Or that he'd just suffered terrible frostbite and nearly frozen to death after falling into a crevasse. All that seemed to matter was that he was with the commander, the only father he'd ever really known. So it didn't bother him much when the temperature dropped to forty below or he got a little wet or even if his skin burned from the sun's reflection off the snow. He was happy with his adopted family and already on top of the world.

"*I* feel like I've been beaten with a gourd," Cora says, arching her stiff back against the car seat.

It took us half the morning to dig the Oldsmobile out. And if one of the park personnel hadn't happened along in his jeep, we'd probably still be wedging branches under the rear tires.

The difference for Bobbie and my mother was that they actually seemed to enjoy slogging about in the muck. They spent most of the time joking with George and Allen who'd stripped to their waists, huffing and puffing, their hairy chests matted with mud.

"The first Holiday Inn sign we see," my mother says.

"The first *anything* we see," Cora says.

When we're less than an hour from Asheville, my sister starts reading to us from the guidebook about the Vanderbilts' famous estate. She's afraid my mother might be too tired to visit it.

"The garden's got every flower known to man," she says, holding up her *Fodor*'s. "You can inhale once and smell the entire northern hemisphere. It'll be like every officers' wives' garden party you've ever been to packed into one."

My mother laughs. "Wasn't he what they called a robber baron? I never understood what that was."

"It means he was a crook," I say. "He stole from the poor."

"Listen," Cora says to me. "You're into orphanology. I'll get one of the guides to tell you all about little Gloria." She drops back against the seat, the dirt flaking from her knees. "I'm telling you, Biltmore's got something for everyone."

That my sister is so enthusiastic about stopping makes me suspicious that she's got something planned with Daniel. Even though there's not been a T-Bird sighting all morning.

Bobbie turns about in her seat. She's said very little since exchanging addresses with Allen.

"What do you think I might like?" she asks innocently. "I guess I don't really care about plants that much."

Cora hesitates, her eyes narrowing the way they do whenever she has to come up with something quick.

"Well," she says, stalling. "I thought I remember reading somewhere how Elvis flew over here from Graceland. He was having a garden put in."

"A garden?" my cousin says.

"Right," my sister says. "He'd heard about Biltmore and wanted to get some ideas."

"Is that true?" Bobbie says.

Cora nods as if still a little fuzzy about the details. "I don't know. Maybe it was the colonel. Anyway, they flipped over the thing and practically stole the whole concept."

My mother appears pleased that her niece is interested in something cultural. Even if she suspects that Cora has made it all up.

"We'll get us a room," she says. "And then after a little nap, we'll all drive over and check this place out. How's that sound?"

"Excellent," Cora says. "Outstanding."

We listen to some call-in talk show. The host's thick Southern accent grates on my sister and she works her crossword instead, plugging the cotton from a bottle of aspirin in her ears.

One of the callers asks the guest psychologist what to do about a husband who she suspects is being unfaithful.

"All I hear is one excuse after another about why he's got to be away so much," she says. "I hardly see him anymore."

The psychologist asks what her husband does for a living.

"He sells shoes," the woman says. "It's not supposed to require a lot of roadwork."

I notice my mother smile sheepishly at my cousin before changing the station.

At the Triple Six Inn outside Asheville Bobbie volunteers to register for the room. She can tell that my mother, whose clothes are badly splattered with mud, is too embarrassed to get out of the car.

"It's the one thing you've got to admire in her," Cora says as we watch my cousin saunter into the lobby. "There's not a self-conscious bone in the woman's body."

"Maybe she just doesn't care what motel managers think," I say.

My sister glances over at me as if at another road sign. "No argument there."

Bobbie doesn't get back into the car but points up at the room on the second floor.

"A couch," she says when I roll my window down. "Best they got."

But I'd rather a bumpy Castro Convertible than a sleeping bag with my twitchy sister. This morning when I complained about all her fidgeting in the night, she looked at me as if I were making it all up. "You were dreaming," she said. "I never even budge." When I turned to my mother to back me up she only grinned. "It's the same thing with your father," she said. "That's just the way they are."

Afterward, I untie the suitcases from the rack (George having used some kind of nautical knots) and carry them up to the room. Cora's already out of the shower.

"Go ahead, honey," my mother says to Bobbie and tells me to turn my head as she strips out of her own muddy clothes. "I'll go last. I want to soak my gams."

"I won't be long," my cousin says.

The room is small and we're all practically on top of each other. But no one complains. After our night in the woods, it feels like the Biltmore.

Later, after Cora has fallen asleep with her earphones still on, Bobbie sits on her bed studying the yellow pages. When she finds what she's looking for she tears the page out of the directory and slips her shoes on.

"Got to quit dilly dallying," she says to herself and then sticks her head in the bathroom door to tell my mother that she's taking her boy out for a milkshake.

"Come on, darlin'," she whispers to me. "I need some company."

But I know that's not the reason. We've already been to a McDonald's drive-thru. My cousin has been thinking about something all morning, and my guess is it's not just her hiker friend.

As soon as we're out of the parking lot, she directs me to unzip her pocketbook.

"Go on," she says, not taking her eye off the road.

I open the large vinyl bag and she apologizes for the mess.

"It's like my life, sugar. One thing piled on top of the next."

There's an amazing jumble of discarded lipstick tubes, broken mascara wands, wadded Kleenex, hairpins, tangled earrings, knotted necklaces. There are parking tickets, Q-Tips, empty prescription vials, breath mints, a how-to book (*101 Ways to Drive Your Man Wild*), a pair of fishnet stockings.

"I can explain all of it," she says. But what she wants me to check is the address she'd torn from the yellow pages. "I figure it's downtown. Usually they get rent cheaper there."

"It's a clinic," I say, unfolding the page in my lap. "The Blue Ridge Woman's Clinic."

"Number'd been changed when I called," she says. "Probably out of business by now anyway."

She takes the business route through Asheville and together we watch for the street.

"When I was your age," Bobbie says, "you'd have to go to Mexico or some other place ten thousand miles away." She glances anxiously out her window, trying to catch the street names. "Now all you got to prove is you're nuts. Which makes it a lot easier on your cousin."

"Maybe we should stop at a gas station," I say finally.

Bobbie puffs her cheeks, exhaling slowly. "You're right. We probably spun by it already."

At the light, she signals and we pull into an ancient-looking service station.

"I guess we could use some gas too," she says. "Why don't you ask the man for directions and I'll fill her up." She jumps out and unscrews the cap from the gas tank. "Go on. Tell the guy I can handle this."

In the small station, a poodle with soiled corkscrew hair lifts its chin at me when the bell rings over the door. There's no one inside and so I step back around to the service bay. An old man in overalls sits in a cane-back chair with his cap pulled around on his head. He's staring at the underside of a pickup that's been raised overhead on the lift. Oil is dripping onto a stack of newspapers beneath it.

"Sounds dead to me," he says. "How's it sound to you?"

I shrug my shoulders. "I guess I don't know a lot about engines."

"Too bad," and he makes a clicking sound with his mouth. "Can't go far without 'em."

I look out at Bobbie who keeps her back to us even though the pump is behind her.

When I ask for directions the man scratches his neck and the pink streaks glow then fade on his fair skin.

"What you looking for?"

I hesitate not really wanting to bring up the actual name. "It's just sort of on the eight hundred block."

He considers me a moment then cranes his neck to see my cousin who's still standing in the dark shade of the station's overhang.

"That place?" he says, his mouth twisting. "You might find that yourself, boy. Seein' as how you got this far on your own."

Bobbie's sitting in the Oldsmobile when I come up to her window.

"It's three exactly," she says, holding out the money. Then she looks back down at her hands on the steering wheel. "I oughtn't to be pushing this off on my sweet cousin."

I look out through the other side of the car. The old man hasn't moved. I can hear the cane chair groan as he tilts back on its spindly legs.

The gas station's tattered sandwich boards feature this month's special on tune-ups.

The old man takes the money from me, turning the bills over as if checking for any counterfeits.

The oil from the raised pickup patters on the newspapers behind us. There's a TV atop the red tool chest. The sound's off and the astronauts are performing somersaults in the gravity-free tunnel to the lunar module.

"Take your right on Patterson," he says grudgingly, lifting his chin exactly as the poodle had. "Gonna be two streets over on your left." Then he rolls his tongue across his teeth as if he'd just bitten into something foul. "You a fool, boy. That woman's old enough to be your momma."

As soon as we leave the station Bobbie starts apologizing for involving her favorite aunt's child in all of this.

"It just shows how it's driving your cousin crazy," she says, shaking her head. "What in the world am I thinking? I'm taking you back to the motel. Pronto." Instead she pulls the Oldsmobile over and sets the shift in park. "What're you smiling about, sugar? What's so funny?"

I hike my thumb back over my shoulder. "That guy. He thought I was the one got you pregnant."

My cousin seems to listen to the car idling for a moment before fingering the buttons on her blouse.

"Honey," she says finally. "You want to bide your time. You want to bide it real good."

When I stop smiling and try to look serious, she reaches over and cups the back of my neck.

"Listen to the one giving all the advice. Like I know what I'm doing."

But if there's one thing anyone can say about my cousin it's that she knows her own mind. My aunt Irene always said that right from the start her daughter possessed an iron will. "All her Daddy and I could do was duck under the table. And it never let up. Not in grammar school not in high school. She did what she pleased. I think that's why the boys were always beating the door down. It's something they weren't used to." My mother agreed. "That and some other attributes your cousin came into the world with," she would say.

The street Bobbie grew up on became known as the Strip because of all the hot rods that seemed forever parked outside my aunt's apartment. Cora claims that Bobbie runs the risk of eventual lead poisoning from the decade she spent draped over the lacquered hoods of every customized car in Chicopee. But I know that it's more than just my cousin's figure that had all the boys revving their engines for so many years. It's how she cocks her head to listen to whatever you say no matter how tongue-tied and awkward you feel in saying it. It makes you fall in love with her. The same way all the other boys in all the dual-carbed El Caminos and juiced up V-8's fell in love with her. That's the kind of person she is. The kind who knows her own mind and makes you feel as if she knows yours just as well and likes everything you're thinking or ever thought about. "In other words," Cora says, "the original bimbo."

But the real question, of course, is how she wound up with Lou. "I got an answer for that," my sister will tell you. "He's her penance. Her sackcloth and ashes. It's her way of exorcising all her guilt. Marry a lazy, no-count, ignorant slob. Lou's your man."

My aunt wasn't happy to see her daughter settle down with an older, divorced, medically discharged ensign but not even my mother heard about Lou until it was too late. They were engaged on a Friday and married the following Sunday. "Too quick for any credit checks," Cora likes to say.

At first, we drive right past the clinic. It's in a section of town that's still partly residential.

"I guess I was expecting something else," Bobbie says and spins back around the block once before finding a parking spot. She slips her sunglasses on even though it's overcast. "You want to wait here?" she asks me.

But my cousin's only being polite.

"I haven't had anything to eat in fifteen hours," she says nervously.

I look down at the crumpled McDonald's sack on the floor. While the rest of us had devoured our breakfast after a night in the woods she'd only sipped at her orange juice.

The building looks like a dentist's office. It's all brick and glass with wooden blinds in the big front window. As we come up the walkway Bobbie reaches down for my hand and her warm palm feels as if she's just taken off a glove.

"I could shoot myself for bringing you along," she says, smiling at me weakly.

There's a smudged slip of paper taped to the door that says to please ring first. My cousin takes a deep breath and presses the buzzer. Her nails, I notice, are unpainted. In fact, as we wait on the steps, it strikes me for the first time that she has on very little makeup. At least for my cousin. Her hair is its usual bubble height but there's no eyeshadow or thick mascara. And she's wearing the smallest earrings I have ever seen on her. No larger than a quarter.

After a loud buzzing sound that makes us both flinch, the door cracks open.

"Lord," Bobbie says under her breath. "It's like a pawnshop."

There's a small carpeted waiting room and a row of chairs against the wall. A young girl sits behind a glass partition, which she slides back.

"Here for a consult?"

Bobbie nods.

"You can start by filling this out," the girl says and passes a clipboard through with a pen attached to a string.

I sit down beside my cousin as she takes up the ballpoint and studies the long form for a moment. It's a minute before she fingers down the string to grip the pen.

There doesn't seem to be anyone else around. The girl had been listening to a radio but turns it off now that she has company.

"How 'bout that rocketship?" she says to me. "Almost there."

Her dark hair is cut short and brushed straight back, her face aglow and clean-scrubbed looking.

"My Social Security number," Bobbie says to herself. She stares at the form as if it's an impossible math problem. "I can't even think of it."

The fluorescent light flickers overhead. There are no plants or posters or even any magazines. Just four chairs and a glass panel to divide the room.

"Nearest living relative," Bobbie says. "I guess that's you, Teddy."

After a while, a man in chinos and a golf shirt comes down the hall and leans over to whisper something to the girl. At first I imagine he's about to kiss her but instead he slowly backs away, grinning.

"I don't know," the girl says, forgetting that the partition is open. "Ask me again at five, all right?"

I pretend not to overhear. Bobbie's concentrating too hard on completing the form to notice.

The man is tall and stoop-shouldered and wearing wire-rim glasses. He turns and walks back down the corridor without introducing himself.

"That was Dr. Peterson," the girl says, lowering her voice as if in confession. "How we doing with that?" she says to Bobbie.

My cousin again smiles at me as if I'd been the one to ask the question. "They want to know a lot, Teddy. Only I don't think I have the answers."

The girl nods as if understanding the *real* problem. "Why don't you let me see how you're doing?" she says and reaches out through the partition.

Bobbie hesitates before handing the form to me, which I pass on.

"Looks like we're doing real fine," the girl says, scanning the long sheet. "Where'd we stop?" And her eyes return to the top of the page. "Number two," she says. "Father's name." She pauses. "You know, you're not required to answer any of these if you don't want to. Entirely up to you. Lots of girls . . . plenty of women skip right past that one. So it's no obstacle. It's just a form."

But Bobbie has stood up. She thinks it would be better if she came back.

Now, suddenly, the girl is apologizing. She didn't mean to give the impression that anything really goes on here. Dr. Peterson's a psychiatrist. The state's very specific about what is permissible and

what isn't. First the doctor requires an interview before anything . . .

The girl scoots her chair back, ducking slightly because she's
too tall to see out through the glass.

But Bobbie's at the door nodding yes. Let her think about
things a little more. And she turns pleadingly toward me.

I thank the girl whose expression says that she's been through
this before. No one should feel bad. It's a difficult time. And all
those know-it-alls and holier-than-thous don't make it any easier.
Just last week one of them barging in with a little stink bomb from
the joke shop downtown and they still haven't gotten completely
rid of the damn smell . . .

Outside, my cousin waits at the end of the driveway. She keeps
her back to me, lifting her hand up like a traffic cop and I stop.
She's wiping her mouth roughly with a fistful of tissue from the
miniature box of Kleenex in her pocketbook.

I turn to see the receptionist peeking through the blinds.

"That's what I mean," my cousin says more to herself than to
me. "I can get myself into things all right. It's getting out of them's
the problem."

And I watch her walk the rest of the way to the car, her arms
crossed protectively over her stomach.

"Cozy," my sister says as we pass between the Biltmore's monumental cast-iron gates. "Cozy without being cutesy."

Bobbie has stayed back at the motel, having convinced my mother that she's suffering from cramps.

After a guided tour of the estate, we spend the morning strolling about the gardens taking pictures of the topiary hedges and bronze sundials. It's hard to believe that anyone ever really lived here. Voices echo in the foyers. Floors shine bright as gymnasiums. "My kind of place," Cora said, gazing at tapestries that covered entire walls. My sister tells me that when Gloria Vanderbilt was a child, her father died and there was a famous custody battle ("As if the kid didn't have it all already.").

While Cora and my mother buy souvenirs, I wait in the car, sitting in the driver's seat. In another year and a half I can apply for a learner's permit. My father promised in one of his letters home to buy me something sporty when the time comes ("Maybe drive your buddies around the island.") and described the small apartment he had in mind for Cora her senior year. "Talk's cheap," my sister said when my mother read the paragraph aloud to us. But I could see the excitement in my sister's face. My father's the only one Cora listens to even when she suspects that he's just "blowing it out his barracks' pipe."

I watch the second hand twitch on the dashboard clock another full minute before reaching over to open the glove compartment.

My mother's letter sits inside fat as a box of Kleenex.

A good son would resist the temptation to snoop. That is what I tell myself as I squint in the direction of the servants' quarters that's been converted into a gift shop. That is what I believe as I unfold the letter in my lap, my heart thumping at the sight of my mother's cramped penmanship. Each entry begins with a new date and the first is already two weeks old.

MONDAY

Darling,

It has not been a pleasant weekend. There are times with the kids when I want to run off and join a religious order but of course I am only in a mood and today has been one of those days when I resent my husband's bachelorhood which allows him to have his cake and his independence too. I suppose there's no one to blame even though you probably feel I am blaming you and yet I've promised myself to try not to be negative in these few pages I'll send before we're off.

I stop to glance guiltily out at the gift shop. My mother can be so casual with where she leaves her letters because of her trust in me. I tell myself this and know that's it's terrible to read another word and yet I allow my eyes to sink back down to the page.

All systems are go. Sears Auto promises that the fluids, air pressure, and filters are checked, my tires rotated and my fan belts tightened. I only wish that the rest of us were in such good shape. Teddy is my sweet angel but his sister has never been more difficult. I try to appreciate how upsetting all of this is for her. She's at that awkward age (but then when has our daughter not been?) when she'd have her mother treat her as an adult or not have anything to do with her at all. Meanwhile her brother frets. He frets about his sister who never lets up on him and he frets about his mother who keeps him from his father and he frets about his father for not seeming to fret about what becomes of any of us. Now you are thinking that his fretful mother exaggerates everything but you have not been there to witness his restless sleep (he's grinding his teeth in bed again) or attempted to answer his questions about his absent father. Cora has put it into the boy's head that there are other reasons why his daddy is so often, as she says, "missing in action." And, of course, on this at least, your anxious son takes after his jealous mother who is always willing to suspect the worst but I must try to close my eyes. They have taken it out of me today.

P.S. I thought this morning of crossing out some of what I wrote to you last night but I want what I say to be exactly how I feel and that is how—

My mother suddenly sticks her head out of the gift shop door, sees that I'm still in the car, and ducks back inside.
I skip to Tuesday.

D-Day is here and Bobbie is still trying to make up her mind. It would be good to have her share the driving but I don't want to influence her on this. If it were up to Cora we would leave under cover of darkness. She's all for her cousin's liberation as long as she doesn't herself have to be in the same car with her. Teddy believes that his sister is only jealous of my affection for her cousin but I'm convinced that it's something more. Cora is an excellent student, of course, but she has always been something of a slow learner with the boys. Having her cousin around will only aggravate the situation.

I skim the next page and jump to the last entry, which must have been while Bobbie was driving. The handwriting repeatedly dips below the blue line.

FRIDAY

I've got some catching up to do. We've had a small setback but everything is fine now. Teddy has had a blackout and it's all that has been on my mind. I don't have to tell you how we all die a little each time it happens. But I think that it affects Cora most of all and naturally she keeps it to herself. How is it that our brave children have such a coward for a mother? I only tell you this now after it's all over because I know that you don't want me to keep anything from you and because Teddy is all right and, as usual, he remembers none of it and only wants to sleep afterward. It's all so very strange as he awakens without the slightest sense of what's happened and I often wish I had the same gift. And so that is our first day on the road. Another one like it and I'll be ready to call the airlines for a ticket (although I see in this morning's paper that number 65 has been hijacked to Cuba) but thinking about it all again makes me weak so I'll stop for now and try to write again tonight.

I replace the letter exactly as I found it in the back right-hand corner of the glove compartment. Although my pulse rate has probably doubled, sleuthing is nothing new for me. Still, it isn't often that I get to hear what my mother actually thinks and not just what she wants my sister or me to hear. My parents are trusting but protective and so even with a stethoscope pressed against our common bedroom wall, I'll rarely pick up more than the crush of mattress springs. And if, afterward, my unsuspecting father should tiptoe past my open door in his boxer shorts, never once has he been suspicious enough to peer in at his eavesdropping son.

I roll my window down and stare at the mammoth, stone mansion with its gargoyles and spectacular landscaping. Gloria Vanderbilt lives in New York now, Cora informs me. She is married, quite sociable, and appears to be well adjusted. This is my sister's way of telling me that if it comes to divorce, it's not the end of the world. In fact, I could possibly grow up, marry, and even prove sociable myself. But as far as turning out well adjusted that is another matter. For Cora reminds me that the civilian Vanderbilt children had something military dependents confined to a post never experience: fame and fortune. Lots of fame and even more fortune.

Gazing out at the reflecting pond, I blink at the water's tinfoil-like flash and the silver T-Bird that disappears into a cloud of white dust before I can lift the stubborn handle on my door.

𝒯𝒽𝓮 gray, monotonous interstate stretches before us like an endless runway from which we'll never take off. More than once this afternoon I've had to keep my cousin from drifting out of her lane. "I'm okay," she said, snapping her head back. "Just give me a little rubdown. I'll be fine." And once again I'd massage her shoulders, working the tension from her strained muscles.

It's dark by the time we pull off the freeway into a Stateline Store.

"I mean I got to go," Bobbie says. "I can hear it sloshing."

She parks between two diesel trucks and hops out of the Oldsmobile, floodlights illuminating the gravel lot like a prison yard.

"How does she find these dives?" Cora says.

My mother slides her camera out from under the seat. "Your father used to stop at Statelines when you were kids," she says. "He'll get a kick out of a picture."

Inside the convenience store, I straddle the white line that's painted down the middle of the linoleum floor.

"Fix your hair," my mother says to me and checks the batteries for the flash.

We're all a little rumpled and I wet my fingers to smooth my cowlick down. Cora sits at the counter, reluctantly spinning about on the stool.

"Say, 'Betty Grable,' " I say when she won't smile.

Bobbie comes back from the ladies' room reeking of perfume.

"Honest," she says as my sister flaps her hand through the air. "I just barely touched the pulse points."

Confederate flags are draped from the ceiling and half the store is filled with Civil War memorabilia: big glass jars of miniballs, brass belt buckles with "Dixie" printed across them. And I can tell that my mother's uncomfortable without my father here.

Afterward, back on the interstate, we listen to a call-in show until a woman quotes Masters and Johnson on the problem of impotence.

"That's enough of that," my mother says and flicks to another station.

"What's impotence?" I say, not recognizing the correct pro-nunciation. The car's suddenly as quiet as if we were watching a UFO descend on the hood.

"Just keep eating your vegetables," Cora says finally.

Even though it's not Sunday there seem to be only evangelists on the radio. And I'm reminded how, crossing the South to our next post, my father would switch the dial to some preacher shouting about communism or atheism in the schools. He'd keep the volume low enough not to rouse the rest of us and paid such close attention that I was always a little suspicious of his own sympathies. In the military you learn not to talk politics. Still, I suspected that my parents were secretly Democrats even if they never found the time to absentee vote.

Cars begin to pass with their wipers on while Bobbie continues to try to follow a minister whose high-pitched sermon fades as we move beyond the local station's broadcasting range. "The road to damnation is paved with . . ."

My cousin imagines that like my mother and sister I've fallen asleep. She struggles to hear the words and winces each time the radio crackles with static from the approaching storm. Leaning over the steering wheel, she tilts her head toward the speaker when my mother wakes from the thunder.

"Looks like we're in for some," Bobbie says as the rain starts to patter on the tarpaulin (George had predicted more bad weather and battened down the suitcases).

"Maybe we ought to stop," my mother says though we're miles from the next exit.

"Just a shower," my cousin says. "We'll drive through it."

But five minutes later, the wind is washing the rain across the road in great, sweeping sheets. The three of us hunch forward, wide-eyed to see the taillights of the truck in front of us. We pass other cars that have already pulled over, their hazard lights flashing.

"I don't like it," my mother says, her forehead only inches from the windshield. "Maybe we should wait it out."

Bobbie has slowed to a crawl as the sky lights up with lightning and I try to make out the billboard in the distance. With the clap of thunder Cora sits up beside me.

"If we'd stopped when we should—"

"Sssssh," my mother says nervously. "Your cousin's trying to concentrate."

"Probably what woke me," my sister mutters.

Bobbie keeps going, afraid of someone else plowing into us if she stops. But we're hardly moving, the speedometer needle barely bumping above zero.

Every thirty seconds the sky flashes white as a flare before thunder rattles the windows.

"I hate this," my sister says. "We're always the one caught in it."

Ahead of us, the dim outline of an overpass appears.

My mother pats Bobbie on the knee. "Let's stop," she says. "The kids are upset."

It's her favorite line with my father whenever she doesn't want an argument.

As we come upon the shelter of the concrete overpass, there appear dozens of motorcycles parked at crazy angles, their riders loitering about, stripped of their wet leather jackets.

When Bobbie eases toward the shoulder, my mother's head jerks back as if from whiplash.

"What're you doing!" she says. "Keep going! Keep going!"

Beneath the overpass, we catch a quick, dry glimpse of the bikers.

"Eyes forward," my mother snaps at me as I spin to see out the back window. "You'll antagonize them."

Unshaven men and pale-skinned women lounge about the concrete girders in studded leather pants and black boots.

"Right out of Fellini," Cora says.

It's another six miles to our exit, which at ten miles an hour exhausts us all. By the time Bobbie signals to turn off we're ready to accept even the Castle Plaza Courts.

While we wait for my mother to get the key ("You can sit, honey," she said to me. "Just keep an eye open."), Cora peers out at the string of rundown bungalows.

"Looks more like a trailer park," she says. "An abandoned trailer park."

"They're a chain," Bobbie says. "Lou and I stayed in one on our honeymoon." She seems to reflect on the memory for a moment. "They're not so bad."

My mother ducks back into the front seat. "Well, the price was right." She brushes her shoulders off. "Ours is all the way on the end. Eleven o'clock checkout."

"No problem," Cora says.

We drive down past the other bungalows, the water lapping at our hubcaps.

"There's no one here," my sister says. "Unless everyone's had their car stolen. Which, come to think of it . . ."

"Long as we got hot water," my mother says, "this'll be one happy girl."

But the shower turns out to be only lukewarm.

"With just a hint of rust," Cora says, stepping back out of the tiny bathroom.

The bungalow has the closed, mildewed smell of a cabin that hasn't been opened all year. The double bed sags deeply. Cora and I will share the convertible couch. The television, a battered portable, is chained to the wall in one corner.

My mother has already explained to the manager that she'll be charging a long distance call in a half-hour.

"Let's get an early start," she says, winding the clock for morning.

"Good idea," Cora says. "Damn good idea."

My mother starts to unbutton her blouse, nodding for me to turn my back.

"Your father and I have seen worse," she says. "When you two were still little we stayed in some beauts, let me tell you."

While Cora changes behind the closet door, I open the couch and uncurl the inch-thick mattress.

The rain has stopped and it feels good to be in bed, even one without springs.

A whining sound comes from the bathroom. Bobbie has decided to brave a shower.

"What's she going to do?" my sister says. "Wash him out of her hair?"

"We want to be real sensitive to your cousin's situation right now," my mother whispers.

She removes her watch, checks the time again, and places it next to the phone.

"I should tell you about the one with rats," she says happily.

She's eager to talk to my father and determined not to let this one end in another argument. "I'm going to be nothing but sweetness and light," she'd said to me earlier. "You're going to be proud of your mother."

"It was in Arkansas," and she smiles. "Another one of your father's marathon drives. The two of you were small enough to stretch out on the backseat. We got caught in the middle of nowhere with less than a gallon in the tank and a hundred miles to Fort Chaffee. So we took what we could find. And boy did we find it."

"You actually stayed in a place with rats?" Cora says. She quickly pads barefoot over to the couch. "What was wrong with the car?"

"That's exactly where I wound up," my mother says. "And I brought you two with me. Only we didn't know about the rats till the lights went out. And your father, of course, told me I was hearing things. He who wouldn't hear a tank come through the door once his head hits the pillow."

"Maybe it's his clear conscience," I say and look purposefully over at my sister.

"Sure," Cora says. "It's what let's him park his wife and children into the Bates Motel and then fall into a coma."

My mother suddenly hushes us, one finger up to her pursed lips. "Did you hear that?"

"Not funny," Cora says, hugging one of the wafer-thin pillows.

"Sssh," my mother says. "Teddy, did you hear that?"

I kneel on the couch to peer out the cloudy window.

"What is it?" my mother says.

"Headlights mostly," I say. "Turning off the road single file."

But now we can all hear them: motorcycles, their tires hissing on the wet highway.

"What in the world are they doing here?" my mother says.

"Probably just come to trash a few bungalows," Cora says, relieved for the moment that it isn't rats.

My mother clicks the lamp out. "What're they doing?" she whispers.

"I think they're checking in," I say. "The manager's showing some of them a room."

"I bet they get hot water," Cora says.

"How many are there?" my mother says.

I count the ones still sitting on their cycles, waiting. "Ten maybe. I think it's probably a club."

"Like those ones out in California," my mother says. She's ready to pack us all back in the car.

"I don't think so," Cora says. "Hell's Angels types generally don't ask to see a room first."

"What're they doing, Teddy?" my mother asks. "Can you tell anything?"

"The one guy's talking to the manager," I say. "Now the manager's nodding at something the guy's saying to him."

"Not to worry about the eleven o'clock checkout," Cora says. "And there's a quaint breakfast nook down the pike they might—"

A great roar of engines ignites and my mother pulls me back from the window.

"Stay still," she says. "Don't let them see you."

I peek back out just as one of them takes a spin down past our car, mud thumping under the wheel guard. He passes close enough that I can see the swirl of tattoos on his forearm.

"I expect they're staying," Cora says. She's crawled to the end of the mattress. "Anybody got a trophy strapped to his handlebars?"

My mother seems to take notice of my sister's pajamas for the first time. They're another of my father's Hong Kong gifts.

Bobbie opens the bathroom door and stands silhouetted in the light, her sheer nightgown aglow. But no one else turns to see. Except her favorite male cousin.

"What's all the excitement?"

It isn't until Bobbie's at the window that my mother glances over at me and then back at her niece. "I want you two girls to put something on," she declares.

"It's those bikers we saw," my cousin says, leaning past me.

Cora draws back to look at my mother.

"You're kidding," she says.

"Just put something on," my mother says, staring blankly at me. "Don't argue."

Cora lowers her chin as if she'd just spilled soup on herself. "Jesus," she mumbles.

My mother then turns to Bobbie. "You too, honey."

My sister rattles the hangers about in the closet.

"Have they gone inside yet?" my mother asks me.

Just then one of the drivers scoops a girl up onto the back of his bike and revs the engine. The others greet this with howls of approval and test their own tires in the mud.

"Maybe if we leave the lights off," my mother says, "they'll just keep to themselves."

"Or maybe they'll burn down every last bungalow and do wheelies on our ashes," Cora says. She's put her blouse on over her pajamas but left the buttons defiantly undone. "What're you getting all worked up about? They don't need us to have a party. They can handle it on their own."

The bikers race back and forth, their splattered headlights bouncing in the dark. The women, hugging their drivers on the banana-shaped seats, swipe playfully at each other.

Bobbie stands before the small door window. "It reminds me of Marvin," she says. "Rosemary, you remember Marvin Cholly? The boy Mom wanted arrested?"

Cora and I both turn to look at my mother who's moved back from the window, too anxious to watch anymore.

"It's what can happen when you get in with the wrong element," she says.

Bobbie shakes her head. "He just got a little rambunctious is all." She recalls how "M.C." used to ride her around on his Harley Davidson. "I was what? About Cora's age?"

"He kidnapped your cousin from the Montgomery Ward in Chicopee," my mother says, taking another quick peek outside. "Your aunt had to get the police after him."

"He was just lovesick," Bobbie says. "I got stuck with the night shift and couldn't go out with him Saturday. Marvin took things like that real hard."

"He practically put Irene in an early grave," my mother says. "She should have brought him to court."

"Kidnapped?" Cora says.

My cousin shrugs her shoulders. "He tracked me down in Housewares and then he got all excited and made me go for a ride with him. I didn't want to so he twisted my arm."

"He twisted your arm," my sister says. "You mean physically twisted your arm?"

Bobbie looks at me as if Cora hadn't heard her. "He put my arm behind my back," she says and illustrates by bending over and thrusting one arm behind her. "Then he walked me out to the parking lot."

"You didn't scream or anything?" Cora says.

"I didn't want to embarrass him. I figured he'd calm down."

One of the bikers blows something that sounds like a foghorn. But my sister ignores it.

"And did he?" she asks. "Calm down?"

"M.C. had what you'd call an excitable nature," my cousin says. "Some boys are like that."

"How long is this going to go on?" my mother says. She's back at the door.

"They're just carousing," Bobbie says. "No harm done."

Couples circle each other warily in the mud. Then there's a kind of soccer scrim with everyone bunched, heads down, shoving toward the center.

"It's ten," Cora says to my mother. "You still going to call Daddy?"

My mother stands beside the phone. "I guess I should," she says, unfolding the piece of paper with the number on it. "This could go on all night."

"Go ahead, Rosemary," my cousin says. "Take the phone in the bathroom."

My mother looks down at the extension cord. "It'd reach, wouldn't it?" and she draws the phone around the bed. "Then that's what I'll do."

"I think this is about to break up," I say.

Someone has turned on a hose and one after the other the bikers slog out of the mud, eyes narrowed, arms overhead like prisoners. They're laughing, peeling their soaked clothes from their bodies as they march half-naked into an opened-door bungalow where music is playing.

My mother steps from the bathroom. "I got through," she says disappointedly. "But your father wasn't in for some reason. I left a message with the duty officer."

Cora flips over on the lumpy couch. "He wasn't there?" she says. "I thought you worked this out?"

"He could be in the john," Bobbie says. She draws the covers back on the bed. "Give him a couple minutes. I bet he rings right back."

"Well, at least he knows where to find us now," my mother says. She reaches in and turns off the bathroom light.

In the dark, we all wait quietly for the phone to ring, listening to what sounds like Glen Campbell coming from outside.

"I'd just like someone to answer me this," my mother says. She's sitting up against the headboard. "What kind of families do these people come out of? I'm curious."

My sister is on her back, staring up at the ceiling. "They don't come out of a family, Mother. They *are* a family."

"Cora's right," Bobbie says. "Same as the ones used to pass through Chicopee. They even called each other brother and sister."

"That and 'mother,' " Cora says. "A disproportionate number of mothers in biker families."

My mother rests on her elbow. "It doesn't look like your father's going to get back to us," she says finally. "Let's try to close our eyes. Big day tomorrow."

It's close to midnight before everyone has fallen asleep. In the tiny room I listen to my mother's and sister's breathing while my cousin gently wheezes in unison. No one snores. Even unconscious we're a polite family. And I run my finger across the edge of my teeth, reminded of my mother's letter.

But I can't sleep. I keep wondering where my father is. He doesn't mean to forget. He just has trouble remembering sometimes the promises he makes. Especially the ones he makes to Cora and me. Which usually leads to an argument with my mother. "You can't get the kids' hopes up on Monday and then forget what you said to them on Tuesday," she'll scold him. "Because *they* don't forget. They rely on what you tell them. You're not some bachelor lieutenant who plays Santa Claus at Christmas." Although that's exactly, Cora believes, the role my father would have preferred.

The bikers' party reminded me of the picture in my junior high civics textbook of a Greek orgy in the sixth century. Women in purple robes lay beside marble baths, feeding batches of ripe grapes to tunic-clad, glassy-eyed senators. Behind them Negro servants waved enormous feathered fans and balanced trays with gold goblets filled with wine. I forget what exactly it was supposed to illustrate: something about what becomes of a democracy when its leaders forsake their responsibilities to the people. At least, that's what I think Miss Clark told us.

Afterward, I sit straight up on the couch, fumbling in the dark for the alarm. But it's the phone and in a moment I hear my mother talking in the bathroom.

"What?" Cora says, squinting at me as if from a migraine.

"I think it's Daddy," I whisper. Bobbie's still asleep.

Cora crawls up close to the clock on the bed table. "Swell," she says. "Four-fifteen. What does he care?"

Still, she tiptoes to the bathroom. I want to tell her to give Mom and Dad some time together but she opens the door and I can see my mother sitting on the toilet seat, listening intently to my father in the dark.

"Come in, honey," my mother says to her and Cora kneels on the tile floor, both of them pressing their ear to the receiver like Siamese twins.

I close my eyes to try to pick up where I'd left off in my dream. We were all living on a farm in what looked like Lancaster County. My father wore his combat fatigues and waved from a Jeep parked out in a field thick with tomatoes. "Go wake your mother up," he shouted to me. But when I shielded my eyes from the bright morning sun, another woman was sitting beside him, holding buggy reins even though there was no horse. "Her name's Sing," my father said when I looked puzzled. "She's just a geisha." And I could see now that she was Oriental. The same girl that appeared in one of the pictures he'd sent back to us. "Better get used to it," Cora said when I rushed into the kitchen. She was sitting at a pine table, leafing through a magazine. "Daddy's probably got one in every port." My sister wasn't wearing Amish clothes like the rest of us. She had her hair up in electric curlers. "The spoils of war," Cora said. "Don't look so surprised." I watched her unpin her hair. "Hot date," she said. "Daniel's got something planned." I stepped back to the sink and stared out the window at a tractor. My father was dark as an oak from hours in the sun and looked happier than I'd ever seen him before.

I step into the bathroom where my mother and sister smile up at me as if drugged by the voice at the other end of the receiver. Already I can see that they've forgiven him. It's almost dawn and Cora is a little giddy.

My mother finally takes the phone away from my sister and holds it out to me.

"Come on, sweetheart," she says. "It's your turn."

I can feel the pulse in my neck as I wait for my father's words to carry the thousands of miles back to America.

"Your mother tells me you're a big help to her on the road," he says. "That's good news, son. You want to look after the girls."

My mother and sister hover nearby, ears pricked to overhear the wonderful sound of my father's voice. But all I can think to ask him about is the Taiwan National Zoo and whether he'd had fun.

"Nothing like the time we're going to have," he says, his voice sounding different suddenly.

And then with Cora frowning at me I ask who he went with and whether they had a good time too. It seems forever before he answers and not just because there's such a distance between us. My mother is staring at me curiously as if wondering whether I might have been awakened from an absence seizure.

I think at first that we must have a bad connection. My father doesn't seem to hear a word I've said. Instead, he starts in on how the freeze-dried food the astronauts are eating was developed at the Natick Labs. But what's really interesting is how the low-residue diet produces few gases and solid wastes. It's not a subject you're going to hear Cronkite or Brinkley talking about but the boys can "just pop a germicidal pellet in the storage bag and there's no bacterial growth or odors. Clean and simple as that."

When I try to change the subject again, my father says something about Luna 15, the mysterious satellite the Russians sent up early Sunday. He wouldn't put it past them to try to collect some moon dirt to steal a little thunder from Apollo. Then he reminds me to "take your sister with a grain of salt" since we both know how she gets. "What do you say?" Before I can answer he tells me to keep my head down in the foxhole and finally to put Mom back on.

Cora is glaring at me as I hand the phone over. But she doesn't say anything in front of my mother and I step back into the bedroom.

Bobbie's gone. It's almost light out. She'd wanted to give us some time together as a family.

I sit on the couch and try to remember my father ever calling me "son" before. It had sounded like something from one of my sister's subtitled movies.

After a while, I hear my mother tell Cora to sit with me for a couple minutes. When my sister backs out of the bathroom, I pretend to be reading one of her magazines.

"You're such an idiot," she whispers fiercely, curling her legs up under her on the couch. "See if I ever tell you anything again."

But I'm not really listening to her. I'm trying to overhear my mother on the phone. Only she isn't saying much. At least not enough for me to figure anything out.

Cora isn't fooling anyone either. All the time she's jabbering at me she keeps one ear cocked. My sister still believes she can get away with anything with her baby brother.

I pull my jeans on over my pajama bottoms.

"Where you supposed to be going?" Cora says.

Outside, the rain has cooled things off and as I walk barefoot down the flagstone steps, a breeze cuts through my thin pajama top. It's impossible to believe that anyone had been sober enough or conscientious enough to pick up after his companions. Yet the grounds have been policed. A single pile of crushed beer cans glitters in the early morning light.

The motorcycles are lined up in a row, their back wheels chained to each other although it's hard to imagine someone tampering with them.

"Hey!"

I turn to see the motel manager standing outside the office shaking his head at me.

"Don't touch," he shouts.

I roll my pants up to test the mud with my big toe like a wary bather. When I finally make my way down to him, the manager studies me suspiciously.

"They're real touchy about their bikes," he says, staring at my feet.

I ask him if he might have seen my cousin but he doesn't seem to hear the question. Instead, he explains how "the boys" were on their way up to some rock and roll concert.

"People think motorcycle clubs don't stay in motels," he says. "Well, it just depends on the club. But they were real understanding about the room I lent you folks," he says. "I knew bikers wouldn't want me putting no kids out in the cold."

I suddenly see Bobbie crossing the road from the gas station. She's wearing galoshes and stops in her tracks when I wade down to her.

"What in the world," she says, pointing her Coke at my feet. "Where's your sense, boy?"

Her eyes are red but I can't tell if it's just from lack of sleep.

"Your momma still on the phone?"

I nod.

"I guess Cora's all excited," she says.

"Off the wall."

She smiles. "Well, that's her daddy she's talking to."

As we come back by the office, the manager winks at Bobbie through the picture window.

"He asked me if I was with the bikers," she says, smiling at him.

At our bungalow we sit down on the steps and look out at the trees that are already steaming in the humidity.

"I thought I'd give Lou an early wake-up call," my cousin says flatly.

"Mom ought to be off the phone pretty soon," I say.

Bobbie looks over at me. "No," she says finally. "I mean, I already did. There's a pay phone over at the service station."

Her voice sounds distant to me.

"I just called collect," she says. "Operator woke him right up."

I flick some of the mud from between my toes. "Was he mad?"

My cousin glances past me. Her hair is pressed to one side and her clothes wrinkled.

"I sort of caught him off guard," she says. "I guess I sort of caught them both off guard."

The sun's come up and birds are squawking in the thick kudzu (an Asian vine, Cora tells me) behind the bungalows. Only when I stop to listen do I realize what a racket they're making. And I wonder how even the bikers can sleep through it.

"Funny how you can tell someone else's voice," Bobbie says. "I don't mean funny ha-ha. I mean funny strange."

I keep trying to see a single bird in the bushes but they're invisible. Still, there have to be hundreds of them to be making that kind of noise.

"Even if it's nobody, for instance," my cousin is saying. "Like someone you used to work with. And you're lucky you can remember her name. But you know her voice soon as you hear it. Doesn't matter if it's just her whispering something in the room. You don't even have to know exactly what it is she said. It just all comes back to you. Bam."

Then she asks me what my dad had to say and I have to think a minute before I can remember a single word of our conversation.

"Trivia quiz," Cora says. "How many cars does the King personally own?"

My mother has warned my sister not to give Bobbie a hard time about Graceland. Cora has seen Biltmore and I've been to the Lindbergh estate. Now it's Bobbie's turn. And so we'll take a short detour through Memphis to Elvis's family home.

"Money doesn't mean anything to him," my cousin declares. "Elvis is a collector. There's a difference."

"Fifteen," Cora says. "That'd feed a lot of starving fans."

Bobbie's face flushes.

"I know you're just trying to get a rise out of me, honey. But Elvis is a true American. He served his country just like your daddy."

My sister drops her knees from against the back of the seat and sits up.

"You know," she says, "I never thought of that. But they do have a lot in common, don't they?"

"She's just trying to be funny," my mother says.

"No," Cora says. "She's right. I mean, let's count the ways." And she bends her pinkie back. "Elvis likes to hang out with the guys. He spends a lot of time on the road. All his subordinates are very fond of him." She hesitates. "Oh, yeah, and he dyes his hair."

My mother flicks the visor up. "Since when did your father ever put anything on his hair?"

Cora leans forward, one arm on the back of Bobbie's seat. "Since those last pictures he sent."

My mother doesn't say anything.

"How about them both having a daughter no one's ever going to hear about?" I say.

Cora ignores me. "Let's see, what else? Despite being married, women are constantly throwing themselves at him."

Bobbie looks across at my mother who continues to stare at the road.

"Whose fault is that?" my cousin asks. "Your father can't help it if he's a handsome man. I don't see how he's to blame for that."

"Who's blaming him?" my sister says. "I'm just pointing out the remarkable similarities between two soldiers. And how no one can resist a man in uniform."

At the next Howard Johnson's my mother signals to pull over although it's too early to eat.

"I just need to use the ladies' room," she says to Bobbie. "Why don't you get us some coffee to go?"

Cora and I wait in the car but as soon as they disappear inside, I tap my sister's arm.

"How about we play a new game?" I say. "How about we play how much Elvis has in common with the 'plain people'?"

Cora glances out her window as if I might have spotted the T-Bird.

"You think you're so smart," I say. "We'll see how much you like that game."

"Hey," my sister says, trying to appear unruffled. "Come to think of it, they both *do* wear a lot of black."

"Why do you have to be such a jerk? Mom doesn't have to be reminded what you think every ten miles. Just keep your big mouth shut, why don't you?"

She rolls her window down and I stare at the back of her head.

"Seriously?" she says. "I mean, did you really see him this morning?"

She's brushed her hair differently.

"You want Mom to know the truth," I say. "You think Dad's got a girlfriend. Okay. How about *your* boyfriend? Maybe she should know about him too."

My sister settles back into her seat but without her smart-aleck look anymore.

Bobbie returns alone and sets the two Styrofoam cups on the dash. She sits staring at the radio for a minute before turning around.

"I think you got your momma a little worked up there," she says to Cora.

My sister yawns extravagantly. "I thought I'd plant a seed of truth," she says. "See if it'll grow."

"You think your momma doesn't see something?" Bobbie says.

"We don't seem to be real experienced at facing the truth," my sister says. "It's never really taken root in this family."

"That's where big brave Cora comes in," I say. "She's going to shine the light so the rest of us can see the way."

"Doing what she can," my sister says brightly.

"It's a hard thing," Bobbie says. She lifts the plastic lid from her coffee. "Being a married woman. Not something I guess we all know that much about just yet."

Cora looks over at me so she doesn't have to look at my cousin. "Maybe some of us are smart enough not to *want* to know either."

Bobbie blows on her coffee but doesn't have anything to say to this.

"Next time," I say to my cousin, "bring a pie too."

Cora throws her head back and laughs. "Taught him everything he knows," she says. But it's not really her laugh. It's some movie star's laugh she's copying.

My mother steps out of the restaurant and for a moment appears lost, as if she's forgotten where the car's parked. It's exactly how she always gets whenever she's distracted. She's thinking about what Cora has said to her. She thinks about everything Cora says to her no matter how dumb it is. "Your sister was a prodigy when she was born," she'll point out to me. "And I still don't know what to do with her. But maybe that's what prodigies are for: to keep their poor ignorant parents on their toes. Well, your sister's certainly accomplished that. Even if she doesn't appreciate her mother, at least she knows I've been on my toes all these years."

Whenever I argue that maybe Cora's just spoiled, my mother won't hear of it. My sister is one of a kind. She was reading the backs of cereal boxes before most kids could handle a bowl and spoon. If I should mention that prodigy can also mean something monstrous, my mother won't deny it. "There's that side of her too, honey. Your sister doesn't suffer fools lightly." Fools, meaning the rest of us, of course. Mother and brother included. The only one not included being my father. She was Daddy's girl from the start.

But now my sister's old enough to suspect that Daddy might have other girls. "His extrafamilial femmes," Cora calls them. "Just like in the movies."

"Somebody in the ladies' room said Elvis flew to Vegas yesterday in his jet," Bobbie says and my sister slumps down in her seat so that her eyes are level with the bottom of the window.

At least the prospect of standing at the hallowed gates of Graceland has gotten my cousin's mind off things. She looks as excited as a teenager. And for a moment I wonder what she must have looked like when she was my sister's age. If anyone was ever my sister's age.

"What do you want to hear?" I say when my mother asks me to find something in the guidebook about Memphis.

"Something positive," she says. "Something uplifting for a change."

And so I read about how the city was judged in a national competition to be the cleanest, safest, and quietest town in America.

"Over Salt Lake City?" Cora says. "Right."

"Let your brother finish," my mother says.

"It was named after Egypt's Memphis," I say, scanning the last few paragraphs. "Because the Mississippi looks so much like the Nile."

"That's another place where I want to go some day," Bobbie says. "I want to sleep in one of the pyramids. There's supposed to be some kind of magical power you get from them."

But my mother's been thinking about a room at the Peabody.

"Paying to see half a dozen crummy ducks waddle across a hotel lobby," my sister says, exasperated.

"I bet that's cute to see," my cousin says.

"It's got to be darling," my mother says.

"Darling," Cora says to herself and looks out her window, shaking her head as if we're all hopeless. "Right."

We pass another motel whose marquee promises round-the-clock Elvis movies and Bobbie glances back at it wistfully.

"Probably cheaper than that Peabody's going to be," she says.

But the Peabody turns out to be booked and we compromise on the Jefferson Davis Inn in downtown Memphis. My mother likes how it's in the heart of the city. There's a twenty-five-inch TV for my sister. And Bobbie notices there's an Elvis impersonator appearing in the nightclub across the street.

When my mother returns to the office to see about the extra cot, Bobbie waits until Cora heads up the stairs to the room and then she asks me what *I* like about the motel.

"I don't know," I say, unstrapping the suitcases from the rack. "I guess that everyone's happy."

It's a moment before my cousin lifts her head out from under the raised trunk lid.

"You don't ask much for yourself, do you, honey?"

I only shrug my shoulders and then suddenly she's crying.

"All of us just worried about what we want and all you want

is for us to be happy." She sets her suitcase down and hugs me, pressing my head against her shoulder. "Where you came from, sugar, it's the Lord's mystery."

I try to draw away, afraid that Cora will return from the room for her other bag.

"No," my cousin says, holding me tightly. "I'm going to get my squeeze. I ain't had many of them lately."

I can see my mother through the picture window of the office. She's collecting tourist pamphlets.

My cousin kisses me on top of the head before at last letting me go.

"It's the only reason I can think maybe I ought to go through with it," she says. "It might turn out to be a little treasure like its cousin." She picks up her pocketbook and slings it over her shoulder. "Probably it wouldn't be, though. Probably it'd turn out to be just another Lou Hammuck, only smaller. Then I'd have two of them on my case."

My mother steps out of the office and waves at us. "Got everything?"

Bobbie smiles sadly at me. "It's your momma's got everything."

Afterward, one of the cleaning ladies wheels the foldaway into the room. Cora has already claimed the other double bed for herself.

"Rank has its privileges," she says.

My mother suggests that instead of showers we take advantage of the pool. This doesn't, of course, include her. Without my father she's too self-conscious to appear in public in a bathing suit. She'll change into shorts and sit poolside in one of the lounge chairs. It makes no sense because even Cora admits that my mother has a perfectly good figure ("Not Natalie Wood or anything but then not exactly Shelly Winters yet either").

Bobbie's another matter. I'm at the end of the diving board

when she tiptoes barefoot across the hot concrete of the parking lot. She's wearing a two-piece suit, a motel towel around her neck. There are only two other men in the swimming pool, both young fathers keeping an eye on their small children. That is, until my cousin stops to lift the latch on the gate.

"How is it?" she says, pointing one toe into the water.

Her stomach's as flat as the board I'm sitting on.

"Jump in," I say. "See for yourself."

She unloops the towel from her shoulders, nods once at her friendly audience, and then dives into the deep end. I watch her sleek form ripple beneath the aqua tint of the water until she comes up under the diving board.

"What's wrong with Cora?" she says, gripping my ankle to keep her head above water.

She'd left my morose sister in the motel flipping through the channels on the TV.

I have to hold tight to the board. My cousin weighs more than I do.

"You don't want to hear it," I say. "It'd take me all week."

She smiles, teeth glinting. And that's when the strangeness begins: the pool tilting slightly to catch the sky's whiteness. So that clouds float in the water like rubber rafts.

"Teddy?" My cousin has released her hold. I've begun to slip. "Teddy?"

I can feel the grainy surface of the board, miniature stones cutting into my forearm as I roll off the side. The fathers in their lounge chairs tumble like striped towels in a dryer before I hit the water and drift gently to the bottom of the concrete pool.

Looking up I can identify my cousin's naked legs, scissoring frantically. She's trying to persuade someone to come to my rescue. There are only the two family men to recruit. And neither as yet seems willing to commit himself. But perhaps it's my cousin's excitement. They can't be certain what it is she wants from them, not having noticed a boy before. So what's all the screaming about?

It's as still as a terrarium in the empty pool. And I'm reminded of the little toy scuba figure I had as a child. Filled with baking soda, it would sink to the bottom of the tub and there sit magically upright, bubbles filtering to the surface. I feel as clear-headed as if I'd just inhaled ammonia. Only my limbs are dead, my arms limp at my sides like wilted plants.

Gargantuan, godlike hands press down upon me and I open my eyes to stare into the face of Elvis. He's dressed in leather, head to foot. Exactly like last year's television special. His purple black hair glistens, the thick, muttonchop sideburns framing his famous face. I'm dead and the Man is king even here.

"Teddy?" My mother lifts the wet hair from my forehead. "Honey?"

Elvis steps back, hip cocked. "How you doing, buddy?"

I try to sit up but my mother opens her hand on my chest.

"Just stay," she says. "Wait."

My cousin stands beside the King, smiling. Behind them Cora paces, stopping only to glance at me menacingly.

I'm stretched out on my back beside the pool. Others come and go, towels wrapped about their pink shoulders. Their children whine, but now is not the time to use the pool.

Elvis speaks to Bobbie. She nods gratefully, her face rapt with attention. He's the King, after all. And he's saved her aunt's only son.

I draw my knees up and nearly pass out. My chest caves in with each breath. When I wince Cora steps forward. She breathes with me until I'm able to handle it on my own again. Then she resumes her angry pacing.

After a while an ambulance appears. Two young men hustle through the iron gate carrying what look like fishing tackle boxes.

They study me a moment then relax. All my signs are positive. They consult with my mother, who's sat down on one of the aluminum deck chairs. They huddle beside her, no longer worried about me.

"Caught your breath, buddy?"

The voice is deep, guttural, unmistakably Elvis.

"Fine." It's my first word and it stabs in my chest. "Good."

Bobbie's beside him now, one hand on his shoulder, and Elvis looks up.

"Takin' care of business."

My cousin is crying. This is all her fault. All her fault.

The King comforts her. "No problem, little lady," he says. "We're back in action."

Cora circles behind me. She holds a robe. Her hair hangs down, touching my face.

"Teddy?" she asks. "Why do you do this?"

The attendants lift me onto the stretcher. This is just a precaution. Routine practice. A quick spin to the ER and I'll be off the high board again in no time.

There's no resisting them. I've no say in the matter. Even Elvis agrees.

"Catch the show tonight," he says. "Got you a front-row seat."

Bobbie is smiling. They wouldn't miss it for the world.

"All right," the King says as I'm wheeled off, my sister's robe spread across my bare legs. "And don't worry about no cover. Just be there."

"*How* about we not mention this to your father just yet?" my mother says.

I'm sitting up in the double bed watching the end of *Viva Las Vegas*.

"He's liable to get the wrong picture," she adds.

But I know that it's the only reason she'd be calling him when they just talked last night.

Cora turns up the TV. Elvis and his bride, Ann-Margret, are kissing in the Little Chapel of the Stars.

For the past hour or so Bobbie's been watching me more than the movie. She'd heard one of the ambulance attendants mention something about oxygen deprivation. Even though the physician in the emergency room assured my mother that "all systems look good," my cousin still doesn't appear convinced. She's been chewing her painted nails all afternoon.

"You keeping something from Daddy," Cora says as Elvis and Ann-Margret hop into a convertible and the credits start to roll. "This I got to see."

"What makes you so sure your mother can't keep things to herself," my mother says. She's been writing a postcard to her sister Irene and her brow's furrowed from the effort.

"Because you don't talk to Daddy," Cora says, "you confess to him. You haven't talked to him since I understood speech."

My mother forgets that she's already licked the stamp.

"If I think it's in your father's best interest not to tell him something, I don't tell him."

Cora flops back down on the foldaway. My mother has informed her that I'm to have the double bed to myself tonight.

"I'll believe it when I see it," my sister says confidently. "And even then I won't believe it."

My mother looks over at me and I mouth the word "Stamp."

She smiles sheepishly then turns to keep Cora from seeing her peel it off the tip of her tongue.

I can hear kids splashing around in the pool outside. The manager had roped off the area until he was persuaded that there weren't going to be any legal consequences. He's already sent up a complimentary fruit basket.

Bobbie changed into her pajamas as soon as we got back from the hospital. As if she wanted it known that she wouldn't be going out again until her cousin could too. But I feel fine. Being underwater for two minutes has cleared the freeway from my head.

Still, I know that I'm confined to quarters at least until Elvis's eight o'clock show. He's the only one my mother might actually let me out to see.

In the emergency room my sister questioned everything the doctor did. She didn't trust any physician young enough to wear a headband. And when he ran a car key up my bare heel, she asked him where he'd graduated from medical school. If he planned on specializing. Why he didn't think to ask if I were on medication. "Is he?" the doctor asked her. And Cora glared back at him. "Why don't you inquire of the patient yourself?" she said. "Depakene," I said. "Ten milligrams, twice a day." The doctor continued to point a penlight at my eye before at last winking at my sister. "You'd make a fine nurse," he said. Cora, who didn't at first acknowledge the compliment, turned her eyes away from me to settle them on the doctor. "So would you."

"So when do we get to see Gritsland?" my sister says, switching off the TV.

It's a sign of my cousin's depression that she doesn't respond to this.

"I'm putting that on hold until your brother gets some rest," my mother says.

Cora stands by the window, peering out at the swimming pool. "Maybe I'll take a little constitutional," she says. "Give Daddy my regards."

"I don't like that tone, miss," my mother says.

My sister sits at the end of my bed and pulls her sneakers on. "Jesus, I just talked to the man. We're not supposed to say anything about the baptism, so what other news is there?"

"You don't think your father just enjoys hearing your voice?"

"No."

My mother caps her pen with the flat of her hand. "Sometimes I forget that you've still got some growing up to do."

Cora makes a face at the wall that only I can see.

"All right," my mother says. "But while you're walking around the block, think about what I've just said."

As soon as Cora slams the door after her, my mother is shaking her head.

"She's getting a little too smart for her own britches. That's what happens when her father's away."

"Well," Bobbie says. "If your daddy being away's what does it, I should have been a genius."

My mother hadn't asked my sister to drop off her postcard in the office and instead tucks it into the road atlas. And so when she steps into the bathroom with the phone, I reach over and slide it out (a picture of a pomaded Elvis beside a guitar-shaped swimming pool). It's addressed to the Spalding plant.

Dear Irene,

Bobbie's had her up and down days but today she's in seventh heaven. Wish I could say the same.

Love,
    R

I wait until my cousin has her back to me and then I slip the postcard into the atlas exactly where my mother left it: between Tennessee and Texas.

The bathroom door's too thin to keep from hearing my mother's voice.

"I'm going to get some coffee," Bobbie says, unbuttoning her pajama top. "What can I bring you?"

Even though I had my stomach pumped I'm not real hungry.

"Sounds like your mom got through," she says when I'm allowed to turn back around.

She's wearing jeans still stiff from the laundromat.

Holding one shoe, my cousin presses her cool hand to my warm forehead.

"You're hot," she says. "Your face is red."

"I've been watching Ann-Margret," I say.

At the door, my cousin glances back at me, unconvinced.

"Why don't you take a nap," she says. "Rest up for Graceland."

I only wave weakly, the sweat trickling down from under my arm.

From the bathroom my mother's voice is typically high-pitched. She'll want to tell my father so much so fast that she'll quickly be out of breath. And because my father will say next to nothing, she'll rush to fill in the dead space. Her sentences will collide with each other until even my mother will understand that she isn't making much sense. And then realizing how foolish she must sound, she'll finally turn to us, asking my father if he'd like to say a few words to "the kids," a signal that their own conversation is over. There can't be anything else to say if it's time for Cora and me.

"Teddy?"

My mother taps on the bathroom door, my first warning. But it'll be another minute or so before she'll actually give up the phone.

"Teddy, honey?"

I sit up, trying to think of something to talk about. My mother has already told my father all about today. Just as Cora predicted. And just as predictable will be my father's not saying a word about it. My mother doesn't want him to get me stirred up and so he will pretend as if nothing has been said about my little accident.

The bathroom door opens and my mother carries the phone over to me.

"It's Daddy," she says, holding out the receiver.

Clearly things have ended between them on the usual unhappy note.

"How you doing, buddy?" My father's voice is as clear and commanding as if addressing his troops on the parade field. And like them I'm brought to attention. "Not letting those hens cackle your ear off, are you?"

It's just as easy to predict how my own conversation will go. Already my heart's racing and I'll get so tongue-tied that my father will finally suggest that we just "put it in writing." Still, like my mother, I try to come up with something.

"We're supposed to get over to Graceland," I say. "Bobbie's dying to see it."

I can picture my father nodding into the receiver. Perhaps gazing out his window in the BOQ. Once again my mother has awakened him with very little to report of interest. And now he's forced to listen to his excitable son prattle on about nothing.

"He was over in Germany when I was there," my father volunteers. "They put him in a tank and let him play soldier for eighteen months."

"You saw him?"

"Hard guy to miss."

This is something new. But then nearly everything my father ever tells me is something new.

"Wait till Bobbie hears it," I say. "She'll probably want to call you back."

"Better keep it to yourself then."

That, of course, is *his* specialty, not mine.

"I mean, did you ever talk to him or anything?"

"Who?"

"Elvis."

"He pretty much kept to himself as I recall. Had an off-base home in Bad Nauheim. You'd see him in the mess hall with a couple thousand other skinheads. I knew his CO. A guy named Templeton. He was a nervous wreck about the whole business. Couldn't wait for the kid to be shipped back."

"How come you never told us any of this?" I say. "Bobbie's going to go nuts."

"What? About some singer?"

"Some singer! Dad! This is Elvis we're talking about."

"He was a buck private."

I look over at my mother. She pretends to be writing another postcard although I know that she's listening closely. Other than her sister there's no one else to write.

"I mean, did you ever hear him say anything?" I ask. "Did you get that close?"

"He was just a kid, Teddy. What would I have to say to him?"

I draw the receiver from my ear and there's almost a pop from the damp suction.

"Listen, tiger," he says cheerfully, "keep up the good work.

You get to the coast without shooting one of them, you're lucky. *They're* lucky."

"I'll try," I say.

"That'a boy." Then he asks me to give him "your mother" and I hold the phone out even more glumly than she'd passed it to me.

My mother retreats to the bathroom, the receiver pressed to her chest so that her heart is thumping long distance in my father's ear.

Then I think of all the things I might have said to engage him so that all he cared about was hearing my voice just as all I ever care about is hearing his. But then if Elvis couldn't hold his interest, what chance was I supposed to have?

Exhausted, I fall asleep while my mother is still in the bathroom. And in my dream, my father's on maneuvers with Elvis, their heads poking up out of their tanks and wearing identical protective earphones. When I try to catch their attention, waving red flags frantically, they seem not to notice and only race past, the tracks of their M26's kicking up the dirt in great clods. "Wasn't that the King?" my sister asks, squinting at the dust storm that swirls by. I nod then shout over the grinding diesels. "Daddy," I say. But Cora is shaking her head peevishly. "Elvis, idiot. Not Daddy."

"Teddy?"

My mother's sitting at the end of the bed, smoothing up her stockings.

"Wake up, honey. You're having a bad dream."

The blinds are drawn and all the lights off.

"Where is everybody?" I say.

My mother turns on the bedside lamp. "You've been out, sugar. It's after five."

I sit up, trying to orient myself. "But what about Graceland?"

"The girls can tell us all about it," she says. "Your cousin's probably gone through ten rolls of film by now."

I swing my legs out from under the covers. "We could take a cab."

But, afraid I'd have a relapse, my mother kept the car.

"I don't want you getting all excited," she says and I can tell that she's tempted to drive us over.

"I feel fine," I say from the bathroom. "Just hand me my stuff."

Only I don't feel fine. And sitting on the edge of the bathtub I stare at my bare feet. They feel like flippers.

"You sure you're all right?" my mother says. She reaches her arm in, holding my jeans and a clean shirt.

Bobbie's cosmetics clutter the counter. Cora had said that she wouldn't be surprised if her cousin winds up fainting dead away.

On the ride over, my mother keeps the front windows down and asks me every other red light how I'm doing. If I told her the truth, she'd make a U-turn on the spot. Everything feels bloated and enlarged. And for once I can imagine how my cousin must feel. Not to mention my sister.

We park right on Elvis Presley Boulevard and I walk beside my mother, keeping my head down.

"Now here's a *real* fan," Cora says when she sees me. She's leaning back against one of the metal notes on the famous wrought iron gate. "Got up from his deathbed."

Bobbie has made friends with everyone in the small crowd of fans, most of whom are from out of state.

"It ain't like the White House where you can take it all in at once," one of the women is explaining to my cousin. "Carter and me lost count how many times we been here."

Carter nods shyly. "Elvis is bigger than any president."

He asks if we plan to take in Woodlawn Cemetery where Gladys is buried.

"It's a heartbreaker," he warns us. "Seeing them dates on that slab."

While his wife recounts each of their annual visits to the site, Cora points out to me the low stone wall that borders the property. It's covered with graffiti: phone numbers and messages to Elvis from all over the world.

"The wailing wall," my sister says.

Bobbie hasn't relaxed her grip on the mesh wiring of the gate and gazes adoringly up the green lawn at the Georgian house.

"When I was a girl," she says. "I used to dream about living here."

"With Aunt Irene?" I say. "Or Elvis?"

"Both," she says.

"Your cousin lost her father when she was younger than you," my mother reminds Cora. "My sister was all she had."

Bobbie slides her arm around my mother's waist. "I always knew where you were," she says. "Mom kept a map on a pegboard in the kitchen and she'd stick a red pin in for every post."

Together with a dozen other fans we gather outside the gates around a self-appointed tour guide. The woman wears an official-looking laminated badge and delivers her monologue in a heavy Southern accent.

"Every Christmas Mr. Presley puts up a nativity scene," she tells us. "As you know, he's away right now but he never misses being here for the holidays. This is the home that he loves and we hope you'll come away with your own fond memories. We know that Elvis wants it that way."

Cora does her eye roll. My sister refuses to admit that she's a fan because of all the bad movies Elvis has made. But she's still managed to collect most of his early records, a fact which she prefers to keep from her cousin.

After a while, Cora asks my mother where the Oldsmobile is. She's seen enough. But there's something else bothering my sister.

And I can guess what it is. She'd claimed she'd be able to draw a composite of the typical Graceland visitor ("Like the ones hanging in the post office."). And she doesn't like thinking of herself as fitting the picture. So she'll wait for us in the car.

Finally, after everyone has asked about Elvis's pistol collection and which window is Lisa Marie's, Bobbie asks the tour guide how she got her great job.

"First of all you have to love Elvis like he was kin," the woman says. "Then you can apply to the Memphis Chamber of Commerce. There's about twenty of us doing this part-time."

In a shop across the street, my cousin buys a set of hound dog salt and pepper shakers and a pair of blue suede bedroom slippers.

As we come back along the sidewalk, the crowd outside the gates is just as big as when we came. At the car, Cora nudges my shoulder for me to glance back at the mansion. The sun has set directly behind it and the chimneys cast long shadows across the front lawn. "There's this sun dial theory," she says. "Come the equinox, it'll tell you the exact time of his return from Vegas."

But I'm thinking about the life-size picture of Elvis's mother he supposedly keeps on an easel in the living room. The guide had mentioned how "her son" could sit and stare at the photograph for hours at a time. And how after her death, everyone agreed that Elvis was never quite the same again. But the question I wanted to ask was about Vernon Presley and why Elvis had refused to attend his father's wedding when he remarried. Did our guide think that Elvis believed that you only had one true family so that stepmothers didn't count? Or did she think that Elvis got so depressed because he began to doubt that his father ever really cared about his mother in the first place? Especially if he could just turn around and fall in love all over again with someone else. But I was too tired to ask.

The Flaming Star doesn't actually allow minors. However, Bobbie's new friend (and my resuscitator) has talked the manager into making an exception tonight. But after Graceland this afternoon unless I get some more rest first, my mother insists, there won't be any performance for me to see. And so I prop the pillows against the headboard and make a show of reading.

I'm at the part where Matt doesn't want to return to the States. He wants to live in the Inuit settlement but the commander won't let him stay behind. That's because if the newspapers back home hear about Matt's pregnant Eskimo wife there'll be no chance of raising any more funds to reach the Pole.

Without looking up I can feel my mother staring at me. She's worried that I've lowered my seizure threshold. For this trip at least I'm cut off from diving into the deep end of any more motel pools.

Later, Bobbie returns to the motel to pick us up for the show.

"Nick had to go straight to the club," she says. "He said there'll be a table up front for us."

"That's awfully sweet of him," my mother says. "I just wish he wouldn't go to all this trouble."

"Makes two of us," Cora says.

My cousin sits down on the bed and takes her shoes off to rub her feet.

"That's what I told him," she says. "But I think he misses his family. He's from Georgia and sort of on the road most of the time."

"He does Elvis on the *road?*" Cora says. "For a *living?*"

"There's a circuit," Bobbie says, resting her head back on the pillow. "He spends a month here, a few weeks somewhere else, and then another week or two someplace else. So he gets to missing his family pretty bad."

"His parents?" my mother says.

"Nick's separated," my cousin says. "He's got three kids."

My mother suddenly busies herself spreading her dress out on the bed.

"Any of them look like Elvis?" Cora says. "Shame if the torch went out."

Bobbie closes her eyes. "I'll just relax for a couple minutes," she says. "We'll have to head on over pretty soon."

Cora's been in and out of the room the last hour for ice or a Coke or something from the candy machine until my mother tells her to stay put. But my sister isn't just restless. Each time she's come back to the room she's looked a little more agitated.

"I guess I'll check the car real quick," I say. "See about the battery."

My mother leans out of the bathroom in her slip. "Don't get anything on you," she says. "Those are your good pants."

And then she tells Cora to go with me.

"All right," my sister says as soon as the door locks shut behind us. "So you figured it out. I'm impressed."

I don't know what she's talking about but when she gets this hyper that's not unusual.

"I told him he's missing a bet," Cora says, already out of

breath on the first landing. "He ought to open up his own private detective agency. Call it Buggy, Inc."

"What?"

My sister doesn't even hear me. "He's a genuine goof," she says, walking backward down the stairs in front of me. "The guy's a primitive. Everything you say to him, he takes it like it's gospel. Which, I guess, makes sense in his case given his—"

Cora stops and I nearly run into her. She's studying me, surprised by my own surprised look. I hadn't, of course, figured anything out until this minute.

"Say one word to Mom," my sister says, "and I'll make your life a living hell."

"How's that going to change anything?"

She leans over the wrought-iron railing. "I keep telling him he's got to go home and he keeps telling me he doesn't have a home. So what am I supposed to do?"

I survey the dark parking lot below us. "You're asking *my* advice?"

She waves her hand in the direction of the large neon motel sign. "See him?"

I do now. By the speed bump in front of the office.

"You mean, you want me to talk to him?" I say.

My sister glances up at our room to be certain my mother isn't at the window.

"He won't listen to me," she says. "What have I got to lose?"

I suddenly feel very tired even though I've been in bed the last three hours.

Daniel is standing with one foot on the bumper of his car when I come up to him. He's dressed entirely in black and puts his hand out to shake.

"Listen," I say. "What're you doing this far from home? I mean, you're going to run out of gas here, you keep this up."

He lowers his foot from the bumper and seems not to understand the question but then points over my shoulder.

"I have come to see your sister."

We both gaze in the distance at Cora who's still up on the landing. When she sees that we're staring at her she crosses her arms and turns her back.

"I think she wonders why you're doing this," I say. "I don't think she really wants you to."

Daniel looks down at his shoes, which must have been a present from his brother. They're military issue.

"Your sister?" Daniel says. "She says this?"

He looks hurt and I feel sorry for him.

"I just think she's kind of confused by you following her this far," I say. "I think she wishes you'd write her when we get overseas. But I don't think she wants you to leave your mother and father and everyone."

He shrugs his shoulders. "I am not a churchgoer. That is my choice."

"Sure," I say. "I'm not trying to tell you what to do. I guess all I'm saying is we're supposed to get on a ship in San Francisco. What would you do then?"

He pushes his fists into his pants pockets and I feel bad for asking him the question. But the farther he tags along the farther it is for him to get back.

"You picked up all our suitcases on the freeway," I say. "That was you, wasn't it?"

He smiles. "One person tries to put something in his truck," he says. "But his was not so fast a car."

"You pulled him over?"

"The man felt sinful for his act," he says.

But then I can hear Cora's voice. My mother, still in her black slip, has stepped out of our room.

"Teddy!" she shouts to me. "Who is that you're talking to?"

Daniel slides into the T-Bird and starts the engine. As I step back, he spins the steering wheel with one hand, the tires squealing.

My mother has rushed down to the landing with Cora chattering at her side.

"What are you doing talking to a stranger at this hour?" my mother says as I walk up to the stairs.

"Why don't we go back to the room?" Cora says to her.

My mother waves a finger in my sister's face. "When I want to hear from you, young lady, I'll tell you. Do you understand?"

Cora looks away.

"I said, do you understand?" my mother says, raising her voice enough to bring Bobbie out of the room.

My sister mumbles something under her breath.

"Answer me, miss," my mother says. "Do you understand?"

Cora backs up against the railing. "I understand, all right," she says bitterly. "You get all this grief from Daddy and then you take it out on me. That's what I understand."

My mother looks down at me and then up at Bobbie.

"What did you say?" my mother says.

"You heard me," my sister says. "You hang up the phone with Daddy and ten minutes later you're looking around for someone to scream at. Well, get yourself another punching bag."

Bobbie comes halfway down the stairs. "Why don't we all talk about this in the room?" she says. "Rosemary?"

My mother is glaring at Cora.

"Somebody had better not say another word," she says. "Somebody had better mind her tongue or she's going to wish she had."

I know the look on my sister's face and it's not the look she gets when she's going to mind her tongue. Not that I'd recognize that look.

"You can't shut me up," Cora says. "I'm not your little whipping dog. You and Daddy can fight all you want. Just leave me out of it. I'm sick of being the middleman."

My sister stands rigidly in one corner of the landing, my

mother across from her as Bobbie steps between them, arms out-stretched.

"You know, it's almost time for Nick's show," she says. "I think he'd be real disappointed if we miss it."

My mother looks at her niece. "That's my daughter I'm talking to," she says evenly. "What I tell her to do, she does."

My cousin doesn't lower her arms. "I think—"

"I don't care what you think," my mother says. "This is between Cora and me."

Bobbie looks at my sister and then back at my mother. I can see that she doesn't want to be where she is but she is. "Rosemary, this is—"

My mother suddenly swats my cousin's arm down. "Don't you put your hand in my face . . ."

I reel back as if I'd taken the blow myself.

"Come on, Mom," I plead, rushing up the stairs. "Let's go inside."

My mother points her finger at my sister, leaning toward her as if into a fierce wind.

"I've spoiled you and this is what I get," she says. "A spoiled, pampered little brat."

Cora is shaking her head, eyes bulging. "That's right," she says. "I owe you everything, don't I? And you don't owe me a thing."

I look up at the second floor. An elderly man has drawn the curtains back at his window and is pressing his forehead to the glass.

My sister pivots, smiling curiously at Bobbie. "Maybe you can learn something here," she says. "This is what happens when you don't call it quits."

"Get in that room," my mother says sharply. "I don't want another word out of you."

Cora steps around my cousin but then stops in front of my

mother. "When are you going to catch on? Everybody'd be a hell of a lot happier. Especially Daddy."

My mother raises her hand but Bobbie wraps both arms around her shoulders while I hang onto her waist.

"Mom, please," I say. "Come on."

Bobbie suddenly loses her footing and we careen into the railing. I clutch my shoulder as we all stand staring at each other, out of breath.

My mother's slip has bunched up on her hip and she smoothes it down.

"You all right, honey?" she says to me.

I nod but keep kneading my shoulder, which had been ground into the iron fence.

My sister staggers up the steps, stopping once to take a deep breath.

"Cora?" my mother says.

My sister doesn't turn around. "What?"

"Are you all right?"

She shakes her head, reaching out for the railing to steady herself. "Oh, for Christ's sake."

Bobbie adjusts the scarf around her neck. "I was going to wear this tonight," she says. "I guess it still looks all right."

My mother lifts the straps up on her slip and waits until Cora is back inside the room.

"Honey?" she says to me.

I'm staring at the aged couple who are at their window, hands cupped at their foreheads.

"What?"

"I want to know who that boy was," she says at last. "And I don't want any nonsense."

Sid the manager of the Flaming Star, leads us down a cinderblock corridor behind the stage.

"It ain't that Nick's act is smutty or nothing," he explains to my mother. "Only sometimes we get an off-duty cop come in. I don't need no more code violations. I got enough with the Health Inspection people."

Since Nick has asked it as a personal favor he's going to let me sit down front. By the exit where it's darkest.

"They want to find mice shit in my kitchen, they find it," Sid says. "They got a question about the wiring, they find a problem, you know what I'm saying? I got more out-of-pocket expenses than a pimp."

Through the crack in the curtains I can see a stand-up comic trying to make a small audience pay attention.

"They come to see Elvis," Sid whispers. "They ain't interested in no jokes."

We pass the dressing rooms and then take a short flight of stairs that leads out onto the floor. The stand-up comic turns as if to say something but Sid's already shaking his head.

"I'll get one of the girls to come by," he says after we've taken our seats.

A cloud of cigarette smoke drifts through the spotlight as couples sit with their backs to the comedian, talking quietly.

My mother's worried about Cora who has stayed back in the motel. They won't speak to each other now and there's no telling exactly how long this will go on. But always it's my mother who will eventually break the silence. Never Cora. That's because my sister is stubborn and immature.

Sid at last strolls back out onto the stage and thanks the comic. Then he tells everybody to get ready for the Flaming Star's feature attraction. Elvis Garon Erwin will be out shortly to bring the King to us in all his glory.

"Nick said it'd be full by the time he comes on," Bobbie says as the empty tables begin to fill up. "He said his regulars wait until the warm-up act is off. They don't care for any off-color stuff."

Sid busies himself checking the two speakers on either side of the stage. Nick has told us that he works with just a cassette and a guitar. "People want to hear the King," he explained to Bobbie. "But you got more look-alikes in this town than you can shake a microphone at. Difference is I ain't in it just for the buck. I'm the twin brother Elvis never knew."

Others are standing in the back of the small club now as Sid tries to squeeze in another few chairs from his office.

A waitress sets a pitcher down before us.

"On the house," she says and winks at me. Her blouse opens to her waist as she leans over with the glasses. "Got you a sweetie there," she says to my mother.

The lights flicker as the speakers crackle with static. Sid taps the mike, squinting painfully into the bright spotlight.

"Lou and I used to go to clubs," Bobbie says. She's been watching my mother closely, afraid to say anything that might set her off. "That was before we got married."

My mother looks over at me. It's the look she gets whenever she's making up her mind whether to say something in front of me.

228

"Just the opposite happened after we got married," she says finally. "Teddy's father started wanting to go out."

This is like hearing a war story from my father. They just aren't told. So both Bobbie and I are leaning forward in our seats.

"I think he was bored early," my mother says so quietly that it's almost as if she doesn't believe anyone is listening. But we are. My cousin and I are all ears. She's said nothing about her conversation with my father earlier. They'd argued again and afterward Cora had said things to her. Now my mother's miserable because of her quarrel with my father and because she has finally come to blows with my sister.

And even as the curtain opens with Nick posed dramatically in the middle of the stage, his guitar slung over his shoulder and the speakers rattling our table with "Jailhouse Rock," I'm thinking that my mother has just confessed that once upon a time my father enjoyed staying home with her but that now he'll go all the way to China just to avoid her company.

"I love this song," Bobbie says, her voice hushed as our glasses shimmy and Nick struts past our table, lip-synching with a sneer, " 'Baby, Let's Play House.' "

My mother reaches past my cousin and gently wipes the tears from my chin.

"Sweetheart?" she says. "Teddy?"

I cork-screw one eye, pretending it's just the glare of the light. Only my mother and cousin know better. It's the kind of sign they've learned to watch out for. And not even Elvis gyrating ten feet in front of them can upstage the real show.

It's useless to argue since I've reassured them before and then have blanked out for the next two hours. And so I can only sit and watch Nick as he mimes a crowd-pleasing string of gospel favorites beginning with "How Great Thou Art." Meanwhile, my mother doesn't look away from me even through an entire medly of "Heartbreak Hotel," "Don't Be Cruel," and "Are You Lonesome Tonight?" When at last Nick launches into, "That's All

Right, Mamma," I turn to smile at my mother but her stern expression doesn't change. She wants to be ready when I spin out of my chair onto the concrete floor.

Perhaps, after all, I *should* fake a seizure. It might get everyone talking again. But then it wouldn't be the first time I wished I could stand in the middle of the living room and fire off a few semi-automatic rounds into the ceiling. The only trouble is I'm not altogether sure what it is exactly I'd want to say. That my mother and father should try to love each other as much as their seizure-prone son loves them? But, of course, it's just not the sort of thing any of us would ever say. Not even if we were all armed and had just lived through our first family fire fight.

In the morning, Cora dresses quickly and walks down to the coffee shop alone. She's still bitter enough not to ask me to come along.

"I guess I get to be the villain," my mother says.

Last night was the first time she's ever raised her hand to my sister. We're not a family to get physical with each other. Although Cora's sullenness is nothing new, my mother's reaction to it is. And she moves about the motel room nervously now, folding then unfolding my sister's clothes as she talks to herself.

When I try to argue that Cora is just high-strung, my mother closes my sister's suitcase.

"What am I going to do with her?" she says. "I haven't got a clue."

Later, while we wait for Bobbie to return from breakfast with Nick, I check the fluids in the car. It's six hundred miles to New Orleans but my mother calls ahead to reserve us a room in a bed and breakfast in the French Quarter. She does this, I know, as a kind of truce offering to Cora.

The dipstick registers only a quarter of an inch of oil and the rear tires are low.

"We'd explode without you looking out for us," my mother

says as I carry a glass of water down to empty into the battery cells. "What chance would we have?"

Cora would have an answer for this if it weren't for her vow of silence.

When Nick and Bobbie come back up, Nick doesn't remove his sunglasses and sits down next to me on the roll-away.

"The King loves the tube," he says, glancing at the TV and then across at Cora who's watching a local game show with the sound off. "The Jungle Room's got half a dozen sets."

My sister ignores him and so I ask what kinds of things Elvis tunes into.

Nick shrugs his shoulders.

"He'd sit with his momma," he says. "But it ain't been the same without her around."

" 'Driving without a license,' " Cora says to herself, solving the puzzle with only three letters showing.

Nick lowers his sunglasses.

"Girl," he says admiringly. "You are *fast*."

"You can't watch anything with her," Bobbie says.

Cora steps over to the window to lift the curtains back. It's the first thing she's said in over an hour.

My mother smiles at Nick. "I'm not going to try to thank you again," she says. "I can't."

Nick stands up. "My pleasure, ma'am." He clears his throat but still sounds like Elvis. "Anytime."

We all trail out of the room into the bright sunlight with Cora well ahead of us.

In the parking lot, Nick loops his arm over Bobbie's shoulder.

"Real fine day," he says. His sunglasses are black mirrors. "Gonna miss you, darlin'."

"Miss you too," Bobbie says.

Nick opens the passenger door for my mother and then jogs around to help Bobbie into the driver's side. He leans in and smiles broadly, one nostril flaring.

"How about I send you folks a record?" he says.

Bobbie turns the engine on. "That would be real sweet," she says.

As the Oldsmobile backs out of the lot, Nick waves to us and then leaps from the curb, slicing the air with a furious karate chop.

"Quite a guy," Cora says.

"Nick's a real gentleman," my cousin says. "He's just like the King that way."

I ask Bobbie what kind of record she thinks Nick has in mind and it's a moment before my cousin confesses that, considering Nick's special line of work, it's a good question.

After a quick stop at the first service station (two quarts of oil and three more pounds of pressure per tire), we head out on the interstate.

An hour down the road, I see our first Fort Polk sign. When we were stationed here, Cora never seemed to leave our Wherry Housing. My mother would get upset with her for not trying to make friends, but my sister complained that finding a kindred soul among Army brats in the Deep South was like looking for a needle in a haystack. All she ever managed to come up with were hayseeds.

Just outside Vicksburg, Bobbie switches off driving with my mother.

"Wasn't there some kind of big war around here?" my cousin asks when we pass another billboard advertising the National Military Park.

"It's where General Grant defeated the Confederates," I say. "He surrounded the city and tried to starve them out."

"Teddy should be a history professor when he grows up," my mother says. "He's like his father. He's real good on dates."

"I wish I'd paid more attention in school," Bobbie says. "It'd make a trip like this mean a whole lot more."

"Tell us something else," my mother says proudly. "Go ahead, honey."

"Well," I say. "The people of Vicksburg wouldn't give up so Grant kept shelling the town for forty-seven days."

Bobbie shakes her head in disbelief.

"The Confederates built caves in the cliffs," I say. "The soil's called loess. Wind-blown silt. It's why they could build them."

"I wouldn't be able to sleep in a cave," my cousin says. "I'd be thinking about bats all the time. I'd have to surrender."

"That's what they finally did," I say. "General Grant starved them out."

Cora reaches under her seat for the headphones. "Probably just tired of bat stew," she says and turns up the volume on her recorder.

When Bobbie tunes a country station in on the radio, I find my place in my book.

By the time he was ten Matt's stepfather had begun to beat him up so badly that Matt decided to run away. He'd heard stories from the field workers about ocean vessels that docked in the Baltimore harbor. Some of them would take on cabin boys even if they were underaged. So one morning before the others woke, he set out barefoot the forty miles to the city.

I stop reading and glance over at my sister who sits with her arms crossed, glaring at the back of my mother's head. Last night, standing outside our motel room, I lied about who Cora had been talking to. It wasn't the first time I'd told my mother a deliberate untruth. Except I couldn't remember ever having lied to her for my sister's sake before. At least not about something that really mattered. But what kept me from getting much sleep afterward was knowing that I'd had to choose between them and that I'd chosen my sister. My spoiled, ungrateful sister. What was worse was that my mother knew that I'd lied. She looked so stunned that for a moment all she could do was stare at me. And I could see that she didn't know what to say. This was something altogether new between us: a bold-faced lie. For what seemed a full minute we both stood as if gazing down into a dark pit at our feet until realizing finally that I was too ashamed to say anything more, my mother let me go.

It's difficult to imagine how Matt must have felt to want to leave his family for a life at sea. He had no memory of his real father and, while he worked in the fields all day, dreamed about ships and the ocean. If he could find someone to take him on as cabin boy perhaps he could find another home. Only this time it would be one that he made for himself and not just one given to him.

We pass the Halls Ferry Road exit and my mother points out the Corps of Engineers research and testing laboratory.

"Your father spent three weeks there once," she says and asks me if I remember.

"They were testing to see what an atomic bomb would do to the river," I say.

Bobbie turns sideways in her seat. "Wouldn't everybody have to leave first?"

I explain how it's all done in miniature. My father had brought home a scale model of Vicksburg made out of cardboard. A mock nuclear explosion depicted what would happen to the levee. Nearly every home in the city was under water, only the steeple of one or two churches poked above the surface.

This was about the same time when bomb shelters were so popular and the Army's Office of Civil and Defense Mobilization was experimenting with the "Family Models of Tomorrow" for dependents to tour on base. Cora's favorite was the one with baffle walls, a special termite shield, and a 12-gauge corrugated steel door to keep out panicky neighbors. "I could move in tomorrow," she would say just to irritate my mother who didn't want to think about any mushroom clouds in her children's future.

What I liked best were all the accessories: the battery-operated radio with the CONELRAD frequencies already marked, the electric lanterns, and the ten-gallon lidded garbage pail for a toilet. The concrete bunker buried under twenty inches of pit-russ gravel was better than any fort I could ever have built on my own. Plus my father had started to travel a lot and it seemed to me our best chance for being together again.

The Oldsmobile's air conditioner pumps full blast as we follow the river down Route 61, the levee winding along the water's edge like an enormous molehill.

By the time we get to Natchez no one is interested in the Indian Visitor Center even though the museum has a sixty-seat auditorium and a film all about the burial mounds.

Instead, we stop for a snack at Mammy's Cupboard, a twenty-eight-foot-tall restaurant in the shape of a black mammy.

The specialty, which Bobbie decides on, is tender fried chicken served with home-cut french fries and presweetened tea.

"Now I feel like a pig," my cousin says when the rest of us just order sandwiches.

"You get whatever you want," my mother says.

It's a popular roadside attraction and people come in just to see the interior, which is like a small lighthouse.

Whenever my sister is upset with my mother she looks for the closest target of opportunity. Which, of course, is always me. So I wait, flipping through the selections on the miniature jukebox at our booth, expecting her to launch in at any moment. Instead, she chews on her thumbnails and sips at her Coke, saying nothing.

Bobbie slides a dime over to me. "N7," she says.

It's a Patsy Cline song.

"She was just so great," my cousin says when it's over. "Momma cried for a week when that plane went down."

My mother nods. "That size falls out of the sky all the time," and she looks over at Cora and me. "And their father practically lives in them."

Bobbie smiles at us as if we were already orphaned. "I guess it's a good thing he's always wearing a parachute."

My mother agrees. "One reason to keep these two on the ground."

Cora nudges me to let her out of the booth and we all watch my sister walk back to the ladies' room.

"She gets like this on the road," my mother says finally. "We'll all just have to live with her."

"Too bad Oldsmobiles don't come with an ejector seat," I say.

My mother leaves a generous tip beside her plate.

"We'll take it easy for a day in New Orleans," she says. "Get us all back on the right track."

"Mom?" My mother turns over, tangling herself in the sheet.

"I'm going to check out the flea market," I say. "I won't be long."

She squints at the sunlight coming through the cypress shutters.

"What time is it, honey?"

"Seven."

She lifts her head slightly to see Cora and Bobbie still in bed.

"I want you back by eight," she says and drops her head back onto the pillow.

Outside, I jump from the top step of the Victorian house, feeling suddenly liberated. The tension between my mother and sister made yesterday's long drive down seem like a week in an armored tank. For hours, no one, not even Bobbie, attempted conversation as we measured our misery by the green mileage markers to New Orleans.

Crossing Esplanade I can see vendors setting up their stands in the crowded corner of the market. The veterans claim the shade of the old federal mint for their folding tables. Those unprotected from the sun huddle beneath beach umbrellas or wear outrageous paraphernalia: huge Mexican sombreros with Army surplus.

I stop at the first bookstall. Like a lot of the wares for sale, even the books look stolen.

"That," the vendor says as soon as I pick one up about the Arctic. "That baby's old." Across its spine is a faded library call number.

He looks down at the rows of mildewed books at his feet. And as he steps into the sunlight I can see the black stubbed toes that poke out from his leather sandals. Everything about him is as grimy as a mechanic and I can't stop staring. He looks like a prisoner of war.

"North Pole," the vendor says and squats down to scoop up several books. Then suddenly behind an old Bunsen burner I notice an Army cot and the back of a man's head. There's a body in the patched sleeping bag.

"That's Wayne," the vendor says, handing me one book at a time. "Wayne's a little under the weather."

The books' covers have the kind of fuzz that grows on overripe fruit.

"Three for five bucks," he says. "Deal of the century."

It's probably the first time the books have been in the sunlight in years and I smear my finger across the cover of the top one. It's about Greenland whalers. The others are too thick with mildew to even read the titles. But none of them look as if they have anything to do with the North Pole or exploration.

Afterward, at the outdoor Café du Monde, I order beignets and read the front page of someone's abandoned newspaper. Right below a photograph of Colonel Aldrin crossing his eyes at a floating toothbrush there's a larger picture of Jackie Onassis stepping onto her yacht in the Isle of Capri. I'll keep the paper for Cora who likes to follow the former first lady's shopping expeditions.

Years ago when we would drive down to spend a Saturday afternoon sitting in Jackson Square, my mother would drink several cups of café au lait while Cora and I got powdered sugar everywhere. My father, meanwhile, would try to interest us all in visiting some historic sites. Places like the Cabildo where we could see Napoleon's death mask. Or the alley behind the old cathedral, which had once been a place for dueling and where William Faulkner had lived. But Cora was more interested in seeing where they'd filmed *Cat on a Hot Tin Roof*. My mother was content just to "visit." It wasn't often, she liked to say, that she could get her family to sit down together at an outdoor table. That was enough for me too: to listen to my parents talk about my sister and me as we sat in the sun eating French doughnuts.

Later, I leave the books (which I'd bought anyway) on one of the ice cream parlor chairs and head back up Esplanade thinking how not so long ago I'd strolled down the very same street holding my father's hand, completely unaware of how miserable he must have been. He was in his early thirties, a married soldier, and a daddy with dependents, which explains, Cora likes to say, why he still jumps out of airplanes.

At the Gumbo Shop on Royal Street, Bobbie asks our waiter about rubbing Marie Laveau's grave for good fortune. My cousin's willing to try anything that might turn her luck around.

"X marks the spot," the waiter says, drawing a map on Bobbie's paper napkin.

He's printed the voodoo queen's name in block letters over a square. The cemetery is several hundred years old and there are thousands of graves but because of the watery soil the plots are all aboveground.

When the waiter returns with our check, my mother asks him what he thinks about visiting the cemetery.

"Let me put it this way," he says. "A lot of the unmarked graves you see over there probably belong to tourists."

The St. Louis Cemetery has become a hangout for drug addicts.

My mother nods. "Not a good idea, in other words," and she looks over at my cousin. "What do you want to do, honey?"

Bobbie slips the napkin into her pocketbook. "You know me, Rosemary. You and the kids take your buggy ride. We can meet back in the room."

My mother's already shaking her head.

"Either we all go together or we don't go at all."

To get to the cemetery from the Quarter we follow Bourbon Street to Conti. There's no point in taking the Oldsmobile. It's only twenty minutes on foot. Besides, it's a lovely, sunny day and we're all sick of the car.

I walk with Cora behind Bobbie and my mother and the only males whose heads don't turn when they see my cousin are those wearing jeans tighter than hers.

"My imagination," Cora says, "or has Lou's wife put on some weight?"

"Your imagination," I say.

But my sister's decided that something is going on in front of her that doesn't meet the eye. At least the untrained eye.

"I don't think so," she says, studying Bobbie's slightly pigeon-toed walk.

On the other side of Rampart, my mother smiles nervously as we pass beneath the rusted wrought-iron gates to the cemetery.

"All hope abandon," Cora says.

The whitewashed crypts, called ovens, are cracked and sunken in decay.

"We're just asking for it," my sister says. "And we've got the perfect guide."

Bobbie stops to unfold her directions on one of the shattered marbles. She examines the waiter's drawing then points in the general direction of the housing project.

"It says that way."

The bleached crypts reflect the sun like sheets on a clothesline. Everything is broken: the slanted crosses, the stone slabs, the endless stacked vaults. It's a small city of crumbling stucco and brick.

Bobbie glances at her map every few feet and leads my mother down another row of tombs. Many of the larger crypts contain several generations that go back hundreds of years.

"The one place I can see a family staying together," Cora says.

In fact, my superstitious mother won't let my father buy us a family plot. "Dad's got Arlington if he croaks," my sister likes to say. "The Army lets the rest of us fend for ourselves." It's true. As a veteran, he's eligible for burial in the national cemetery. But he likes to taunt my mother by saying that if ever his chute doesn't open, he'll just point his toes and save us all the expense.

Bobbie makes a surprising, little whooping sound. She's stopped before a large live oak whose great aboveground roots have raised one corner of a vault.

My cousin reads the grave's simple marker. "Marie Laveau, Voodoo Queen, 1779–?"

The metal fence around it has been trampled down and only one rusted fleur-de-lis is still upright.

"Honey," my mother says. "Why don't you make your wish so we can go."

But now that she's found it Bobbie's hesitant about actually touching the grave.

"I really want us to start thinking about getting back," my mother coaxes her.

My cousin at last steps across the fence and bows her head, making a brief, silent wish beside the vault.

"Okay," my mother says. "Now which way's out of here?"

But she doesn't move when she turns to see what Cora is staring at.

A man has slunk out from behind one of the mausoleums. He's barefoot and wearing only faded jeans.

When none of us says anything, he leans back against the vault that's the size of a tool shed.

"How you folks doing?"

Only Bobbie smiles. "Kind of hot," she says. "How you?"

Against the glare of the white stucco he's almost invisible, his skin is so pale.

"Real fine," he says and starts rocking back and forth on the balls of his feet.

My mother herds me closer to Cora.

"It really is a nice day," she says.

The man raises his chin to study the cloudless sky.

"You got that right."

My sister has taken her sunglasses off and is silently twirling them by the stem.

"Nice place," Bobbie volunteers, gazing about her as if in the showroom of a furniture store.

The man digs his toes in the dirt and I notice that each nail is painted a different color.

"Folks dying to get in," he says.

I dip my shoulder under my mother's tight grip. Her fingers are cutting off the circulation.

"So," she says genially. "We were on our way back to the car."

When the man smiles, his teeth are brown and jagged. "Don't want to keep you."

But he's blocking the path.

Bobbie turns and winks at me. "How long your daddy going to take to finish that cigar?" she says. "He promised just a minute."

The man only moves away from the vault.

"Here's what I got in mind," he says, crossing his long, bony forearms in front of him. "We all chip in for a contribution. See what it comes to."

"What a slime," Cora mumbles.

My mother grabs the back of my sister's blouse and yanks it like a subway cord.

"That sounds good," she says, unzipping her bag. "That's reasonable."

"Just pitch the thing over here," the man says and taps his foot on the ground.

My mother slides the strap from her shoulder. "It's just mostly credit cards," she says.

"We accept them all," and he curls his finger at my cousin. "Don't disappoint me now."

Bobbie has tucked her pocketbook under her arm.

"Honey," my mother pleads. "Let's just do what the gentleman says, can't we?"

My cousin reluctantly lifts the flap on her pocketbook and takes out her wallet. It's the one with her name in rhinestones and she slips out a single five-dollar bill.

"Don't think so," the man says, his voice less playful.

Bobbie flings a ten at him but then snaps her purse shut.

When the man steps toward her, my mother swats my cousin's purse from her hand and it spills open.

"Don't touch it," my mother screams and even the man looks startled. "Nobody touch it."

Bobbie stands back up slowly. My mother's jaw is twitching.

"I'll make it up to you," she says to my cousin. "It's only money. That's all he wants."

We watch the man rip the rest of the bills from Bobbie's thick wallet when someone else suddenly appears in the deep shadow of the vault. He's taller and wearing dark clothes but he doesn't come any closer.

"Well, look who's here," Cora says, spinning her sunglasses again. "Where you been, Daddy?"

The thief remains on all fours in the dirt, gathering up my cousin's money. He doesn't want to appear to fall for my sister's lame trick and only glances casually over his shoulder.

As if to introduce himself, the taller man steps out of the shade and into the sunlight, lifting the black hat from his head.

It's Daniel.

"Good day."

His clothes are too short, making him look gangly and slightly crazy.

The man drops Bobbie's wallet as he lunges past me, my mother's pocketbook thumping against his sunken chest. Cora tries to reach out for him but my mother catches her arm.

"No!" she shouts.

Daniel abruptly spins about, the sand flicking up from his sandals.

"Wait," my sister calls after him but he only flings his hat off.

Afterward, my mother staggers over to one of the marble slabs and sits down. No one bothers to pick up the rest of the money.

"I'm sorry, Rosemary," my cousin says, kneeling in front of her. "I should have listened to the waiter."

My mother is breathing shallowly and holds her hand up. "I just need to catch my breath," she says.

Cora wanders over and sits at her feet but doesn't say anything.

My mother unexpectedly wraps her arms around my sister's shoulders, pulling her toward her.

"You're just like your father," she says and sobs loudly. "You're exactly alike."

Bobbie brushes the dirt from her knees. "Nobody'd of messed with us if your daddy'd been here," she says.

"But of course, he wasn't," Cora says quietly.

"Daddy would have killed him," I say, unable to keep my voice from quivering.

Then we're all silent. It's as if we're back in the car, staring dumbly out at the scenery.

"I've seen that boy before," my mother says at last.

Bobbie nods. "I thought it was Johnny Cash," she says. "Everything he had on was black."

I stare at the back of my sister's head.

"I don't think he was with the police department," my mother says. "He didn't look old enough to be."

My cousin slips one of her shoes off. "Maybe he was undercover or something," and she rolls her sock down to her heel.

"He was just a kid," my mother says. "A big kid but still just a kid."

My sister peers over her shoulder at her but then looks back at me. "His name's Daniel," she says. "He's the little friend I was talking to. All right? Everybody happy now?"

My mother is nodding. "In the parking lot," she says to herself.

Bobbie continues to rub her toes. "That boy must be in love," she says, grinding her foot back into her shoe.

My sister raises both hands and brings them down flatly on her thighs. "Give me a break."

My cousin looks dumbfounded. "Honey, ain't nothing in the world wrong with a boy crossing state lines to keep in touch." She walks over to where she can see down the row of crypts. But there's no sign of anyone. "Besides, I never found you could tell a boy with a car what to do."

My mother smiles at me the way she does whenever what she's about to say is actually meant for Cora. "He has to go back home," she says. "That has to be made clear to him."

My sister springs to her feet. "Fine," she says to me. "Someone make it clear to him. Tell him to go back to his loony family. See what happens."

My mother keeps her voice down as if speaking to a spoiled child, which, of course, she is. Although she still addresses everything to me. "I think that's your sister's responsibility now. He's her friend. He's not here because of us."

Cora kicks the stone marker and dust puffs up from the toe of her shoe. "I'm going back to the room before I get a sunstroke," she says.

My mother nods. "We're all going back together," she says

and then lowers her voice again as if to keep from getting my sister any more worked up. "We've had a full day."

But she waits for Bobbie who's turned back to stand beside the voodoo queen's tomb where this time my cousin forms the sign of the cross on her forehead before making a second silent wish.

Standing in the door of our room, Daniel thrusts my mother's pocketbook out as if it were a bouquet of flowers. The zipper is torn and the leather scuffed and dusty. But nothing, my mother declares after emptying its contents out on the bed, appears to be missing.

"What's left for you to rescue," Bobbie says, coaxing Daniel into the room. She's been rolling her hair and holds one of the curlers like an antenna over her head. "Honey, you're a one-man lost and found."

But Daniel is typically close-mouthed and will only say that the man was sorry for having stolen it. He remains by the door shrugging off our appreciation as if recovering six pieces of luggage from the freeway and wrestling a pocketbook back from a drug addict were nothing.

"Everything's here," my mother says, still unable to believe her good fortune. "Even the pictures."

It's what she checked for first: photographs taken of the family together from each assignment since my sister was born.

While Daniel submits to our questions, Cora only sits on the bed and listens. But every once in a while I catch her studying him the way a director might study an actor during an audition. No doubt she has her own list of questions but they're not ones she'll ask in front of the rest of us.

My mother surprises us all by not bringing up the subject of Daniel's running away from home. Instead, she insists that he at least let her cover some of his car expenses and before he can protest, she tucks a wad of bills into his fist.

Finally, Bobbie suggests that we all walk down to Jackson Square before it's too dark for a buggy ride.

"Course I guess that'd be kind of old hat for you," she says to Daniel. "I mean, buggies and all."

"Why don't we let you two get a head start," my mother adds. "We can meet a little later for doughnuts. How's that sound?"

Cora isn't speaking to her, of course, and only tells us not "to wait up." She'll see us when she sees us.

Afterward, as we arrange ourselves in the backseat of one of the rental carriages lined up across from the cathedral, my mother is optimistic about Daniel. In fact, she's worried more about Cora.

"Your sister's not used to boys saying good-bye to her," she points out to me. "I don't want to see her get her feelings hurt."

"I guess it's easier to say than do in this world," Bobbie says. "Least that's been this girl's experience."

My cousin's wearing the large straw hat she picked up in a novelty shop on Bourbon Street. "New Orleans: Shucking Capital of the World" is printed across its wide brim.

The carriage driver, a light-skinned black man with a red bandanna tied loosely about his neck, appears to doze off, trusting his ancient horse to handle the route on its own. Only occasionally does he snap his head back to point out a historical landmark. The site, for example, where Tennessee Williams "wrote that movie *Streetcar*."

I know that Matt Henson once lived in the Quarter but when I ask the driver about the great explorer, he only shakes his head ("Never heard the man") and calls our attention to a small restaurant where Napoleon regularly dined.

When we were stationed at Fort Polk, Cora argued that the reason my father loved coming to New Orleans was because he could fantasize about living in Europe instead of being stuck Stateside with the rest of us. But my mother believed that it was just because it always seemed hotter in the city and my father loves the heat. It was only one of the reasons he would have made such a good farmer, she contended. The idea of lounging on a tractor in the middle of a blistering field actually appealed to him.

My eyes droop with the rhythmic clopping of the horse along the cobbled street.

Right before we were reassigned from Fort Polk, my father took us down to the city to spend one last day in the Quarter. We were sitting in an outdoor café eating beignets when one of the carriage horses reared up and took off down Decatur scattering tourists like bowling pins. The driver frantically cracked his whip and screamed obscenities but couldn't reign him in. Then, practically in front of our table, the horse hit a fire plug on the corner and buckled at the knees, sending the driver hurtling from the bench and skidding across the sidewalk on his elbows. I don't recall what became of him. All I remember is my father teasing my mother about the horse. "That's what happens when you get one with too much get up and go," he said to her. "Eventually, it'll want to get up and go." My mother didn't find this particularly funny and in fact spent the rest of the afternoon sulking. My father finally won her back but not without a lot of affectionate banter at a nice restaurant. "It's good for all of us to get away now and then," he said, scooting his chair closer to hers and looping his arm over her shoulder. "That's all that horse was probably saying."

"Teddy?"

I lift my chin from my chest to see both my mother and Bobbie leaning toward me in the carriage.

"You sleepy?" my mother says.

The driver's pulled into the back of the line of buggies parked alongside the levee. He straightens the horse's harness, waiting for us to get out.

"It's probably all those foldaways," Bobbie says.

To reassure my mother I grip the seat handle and bound out of the carriage, landing feet together on the sidewalk like a paratrooper.

We walk through the small park to the cathedral, supposedly the oldest Catholic Church in America. Or at least that's what all the buggy drivers will tell you. In the vestibule my mother opens her change purse and gives Bobbie and me a couple of quarters.

"Make a wish," she says.

For fifty cents you're allowed to light one of the candles arranged on a table outside the confession booth.

"Marie Laveau was cheaper," I say.

My mother shakes her head, holding one finger up to her pursed lips. "You're in a church," she whispers.

"To everybody's health," Bobbie says and lights one of the wicks with a thin taper. When she says this I notice that she touches her stomach with her other hand.

"You're not supposed to tell," my mother says, making her own wish. "Didn't Irene ever teach you that?"

My cousin steps back from the bank of flickering candles, her palm still flat against her stomach. "There's a lot of things Mom got around to too late," she says.

My mother has pinned a handkerchief to her hair even though not even the female tour guides have their heads covered. " 'Old-fashioned' doesn't *begin* to describe the woman," my sister likes to say.

I light one of the back candles.

"Now *Teddy* keeps *too* much to himself," my mother says as we wait in front of the sign for the next available tour guide.

My cousin has snapped open her compact to apply a fresh coat of tropical red lipstick. "People are always going to be telling that boy their secrets," she says and dabs her pinkie at the corner of her mouth. "It's a curse and a blessing."

"My boy would make a wonderful priest," my mother says.

"What're you talking about?" Bobbie says. "And deprive all the girls?"

My mother half smiles at me. "No," she says and looks away. "I guess not."

Our guide turns out to be part Cajun, and my mother and cousin have to concentrate to understand her. But the woman jokes that "God speaks only French here" as she draws our attention to the magnificent stained glass windows and frescoes of the "divine family."

After a while, my mother tells Bobbie and me that she wants to sit down for a few minutes to rest her legs.

"You can wait for me out in the square," she says. "See if you like any of the artwork."

What she really wants to do, of course, is say a few prayers. One of my mother's fears is that she's failed her spiritual obligations to her children. "She thinks we'll get struck by lightning if we don't at least make it in at Christmas and Easter," Cora says whenever my mother insists that we attend mass during the major holidays. "Like that's going to square things with the Supreme Commander." My father, who had been an altar boy at my age, stopped putting up a fuss when we were assigned to Fort Campbell ("Check out the organist," Cora said, pointing out to me the buxom assistant choral director. "Mystery solved.").

"Irene's the same," Bobbie says as soon as we're back out in the fading sunlight. "There's a church streak runs through those two. I guess it just missed us."

"By a mile," I say but I can tell that she doesn't like to hear this from me.

"Maybe I believed in the right things a little more," she says, opening her sunglasses, "your cousin wouldn't be in the fix she's in today." She stops to look out at all the artists who've set up their easels around the square. "I guess it's why I haven't tried to talk to your momma about it either."

I'm a little confused by all the "its" but I know what she means. Like my aunt, my mother would probably volunteer to raise "it" on her own. And so my cousin will keep her secret to herself.

As a personal favor, Bobbie asks me to pose with her for one of the portrait painters.

"I'll send it back to Irene," she says. "Picture's worth a thousand words, right?"

But she's not very cheery and the whole time we sit on the two folding chairs, the artist has to keep telling her to smile.

"What you so glum 'bout, cher?" he says, smearing the pastels on the foolscap with his thumb. "Girl pretty as you."

He's lacquering the portrait with hairspray when my mother steps out of the cathedral and unpins her handkerchief. Standing on the stone steps of the church in her yellow sun dress and sandals, she reminds me of her favorite wedding picture with my father, the one where she's squinting into the sun still holding her spray of flowers. But even with her eyes half closed, you can still see how completely happy she was that day. "You could practically circle her waist with your two hands," my aunt told me once of her sister. My mother hasn't gained that much weight over the years. She's changed but the change isn't in her waistline. It's in her eyes. They don't make you think of her wedding picture anymore.

"Look at my sweet boy," my mother says as Bobbie unfurls the pastel portrait for her.

And she and my cousin study my likeness as the artist hides his money box back under the tarpaulin at his feet.

"What do you think?" Bobbie says, nodding thoughtfully at

the drawing. "I think he's getting to be the spitting image of his momma."

But my mother's chin is already beginning to tremble.

"It's his eyes," she says finally and smiles at the artist as if he'd just baptized her baby. "They're filled with sunlight."

"I blame myself," my mother says, peering through the curtains again. "I never should have let her out of my sight."

It's after eleven and Cora is still not back.

"They're probably just out in the car," Bobbie offers. "When you're cruising it's easy to forget the time."

But my mother fears the worst. "He's kidnapped her," she says. "That's why he followed us all this way. He barely knows the girl and he's chasing halfway across the country after her."

"It wouldn't be the first time, Rosemary," Bobbie says. "Boys get something in their head and there's no talking them out of it."

"That's exactly what I'm saying," my mother says. "He's crazy."

She stops twisting the curtain in her hand and looks over at me. It's my turn to say something reassuring.

"I think he's come this far, Mom, he probably just wants to bend her ear as long as he can."

"You don't think he's crazy then?"

Bobbie suddenly points at the TV.

"I saw this with Lou," she says.

Johnny Carson stands over a man who's stretched out on an operating table.

"It was on 'Steve Allen,' " my cousin says and turns up the volume.

A magician is explaining something called "psychic surgery" that people are being duped into giving up their life savings to have performed.

My mother steps over to where she can see both the TV and, through the window, the street.

The magician dramatically works his white shirtsleeves up to his elbows before plunging one hand into the heavy fold of the man's pale belly. The audience groans but then it's quiet again as the magician sinks his hand so deep that all you can see is his wrist.

"It gets worse," Bobbie says.

My mother glances out the window and then back at the set.

The color on the TV isn't very good but you can see the blood on the man's white skin. It gushes out as the magician pretends to be feeling for something in the patient's stomach.

I try to adjust the picture. It's at least gotten my mother's mind off Cora.

"There," the magician says and pulls up what looks like a gray worm.

The audience moans again but this time it's followed by a mixture of laughter and applause.

Johnny lets his guest do all the talking and only stands to the side like a worried relative.

"There's more," the magician says, seeming astonished by all that he's pulling out. Both hands appear submerged in a mess of intestines. The sheet covering the man's lower body is soaked with blood. At least a gallon has flowed over the side onto the white cover. "What have we here?"

And he twists out several more seaweedlike strands, arranging them on the table beside the patient.

"You wonder how they let them do that on TV," Bobbie says. "Even on 'Johnny.'"

"What he's saying," my mother says, "is that there are lots of naive people out there. People who think you can trust other people. People like me, for example."

The magician raises both hands overhead. They're dripping with blood or at least what looks like blood.

"You can sit up now," he tells the patient who rolls over onto his side, kicking the sheet off.

"You've been a good sport," Johnny says to him.

The man nods shyly as he wipes the gore from his large belly and the audience sees that it's only a trick.

"It's all done with props," the magician says. "It's what you get in any Hollywood movie."

Johnny jokes that he'll shake his guest's hand later. "We'll be right back," he says, finding the camera before the cut to a commercial.

My mother turns the TV off.

"What time is it?" she says even though she's still wearing her watch. "If they're not back in ten minutes, I'm calling the police."

"Mom," I say. "Cora's not exactly a baby. I mean, she could get a learner's permit if she wanted one."

"Your sister's a minor," my mother says. "That means that boy's in big trouble. I don't care *how* old he is."

"My guess is seventeen," Bobbie says. "I think he's probably just a little big for his age."

A car backfires outside and my mother leaps to the window. But it's not Cora.

"Your sister knows better than not to call," my mother says to me.

"Cora's an idiot," I say. "Which means she's stupid enough not to."

"Five minutes," she says. "Then I start dialing."

Bobbie steps into the bathroom with her pajamas. She's put off getting dressed for bed. "She'll probably be here before I wash my hair."

But she isn't and for the next twenty minutes, my mother and I sit listening to my cousin in the shower.

"They'll be here," I say finally.

My mother taps on the bathroom door. "You can turn that off now," she raises her voice. "You're going to get waterlogged."

A moment later, my cousin sticks her head out.

"Rosemary?" she says, pressing a towel to her chest when my mother picks up the phone. "You know they're not going to do anything this soon." She flips her wet hair back. "If she was twelve years old or something it'd be different. Irene went through this with me half a dozen times. They won't even come out."

But my mother's already dialing.

Bobbie looks over at me and I shrug my shoulders.

"Yes," my mother says into the receiver. "Who do I talk to about my daughter? She's been kidnapped." She listens for a moment and then nods. "Since early this afternoon." Her hand is shaking so that it looks as if she's banging the phone against her ear. "I understand that," she says. "I'm just telling you that I want to talk to someone in authority." She waits again and then sets the phone back down into the cradle.

I watch her walk over to the door, test the doorknob then turn and stare at me for a moment as if trying to remember something I might have asked her.

"They said exactly what your cousin said they would," she says at last.

Bobbie steps barefoot out of the bathroom in her pajamas with a towel wrapped like a turban about her head.

"They'll want you to come down and fill out some papers," she says. "But they're not going to use up any squad cars or anything. Not for forty-eight hours. It's just the way they do this kind of thing. They don't get too excited about kids not coming home when they're supposed to."

"Cora doesn't do this every day," my mother says. "She's not that kind of kid."

My cousin stares at the mound of dirty clothes stacked on her suitcase.

"Why don't we do this," she says, looking back up. "Why don't I throw something on and we drive around a little. See what we see."

My mother moves over to the door and unlocks it. "What if she calls and we're out?" she says.

Bobbie unravels the towel from her head, shaking her hair out. "Teddy can man the phones," she says. "We won't be gone that long." And she squats down to get her shoes out from under the bed. "What do you say, Teddy?"

"Sure," I say. "If it's going to make Mom feel better."

My mother starts to say something but her voice catches and she studies her feet for what seems like two minutes.

"At least I'd feel like I was doing something," she says finally.

"Good," Bobbie says. "Two minutes." And she steps back into the bathroom.

My mother looks over at me. She doesn't smile and her eyes look the way they do after she's been on the phone with my father for one of her marathon calls. "Do you think your sister would run away?" she says.

Cora has always seemed unhappy to me but I guess I never considered that she'd do anything drastic.

"Run away?" I say. "Why would she run away?"

My mother sits down on the bed and folds her hands in her lap. "Because she hates her mother."

I glance at the bathroom door.

"Cora's all talk," I say, keeping my voice down. "She doesn't mean half of what she says."

My mother seems suddenly calm.

"I think your sister feels I'm trying to live her life for her," she says. "I think she feels that I put too much pressure on her." She hesitates as if weighing her words carefully. "But what do you think, honey? Tell me the truth? Does your mother expect too much?"

Bobbie hops out of the bathroom on one foot, trying to slide her shoe on. "Let's go," she says.

My mother wipes her eyes with the corner of the bedspread before standing up.

"I don't want you anywhere near that door while we're gone," she says to me. "Do you hear what I'm saying?"

I nod.

"You keep it locked. You understand?"

"Yes."

Bobbie grabs her pocketbook. "Ready."

My mother hasn't taken her eyes off me. "We won't be gone more than thirty minutes. I want you to promise me you won't leave this room."

"I promise."

"And keep the TV on. I want to be able to hear it outside. And don't go anywhere near that window."

"Let's go, Rosemary," my cousin says. "The faster we'll get back."

"And if your sister calls . . ." My mother stops and gazes up at the ceiling, blinking rapidly. "Promise her I won't say a word about this. Not even to her father."

As soon as they step outside the room, I lock the dead bolt. My mother tries the knob several times, leaning heavily against the door to test it.

"Rosemary, it's not going to open," I hear Bobbie whisper from the street.

It's exactly midnight.

I find my book and prop the pillows up against the headboard. Matt's trudging back through a snow storm after Peary has again failed to reach the Pole. The commander is sick and has to be carried on one of the sleds. Matt's own hands and feet are frostbitten and his nose dangerously numb.

To keep from thinking of his ailments, Matt daydreams about his Eskimo mistress who was seven months' pregnant when he left. The boy would have been born by now and Matt wonders whether it looks more like an Inuit or a Negro. He doesn't know what he'll do when he returns. The commander will expect him to board the ship with the rest of the crew and sail back to the States. But Matt will tell him that he wants to stay with his new family.

When the phone rings I have to sit still for a moment before I'm able to pick up the receiver.

"Teddy?"

It's Cora.

I can hear a humming noise in the background.

"You all right?" my sister says.

I breathe in and in a rush ask her why she's on the phone instead of back here in the room.

"Listen," she says. "Just tell Mom I'm fine."

"Are you kidnapped?"

I hear a male's voice. Daniel's. But I can't make out what's being said.

"Does he want us to pay money?" I say as soon as my sister comes back on. The question doesn't make any sense, of course. Daniel's the one who returned my mother's pocketbook.

"Look," Cora says. "Just tell her it's like one of Dad's little junkets. I'll be back. You guys keep going and we'll stay close. Tell her that."

I wipe the tears from my chin and try to keep my voice from embarrassing me.

"You'll get lost," I say. "How are you going to know where we are?"

"Teddy, I've seen the itinerary. Mom's already got reservations in Vegas. Probably in the room next to Elvis."

"You're going to meet us there?"

She holds the phone away again.

"Just tell her I decided this on my own," she says finally. "Nobody's twisting my arm."

"Is Daniel . . ."

She waits but I can't finish.

"Is Daniel what?" she says.

But I can only make a kind of gurgling sound.

"Listen, Teddy," she says. "I can't take another ten minutes in that car with her. Honest to god I can't. It'll be better this way for everybody."

"She said she wouldn't say anything," I manage. "She just wants you to come back."

Cora hesitates and then whispers something with the receiver covered. "Okay," she says. "Just tell her not to have a cardiac. Daniel's a safe driver."

She wants to hang up but I'm afraid to let her go. I'm afraid I'll never hear from my sister again.

"Mom'll call the police," I say. "She'll—"

"Teddy, I'll call you when you get to San Antonio. You're staying at the Stuart Inn there. Mom's got everything mapped out. It's only one of the many things I admire about her."

"Cora—"

"Just stay out of the motel pool," she says and then the line goes dead.

Less than ten minutes after I set the phone down my mother's pounding on the door.

"Teddy! Teddy?"

I draw the dead bolt back and she bursts in.

"Why was the line busy when I called?" she says, rushing to the phone as if I hadn't already hung up. "It was your sister, wasn't it?"

Bobbie steps calmly into the room.

"Tell me, Teddy," my mother says, trying to catch her breath. "What did she say? Is that boy with her?"

From the door I can see the empty public phone booth across the street, the light bulb inside emitting a faint humming sound as if it's about to go off for good.

"Cora's okay," I say, keeping my back to them both. "She just called to say she's fine."

When the air conditioner starts blowing only warm air, my mother tells us just to roll our windows down. There's no time to have the Freon checked.

I sit in the backseat, eyes slitted and head ducked against the rush of dry Texas air. Even Bobbie has tried to hold it in until the next stop for gas. Both breakfast and lunch have been ordered through drive-in windows. We haven't seen a waitress in twenty-four hours.

I've counted seven T-Bird's since we checked out of the room at dawn. Only one of them was the same color as Daniel's but it was driven by a middle-aged woman with New Mexico license plates. If they're trailing us then they've kept out of sight. My mother's only briefly switched off driving with my cousin. It's easier on her, she claims, just to stay behind the wheel.

"I'm going to set the motel thermostat at fifty," Bobbie says, raising her voice to be heard. "Then I'm going to take an ice cold shower."

My mother adjusts the outside mirror, something she's done every ten miles or so. Right before we pass the Martindale exit, she points up at the green sign.

"When your father was at the airfield here," she says, shouting over her shoulder, "we drove down nonstop from Fort Campbell. It took us twenty-seven hours. Of course, we didn't have to worry about two kids."

No one has said a word about Cora all day. My mother is too much on edge to talk about my sister and drive at the same time.

Bobbie holds her hair back to keep it from flying in her face. "What'd you do that for?" she says.

My mother takes off her sunglasses to rub her eyes. She's exhausted and nearly everything seems to set her off. "We didn't have two sous to rub together for a motel," she says finally, "so we just drove in shifts."

"And you made it," my cousin says.

"We did," my mother says, hesitating to finish the sentence. "But then we were young and had a lot to talk about back then."

I pin a corner of the map under my leg. We're getting close to our turnoff and my mother asks me to reread the directions the motel manager gave us over the phone.

"Where 10 crosses 37," I say. "Exit 12. Then the second light past the Alamo."

"Irene took me to see the movie when I was a kid," Bobbie says.

My mother glances at me in the mirror. "Your father used to drag me down all the time," she says. "He knew the place better than his own backyard. I could never understand the fascination."

"I wouldn't mind seeing it," I say but my mother pretends not to hear me. She'll want us to head on to El Paso early if Cora doesn't contact us.

Last night, she made me write down everything my sister had said over the phone. When I read it back to her she constantly stopped me to get the exact wording right. Later, lying in bed, she held the sheets of motel stationery up like an actor studying his lines. "What did she mean by 'pressure,'" she would say and I'd try to explain all over again what I thought my sister was complaining about. Then, right before I finally closed my eyes, she wondered aloud what Cora was going to wear. "Your sister left everything with us," she said and broke down again for the hundredth time.

My mother has put off telling my father the news since there's nothing much he can do ten thousand miles away. Unless, of course, it turns out that I've completely misinterpreted what was said to me by my sister. And that it *is,* in fact, a bona fide kidnapping we're talking about. At which point she'll have my father (or whatever state representative necessary) call out the entire armed services.

In the meantime, she tries not to fall asleep at the wheel by mulling over all the possibilities of my conversation with Cora. That, for instance, my sister was afraid to say what she truly felt in front of Daniel. That he was physically threatening her even as she held the receiver. If that was the case, I'd argued, how come there was no mention of any money? Or how come he would even let her call us in the first place? My mother didn't have any answers to my logical objections but that hasn't kept her from doubting my reliability as a witness.

Bobbie has said little from the start, choosing instead simply to hold my mother's hand without offering any advice. This is a family matter, she seems to say. And strictly speaking she isn't family. At least not immediate family. However, the real reason she's kept her thoughts to herself, I'm convinced, is because she feels Cora's running off might be partly her fault. She believes that when my sister said that she couldn't stand being in the same car with her anymore, she meant my cousin.

"Cora knows what she wants," Bobbie said when we walked down to the Coke machine to let my mother be alone for a few minutes. "And I'm everything she doesn't want. She doesn't want to spend the rest of her life in some place like Chicopee. She doesn't want to wind up working tips for a living. She wants to be her own person." My cousin put her quarter in the machine and stared at the different pictures of soft drink cans. "I can't even make up my mind what to drink," she said and then punched her selection with her fist. "I'm no teenager anymore. I've got to make up my own mind about some things. And if I was honest I'd tell your mother that I'm *glad* your sister's done what she did. Cora's going to be all right. Nobody's going to push her around. I was her age I'd hit the road too. Only this time around I'd get farther than Worcester."

It's dark when we pull into the motel and my mother asks me to come with her to the office. She gets out of the car, looking about as if expecting Cora to be waiting for us.

"Where are we?" she says and leans against the dusty Oldsmobile as if suddenly afraid her legs might give out.

"Texas," I say.

She smiles at my cousin through the dirty windshield. "I thought we'd never get here," she says.

In the office, my mother tells the desk clerk that she's expecting a very important call.

"It doesn't matter what time it comes through," she says, "you're to wake us. Do you understand?"

The man is wearing a T-shirt with "Remember the Alamo and Don't Forget the Stuart Hall Inn Either" stenciled across it.

"Gotcha," he says and hands my mother the key.

"You're on duty the rest of the night?" she says.

"Totally."

My mother opens her pocketbook and places a five-dollar bill on the counter.

"That's for you," she says.

The man looks down at the money and then over at me.

"Sure," he says, covering the bill with his palm. "I'm going to see to it personally."

Back outside, I take the room key from her.

"I'll open up," I say, louder than necessary. But my ears still feel as if sea shells are clamped over them. "You show Bobbie where we are."

My mother considers each of the half-dozen cars in the lot before turning to smile at me.

"Your sister's broken my heart," she says and then walks back to the Oldsmobile.

It's a clear, warm night and I'm reminded of the proving ground in Arizona when I would lie out on the sun-baked driveway and watch the sky slowly fill up with stars. You could see entire constellations in the desert. It's not the same in a city where the smog and the lights keep you from seeing anything. "Nice if you're an astronomer," Cora would say, "or a piece of petrified wood."

I don't really feel angry at my sister. And so there's nothing to forgive. It doesn't matter to me that she's always unhappy or that she can't live with my mother. I only want for us to be together again even if she's right and we'd all be better off just to let nature take its course and scatter us to the four corners of the globe: my father to live with his geisha in the Orient; my mother to the opposite coast from my sister's boarding school in the Hollywood Hills; and me to some friendly, communal home like the Lindbergh's estate for delinquent boys in Hopewell.

At first, I imagine the two bright lights bearing down on me to be the twin stars, Castor and Pollux. But they merge into one like the single beam of an oncoming train. And as I try to locate the North Star to get my bearings, it's already too late to soften the hard contact of concrete.

"I'm ready just to pack it in," my mother says, pressing a cold facecloth to my forehead. "Honest to god I'm ready to turn us all around and head back to Irene's."

But she doesn't mean it. She's just upset about my latest blackout. It was only a slight seizure. Probably from not eating. Or more likely, my mother insists, from worry.

"And what about Cora?" I say.

My mother lifts the rag from my head and wipes her own face. "At this point, sweetheart, I'm thinking that your sister can do what she pleases. It's probably just as well that I stay out of it. That's what she's always telling me to do, isn't it?"

"You know what I feel like?" Bobbie says. "I feel like jumping in the pool."

My mother stretches out on the bed beside me and unfolds the washcloth over her brow. She's taken several sips from her flask to try to help her sleep.

"I'll come with you," I say, throwing the covers back.

My mother opens her eyes but they droop shut again.

"You're not to go anywhere near the water," she says. "Bobbie?"

"You rest, Rosemary," my cousin says. "We won't be long."

My mother's exhausted from having done all the driving but can't seem to drop off.

Bobbie changes quickly in the bathroom.

"Let me grab some quarters," she whispers, tiptoeing across the carpeted floor to her pocketbook. "You can get us a couple soft drinks."

"No swimming," my mother mutters.

I fold the complimentary newspaper under my arm and ease the door shut behind us, double-checking the lock.

"I like a man looks out for his girls," Bobbie says.

I hold the paper out and we both stand reading the large head-lines. The *Columbia* has fired its main engine and for the first time gone into orbit around the dark side of the moon.

This seems even more amazing to me than walking on the lunar surface.

"No one has ever seen what they'll see," I say. "Think about that."

Bobbie seems to for a moment but then asks what channel the Miss Universe beauty pageant comes on tonight.

"I don't want to miss it," she says and walks ahead of me like one of the finalists in the swimsuit competition, her bare heels never touching the ground.

Although the pool's still lighted there's a chain looped between two metal posts with a "closed" sign hanging from it. Bobbie waves and makes a tipping motion with one hand to remind me about the drinks.

While my mother held an ice cube to the welt on my elbow (which apparently had hit before my head), she asked me what the Lindberghs did to pass the time while they waited to hear from the kidnappers. She'd just uncorked her flask and had that tired look she gets whenever my father is off earning his hazard-duty pay.

"They had a lot of people in the house," I said. "Hundreds of cops and investigators. Everybody in the world wanted to be there."

My mother nodded, moving the ice cube across her own forehead. "Whereas we don't even have your father," she said. "That's the difference."

I told her it wasn't the only one. For example, Cora wasn't exactly a baby. And she didn't get carried out a window in her pajamas. Not to mention there not being any ransom note. However, the biggest difference was that she hadn't been kidnapped in the first place. She was just going where we were going in a different car.

I didn't know how much I believed any of this but it made me feel better to have said it. Which is probably what all the people at the Lindberghs' were doing most of that first night too: trying to comfort the parents with lies.

Bobbie's floating in the deep end when I set her drink on the diving board. Her arms are stretched out, palms up, her legs slightly parted and her toes curled back. My cousin's stomach appears to rise slightly out of the water like a small island.

I take my shoes off and roll my pants up. The pool's surrounded by palm trees and I sit by the board and dip my feet into the warm water, mosquitoes humming at my ear.

"Teddy?"

My cousin gives me a wary look as she comes up the ladder, the water washing down her tanned limbs.

I glance at my feet in the pool bent at the ankle from refraction.

"I'm thinking we better keep an eye on your momma," my cousin says and takes a swig of her drink. "What do you think?"

I nod.

"She's like Irene," she says. "Usually it'll be a day or two later before things really kind of hit her. So I think we better watch out for her."

"Maybe you ought to drive then," I say.

She wipes the moisture from the aluminum can. "Once, when you and Cora were little, your mom and dad rented a place out at the shore. They took Irene along to help baby-sit."

In my cousin's version it's my sister who wanders off. And this time it's my aunt who has the conniption.

"Irene never learned how to swim so she panicked," Bobbie says smiling at me, the Coke between her legs. "I guess I would have too. But two minutes later Cora showed up. She'd just found someone else's beach umbrella to sit under. Anyway, it wasn't until the next day when we're all back in Chicopee that Irene got the shakes. It took that long for everything to finally sink in. She couldn't sleep for a week."

I lift my feet out of the water and rest them on the drainage gutter. "And so you think Mom might crack?"

"I think she's a lot like her sister. I guess I'm saying it's just something that kind of runs in the family. And we're all of us in the same family. Right?"

She collects the towel from the folding chair and wraps it around her shoulders.

"My sister's an idiot," I say. "All she thinks about is herself. That runs in this family too."

I stand up too fast and the palm trees do a little dance.

"All right," my cousin says, catching hold of me. She braces herself on the slippery tiles, one arm about my waist. "How we doing?"

I point to the chaise longue and she leads me over to it.

"I didn't have much lunch," I say.

She kneels in front of me on the chair. "I guess I got somebody else to keep an eye on," she says.

The mosquitoes buzz about us and I wave my arm weakly.

"This boy your sister's with," my cousin says. "You think he's all right then?"

"I guess so. He's a pacifist."

Bobbie smiles. "That's what they all say. But I never knew one didn't make a pass eventually."

I hand her the entertainment section of the paper.

"Good," she says when she finds the write-up on the beauty pageant. "It comes on at nine."

I read about how the spacecraft has been coasting at twenty-four hundred miles an hour. The article explains how sunlight is unfiltered in space, and so Mike Collins, the pilot, has had to keep the ship rolling slowly so no one side gets overheated. I tell Bobbie it's how I always feel around Cora: that if she stays in one place too long she's liable to explode.

"Cora's going to be all right," my cousin says. "Your sister can take care of herself."

I want to believe this too but my sister's never really been on her own before. She talks big but she's spent all of her life living on one post or another protected by MP's and guardhouses. It's my cousin who's been out in the world even though she's never gotten much farther than Chicopee's city limits. Cora and I are brats. We follow orders. That's what makes us dependents.

My mother's standing beside the bed when Bobbie unlocks the door.

"Somebody just called and hung up," she says. "I don't think it was a wrong number."

"Cora?" I say.

She looks back down at the receiver as if expecting it to ring again.

"I called the office and the boy said someone asked for our room."

Bobbie steps into the bathroom for a dry towel.

"Did he say if it was a girl's voice?" she asks.

My mother nods. "A female's, yes." She looks at me. "Next time I want you to answer it."

My cousin bends over to dry her hair. "That's probably a good idea."

My mother sits back down on the bed and leans against the headboard. "It's probably the first good idea I've had since we pulled out of Chicopee."

"*Just* tell her Daddy doesn't have to know," my mother says as I lift Cora's suitcase into the back of the Oldsmobile. "Tell her there won't be any questions asked. Just tell her . . ."

But she has to stop.

"Mom," I say. "It's no big deal. You know how she is. She's just crazy. That's all."

My mother lowers her hand from her forehead. "Okay, sweetheart. I'll wait in the room. Just promise to come straight back."

Bobbie's been watching all of this in the side mirror and starts up the engine.

Last night, just after the new Miss Universe was crowned, Cora called. Only this time I answered the phone and Bobbie quickly lowered the sound on the TV.

"She's right there breathing down your neck, isn't she?" Cora said.

My mother didn't say anything but kept her ear next to mine on the phone.

"Where are you?" I said.

"She's going to smother you, Teddy," my sister said. "And I'm beginning to think she's not even aware of it."

"Where are you?" I said. "San Antonio?"

"No, I'm in Taipei. Where the hell do you think I am?"

I almost wanted to say that I didn't care. That she could go back to Amish country if it was up to me. But, of course, nothing was up to me.

"Why are you calling?" I said. "What do you want?"

My mother suddenly stepped back, gazing at me dumbstruck.

"Are you mad at me too?" my sister said.

"What am I supposed to be? You don't tell us anything, you just disappear."

"Your day's coming," she said. *"Theodore: 27."*

I could hear a TV in the background. She had the pageant on.

"I'll see you at noon," Cora said. "Just remember the suitcase."

Bobbie was trying to read Bob Barker's lips as he straightened the crown on Miss Philippines's teased hair.

"Nose job," my sister said when the new Miss Universe started down the runway. "Right out of the box."

I wanted to ask about Daniel but decided against it with my mother there.

"So just leave Mom at the motel," my sister said. "I'm not up for *Rigoletto.*"

I couldn't think of anything else to say.

"I guess I'll see you then," I said finally.

"I'll be the one in the wrinkled clothes."

My mother stands back from the car and I roll my window down.

"Maybe I should just bring a gun and shoot her," I say.

She doesn't smile. She'd spent most of the night pressing my sister's clothes with her portable iron.

Bobbie waves to my mother and makes a face at the broken air conditioner.

"Going to be a hot one," she says.

We take Route 37 straight downtown. The Alamo's in the heart of the city.

My cousin flips the visor. "The way I figure it," she says, "I'm only halfway through the first trimester. I could still do something about it."

She avoids giving it a sex. It's her "problem" or her "condition" or even her "pain." But she thinks Las Vegas might be best for where she's headed. At least right now. It's the place that's kind of stuck in her mind. And, besides, Elvis will be at the Resorts International, his first public performance in nearly a decade. She considers it a kind of omen.

"You know what I mean?" she says. "Just think of what *he* must be going through."

But I'm having a hard time concentrating.

"There's no rush," she says. "I got some more thinking to do between here and there anyway."

In the distance, I can see the seven-hundred-and-fifty-foot Tower of the Americas left over from the Texas World's Fair. The motel manager had told us if we found the tower we couldn't miss the Alamo.

"How about I do a little sight-seeing," Bobbie says after parking the car in a pay lot across from the museum. "It'll make it easier on your sister."

We agree to meet at the Cenotaph in the plaza. It's the monument with all the names of those who died defending the fort.

"Tell Cora I'm sorry," my cousin says. "I know she wasn't real crazy about me coming along."

"Who cares what she thinks," I say. "My sister's a spoiled brat."

But Bobbie's already across the street, her long-strapped pocketbook bobbing at her hip.

I don't remember the Alamo. I was only three when my father was assigned to Martindale. But it surprises me how small it looks when I cross the plaza and see its yellow stone facade shining in

the sunlight. It's hard to believe that the Mexican army took thirteen days to overrun it.

I'm sitting in the grass beneath one of the palm trees when I see
my sister stride up to the wide oak doors to the mission, turn
about and walk back out into the middle of the courtyard. Daniel's not with her.

I hesitate for a moment watching her glance about as if put off
that she has to wait for her younger brother. As soon as I step out
of the shade into the light Cora sees me and heads over.

"So," and she waves back at the famous landmark. "Looks a
lot like the one they used in the movie, doesn't it?"

But the "real" one, the one the studio built for the movie, is
over near Brackettville.

"The guides don't like to tell you that," she says. "They're
afraid it'd be a letdown. And, of course, it is. Hollywood does
everything better."

Then she tells me how John Wayne hired a Marine drill sergeant to handle the four thousand extras and that production was
threatened when Laurence Harvey had a cannon wheel roll over
his foot.

My sister's talking a mile a minute, a sign that she's nervous.
But she can see that I'm by myself.

"So," she says. "Still mad?"

"I guess not."

She lifts her sunglasses and it's obvious that she hasn't slept
much.

"Mom all right?"

"She just wants you to . . ."

My sister looks away, embarrassed for me.

"Listen, Teddy," and she's shaking her head. "You're making
a big thing out of this. I'm just taking some time off, that's all.
You'll come to a point when—"

"I'd never hurt Mom," I say angrily. "I'd never do what you
did to her."

She stands facing the Alamo. No one's entered or left the place the whole time. It doesn't seem that popular an attraction.

"Let me explain something to you, Teddy." My sister stops as if uncertain whether it's even worth trying. "How can I phrase this delicately?" She taps her fingernail against her front tooth. "All right, here it is. Mom and Dad are kaput. This whole trip's a joke. We'll get over there and even *Mom'll* be able to figure out Daddy's little domestic scene. And, believe me, there won't be a fan big enough for what's going to hit it. Which leaves the kiddies—us— where? On another slow boat back to Chicopee. You can't see that?"

"I see what you've done to Mom."

My sister drops her hands to her sides. "What *I've* done to Mom. That's rich. Listen," but she gives up. "I'm not even going to get into that. Just think of it as coming attractions. And your turn's coming."

"I don't know what you're talking about," I say.

She looks past me to where I've left her suitcase under the palm tree. "No, I guess you don't," and she steps around me.

"What about Daniel?" I say. "Did he make you leave?"

She's ducked into the shade and is kneeling in the grass.

"He's just along for the ride," and she unlocks the suitcase. "He'll take me as far as Vegas. That's the deal."

She opens the suitcase and for a moment just stares at her folded clothes.

"This is what I mean," my sister says, her back to me. "This is typical."

"What?" I come around in front of her. "That Mom does something nice for you? You're just a brat, that's all."

She stands up, dusting her slacks off. "You don't see what this is all about, do you?"

I look back down at the blouse I'd watched my mother spend half an hour ironing.

"This is how she keeps her claws in you," my sister says,

sweeping her hand low. "This is how she won't let you go." She bends down to close the suitcase. "Just tell her I'll see her in a couple days."

"Tell her yourself."

Cora looks at me then yanks the handle up and her clothes spill out at her feet.

"Shit."

A Japanese couple, cameras crisscrossing their chests, start over toward us but Cora waves them off.

"Everything's under control," she says and rolls her eyes at me. "They're so goddamn polite it's nauseating. And I'm supposed to spend two years of my life with that?"

"We're going to Formosa," I say and can see my mother has even pressed her underwear. "Not Japan."

"*You're* going to Formosa," and she pounds the snaps shut with her fists. "Where I'm going is another matter." She straddles the suitcase like a hitchhiker. "Look, little brother. I don't blame you for anything. Believe me, I know what you're up against. It's just I've been at this a little longer than you. So we're coming at it from different angles. You got yours, I got mine."

I reach into my back pocket. "Mom wanted me to give you this," I say.

Cora smiles crookedly. "Gee, I wonder what that could be," and she holds the white envelope to her forehead. "A bribe?"

"Why don't you open it later," I say. "I don't need to see it."

She opens the envelope anyway and we both stare at the thick wad of money.

Cora takes two ten-dollar bills and hands the rest back to me. "She's probably memorized all the serial numbers anyway." My sister picks up her suitcase. "Look, tell her not to worry about Daniel. He's what she'd call 'a nice boy.' "

But Daniel's suddenly frightening to me. "If he hurts you," I hear myself say, "I'll kill him."

My sister's expression isn't really a smile. It's more pitying.

"Teddy," she says finally. "I'll see you in a couple of days, okay?"

I don't want her to see me crying and so I turn my back and walk away.

"Forget about Elvis," she calls out. "We'll look Howard Hughes up."

My mother frames me in the rearview mirror. She's thought about our situation the past three hundred miles and can come to only one conclusion. My father will have to finish off his tour of duty alone and rejoin us Stateside in eighteen months. Tonight she'll call him so that he might contact whoever he has to contact to cancel our berth aboard the USS *Anderson*.

Neither Bobbie (who acts as if Cora's headphones have been up too high to have heard a word) nor I say anything in response. I only stare out at the cactuses and creosote bushes and rusted barbed wire of the airless Texas landscape. But mostly I'm mum because I don't want to believe that my mother is really serious. And yet I know that she is and that she's terrified of my sister winding up an MIA.

After rereading the same sentence half a dozen times (the commander has forbidden Matt even to raise the subject of remaining behind with his Eskimo mistress and infant son), I fold the corner over on the page and slump down in the seat. Keeping my head below the half-open window, I apply another coat of ChapStick to my cracked lips. It's impossible to read. All I can think about is that my mother is upset enough to actually go through with her threat.

Later, after a climb of nearly twenty-five hundred feet into the Apache Mountains, the temperature gauge has inched into the red again when we pull into a small filling station. The attendant, a boy not much older than me, wraps a wet rag about his fist to keep from scalding his fingers on the radiator. But he can still only back off from the raised hood. And so for the next half-hour, my mother, my cousin, and I sit in the shade of an ancient Sinclair station waiting for the engine to cool off enough that the metal cap can be unscrewed.

Usually his mother's here to work the register, the boy tells us, but today she's in a hospital in Odessa with a mysterious ailment that causes her nose to bleed. When Bobbie asks about his father, he only smiles broadly, his brown teeth stained from chewing tobacco (he'd pried the flat round tin from his back pocket as he pumped the gas). "My old lady don't want him around," he says and spits a long stream of juice at his feet.

"How far's El Paso?" my mother asks. She changes the subject because she's distraught and doesn't want to risk feeling overly sorry for him.

"Never been," the boy says, returning my mother's credit card with a smudged thumbprint on it. "Nobody ever took me."

Later, as we coast back down the mountain, I look up Odessa on the map. It's less than a hundred miles due north. "One thing brats got over the population at large," Cora likes to say. "The house number changes."

I try not to look for T-Birds but can't help craning over my shoulder whenever a car moves up behind us. Every hour or so we stop to prevent the engine from overheating and to restock the ice chest but my mother refuses to share the driving with her niece. And with the humidity and the hypnotic drone of the tires, I keep my eye on the mirror to be certain that she's still conscious at the wheel.

Not another word will be said about her decision, of course. It's just the way we do things in this family. "And what I so much love about the life," Cora has always complained of the military. "You get your orders from on high. You don't ask questions. You march into the sunset."

We stop for dinner at the Pecante Corral, an old hunter's lodge that's been converted into a Mexican restaurant. Thousands of patrons' clipped ties hang from the timber rafters. My mother vaguely recalls stopping here once when my father was only a captain and Cora still in diapers.

"All I really remember is that your sister was a lot easier to handle," she says.

It's still early for dinner and a mariachi band plays without much enthusiasm to the empty dance floor.

After ordering the jumbo fajitas, Bobbie dips the corner of her napkin into her ice water and dabs at my red forehead.

"We need to get this boy some skin balm," she says. "He's been wind blown."

My mother quickly downs her margarita and rises in the booth to wave at our wandering waiter. "It'll be cooler soon as the sun goes down," she says.

"You don't want to get a room?" my cousin says. Once we're on the other side of El Paso there doesn't look to be much to recommend itself.

"I've decided to go by way of Yuma," my mother says. "It's a little bit of a detour but Cora knows the route. Teddy's father used to command the proving ground there." She studies her silverware then looks up at me guiltily. "You remember how lovely the desert was at night, honey. Anyway, you two can sleep."

Bobbie catches my eye but doesn't say anything. El Paso's still another four hours off.

When the waiter trots back over, my mother asks him if the margaritas come in a pitcher. "It has a very nice taste," she says, plinking her glass. "Usually I'm not that fond of mixed drinks."

In fact, until recently my mother's not been that fond of anything stronger than a Tom Collins. The only time I've ever really seen her with what my father called a "snootful," was the night she won the exacta at Jefferson Downs outside Fort Hood. On the ride home they'd stopped by the officers' club to celebrate and she'd tried the spiked Hawaiian Punch left over from the usual Friday night Luau Hour. "We ought to keep it on tap," Cora said to me as we watched my mother paper the kitchen table with twenty-dollar bills. Ride 'em Cowboy and Bonus Bonanza, a couple of longshots, had paid over sixteen hundred dollars and they'd collected their winnings in cash. "The ponies will make you free," Cora said as my mother kicked her shoes off and twirled her sweater overhead like a lasso before puking into the kitchen sink. This was also her final weekend with my father before he would fly alone to Burma for a nine-month solo tour of duty.

"We're going to have to watch her," Bobbie says when my mother heads back to the rest room. "She's like Irene. They don't have a real high tolerance."

I pour the rest of my ice water into the pitcher, studying my cousin for any sign that she knows more than she's letting on.

"I guess that makes you the driver," I say.

My mother takes the long way back around the dance floor, waving to the mariachi players who are tuning their guitars for a second set.

"It's very nice," she says, easing herself down into the booth. "Very homey." And she examines the pitcher for a moment. "The waiter refill us?"

My mother's eyes already look a little squirrely but then she's been driving nonstop since this morning.

"If you two want to order something for dessert, go ahead," she says and swigs her drink as if it were Kool-Aid. "Everything looks real appetizing."

I can tell that we're only making her nervous.

"What do you think?" she says at last. "Your sister going to be there ahead of us?"

Cora, of course, has *always* been there ahead of us but that isn't what my mother wants to hear from me.

"They're not loaded down like us," I say. "They're traveling pretty light."

My mother takes this as the good news she was looking for.

"You're right, honey. They'll probably pull in late tomorrow."

Bobbie declines another iced tea and asks the waiter when the place fills up.

"Saturday," he says, peering at my mother who's built a small house out of the packets of sugar.

My cousin glances across the floor at the band and all four of its members raise their instruments at her.

"Maybe we ought to get back on the road," I offer. "Radiator's got to be cooled off by now."

My mother taps the bottom sugar packets with her spoon and they slide across the slick table.

"Teddy's worried his mother's having too much to drink," she says when she sends the waiter for another pitcher. "And he's right."

"We could maybe make another fifty miles or so," my cousin says. "Then find a motel with a great air conditioner."

"I guess I don't know my own child," my mother says. "One minute she's in my rearview mirror, the next she's in some stranger's car."

"Cora lives in a dream world," I say. "She thinks we should be going to Paris, that's all. She'll get over it. You know her."

My mother palms her glass. "I don't even know her father," she says more to herself than to us.

Bobbie reaches across the table to squeeze my mother's arm.

"You know them fine," she says.

But my mother's shaking her head. "I didn't listen to her," she says. "Same way her father doesn't listen to me."

Our waiter returns to inform us he'll be going on his break now and asks if there'll be anything else.

My mother prints her initials on the frosted pitcher. "That's what I need," she says. "A nice long break."

The waiter exchanges our paper napkin dispenser for a full one then places the check face down in front of Bobbie. "Very good," he says, backing away and bowing awkwardly.

"Your grandmother was part French," my mother says to me as I watch the letters run down the wet pitcher. "I've always thought that was who your sister took after. My mother was very temperamental. She wanted to be on the stage. But her parents wouldn't have anything to do with it."

"Was she talented?" I ask.

"She thought so," my mother says.

"That *does* sound like Cora," I say.

Bobbie draws the pitcher toward her. "One drink's not going to kill me," she says and fills her iced tea glass.

My mother smiles at her niece. "You're going to like it," she says. "It's very south of the border."

"I hate to see anyone have to drink alone," my cousin says. "That's something Lou started doing with me."

My mother looks up. "Lou not take a drink!"

"Just to annoy me," Bobbie explains. "Then I'd find half a dozen cans in the garbage the next morning. He'll wait till I fall asleep before he has a few."

"Terrible," my mother says sympathetically.

My cousin folds her napkin into a triangle. "Well, I can do a few things on my own, too."

My mother lifts her glass in a toast. "I'm going to drink to that. That sounds like an admirable idea." And she looks across at me. "It's curious but one thing alcohol will do to your mother is to make her speak quite clearly. My vocabulary actually improves. I'll come up with words I didn't knew I know . . . know I knew. Your father was the first person to notice this."

We sit and listen to the band play several Tijuana Brass tunes and when our waiter doesn't come back from his break, Bobbie carries our pitcher into the kitchen, allowing the swing doors to whoosh shut behind her.

"Your cousin has what your mother lacks," my mother says. "Do you know what that is, sweetheart?"

She's gazing at me the way she gazes at the highway after two hours without a stop.

"No."

"Chutzpah," she says. "And you want to know why your mother's a failure?"

My cousin suddenly explodes out of the kitchen, a new pitcher of margaritas swaying dangerously in her hand.

"Because your mother's all talk," my mother says. "All talk and no action."

Bobbie slides into the booth without spilling a drop.

"Hector's back there puffing away on a cigarette reading the racing form," she says. "He told me to help myself. It's on the house."

"Very good," my mother says. "Let's drink to the house."

My cousin chugs her margarita. "One thing I hate to be is behind."

My mother raises her voice as if we're still in the car. "It's what can happen to you," she says. "You get left behind."

By Bobbie's third glass I'm fairly certain we'll be spending the night in the nearest motel. When Hector returns, I ask him which one that would be.

He looks at Bobbie then over at my mother. "The Hacienda Inn," he says. "You can leave the car in the lot."

By the time Bobbie pours the last of the pitcher my mother's resting her head back against the booth, her eyes closed.

"It's different," my cousin says, examining her drink as if something is puzzling her. "It feels light on your tongue until you swallow it. Not like any margarita I ever had. I don't even think this *is* a margarita. I think Hector's pulling our chain."

She opens a paper napkin and waves it overhead to get Hector's attention. Our waiter finally drifts over.

"Yes, ma'am?"

"Hector," and my cousin rests her hand on my mother's shoulder. "What have you done to my aunt?"

But Hector only tips the pitcher and asks if "madam" would care for a refill.

Bobbie studies him for a moment as if to detect any sign of sarcasm.

"Yes," she says at last. "One more for the road."

I watch Hector circle the dance floor. It's Happy Hour and the band reminds everyone to take advantage of the Two-for-One special.

"That's what I am," my cousin says when Hector sets the new pitcher down. "A Two-for-One special."

Hector retallies the check. "Yes, ma'am," he says.

But there are other tables to tend to now and he does his little retreating bow.

"Lou's like that," my cousin says to me. "He never looks at you when you talk to him." She dips her entire glass into the pitcher. "That's why I love my cousin. He even looks at me when I'm *not* talking to him."

"Yes, ma'am."

Bobbie laughs. "You're your sister's brother," she says. "It's how come you're so quick."

"Without her I'm nothing," I say.

She looks over at my mother who's making a slight hissing sound with her breathing. "So who'd you like last night? I'll bet you anything Lou picked the one from Israel."

It's a moment before I understand she's talking about Miss Universe. Cora had waited until the winner was announced before she called. Next to the Academy Awards my sister loves beauty pageants.

"I guess I wasn't really paying that much attention," I say. "Cora said Daddy would have gone for Miss Thailand."

Bobbie takes a napkin from the dispenser to dry her elbow. "That's where Lou and your father are so different," she says. "Lou likes his girls big," she says. "The bigger the better. As long as it's the right kind of big."

"Big," I say.

"Buxom's the word he'll use," she says. "He used to say I was buxom. Now I guess I'm something else far as Lou Hammuck's concerned."

"I'd pick you over Miss Israel any day," I say.

My cousin smoothes the wet napkin out thoughtfully. "That's because right now you like big," she says. "But you'll grow out of it. The time you're your father's age you'll pick Miss Thailand too. You'll have good taste."

"I already have good taste."

My cousin listens to the band play another Herb Alpert song before directing her gaze back at me.

"You're thinking I should watch what I drink," she says.

I don't say anything.

"That's what I'm doing," she says. "I'm watching what I drink."

Like a Muzak tape, the band plays the same Tijuana Brass tunes in the exact order they'd played them earlier. In the meantime, someone periodically strays over from the bar to ask Bobbie to dance but she turns them all down. "Then how about your girlfriend?" one of them wonders and both my cousin and I look over at my mother who sits with her face cradled in her arms on the table. When the man rejoins his friends, Bobbie smiles lopsidedly at me.

"Ask me how I know I'm drunk," she says. "Go ahead."

My mother hasn't moved or uttered a word in over an hour and my cousin has done most of the talking.

"How?" I say.

"Because my scalp itches. And because my shoes feel three sizes too small." She scratches the back of her head. "And I can tell you something else."

I feel under the table for my mother's pocketbook. "What?"

"This," she says. "I'm going to fall asleep very soon. I don't want to scare you. I just want you to know what's probably going to happen here."

I find some cash in my mother's wallet and set the ashtray on top of it.

Hector immediately hustles over and, when he sees his tip, helps me slide my mother out of the booth.

"The Hacienda Inn," he says.

While we wait for the courtesy van Hector explains how the arrangement keeps everybody happy.

"We clear the lounge and they fill their rooms slow nights. Which is when we schedule Happy Hour."

At the motel register, Bobbie stands with her back to me, swaying slightly, both elbows on the high counter. The van idles outside, my mother's head resting against the back of the seat as if she's about to have her hair done.

The driver, a woman in her late sixties wearing pin curlers, drops us off directly in front of our room and I unlock the door and throw the bedcovers back before Bobbie and I steer my mother in.

"Double's all yours," my cousin says and sits down on the mattress. She stares at her feet for a moment and then focuses hazily on me. "A favor?" She drops backward onto the bed, just missing my mother. "Shoes."

I cup my hand under each heel and before I can slip them off she's asleep.

My mother lies with her arms and legs spread out in a kind of free fall. Luckily, it's a generous queen, the two beds taking up most of the room. "You've seen one link," Cora would say. "You've seen the chain." And it's true. In most budget motels you can find your way about in the dark. It doesn't matter if you're outside El Paso or in downtown Reno. There's always going to be the same glass in a slip jacket on the metal shelf over the bathroom sink. When she was my age, Cora collected the paper banners across the toilet. She kept them in a large scrapbook with the date, city, and "County Seat" printed under each one. "Most girls would save the matchbooks," my mother would say to her. "Or even the paper place mats."

Outside, I check to be certain I have the room key and then I lock the door behind me.

I've crossed the country half a dozen times, watching my father drive with just his palm lightly resting on the bottom of the wheel. It's no mystery how to handle an automatic. You point the little red arrow at "D" and then you press the gas, keeping your foot poised above the brake (not "riding" it as my father accuses my mother of doing).

And yet when I finally settle into the front seat of the Oldsmobile, nothing looks that easy and I sit for a moment, considering my best route.

But I'm not prepared for the jet engine explosion of the motor and my wet palms slide around the wheel as if lubricated. I wipe them on my pants before easing the shift arrow from "Park." The trick is in not pressing down too hard on the gas. I've learned at least that from taking several passes in the driveway.

And yet as I gently apply gradual pressure to the accelerator, there's no acceleration. The car doesn't budge. I try to recall how Buzz Aldrin always contemplates a mental checklist before docking procedures, and I run through my own: foot on proper pedal, gas in tank, no concrete parking block in front of the car, no lights on the dashboard . . . The emergency brake. I reach under the steering wheel and unlock it.

It's my mother I get my cautious streak from. This time the car lurches and I slam my foot down. There's no one in sight. Cora learned how to drive just before we came up to Chicopee. My father would take her out on Sundays to practice in the Pentagon's parking lot. As with everything else Cora was a quick study even though my mother refused to allow her to get behind the wheel this trip. "When we're with your father again and he's sitting in the front seat with you," she promised my sister, "we'll see about a license. And not a minute sooner."

My father joked that when the time came for me to get a learner's permit, he'd try to get assigned to another proving ground. But my mother didn't like him talking about driving lessons when I wasn't even a teenager yet. "He doesn't need to be thinking about licenses," she protested. "There's plenty of time for that." Later, Cora would tell me that I should prepare myself. "She'll put every kind of roadblock in your way she can come up with. Believe me, anything that could possibly loosen the apron strings, you can forget about. She'll be tying you in knots every chance she gets."

I carefully press back down on the gas. The speedometer flicks then settles just under the ten as I turn the wheel to bump over the curb and out onto the access road. It's an easy three blocks to the motel lot and I manage to steer the car into the slot closest to our room and turn off the engine. Then I take my foot off the brake and listen to the clicking sounds of the engine as it settles down.

There are no cop cars or flashing red lights. No dented fenders. I've managed to retrieve the Oldsmobile without arousing any suspicions. And all of this without a teacher. Even Cora needed my father as coach the first few times out. But I've done everything on my own. Just by talking myself through it and not getting excited.

Still, when I lock the door after me, I feel a drop of sweat burn down my side, and my legs are as light and hollow-feeling as from a seizure. But I'm not out of it. All I've really been is on my own for ten minutes. And for that to happen, my mother has to be unconscious, my sister kidnapped, and my father in China.

I listen to my mother talk in her sleep. Despite her fierce hang-over and aching legs she has pushed across what Cora used to call the Arizona Outback. But when no word came from my sister in El Paso there seemed no reason not to press on. "We'll let your father decide," she mumbles, her toes poking out from under the sheet. "We'll leave it to him." My cousin grunts her husband's name then turns onto her side. "You can come after me," she says. "Maybe you'll find out something. Who knows?"

Our little motel is less than a stone's throw from Yuma's noto-rious territorial prison, the only thing that Cora ever found re-deeming about the place. And only because it's where they filmed the popular television series with Nick Adams. This was the period that marked the onset of my sister's "condition," a mysterious ailment for which every Army doctor consulted blamed an overac-tive thyroid. But having read all of the medical literature in print, Cora came up with her own self-diagnosis: psychological stress from an insufferably overbearing parent had caused all her pres-sure-related symptoms. Each day she stared at her swollen eyes in the bathroom mirror and cursed my mother. For once upon a time, she'd had my father's eyes, brown and movie star beautiful. Now they bulged like a bullfrog's and there was only one person to blame.

Whenever my sister felt most vulnerable she'd seek out her younger sibling for the truth. *Did* they look puffy to me? But when I could only shrug my ten-year-old shoulders, she would glare venomously and accuse me of holding out to spare her feelings. "She'll get over it," was all my mother would say whenever I asked about my sister's mercurial mood swings. "It's just a phase."

I find my mother's penlight on her car keys (next to the tiny can of mace) and rest my book on my chest in bed. Matt's back aboard the *Roosevelt* and the ship is working its slow progress through the dangerous ice floes that clog their route home.

Despite countless hazards along the way, the commander has retreated to his cabin and allows his navigator to make all the crucial decisions. For two months Peary avoids contact with any of the crew including his bewildered Negro assistant. His aloofness has plunged Matt into deep despair. He'd forsaken his Eskimo wife and child to accompany Peary in his life's ambition and now the commander seems to want nothing more to do with him. Nearly all of his waking hours Matt spends going over in his mind his actions during their final assault on the Pole and what he must have said or done to cause the commander's shunning of him.

I roll over to see my mother reach out from under the covers to silence her travel alarm (she wants to take advantage of the cooler morning temperatures).

"Six o'clock," she says groggily. "Let's see if we can be out of here in twenty minutes."

After a drive-thru at McDonald's, we pass over the Chocolate Mountains and head toward Blythe.

It's the same road Cora and I traveled each day to the public school in Yuma. Inferno High, my sister called it, and along with the rest of the brats from the proving ground, we were in classes with mostly poor mestizos who could barely speak English. But even harder for Cora to take was being so tantalizingly close to her Mecca, Los Angeles, just across the river. "There is no God," she would lament as we bounced about in the backseat of the swelter-ing Army bus. "Otherwise she'd have aimed a *real* meteor at this hellhole."

My mother watches the temperature gauge, keeping the speed-ometer needle perched at a cautious and steady fifty. She has detoured up 95 instead of the shorter route through Phoenix in hopes that Cora might be nostalgic about our old assignment. But my guess is that given my sister's memories of the place she'd be more likely to come by way of Canada.

Bobbie has lost interest in Cora's tapes and allows my mother to choose the station on the radio. For the first few hours, my cousin doesn't appear to blink behind her dark glasses and only stares out at the relentless dunes.

As the heat shimmers above the highway in a silver wave, I accomplish something rare for me in a moving vehicle: I doze off. The backseat is already as warm as the sand that sifts across the asphalt and just as monotonous. And I know that even if my mother should fall asleep, the odds are against her finding any-thing to hit.

In my dream, we are all at sea, halfway to China on an ancient military cruiser. About to give birth, Bobbie moans pathetically in the bunk below me.

"It'll be just her luck it'll look like Lou," Cora is saying. "And have a weak back."

Through the porthole I can see first the gray water and then with the heavy roll of the ship, the grayer sky. The Dramamine isn't working and I grip the metal frame of the bunk bed to keep from being pitched out.

"How we doing?"

It's my mother's voice and I open my eyes.

"Feel better?" Bobbie asks.

I sit up to see that we're parked outside a diner.

"You've been resting," my mother says.

I'm wearing my pajama top.

"You had a little accident a ways back," and she feels my damp forehead. "We had to change shirts."

I still have on my jeans although my pants leg is wet.

"I was sick?"

Bobbie's nodding. "I think it was the sausage with your pancakes," she says.

But my mother's shaking her head.

"Probably a combination of things." She has a short sleeve shirt which she sets down beside me. "The heat. The car. Your . . ." She shrugs her shoulders. "How about we take a little break. Try to get something back on your stomach. You feel like toast?"

In fact, I have the kind of empty sensation that only comes after a seizure.

"Quite a while," my mother says when I ask how long I've been out. "But we've made very good time."

When I swing open the door, I feel weightless, as if my limbs are pumped full of air like one of the astronauts' pressurized suits. And I float into the restaurant.

Bobbie heads directly to the ladies' room. She'll just be having coffee.

In the booth, my mother anxiously straightens her silverware.

"I don't think we're going to see your sister again," she says as soon as the waitress is gone. "I've only been fooling myself." She doesn't look up from folding her napkin into a tight square. "I thought it was just something she'd grow out of."

With her head down I can see the white streak of hair that looks as if it had been done at the beauty parlor. But my mother has never used even a rinse. "Less is more," she tried advising Cora on makeup. "You don't want to muck it up." This was when my sister had first persuaded herself that her thyroid had ruined her looks. She would be a freak the rest of her life. And all because of a mother who smothered her young.

"I guess your sister and I just never spoke the same language," my mother says, speaking ominously in the past tense. "But I just have this feeling that she's not going to show up. That we're going to sit in the desert and wait for nothing."

I can smell our order. The cook has set the plates out for the waitress to carry over to us. My stomach has been growling since I closed the menu. I can't concentrate on sympathizing with my mother. I only want to eat.

Bobbie returns from the rest room having relined her eyes and added a new layer of lipstick. When she was Cora's age, she told me once, she could go through an entire tube of lipstick on a good Saturday. "That's when the boys were all over the place. You couldn't swing a stick and not hit one."

"They got some slot machines in the ladies' room," my cousin says. "I guess we crossed the border."

"Teddy and I were talking about his sister," my mother says. "I was telling him I don't think we're going to be seeing her this stop."

Bobbie looks over at me and then back at my mother. She's not sure how to take this.

"Well, I think we ought to wait and see," my cousin says. "Maybe she'll surprise us. Cora likes surprising people."

My mother's face brightens.

"You think so, honey?" And she's nodding at both of us. "Honestly?"

The waitress whisks in with several large white plates balanced up her arm like a street juggler.

"The 'Manly Breakfast,' " she says, setting each piece of crockery down with a clatter. "Enough here for an army." And she unhooks two coffee cups from her thumb. "Caffeine for the ladies." She steps back to survey her work proudly. "Now what else?"

"Just the check," my mother says and pushes her coffee to the side.

The waitress watches me launch into the tall stack of pancakes.

"Got yourself a hungry jack there," she says.

And I suddenly realize that they're all watching me as a stream of syrup curls from the corner of my mouth.

"You eat up," my mother says and both Bobbie and the waitress smile approvingly.

I don't stop to look up again and barely chew the first few mouthfuls, washing everything down with eye-watering gulps of cold milk.

"He's got an appetite," my cousin says when I start in on the mountain of scrambled eggs, feeding the stiff bacon into my mouth like lumber into a shredder.

My mother slides the small side plate of biscuits in closer. "It counts for two meals," she says. "You figure he missed one."

But afterward, in the men's room, most of it gets heaved back up into the john. Great stinging upchucks that I try to drown out by running both faucets and flushing the commode.

"Maybe we went at it a little too fast," my mother offers when I struggle back to the booth. "Why don't we sit for a while and then you could try a little dry toast."

What I would really like is just to lie down in the back seat of the Oldsmobile.

My mother pulls some cash from her pocketbook for the tip. "Here's what I'm thinking," she says and irons two singles out on the table. "I'm thinking I ought to just turn the car around right here and head us back to Chicopee."

Bobbie's been studying her hands on either side of her plate. Her nail polish is chipped, which is unusual for my cousin. She's as tidy as a cat about her personal hygiene.

"I mean, what's the point?" my mother says. "I've already decided not to take the kids . . . Teddy over."

Bobbie smiles across the table at me. "I don't think your

mother really means that," she says. "I think she's just a little upset right now."

My mother leans back to look at me and then she starts nodding. "Your cousin's right," she says finally. "Don't listen to your mother. Nobody else does."

Outside, it's overcast but still in the nineties.

"I can't stand this heat," my mother says, opening all the car doors before we get back in. "I don't know what I'm doing out in it."

I'm tempted to say that jets are air conditioned but I don't. My mother can't help it if she has a phobia. "That's the fatal flaw in all families," Cora would argue. "One suffers we all suffer. And in this family it's a guaranteed constant affliction."

When we pass Buttercup Valley, my mother doesn't say anything. But it's probably the reason she came this way. The first summer we were at the proving ground, they were filming parts of *The Flight of the Phoenix* here and my sister constantly pestered my parents to drive us over in the morning and then pick us back up at the end of the day. This went on for nearly a month when the double for Jimmy Stewart crashed his single-engine plane trying to bring it down too close to the camera. My sister was only a couple of hundred feet away, hobnobbing with the extras when the plane nosedived into the sand killing the pilot instantly. When, weeks later, they finally resumed filming, my mother wouldn't allow Cora or me anywhere near the set. My sister badgered my father daily until he finally relented, sneaking us over in his staff car when my mother believed he was only dropping us off at the post theater.

Half an hour down the road, we see something we haven't seen in days: hitchhikers. Two of them walking slumped over with their heavy backpacks.

Bobbie twists about as we pass.

"Lord have mercy!" she shouts. "Stop the car!"

My mother turns the radio off. "What?"

"You didn't see who that was?" My cousin's looking at me. "What?"

"Those two guys," she says excitedly. "Back there."

But they're only big as my thumb now.

"It was George and Allen," Bobbie says. "Stop the car!"

My mother lifts her eyes to the rearview mirror.

"It was them," my cousin says and her voice cracks. "I saw them, Rosemary. Stop the car!"

As a concession, my mother drops down to thirty.

"Now how could they be anywhere around here?" she says. "They've been on foot."

"I don't know what they've been on," my cousin says. "But that was George and Allen."

My mother gazes at me in the mirror. When I shrug my shoulders, she allows us to coast to a stop. We haven't passed a car since breakfast and we all sit in silence for a moment before my mother turns on the hazard lights.

"And if it's not them?" she says. "Then what?"

But Bobbie already has her head out the window.

"They looked pretty beat," she says. "Like they were really struggling there."

"Let's put the windows up," my mother says. "Let's just be on the safe side."

We're all turned around, trying to see out the back window.

"Here they come," Bobbie says finally.

My mother keeps the engine running, ready to dart back up onto the road.

The hitchiker in front blocks out his companion behind him.

"It's George," Bobbie says, unlocking her door but my mother's latched onto her arm.

"Wait," she says.

Only now I can see that it's George all right and Allen behind him. They're both dusty and haggard-looking and begin jogging toward us.

Bobbie leaps from the car.

"It's them," I assure my mother. "Really."

But she still punches the lock down on the door anyway.

"Mom," I say. "It's George and Allen."

She has her hand up to her forehead to shade the sight of three figures hugging each other alongside the road.

"Okay then," she says at last. "But your eyes can play tricks on you out here."

$\mathcal{G}\textit{eorge}$ and Allen are no longer on speaking terms and sit in the backseat separated from each other by my cousin. They keep the reason for their falling out to themselves but my mother persists in trying to break the conversational ice.

"It's just amazing to me," she says, raising her voice in the noisy Oldsmobile, still unable to believe who we've picked up in the middle of the desert.

George leans forward to within inches of my mother's ear.

"Yes and no, Rosemary," he says and reminds her that there are really only two routes to take. "We knew where you were headed and just figured you'd want to take in Yuma along the way."

"But you made better time than we did," my mother says. "And we haven't exactly dillydallied."

He explains how eager truckers are for company at night and that their first ride hauled them all the way to El Paso nonstop.

"And real pleasant company too," Allen says to Bobbie. "He wanted to nuke the Commies over the *Pueblo*."

"Some of us were grateful for the lift," George says pointedly.

My peacemaking mother glances back and forth at them in the mirror.

"Your being here," she says, shaking her head in disbelief. "It's just remarkable. There's no other word for it." And she looks over at me. "What would the odds be in the casinos, Teddy? It's not something you'd bet on."

I only nod that it wouldn't be.

"Some of us are willing to stick around," George says to no one in particular. "Then there are the others who hightail it at the first sign of trouble."

"Excuse me," Allen says to Bobbie. "But what was the body count this week? Two hundred? Two fifty? I guess some of us read the signs differently."

"It was okay when their country was right," George says to himself. "But as soon as they decide it's wrong they suddenly want nothing to do with it. Well, they're only hiding from the truth."

Allen forces a smile but this time actually *does* speak to Bobbie.

"I guess that's what draft dodgers and bad marriages have in common," he says. "They're not really going anywhere."

It's clear from my cousin's expression that the comparison escapes her.

"I didn't think you guys believed in hitching," she says instead.

"This has just been a little detour," Allen says. "*I'll* still head on up to the border. Someone else can do what he likes."

"Someone else *always* does what he likes," George says, pretending to speak to my mother.

"Which is it in a nutshell, isn't it?" Allen says. "As if our actions don't have consequences for others . . . But why am I bothering you people with this?"

My mother's shaking her head. "You're not, Allen," she says. "We *want* to hear."

But my cousin's still curious about why they'd thought to come this way.

"You were going to look for us in Las Vegas?" she says.

Allen adjusts the backpack at his feet, shifting his cramped legs. "Pretty crazy, isn't it?" he admits.

Bobbie loops her arms over both their shoulders. "We're three little kittens who've lost their mittens," she says.

George guffaws. "Trouble is," he says, "I don't think someone's going to find them in Canada either."

Sitting up front for the first time with an unobstructed view of the interstate, I'm reminded of something Cora once pointed out to me. We were headed back to the proving ground on the school bus with all the windows wide open and my sister's hair frazzled by the scalding desert sun when she suddenly turned to me and wondered if I'd ever noticed how everything outside always changed except for where the road met the horizon. It was the only piece of scenery that ever stayed the same.

"Brats are always staring at a vanishing point," she'd said. It was the Army's eternal triangle, a patch of concrete that remained forever before us. The illusion ("a military specialty") being that we were making up ground. But, of course, we were only standing still. That was why posts were indistinguishable. They were the same one. We only *thought* we'd crossed the country to a new assignment. But if you *really* thought about it ("Not something I encourage little brother to try"), in a car you're trapped between two vanishing points. The one in front was just being fed into the one behind. And who occupied the time warp in between? Your all-American dependent military family.

George has a question for us.

"Here we are unloading our troubles on you people," he says. "And it finally dawns on me that someone's missing." When I turn around, he's looking at me. "Where's your sister, for heaven's sake?"

But a huge billboard of Steve and Edie very nearly takes my breath away. Their heads are the size of Mount Rushmore.

"Cora?"

My superstitious mother reaches up to touch the St. Christopher's medal on the visor.

"You two would appreciate this," she says and smiles first at George and then at Allen to be certain they've heard her. "Teddy's sister has struck out on her own."

Both men seem to hope that the other will say something first.

"She's run away?" Allen volunteers.

We all listen to the whistling of the air through the car.

"She's gone back home?" George says.

My mother only drums her fingers on the steering wheel. But I'm tempted to ask her the same question. Where *would* my sister go if she decided to go back home?

"She's meeting us in Las Vegas," Bobbie says. "She just wanted to be by herself for a little while."

"I can appreciate that," Allen says. "Honest to god."

And then for several minutes no one speaks. Our throats are parched from yelling to make ourselves heard and so we simply stare out our respective windows.

Twenty miles outside the city, billboards flash past like cartoon panels. Frank Sinatra rises a hundred feet above the sand, a microphone the size of a tree in his fist. Enzo Stuarti's pinkie ring looks more like a diamond hubcap. Shirley Bassey and Leslie Uggams are ten stories high. Everyone is larger than life but then everyone is a celebrity.

Although it's only noon, my mother wants us to get situated first, which means checking into our hotel. She's anxious to see if there's any word from my sister.

"Don't worry about us," George says when Bobbie reminds my mother that we have company. "Really, you can let us out wherever."

Allen reaches down for his knapsack. "I'll speak for myself," he says sharply. "You can let *me* out wherever's convenient."

But my mother won't hear of it. They're at least to have something to eat with us at the hotel. She pretends that this was a given from the start.

The Strip appears unchanged since my father used to drive us up from the proving ground. If Cora were with us she'd be groaning at all the washed-up acts still headlining in the same big hotels. The only way to explain their longevity, she would argue, was by their mob connections. "Know who their favorite moll used to hang out with?" she'd ask the rest of us and, of course, none of us did. "Who, honey?" my mother would say, ever willing to humor her high-strung, testy prodigy who even at thirteen had all the answers. But it was my father Cora wanted most of all to impress and he played along less convincingly. "I bet it was somebody really big," he'd say. "Try the President of the United States," and my sister would watch my father closely to see how this registered. "No kidding!" And he'd wink at me as if to say that we were the only ones in this family still in the same solar system.

My mother pulls into our hotel and the parking attendant hustles around the Oldsmobile to open the driver's door. He's dressed in what looks like a drum major's uniform and holds his palm open for the keys.

But my mother's been here before.

"You can take the suitcases down," she instructs him, unlocking the trunk. "I'll hold on to the keys till we get our room."

The attendant has already slid into the seat to get a closer look at my cousin. "House rules, lady," he says, his arm thrust out the window.

My mother looks as if she is wearing a fright wig, her face is beet red, and she hasn't slept soundly since my sister disappeared. She is not in the mood for someone Cora's age clicking his fingers at her.

"I have my own rules," she says and about-faces without looking back.

The rest of us have all stepped into the shade of the hotel's gigantic marquee as the gangly parking attendant draws his long legs back out of the car.

"Hey," he says to Bobbie over the hood. "I'm flexible." And he wheels one of the luggage dollies around to the back of the car.

My cousin has sat down on the curb and is fanning herself with the road atlas. She's been talking quietly with Allen who quickly collects his backpack as soon as George reaches past the attendant and pulls out their gear.

"Good question," she says. "Only I don't know." And she smiles meaningfully up at Allen as he sets his bedroll down beside her. "But I guess I don't have the answer to a lot of questions."

My mother suddenly appears at the lobby's large brass-trimmed revolving door. She's waving an envelope and I can see that she's been crying. George hustles over to whisk my mother out.

"It's from Teddy's sister," she says and directs Bobbie to find something in her pocketbook for the car hop.

I take the keys from her and hand them to the attendant who's had to push a second dolly up behind the first.

"I opened it, honey," my mother says to me.

The envelope had been taped shut with "For Teddy's eyes only" printed across it in Cora's handwriting.

"There's just a phone number," my mother says excitedly. "But she's here."

I look back at my cousin.

"How about we take these guys to lunch?" Bobbie says.

George stands beside his gear and I'm reminded of how little they'd packed for their trip. They hadn't expected to come this far out of their way but then just like us their plans had changed.

If it will make things any easier, my mother tells me, she'll join the others downstairs.

She holds two fingers up. "Scout's honor, honey. Not another word." But before I can dial the number she's flapping both arms again as if a train's coming. "Just one last thing. Make her under- stand . . ."

I set the receiver back down.

"Tell her I'll get off her back," my mother says. "Tell her from now on things will be different. She'll see."

She stops and raises one hand as if to shade her forehead from the sun.

"Mom, it doesn't have to be a big deal."

"You're right, sweetheart." She sits down on the sofa but then just as quickly springs back up. "I promised not to interfere and here I am interfering."

"All right," I say. "I'm going to start over. Everything okay?"

She looks around the room once and notices that the televi- sion's still on. Before heading down for lunch with George and Allen, Bobbie had been watching "Days of Our Lives" ("It's how I keep up to date with Lou.").

My mother switches the channel back to the local station. Every fifteen minutes they show the tape of Elvis being driven from the airport in his limousine surrounded by a motorcycle escort. He's all in black and wearing enormous gold sunglasses. He only waves at the hoard of photographers before being hustled into a side door of the hotel. In this town, the reporter announces, the King's landing is bigger news than Apollo's.

"Go ahead, sweetheart," my mother says to me and steps over to the bathroom door. "Go ahead."

I dial 9 to get outside the hotel and already my mother's pacing again.

"Hello?"

The sound of my sister's voice stops my heart and I squeeze the phone to keep from dropping it.

"Cora?"

When I look up, my mother is staring at me. She's kneeling on the mattress as if her legs have suddenly given out.

"What do you say, kiddo?"

For a moment, I'd almost thought it was my father.

"Good," I say, rocking slightly to steady my own quavering voice. "Copacetic."

"You sound like Daddy," she says.

Although the curtains are drawn, the room seems remarkably bright (a bad seizure sign). But first I want to tell her that like Mom I'm sorry for everything. If she'll just come back, I'll be different. Mom promises to be too. And Bobbie's even talking about flying home early after the Elvis concert.

"You still there, buddy?"

I nod before managing a feeble, "Yes."

"Mom's doing low passes, isn't she? I can hear her wings flapping. Two to one she opened your mail. Am I right?"

I hold my breath, afraid that she'll hang up no matter what I say.

"Better get used to it," she says. "You're up next. But listen, meet me in the lobby of the Stardust at eight. It's walking distance. *Sans* Mom, of course. I'd like to get a word or two in edgewise."

"Okay," I say. "She'll let me."

My sister makes her snorting sound. "Sure she'll let you. Long as you've got a gun pointed at her head."

My mother has crawled across the bed to hover closer to the phone.

"You can tell her that my little friend is out of the picture," Cora says. "Not that he was ever really in it. That should make her happy. Anyway, the Stardust at eight."

When the line suddenly goes dead my mother rips the receiver from my hand as if to catch the faintest echo of my sister's voice.

"Nothing," she says, staring at the phone.

"Mom, everything's fine," I say. "Cora wants to see me tonight. Everything's going to be okay. Daniel's gone."

"She said that? The boy's gone?"

I nod. "I don't think he really mattered that much."

"No," my mother says. "That's not the problem, is it?"

I tell her that Cora wants to get together at eight. But that I'm to come alone. My mother listens to this and then walks unsteadily into the bathroom to splash water on her face. She lowers the towel and talks to me in the mirror.

"Your sister hates her mother," she says. "But I guess that's no big secret anymore."

"I don't think so, Mom. I think she's just—"

"All this has been building up for some time now, honey. It shouldn't be such a surprise to me. But it is, of course. I guess I just didn't want to believe it. That a daughter could feel this way about her own mother."

"Mom, I think—"

"I'm going to stay out of it. I've learned my lesson. She wants to talk to you, not me. I understand that. You just tell me exactly what she wants and there won't be any pressure from this end. That's a promise."

I stand up slowly as if trying to catch my balance in an elevator.

"Teddy?"

My mother has her hand on my face.

"You're sweating, honey. Your skin feels clammy." And she eases me back down onto the bed. "You need to sit still."

But I'm staring at her mouth.

"You're bleeding," I say.

My mother touches her lip. "I must have bitten it," she says dreamily and hands me the large menu from the desk.

She'll run downstairs now and have a quick sandwich with the others. She's not real hungry.

"Pick out something that'll be easy on your stomach," she says. "Just have them bring it up." She tugs my shoes off and pulls Bobbie's quilt from the other bed. "I'll lock the door behind me. I don't want you answering for anybody but room service. Understand?"

I nod.

She leans on the TV. "Did you say you wanted to see this again?"

It's the clip of Neil Armstrong coming down the ladder.

I didn't.

My mother watches the astronaut delicately test the lunar surface with his foot before she looks back at me.

"I must be losing my mind," she says.

After a moment, she opens the door, steps into the hall, hesitates, then comes back in. "I forgot my shoes." And she fishes them out from under the TV stand. "Your sister has me so I don't know whether I'm coming or going."

"You were going," I say.

She studies the thick carpet. "I hope your children go easier on you," she says.

"I'm not having any."

My mother doesn't smile. "You have a head on your shoulders," she says solemnly. "I thank my lucky stars for that."

"Well, you feel so lucky, why don't you bring all those socks full of quarters up from the car? You could feed the slot machines."

But she'd completely forgotten about them.

"I guess I get that from Cora," I say. "I never forget about money."

She looks back down at the shoes on her feet. "That's good, sweetheart. You can take care of your poor mother when she's old and gray and you're a lawyer."

"Or a movie star."

Her eyes get shiny and she pinches her lip gingerly.

"Whatever either of you want, Teddy. I know your sister doesn't believe that but it's true. All I want is for the two of you to be happy."

"There's still a little blood," I say.

Her face is contorted. "Your sister hasn't turned you against me, has she?" She doesn't try to stop the tears now. "Cora hasn't made you hate me too, has she?"

"Come on, Mom."

"Because your sister gets these ideas in her head . . ."

"Mom. I'm not a baby. I can figure out a few things for myself, you know."

She's shaking her head, biting down on her lip again.

"Because you two are all I have. You're all I have in the world."

It's not the first time she's said this and so I ask her about Dad.

"You have him too," I say. "Don't you?"

My mother lifts a corner of the quilt up to dry her face. "Your father's in another world, sweetheart."

"Taiwan's not another world. It's just a different country. We could get there tomorrow if you'd let us all fly."

She sweeps the quilt back over my legs and kneels beside the bed. "I'm trying to keep you from your father," she says finally. "That's what your sister's made you think, isn't it?"

"Why do you keep bringing Cora up? Is she supposed to have me programmed or something?"

When I kick the quilt off she patiently gathers it back up from the floor.

"Your sister blames her parents for everything that's wrong with her life right now. She's just going through a difficult time, that's all."

I recognize the tone. She's afraid of a seizure.

"Well, maybe you're the one making it difficult," I say. "Maybe we wouldn't have to go all the way to China if Daddy wasn't so unhappy here."

She stands over me like a mother over the cradle of a colicky child.

"And that's what you honestly think, Teddy? Or is it what your sister's telling you to think?"

I reach up and feel my throat but drop my hand when I see my mother's frightened look.

"All right, honey," she says abruptly. "End of discussion. That's enough for today."

But for once *I* want to be the one to end the discussion. For once *I* want to be the one who says when's enough.

"Cora thinks Daddy has a girlfriend," I blurt out. "She thinks he doesn't want us to come over because he's happier there with her. She thinks that's why Daddy wanted to go overseas. To get away from you. What I—"

My mother tries to take my hand but I scoot farther over into the middle of the bed, glaring back at her.

"She thinks that's why you've kept us here. Because you know that Daddy doesn't really want us to come over even though he says he wants us to." I draw my knees up against my chest. "She thinks this whole trip was a joke from the start. She thinks that when we get to the Coast you're just going to put us all on a train and head back to Chicopee. She thinks that you're just playing games. But that you don't love Daddy and he doesn't love you. And since you asked, that's what she thinks."

My mother's standing the same way she stands whenever she argues with my father: with her arms crossed and her shoulders slightly in-turned as if expecting things to come to blows.

"And that's what you believe?" she says softly. "What your sister believes?"

I crawl off the opposite side of the bed and look back at her.

"I believe that Daddy's not with us and that we're not a family."

My mother doesn't take me as seriously as she does my father or Cora. And even though I know to expect this whenever we argue it still only makes me angrier.

"We'll always be a family, Teddy," she says. "It doesn't matter where we are."

"Sure," I say. "That makes a lot of sense."

She opens her pocketbook to see that she has cash in her wallet. "We can talk about this some more later, honey. After we see your sister everything—"

"I don't think she wants to see you."

My mother turns the room key over in her hand. "You're right, Teddy," she says. "You're absolutely right. And that's the way we'll handle it. I won't be anywhere involved." She walks over to test the lock on the door. "I just meant that maybe now that we're all here we can start to work some of these things out." She puts the key in her pocketbook. "I want you to double lock this after me. And use the peephole with room service."

She steps into the hall again and closes the door, waiting for me to set the chain lock.

"Okay, honey," and she jiggles the doorknob from the other

side. "Just remember what I said and stay put. We'll talk about seeing your sister when I get back."

I sit down on the bed and watch Aldrin holding the flagstick as he pretends to play golf. But I've seen it a hundred times already and find a channel that isn't covering Elvis or the moon landing. There's only "Concentration" and I turn the volume off. Cora once said that watching close-ups of contestants with the sound muted was like talking to Mom. You could see the wheels spinning only it was anyone's guess what she was really thinking.

But what *I'd* been thinking while I talked to my mother was how for the first time in my life she seemed completely at my mercy. After all, I was to be the one to argue her case with Cora. It would be entirely up to me to win over my hypersensitive sister and somehow persuade her that all would be different from here on out. Like the go-between in the Lindbergh case, I would speak for the family. But my mother had made only promises. The same kinds of promises that she'd made all along to my skeptical sister. Why they were supposed to be any more convincing coming secondhand from her brother was the real question.

When the phone rings I blink at the television screen but there's only Ed McMahon soundlessly pointing the microphone at a rebus puzzle.

"Guess who I just saw step out of the elevator?"

It's Cora and she's in the lobby.

"My goodness the ladies must have cast a spell," she says. "They're all down here with their happy campers."

But she wants to know if I'd like to get together a little early.

To steady myself I reach out to touch the glass door to the balcony. Cars move along the Strip, their windshields catching the sun like quicksilver.

"Mom told me to stay in the room."

My sister is silent.

"She made me promise," I say.

"Hey, sports fans," Cora says. "You make the call."

After hanging up, I study the room service menu before drawing one of my shoes out from under the bed. Then, in the drawer of the desk, I find some hotel stationery and write my mother a brief note in case she comes back before I do. But she's not to worry, I promise her. I'm not going far.

𝒯𝒽𝑒𝓇𝑒'𝓈 something different about my sister.

"What a character," she is saying. "As screwed up an Amishman as they come."

We're sitting in the Silver Dollar coffee shop just down the street from the hotel. There's no clock and I've lost track of the time. But Cora's been going on for at least an hour. She's had little sleep the past two days and yet she doesn't look tired. She looks different.

"He's met some people that are heading on up to this settlement near the Utah border," she says. "Some kind of ragtag descendants of Mormonism. Apparently there's a whole gaggle of polygamists living together up there. Anyway, it's struck a chord and Dan's got his heart set."

When I ask my sister if he wants her to come along, I keep my hands flat on the Formica table to prevent them from shaking.

"It crossed his mind," she says, eyeing me over her cup of coffee. "I came this far with him."

I look out at the empty street. Everyone stays inside the dark, air conditioned casinos. By now my mother has probably discovered the note and alerted hotel security.

"You'd rather stay with him?" I say finally.

Cora wets a paper napkin to clean her sunglasses.

"Daniel's lost," she says. "His family's got religion. But he doesn't. And in Dutchville you can't have one without the other." She laughs hoarsely. "One thing I got to hand Mom and Dad. They at least never crammed God down our throat. And that's probably just because they had such a bad experience the last time they were at the altar." She stops. "What's the matter with you? You got a chill or something?"

I tell her I'm just not used to stepping out of the heat and into air conditioning.

"Anyway," she says, putting her sunglasses back on to study me in a different light. "Dan's with the rest of the crew, and a very fine crew it is, out at this . . . I don't know what you'd call it. An encampment? It's ten minutes from here. I've got the car."

"You've been out there?" I say.

"Only long enough to turn around and come back. It's just a bunch of teepees." She shakes her head. "Poor Daniel. Now he thinks he's going to find happiness with the Smith Family Robinson."

And what about her, I say. Where's she going to find it now?

"Find what?"

"A happy family."

My sister lets the sunglasses slip partway down her nose to give me one of her patented looks.

"Teddy," she says. "Even at your tender age I knew that was a contradiction in terms. Unlike our mutual friend I'm not running *to* anything. I just want to be able to take in the sights on my own. And that's something Mom fails to comprehend. *To this day.* That her children aren't appendages."

I've never seen my sister so tan. Her dark hair appears almost knotted from being whipped about in the T-Bird. But that's not what's different about her. It's something else.

"No doubt you've been getting the full media blitz the past

forty-eight hours," she says. "Propaganda from the home front can be a little mind bending. Believe me, Mom honed her act on her firstborn. You have my sympathy."

"You don't think I can think for myself."

She looks back out at the large neon arrow that's pointing down at one of the casinos. "The deck's stacked against us, kiddo."

"Mom misses you," I say.

My sister's profile is my father's. There's none of my mother in her at all.

"Don't get gooey on me, Teddy. I've heard that pitch from her before."

"What do you want her to say then?"

"I don't want her to *say* anything. She's been *saying* for sixteen years."

A delivery boy backs into the coffee shop tugging an aluminum cart after him.

"You want her to change," I say. "And she wants to change."

My sister gazes at the rows of powdered doughnuts aligned on the metal shelves of the wagon.

"Mom's Mom," she says wistfully. "I know better than to get my hopes up."

Other than after a seizure, my sister never feels sorry for me. At least not that I'm aware of. But the sad expression she has when she stands up from the stool makes me think that this is what she'd look like if she did. It's a pitying look for her pitiable baby brother who's afraid his big sister is about to run away for good.

But then I see that my hand is holding her arm and that it's the real reason her expression seems so foreign. I'm keeping her from going her way and that is what caused her surprise. My sister and I are never physical with each other. It's only one of our family's unspoken rules. And so my hand on her arm has taken her aback.

"Mom promises," I say. "She promises, Cora."

She doesn't take my hand away but I can see that she feels awkward.

"Look, Teddy. I don't know what's going to happen right now. Let's just go with the flow for the time being."

"What does that mean? I don't understand."

She glances at the delivery boy who's carefully arranging packs of peanut butter cookies in the display counter under the register.

"It means I've got to deal with a crazy Amishman first."

"Daniel," I say.

"Right."

"So what should I tell Mom?"

She steps away from the stool and I let my hand slide from her arm.

"How should I know what to tell her?" And she reaches into her pocketbook for a dollar bill. "Tell her to put everything on red."

Outside, the heat seems to crackle about everything metal: stop signs, buses, the car key in my sister's hand.

"You're driving?" I say.

Cora presses the key to her forehead. "I see a silver T-Bird. Circa '57."

"You don't have a license," I say.

"The secret's in not getting stopped, Teddy. Let that be a lesson to you."

In fact, she drove most of the way.

"Unlike Mom, Dan's willing to let someone else take the wheel. So I took it. And here we are. Still in one piece, no less."

She steps from the curb without waiting for the light to change and I catch up with her in the crosswalk.

"Where you going?" I say.

"I'm parked around the corner. A meter."

I have to trot to keep up with her. My sister's a fast walker. It's one of the reasons she believes she was meant to live in L.A.

"Mom hasn't told Dad about any of this," I say. "She hasn't even called him."

Cora checks over her shoulder. "Good. She should do more of that."

"Mom will do more of anything you want," I say. "She wants to change. You wouldn't recognize her. She's not like she was."

My sister slows down and then finally stops. "Teddy," she says, looking past me. "Mom and I go way back. You don't teach her new tricks. She *knows* all the tricks. Including remorse. She could take that one on the road. What am I saying? She's *taken* it on the road, for god's sake."

We're standing beneath the awning of a pawnshop. Guitars and electric keyboards hang in the window.

"What if she said we weren't going overseas?" I say. "What if she said we were moving to Los Angeles so you could go to your boarding school?"

But my sister's lifted her sunglasses and is straining to see something in the distance.

"That's Bobbie, isn't it?" she whispers.

"What?"

"Outside the coffee shop," she says. "Who's that with her?"

But the reflection off the concrete is blinding and my eyes water.

When I step out to the curb Cora pulls me back.

"Look," she says. "I'll call you later. Tell Mom everything's cool."

"No," I say and seize my sister's arm. "Don't go. Please."

"Teddy, let go."

A pedestrian steps around us, tucking his casino cup under his jacket protectively.

"Let me come," I say.

"Teddy, relax." And she pats my hand. "I'll call you later. Honest."

When I won't let go, my sister drags me several steps.

"Teddy!"

"No," I say. "I'm coming."

The glass door to the pawnshop suddenly swings open.

"This guy bothering you, sweetheart?" A man with a croupier's visor and thick bifocals is leaning out of the shop.

"It's just my brother," Cora says.

He scratches the folds of his neck.

"Be sweet now," he says to me.

But my cousin has come halfway down the block and is waving.

"Teddy!" she shouts.

Cora glares at me. "Did you tell her?" And she shakes her arm free. "Did you?"

I turn to see someone dressed entirely in white beside my cousin.

"Teddy!" Bobbie yells. "Wait!"

A stretch limousine swings out of one of the hotel garages and my cousin's friend wraps his arm about her waist.

"It's okay," I shout back. "Stay there!"

Bobbie glances both ways as if to cross but hesitates.

Cora moves cautiously away from me.

"It's all right," I say to stop her. "They're not coming."

We watch the person holding on to Bobbie hike his thumb up.

"Hey, buddy," he says, his enormous silver buckle catching the sun like a fishing lure. "What you know?"

And he sweeps his black wraparound sunglasses off with a flourish. It's Nick.

"Jesus!" Cora says.

Nick karate chops the air. "Special appearance."

I stand between them.

"You can go back to the hotel," I say to Bobbie. "I'm just talking to my sister."

"Hey," my cousin says to Cora. "You got a nice tan."

"Lookin' good," Nick says.

Cora takes several more steps away from me.

"I'm out of here," she says.

As if covering my sister in a getaway, I walk backward behind her. "I'll see you later," I tell Bobbie. "We're just going to talk a little more."

But I can tell that my cousin doesn't know whether to unleash Nick or to let us be.

"Your mother's real upset," she says, trotting after us but at the same time careful to keep her distance. "Maybe you could let her know everything's all right."

"Everything's fine," I say. "You can tell her for me."

Nick suddenly whirls his arms about in one of Elvis's karate moves. "Speakin' of the devil," and he freezes, pointing like a mannequin back down the street.

At first, I see only Allen standing outside our hotel trying to hail a cab. Then my mother appears with George, looking exactly as I imagined she would: frantic.

"Just tell her I'll be right back," I say to Bobbie. "Honest."

My cousin grips Nick's elbow.

"You better hurry," she says to me.

Cora is already around the corner and I cut through an open-doored bingo parlor, the cold air hitting me like an ice pack before three steps later I'm back out on the street.

I spot my sister tossing her pocketbook into the T-Bird. When I shout her name she bounces into the front seat and starts the engine just as I come up to the passenger door.

"Open it!" I shout, yanking the handle.

She leans down to see out the window at me.

"I'll jump on the hood," I say. "You won't be able to go any-where."

When she sees that I'm not going to let go, she reaches across the seat and unlocks it.

"Christ, Teddy!"

The door won't open completely against the curb and I have to slide in sideways.

"Hot," I say. The vinyl seat is scalding.

Cora glances up at the mirror and then nudges the bumper against the car parked in front of us.

"Goddamn it!" and we drift back slightly when she wrenches the wheel violently.

I turn to see Allen loping toward us as Cora rocks the station wagon behind us before finally peeling out onto the street.

"I'm running the light," she screams at Allen as he ducks down to see in at her.

"Your mother—" he says but my sister only shifts into second.

"It's okay!" I yell.

Allen seems to think twice about risking traffic and jumps back up onto the sidewalk.

The car's been baking in the sun and I can smell the fast-food wrappers on the floor.

The light stays green and we glide through the intersection.

"So where we going?" I say, watching Allen recede in the dis-tance.

My sister doesn't say anything for two blocks and then glares at me.

"I promised Dan I'd bring the thing back," she says and tucks her hair behind her ear. "And I never break a promise. Unlike *some* people I know."

I sit still, afraid to inhale, afraid suddenly to discover that there will be nothing left to breathe. And I think of how it must have been for the astronauts yesterday opening the capsule door not knowing what to expect.

The air sears my lungs and Cora turns as I double over coughing.

"All right?" she says when I swallow painfully.

And only then does it strike me what is so different about my sister. It's her eyes. They hardly look swollen at all. But even if I weren't so choked up I'd still know better than to ask her why.

My sister drives with remarkable confidence, twice passing Nevada state troopers without flinching. When I compliment her coolness, she turns her head slowly to gaze over the top of her sunglasses at me.

"How I've missed you."

We turn off the interstate onto a single-lane access road and I bring up how she must have gotten to know Daniel pretty well by now.

"I mean, the two of you being together for two days."

Cora flicks the visor to fan herself.

"As a matter of fact, I don't have a *clue* about the guy."

We both stare out at the familiar mirage that floats above the flat black highway ahead. Ten miles outside the city and once again there's only mesquite and sand in every direction.

My suntanned sister slouches in the driver's seat with her elbow thrust out the window. For the first time in her life, she's been completely free of us. And the change is everywhere in her face. It's the identical look my father gets whenever he returns from maneuvers or some out-of-state inspection. Gradually, of course, he becomes his old self again: just a little less lively and slightly subdued.

"Bobbie must be in hog heaven," my sister says. "Going to see Elvis *with* Elvis."

I tell her it's the first I'd seen of Nick.

"It's probably like Plato's forms for her," she says. "She can only handle the Man's imitation."

Bobbie had mentioned Nick's teasing her about catching a red-eye to Vegas. Apparently with Elvis's shows all being sold out there was plenty of work for impersonators. They were coming in from all corners of the globe to handle the overflow. She just hadn't taken Nick too seriously.

"There's a turn up here somewhere," Cora says. "Another mile or so."

Mountains hundreds of miles off appear gray and flat as aircraft carriers.

My sister lifts her foot off the gas.

"To the best of my recollection that's it," she says and the T-Bird bumps onto a cracked blacktop road that parallels a canal.

A citrus farm appears out of nowhere, a network of rusty sprinklers arching over it like a giant praying mantis. Very soon the pavement ends and there's only a gravel road with deep ditches on either side.

"Dan thinks it's going to be different in the desert," Cora says. "I told him he has a very dry sense of humor. But I don't think he got it. Among other things."

The people he's hooked up with, she explains, are just passing through and will join the parent family up near the border.

"I can't turn my back on him five minutes," she says, "and he's ready to be blood brothers with some loon he bumps into at a washateria."

She attributes this to Daniel's upbringing. All it took was for him to get out of the house to hear a new siren song.

We are driving along the edge of the citrus grove where the sprinkler system is fed by a broad, concrete canal. With all the dust, Cora turns on the wipers but it only streaks the windshield.

"Shit."

"You better slow down," I say when it's impossible to see.

The road's become ridged and grooved and we sway and bump as if on a carnival ride.

"This is ridiculous," my sister shouts.

But before she can stop, something, the muffler, rips out from under us and the car catapults completely over, tumbling us about until there's a sudden stillness, a silent floating as if we've been hurled about the dark side of the moon.

I feel a body pressed against me as water gushes in as if from an open hydrant. The car has settled to the bottom of the canal and I pull myself through a window but nothing is where I imagine it to be. There is only a murky light to push toward until the water at last opens and the sun and the heat singe my face.

Gasping, trying to catch my breath, I jerk my head to see where the car broke off a chunk of concrete. The water bubbles up about me and I gulp one last lungful of air before dropping straight back down into the brown water. There are only shapes. And I reach out to touch the hard blackness of a tire, trying to think if it's the driver's side. But I can't picture anything except how my sister's thick hair had swirled about like seaweed. Unable to hold my breath a moment longer, I burst back up to the surface, algae draped over my shoulders.

The car can't be any deeper than six feet. At least this time down I have some bearings and when I wave one arm about inside the window my hand brushes against a foot. Cora's kneeling on the dashboard, her body arched back. But when I try to pull her toward me, she resists and I have to let go.

Back up out of the water I fill my lungs with air and can feel the pressure behind my eyes. Everything is as bright as a dream. My sister will drown if I faint, I tell myself. She's freed herself from the collapsed steering wheel and is only inches from the open window. But she can't see the way out.

I drop back down into the water until my toes settle into the thick silt. The car is tilted backward, the front end resting against the side of the canal. This time my sister doesn't pull away and her body comes weightless through the window as we rise slowly, twisting about each other, ascending.

We break into the light and I slash my elbow on the jagged wall of concrete. My chest heaving, my eyes burning from the poison of the stagnant water, I look down to see the algae covering her like a black wig, her bruised legs half submerged in the slime.

I sit up, holding onto her arms to keep her from sliding back down the slope of the canal. But she's not breathing. And I quickly raise both her arms, rolling her over onto her stomach. With my hands splayed out on her back, I nearly tumble over pressing with all my weight between her shoulder blades.

The black water still reaches to her knees and her clothes are fouled by its stench. My sister looks pathetic and lost to me and I start to cry as I lift up then press evenly down, counting to keep an even rhythm. Bubbles balloon up from the car and I tell myself that with the air pocket she could have been breathing the whole time.

But I try to think of something else. Something to keep from falling into a seizure. My sister's body is as fragile as a child's as I thrust the heels of my hands into her. There's no tension in her muscles. No life.

And so I think of when we were children and lived in Wherry Housing without air conditioning. At night unable to sleep beneath the warm mosquito nets my father strung over our beds, we took turns gently rubbing each other's arms. And always I was first to close my eyes. But my watchful mother soon decided we were too old to share the same bed. It would be my last memory of any physical intimacy between us.

Something warm makes me draw my hand up and I look down to see water trickling from my sister's mouth.

"Cora," I whisper, lowering my head next to hers. I can smell the terrible odor of the canal on her breath. Then her eyes flicker as I pick the strands of hair from her mouth. "It's me."

Her Adam's apple slides in her throat. Only nothing happens and I suspect that all of this is only my dream then a great gush of bile erupts from her lungs so forcefully that it lifts her head. And I wedge my hand to keep her jaw from striking the concrete as her whole body trembles, her legs quivering.

"Cora?"

Her arm twitches as she turns onto her side and I kneel beside her, wishing there were something I could cover her with. She is shaking badly. But then she stops and gazes up at the empty sky.

"How do you feel?" I say finally.

My sister flops her arm across her waist before at last lifting it to shield her eyes from the sun.

"Like you," she says.

And I nod, knowing what she means.

"*Elsa* Lanchester," Cora says. She's wearing my sneakers and they still creak with sludge. *"Bride of Franken-stein."*

She stops again to rub her sore legs.

"Now you know how Mom feels," I say.

My sister wipes the mud from her knees. "Go ahead," she says. "Kick a girl when she's down."

The camp can't be more than a mile off and she wants to keep moving. Despite the bruises and stiff muscles, she doesn't feel all that bad ("I never realized how cathartic puking could be."). Still, I keep my eye on her. She's coughed up a plateful of algae.

Cactuses sprout magically beside the road, their limbs riddled with buckshot. A vulture big as a dog sweeps down to check on our progress.

But mostly I worry about stumbling over sidewinders sunning themselves in the sand. Crossing the proving ground on our way back from school, we would hang out the bus window to count the number flattened on the highway.

Cora stops to point at a sudden cloud of dust approaching us.

"A pickup," I say when the truck is close enough to make out its battered cab.

We shuffle off the road.

"A pickup would be nice," Cora says.

It's an old truck. The kind with wooden door panels and head-lights the size of hubcaps.

The driver pulls up and leans out the window, a red bandanna at his forehead.

"Look like you could use a lift," he says.

"I guess we're going the same direction," I say.

He wipes his side mirror with his palm. "You were out here before," he says to Cora as she struggles into the seat beside me.

"Got a little turned around back there," she says.

The man fingers the ponytail that loops out from under his feed cap. His khaki pants are shredded at the knees and he doesn't seem at all curious about our own ragged condition.

"You with the group?" he says.

Cora picks a clump of dirt from her hair and flicks it out the window.

"Just paying our respects," and she turns to look at the sacks of concrete mix stacked as high as the cab window. "You still working on that gazebo?"

The man nods. "Whatever they want to call it. It's their money."

When he shifts gears, the engine makes a low, moaning sound.

"Out here you run into some different kinds," he says. "Maybe some lose it at the tables. Others get a little sidetracked one way or another. You know what I'm saying?"

"Sort of a melting pot," Cora offers.

He nods. "Usually, they don't last long. The heat gets to them. Only these ones been camping awhile now. But I guess you know that."

"Actually, no," Cora says. "But let me ask you something."

The man lifts a pack of Camels from his rolled-up sleeve and gums one out. "Shoot."

"They strike you as basically peace loving?" my sister says, declining his offer of a cigarette. "Because mostly we're here just to say a quick good-bye to a friend."

The truck hits a rise and we're all three lifted an inch from the seat.

"Well, speaking personally," he says. "I don't pay much attention to all the chanting and the bells and stuff. But in answer to your question, I'd have to say yes."

Less than a mile farther we come upon the camp. Sears pup tents are mixed in among several authentic-looking Indian teepees.

"Got me a flat last time I went too far off the road," the driver says and backs the pickup around before setting the brake.

"Anybody home?" Cora says.

Our friend unhooks the tailgate, leaning one of the shovels against the tire well.

"Not many leave their sleeping bags all that much," he says and points out a small group of them sitting in a semi-circle away from the tents. "Far as I can tell they're inclined to stay out of the sun."

There are no other vehicles in sight and I ask him how they got out here.

"Walked, I guess. It's why I keep the key in my pocket."

There's a slight breeze and we both turn at the tinkle of a wind chime.

The driver straps a carpenter's belt around his waist then fills one of the pouches with a fistful of fourpenny nails. He's ready for work and I follow him over to the construction site. Cora stands in its sparse shade watching the prayer session in the distance.

It's uncertain what exactly my sister wants to do next. For the moment, she appears content just to sit on a stack of treated lumber and rest her bruised limbs.

"He reminds me of someone," I say as we watch the carpenter drag prefab lattice from his truck. "A foreigner."

Cora's as suspicious of my condition as I am of hers and only nods, eyeballing me.

Even with all the banging and sawing, no one is curious enough to poke a head out of one of the tents.

After a while, to make conversation, my sister asks the carpenter if living this close to the casinos it isn't tempting to squander all his earnings. Before he can answer, someone gets up from the group, bows to the others, and starts toward us. He's wearing what looks like a sackcloth.

"What do you know," Cora says. "The Amish convert."

It's a moment before I recognize him. Daniel keeps his hands buried in the folds of his robe like a monk.

"So," he says, smiling brightly at my sister. "You are here."

Cora's ratted hair hangs down in front of her face and she looks as if she's recently fallen into a polluted canal. But Daniel seems oblivious to her appearance.

"And see who I brought," my sister says.

"Yes," Daniel says, smiling at me. "But I did not see the car. Only the truck."

Cora taps her fingernail on her front tooth, gathering her thoughts.

"I got some bad automotive news," she says and then quietly explains about the T-Bird.

Daniel comes over to shake my hand and seems only to half listen to the story of his car's total loss. He has his own story to tell and waits politely for Cora to finish.

"I'll, of course, reimburse you," my sister is saying. "You can get yourself some replacement wheels. I know what they mean to you. So I'm real sorry."

It's rare to witness my sister apologizing for anything. I don't blink the entire time.

"It means nothing," Daniel says, his back shielding the sun from her. "I have no more use for it."

Cora looks down at his bare toes, which peek out from beneath the frayed hem of his robe.

"I'm still writing you a check for the Blue Book value," she says. "Soon as I find it out."

The carpenter takes several measurements with his extension tape, recording his figures in pencil on the wooden railing.

He slides the tool back into the loop on his wide leather belt and I at last think of who he reminds me of: another itinerant carpenter with hooded eyelids and a kidnapper's face.

When Cora insists that we not get in the way of his work, he sticks a nail between his teeth and unsheathes the hammer.

Daniel's eager to tell us about the Lama as he enfolds his hands, resting the tips of his fingers under his chin to bow slightly from the waist.

Cora and I glance at the group that's still sitting in the sun.

"Lama Shing," Daniel says and explains how the Sensei has been touring the Southwest the past year, visiting others willing to take him in for no more than the cost of a bowl of unwashed brown rice. Along with his friend, Mike, he will return eventually to an apartment building they own jointly in Canada.

Cora listens despite the distraction of all the hammering. Surprisingly she puts no damper on Daniel's newfound religion. And even occasionally adds an "interesting" or an "impressive" to some truth the Buddhist Zen master has revealed to him. Just this minute, for instance, the Lama had been explaining the mystical nature of *powha,* or how the soul migrates.

But what is even more astonishing to me than the belief in being able to "psyche phrenically" open the top of one's head to permit the soul to depart at death is how Cora doesn't once roll her eyes or make a snorting sound.

"What do you think, Teddy?" she says instead. "Sound like something Mom might get into?"

I've stopped worrying about my sister. She already seems her old self again: restless and slightly bored as she sits through Daniel's long story of how the Lama and his companion had come to bid on a bankrupt bank, which they now rent out to tenants in Toronto. Only the part about a famous movie star who was a devoted follower of the sect and had helped finance the transaction seemed to perk her interest.

"Teddy and I probably ought to head back," she says finally. Her legs have tightened up and she gets to her feet cautiously. "But it sounds like you've found yourself a home. That's great."

For an instant, Daniel appears confused as if my sister is abandoning him. And when she offers her hand to shake, he looks over at me as if for help.

"Mom's sort of expecting us," I say.

But he's turned back to Cora who's borrowed a pencil from the carpenter and is copying down our forwarding address on a patch of silver duct tape.

"Who knows where we'll wind up," she says to Daniel. "Just write and I'll write back."

Only Daniel can't seem to raise his sad eyes from my aunt's address in Chicopee.

"She will," I try to reassure him. "Cora used to write to half a dozen fan clubs every week. She's real faithful that way."

My sister gives me one of her withering looks. "Odds are it won't be a foreign address," she says. "Maybe you could come visit when I send the check. Scout's honor, it's practically in the mail."

Not even this seems to lift Daniel's spirits, having envisioned Cora joining the sect herself.

"So," my sister says, and nudges me to get moving. "What do you guess it is? A mile back?"

She doesn't want to get banged around in the truck again and thinks walking might help prevent any more charley horses. At least as far as the interstate.

"They're going to cramp otherwise," she says.

My sister waves to the carpenter who's kneeling in the center of the unfinished gazebo, a nail dangling from his pursed lips.

When it sinks in that Cora and I are leaving, Daniel suddenly seems to snap out of his reverie.

"Please," he says, holding his hand up, the silver tape still stuck to his palm. "There is something for you."

We watch him low-crawl back into one of the tents.

While we wait I point out to my sister that we have a real secret between us now. We've broken Mom's first commandment.

"You mean getting into a truck with a stranger?" Cora says.

I nod.

"You know," she says. "I was thinking that on the way over. That if this guy didn't dismember us Mom would."

When Daniel duck walks out of the tent he almost looks surprised that we're still here.

"For you," he says and places a pair of handmade thongs at Cora's feet. "The Lama made them."

My sister slips out of my back-flattened sneakers.

"I wreck his car so he gives me a new pair of shoes," she says. "Who says a good man's hard to find?"

But we both turn to see that Daniel's meditation group has broken up and is heading over. They're led by the Lama, the only one in a different color robe.

"Well," Cora says and stuns Daniel by patting him affectionately on the arm, "it's been groovy. Only we gotta run."

"I will show you the way," he says but my sister's shaking her head.

"No, really," she says. "Stay. We'll find it."

And I have to trot to catch up with her, spinning about to wave to Daniel. "Write," I say. "She'll write back."

When I turn around again, my sister is glaring at me.

"And who the hell gave you power of attorney?"

But twenty feet farther, she waves back at Daniel's forlorn figure.

"Write," she says. "I'll write back."

The others have come up to stand beside their new brother as the Lama works his arm out from under his robe to loop it consolingly over Daniel's slumped shoulder.

"He'll be fine," Cora says and wiggles her foot to tighten her toes on the thong. "Course it would help if he were a movie star."

We pass the carpenter's truck and follow the path out to the road. There's an awful stench from the canal.

"It's amazing, how it all comes back to you," Cora says, making a face.

But she doesn't mean having practically drowned in the T-Bird. She means our years at the proving ground.

"Everything that happened to you when you were a kid," she says. "It all comes back with just a smell. You can't get away from it."

And it's true. We would step from the post theater at night and there would be that terrible odor. The Milky Way shining like a chandelier and still we'd have to inhale through our mouths. "Only way you're going to get the sand to bloom," my father would say of the desert's vast and foul-smelling irrigation system. "You dig a big ditch and then you pump water in it."

But what I remember most about that time wasn't the desert or the putrid scent of the Army Corps of Engineers' handiwork. What I remember most is turning ten years old and my sister beginning to speak to me in an altogether different way. "You're double digit now," she said after I blew out my candles, "even if your IQ isn't." And yet soon she would confide in her baby brother her very darkest suspicions about the military in general and our sad family in particular. Suddenly Daddy was a lady-killer, a Don Juan (pronounced Ju On), a philanderer. And Mom a psychosomatic, a shrew, a hysteric.

Cora's First Principle held that nothing ever happened by accident. Dig deep enough and you found a conspiracy. At the very least a plot. For instance, we wound up in the desert because my philandering father was trying to dump my hypochondriacal mother. He knew that she couldn't take the heat and this was his way of getting her out of the kitchen. And when after a year and a half in the desert he hadn't succeeded in dehydrating his spouse, he conspired a transfer to Canada to try to freeze her out.

Our assignments, my sister was convinced, were always finagled by Daddy's buddies in Washington who secretly stuck together being ball-busted husbands themselves. What better test for the dependents than to send his seasick-prone son and xenophobic wife on a slow boat to China. There may not be a God, Cora liked to say. But the Pentagon came pretty damn close.

I didn't believe any of this, of course. Partly because the Army brass I bagged groceries for or handed bowling shoes to at the post lanes never struck me as smart enough to be successful conspirators. But mostly I didn't want to believe that my father was a miscreant (nine down) or my mother a termagant (the same across). It was easier to accept that my sister was a paranoid, too-smart-for-her-own-good spoiled brat. At least I didn't need some harebrained plot to explain what I could see for myself.

"I've decided to rejoin the circus," Cora says.

She stops to adjust the thong between her black toes.

"As far as Los Angeles, anyway," she adds. "Then F. Lee Bailey and I will sit down with Mom and see how serious she is."

I'm afraid to say anything and so I don't.

My sister is crazy but she's my sister and not even her wildest conspiracy theory has ever disproved that I'm not her only sibling. And since she's almost three years older I'm used to walking in her shadow and letting her find our way home.

Still, I keep my eye on the canal that snakes off to our right.

There are no other landmarks. No telephone poles. No billboards. Not even the distant hum of traffic. The dusty road isn't distinct enough for me to be certain when we're really even on it anymore.

Yesterday, in the papers, someone was saying how Charles Lindbergh was probably the last of the lonely adventurers. Crossing the Atlantic he didn't carry a radio and the only people to hear from him the whole time were a few fishermen when he passed over the Irish coast. The Apollo mission was different. Everyone rode with the astronauts all the way to the moon. You can't do anything on your own anymore without the world coming along.

On his famous victory flight back across the country, Lindbergh needed to refuel and came down in a sandstorm just west of Las Vegas. There weren't the kind of interstates we have today to pick up his coordinates from. He just seemed to have a sixth sense about geography and always seemed to know roughly where he was. After half a mile I'm already turned around and if it weren't for the canal I'd be lost.

But not Cora who hasn't once looked back to check her bearings. Even if there were a traffic cop around my proud sister would never ask directions. She has always hated being called a dependent.

The sun almost loses its shape against the bleached cloudless sky. In the Arctic, explorers were often blinded by its relentless reflection off the snow. They would trudge across the ice, eyes slitted against the glare and crevasses would open at their feet too late for them to see.

I'd read how more than once Matt had pulled the commander from a sudden crack in a floe and quickly rubbed the circulation back into his frozen limbs. In the beginning, Peary had always taken the lead on each of their treks north. But in the end it was Henson who pulled the crippled commander to the Pole. Or at least to that place Peary would call the top of the world.

I don't think that Matt ever really believed that they'd gotten there. I think he lied to himself rather than believe that the commander had lied to him. It was just a patch of ice anyway. A spot they'd been trying to reach for twenty years but never quite managed to attain. It didn't really seem to matter to Matt all that much. What he cared about was the commander. You only have to look at a photograph of him standing next to Peary to see that he loved the man despite everything.

"Check out Mom," Cora said the last time she caught me looking through one of our albums. It was the picture my aunt Irene took of my parents right before my father left for Taiwan. "Portrait of a mad housewife. Notice the slightly crazed half smile. The desperate shadow beneath the swollen eyes. Ladies and gentleman of the jury, this is a woman who could suffocate her own children."

But my sister would say nothing of the other picture on the page developed from the same roll. It's of Cora and me on the steps of our place in Chicopee. I'm looking up at her, laughing at something she's just said. And what the camera shows is how much we're a pair. We don't look that much alike, especially in the coloring, but clearly we're brother and sister. And at ease with each other. Cora's expression can't hide her delight in my finding her quite so amusing. And obviously I *am* delighted to be in her company. She is the smartest, funniest, and most interesting person I know, and all of that is in the picture. Anyone can see it so there's nothing to say, and in this family, at least, neither of us ever will.

But I've been daydreaming again and my sister is up ahead in the road waving her arm petulantly, her long shadow connecting us like a dark umbilical cord.

"Catch up," she shouts.

So I do.

Epilogue

"I give you Zsa Zsa's," Cora says, pulling the Oldsmobile into the scorched driveway of the movie star's former estate.

But our headlights reveal only a scattered pile of charred bricks. Like a lot of celebrities' homes this one was reduced to rubble by last season's brush fire.

"There was just her gardener out here with a hose," my sister is saying. "So we started a bucket brigade and practically emptied the swimming pool before they evacuated everyone."

"The sisters let you get that close?" my mother says. "I don't like that, Cora. I don't like that one bit."

Mount St. Mary's Academy is just up the hill but the fire was never really a threat to my sister's school. Even the nuns were out pitching in.

"Quite a scene," Cora says happily. "Sister Elizabeth Joseph trying to get Zsa Zsa's pool pump unplugged. She's got a doctorate from Cal Tech in mechanical engineering. But the gardener doesn't speak English. So she's screaming at him in some kind of Pidgin Spanish with her habit rolled up to her elbows."

Despite the devastation much of the neighborhood has started building back up.

"I guess money will do that," my mother remarks.

"That," Cora says, "and *so* much more."

It's expensive real estate all right and my sister's school perches atop the mountain that overlooks it. You can even see the famous Hollywood sign across the canyon. Not that Cora's crass enough to point this out. She considers herself a native now and natives aren't impressed by tourist attractions put up by the Chamber of Commerce.

"Steve's place is right up here," my sister says.

Steve is Steve McQueen, of course, whose daughter Cora has twice baby-sat. But this is nothing to get excited about, my sister modestly asserts. All the girls at the academy have baby-sat for the McQueens at one time or another. For the McQueens and the Zanucks and the Bronsons and the Goldwyns and even for Dick and Liz for that matter. Notices are posted on the bulletin board downstairs in the dorm and if you're interested it's all handled by Sister Mary Clare who makes the callbacks (the phone numbers being, naturally, unlisted).

Cora dims the headlights as we pass a huge white colonial that looms out of the dark on the winding mountain road.

"What's it like inside?" my mother says, craning about in the backseat. "It looks lovely."

"Very unpretentious," Cora says and casts a casual, nativelike glance over her shoulder. "They only have the help in when absolutely necessary. They're very private people."

My mother forgets if Steve is still married and so Cora fills her in on the famous actor's complicated marital history. Plus the decor of the upstairs master bedroom and the couple's favorite choice of wallpaper throughout. They're details that my sister recites only because of my mother's interest. Cora's own bent is more along the lines of who comes to whose private dinner parties. It's a way for her to see firsthand how the power brokers really run the industry. And *that* is something worth learning.

"You'd be surprised what a fly on the wall can pick up," she says.

"Exactly," I say but my sister ignores me.

"The head of Warner's little pied-à-terre," Cora says, directing our attention to a vast garrison-like estate built in the twenties. "They had me watch the twins while they screened some uncut new film for their media reps. They hadn't even done the post dubbing yet so it was pretty raw footage."

My sister has never looked happier to me. My mother's presence in the backseat helps to remind her of how far she's come in just the past six months alone. Geographically from Chicopee Falls, Massachusetts, to the City of Angels, California. But psychologically the whole hundred yards. She is living on her own in the one place in the world she's always wanted to be. And in the glorious future my sister foresees for herself, she is going to try very hard not to forget all the little people, and what better place to begin than with her own family.

"I could move into that one tomorrow," my mother says, nodding at an enormous house with a tiled, mansard roof.

"He made his wad on spaghetti westerns," Cora says dismissively. "Sister Mary Clare won't even pin his ads up on the board. She thinks there's something kinky about him."

After a while, when I've stopped contributing to the conversation, my mother asks me if I'm feeling all right.

"You're awfully quiet," she says. "You're not getting carsick on us, are you?"

This gets my sister's attention.

"Maybe you ought to crack your window," she says.

We've been taking sharp turns for over an hour to rubberneck at how the other half lives. Or at least my sister's running rendition of how they live. But many of the places look deserted. As if their owners must be off doing what they're famous for: making movies. I haven't said anything because I know that this would somehow detract from my sister's whirlwind guided tour. Part of the excitement for her is in speculating about just what Julie and Warren and Bob and Natalie are most likely up to as we brush so closely by their glamorous lives.

My father would have had Cora head home by now. Unlike my mother, he only puts up with my sister for so long. But, of course, my father's not here to bring her back to earth. And it doesn't look as if we'll be joining him any time soon. When my mother decided that it would be best for us just to wait for him here, she rented a small, two-bedroom bungalow in Santa Monica where I attend the public junior high school. Mostly my classmates like to collect troll dolls and fantasize about dream dates with the Monkees. So I've pretty much kept to myself although I'm quite fond of my teacher, Miss Grega, who, coincidentally was an Army brat herself.

Whenever my mother pesters Cora about never having time for us on weekends, my sister tells her to "Let Mohammed come to the mountain." Which is what we're doing here tonight. Even though she doesn't have her own car yet, driving the Olds is no big thrill for her. "It's not what I had in mind passing the road test," Cora said when I called to congratulate her on her new driver's license. "That wasn't the real incentive."

My mother describes our present status as a holding pattern. But being in the military, she argues, we should be used to the situation by now even if we're not. Every other week my father calls sounding sunny and optimistic until I hand the phone back to my mother.

"*Déjà vu*," Cora will say each time I relay the latest hostile exchange between them. And then to try to cheer me up she'll do her Julie Andrews imitation of "My Favorite Things" or make some other fun of our parents' long distance battles. But mostly she advises me to take up a hobby other than eavesdropping ("Bad karma, kiddo."). Because if I don't get a life of my own, she knows somebody more than willing to make one for me.

Still, I try to appreciate how it is for my mother too. After all, who else does she have? And is it such a sacrifice to go to bingo with her at the "Y" or to be her date Saturdays for a movie in Westwood? It's not as if she's keeping me from bringing any friend home I want from school. Although she'd prefer that I hold off on getting serious about the girls just yet. I've got a whole lifetime ahead of me and they'll be banging the door down soon enough anyway. So what's the hurry?

When I argue this, Cora wonders if I remember the scene from *20,000 Leagues Under the Sea* where the giant squid curls its monstrous tentacles around the submarine. We've had this conversation before. "True," she'll say. "It's just I never cease to be amazed at how an audience can see a picture and yet not really see it. You know what I mean?" I do but allow my sister to lecture me anyway, imagining her standing in her pajamas at the end of the dark hall of her dormitory, having come from wanting to "throttle some executive producer's little demon seed."

"Liz's old place," Cora says and nods at an elaborate wrought-iron gate that keeps us from getting a glimpse of the hacienda-style house. "An MGM accountant bought it from Mike Todd's estate. I'm thinking of sitting his joint-custody six-year-old."

It's impossible to know when Cora is pulling our leg. She goes on as if making up stories and even imitating Rona Barrett's Bronx nasal drone. By now, my father would have had us trying Baskin-Robbins' new lunar cheesecake flavor somewhere on Sunset Boulevard but my mother is afraid to be critical. There's a new, unspoken agreement between them that has changed all the old rules. Cora tells me that on my sixteenth birthday I should seek out a good contracts lawyer expert in family law ("Maybe the same guy who handled Lee Marvin."). Otherwise, with Mom in the director's seat, she can already envision how my own little melodrama will play on the big screen.

My mother laughs at something Cora says about Sonny and

Cher's gaudy Italianate "marble mausoleum" being just the ticket for Bobbie and Nick.

Last night, my cousin called to tell us that she's experienced another false labor but that her obstetrician is still predicting Sunday as her due date. Lou continues to phone on the hour and remarkably has become quite close with Nick who, it turns out, once managed a shoe store himself. "You wouldn't believe what all this has done for Hammuck," Bobbie insisted. "I hardly recognize his voice when I pick up the phone anymore." But she refuses to let Lou fly out for the big event. It's his baby, all right, but she's the one having it and she'll be the one decides when he can see it. In the meantime, Nick's got her taking croupier lessons at a reputable school on the Strip that boasts a 100 percent employment record for its graduates. The casinos are always short of quality dealers and Bobbie has her heart set on Caesar's where Nick's been packing them in in one of its smaller, side lounges. Apparently there's been a real boom in the impersonator market ever since Elvis left town.

"I never thought so clear in all my life," Bobbie confessed to me during one of our recent marathon phone conversations on Nick's hotel courtesy line.

"Must be all that clean desert air," I told her.

My cousin suspected it was something else.

"Tell you the truth, I think it's got more to do with nobody breathing down my neck for a change. Like what Allen must have felt when he finally crossed the border."

My mother still gets letters from George written on "Remember the *Pueblo*" stationery. He hadn't followed his son to Canada and has refused to visit him in Winnipeg. Allen had been brainwashed into believing all that nonsense about Woodstock, he wrote my mother. "We got different ideas about what makes a nation never mind a family."

Cora's own letter to Daniel was twice returned unopened from the barbershop in Lancaster. She's since deposited his check in a savings account in the Bank of Beverly Hills ("We'll see if the Lama pays him as much interest."). Still, my sister wouldn't be surprised if he someday turns up on her studio doorstep looking for a part ("But then aren't we all?").

"Nick's been through what I'm talking about," Bobbie added about her divorced friend. "Four times as a matter of fact. I've even got to know one of his ex's. She's a bail bondsman over in Carson City. Anyway, Nick lets me be. We see each other when we want to see each other. Right now that's a lot but probably it'll be less later on after the baby comes along. Nick's honest about kids. Says he'll be happy to play uncle but not even the King's much good at being a daddy."

I asked her what she thought would happen on the home front.

"You mean Lou?" she said. "Who knows. Irene's taking the bus out so we'll see."

Then she tried out some more girls' names on me from a long list she'd been collecting on the back of one of Nick's room service bills. Priscilla was Nick's suggestion and amazingly Lou came up with Irene, but none of them really set right with her. Not even Rosemary.

When I told her my favorite was Cora, she made a snorting sound in the receiver that actually reminded me a little of my sister.

"It just better be a boy is all I got to say," she said finally. "I got my little teddy bear's name all picked out."

But I suddenly notice that we're headed away from my sister's school. Cora has talked my mother into a quick spin through Laurel Canyon before heading back up to the dorm.

"It's less twisty," she says and glances over at me. "Even for Neil Armstrong here."

"Leave your brother alone," my mother says, reaching over

the seat to feel my forehead again. "And I don't want us going anywhere near the Tate place. You can just scratch that off the list."

According to my sister the cops still have the road cordoned off with yellow streamers.

"How about Inger Stevens then?" and she rattles off a list of other suicides in the neighborhood. "Or Johnny Yuma himself."

But I hadn't heard about Nick Adams.

"Some rebel," Cora says. "Enough paraldehyde to kill a horse."

"If you're going to be morbid," my mother says, "just turn the car around right here."

Instead, Cora wonders if there's anything like a Hollywood Hills in Formosa and if Daddy ever cruises for fun.

"Your father?" my mother says, trying to glean just what Cora is getting at here.

But I know that edge to my sister's voice.

"I guess there's got to be some geishas heating up the cinema over there," she says. "I just have a hard time picturing Taiwanese starlets with big boobs."

All of this is for my mother's benefit, of course. To give her something to think about until my father's next disappointingly brief letter.

As we scale the tortuous, vegetation-singed canyon, Cora enlightens us about the money men who really run the picture. My mother sits nodding at all the electronically controlled gates and imposing guard huts with their private security officers who cast us suspicious glances as we pass in review. When I note that the only thing missing is a decorative cannon and a loudspeaker blaring taps, Cora rolls her eyes without comment. It's a world of difference, we're to understand, between the pathetic life of military dependents and the exalted existence of such civilians as live behind *these* walls. But because I'm feeling a little lightheaded I try another comparison. The area looks a lot like the hills around

Lindbergh's home which was similarly isolated and purposely selected to keep the riffraff at bay.

My sister suggests that I try breathing into a paper bag, and not until I mention how all the walls remind me a little of the Kennedy compound does she grudgingly admit to some parallel. But only because there were stars hanging out with the boys when Jackie wasn't around. At any one time, Jayne or Angie or even Marilyn herself might drop by. All of which went down the drain with baby brother Ted. It's water under the bridge and now there's left just a bunch of extras trading in on Camelot reruns.

For the first time in her life, Cora envies me. I go to school with the children of people actually responsible for making films. And not just actors but the real meat and potatoes of the industry: sound technicians, best boys, cinematographers, grips, mixers. Although I don't tell my sister this, I've noticed that they're all a little like military brats in the way they wear their parents' rank on their sleeves and rarely socialize with anyone lower than them on the credits.

But my mother promises that if I can just get through the rest of the school year, she's convinced that my father's next tour of duty will be Stateside and some place we'll all like. This doesn't affect Cora whose contract includes a no-move move clause which means she can't be uprooted without her consent. And it's impossible to imagine any assignment more enticing for her than here ("There being no Fort Cannes that I'm aware of.").

My sister predicts that we'll all just revert to form anyway. That psychosomatic Mom will continue complaining about her legs while Daddy keeps in shape chasing younger and longer ones behind her back. Meanwhile, everybody's dutiful son will go on fantasizing about his voluptuous junior high school teacher while losing himself in his extra-credit homework. There are rich filmic possibilities here, my sister believes. All it will take is for a fresh and talented new director to put her gimlet eye to the camera.

Although Cora laughs when I tell her, Miss Grega has already approved my honors term paper: an original screenplay based on the life of Matthew Henson. I want all the locales to seem authentic and so my mother has proposed combining the research with a car trip back East to get a few more things out of storage. But I guess actually detouring up through the Canadian Arctic will be out of the question (although my father has some quartermaster contacts in the Northwest Territories he said I could call on).

What I'd like the film to show is how Matt was always trying to get to a place that doesn't really exist. The North Pole changes every day. It's never the same spot on a map. At least what you'd find there isn't the same. Not that it mattered to Matt. He was more interested in the company he kept along the way. Cora suggested Sidney Poitier as Henson and somebody like Rod Steiger as the commander. Mom, she said, was born to play Peary's long-suffering wife.

We've come around the other side of the mountain now and my sister has picked up on her running commentary again when I catch sight of the remarkable grid of lights below us. We're up about as high as you can get in a car and the cool night air's just about perfect but depending on your angle, the city always looks a little different from the hills.

I'm studying how the lights shimmer in waves when both wipers suddenly flare up like Fourth of July sparklers. I should have known what was coming as soon as my toes started prickling. Then the hair on the back of my neck sticks straight up and it's too late to signal either Cora or my mother. Their voices are drowned out by the whistling sound in my ears, the same sound I'd heard when the T-Bird cleared the canal like a howitzer shell. My mother's behind me while Cora's too fixed on the road ahead to notice anything unusual, and I'm thinking how it must have been like this for Matt each time he saw the Northern Lights and felt as if all he had to do was just get a little closer, stretch out his arms, and for once he'd be able to touch them.

KNOX COUNTY PUBLIC LIBRARY

5 0551 01458384 4

FICTION   LML
Bennett, James Gordon
The moon stops here

MAR   1995

LAWSON McGHEE LIBRARY

GAYLORD S